# Praise for *The Girl Who Wrote in Silk*

"Vibrant and tragic, *The Girl Who Wrote in Silk* explores a horrific, little-known era in our nation's history. Estes sensitively alternates between Mei Lien, a young Chinese American girl who lived in the late 1800s, and Inara, a modern recent college grad who sets Mei Lien's story free."

—Margaret Dilloway, author of *How to Be an American Housewife* and *Sisters of Heart and Snow*

"*The Girl Who Wrote in Silk* is a beautiful story that brought me to tears more than once and was a testament to the endurance of the human spirit and the human heart. A powerful debut that proves the threads that interweave our lives can withstand time and any tide and bind our hearts forever."

—Susanna Kearsley, *New York Times* bestselling author of *A Desperate Fortune* and *The Firebird*

"*The Girl Who Wrote in Silk* is a beautiful, elegiac novel, as finely and delicately woven as the title suggests. Kelli Estes spins a spellbinding tale that illuminates the past in all its brutality and beauty, and the humanity that binds us all together."

—Susan Wiggs, *New York Times* bestselling author of *The Beekeeper's Ball*

"A touching and tender story about discovering the past to bring peace to the present."

—Duncan Jepson, author of *All the Flowers in Shanghai*

"It was one of the best books I have read in a long time. I can't stop gushing over it… such a beautiful and engaging story."

—Samantha Scott, Auburn University Bookstore (Auburn, AL)

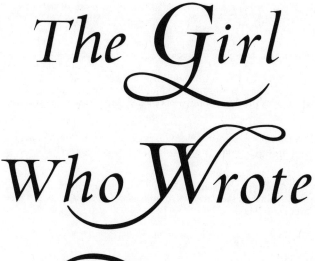

# The Girl Who Wrote in Silk

KELLI ESTES

sourcebooks
landmark

Published by Sourcebooks Landmark, an imprint of Sourcebooks, Inc.
P.O. Box 4410, Naperville, Illinois 60567-4410
(630) 961-3900
Fax: (630) 961-2168
www.sourcebooks.com

Library of Congress Cataloging-in-Publication Data

Estes, Kelli.
  The girl who wrote in silk / Kelli Estes.
    pages cm
(pbk. : alk. paper) 1. Chinese American women—Fiction. 2. Chinese Americans—Fiction. 3. Immigrants—United States—Fiction. 4. Family life—Fiction. I. Title.
PS3605.S7355G58 2015
813'.6—dc23
                                        2015003432

Printed and bound in the United States of America.
VP 20  19  18  17  16  15  14  13  12

For my husband, Chad.
Without you, I wouldn't be me.

# Prologue

*Sunday, February 7, 1886—just past sunset*
*Puget Sound, Washington Territory*

M ei Lien felt the steamship shudder beneath her feet and wondered if the quaking of her own body had caused it.

"You don't have a choice," Father hissed. Before she knew what was happening, he'd prodded her to the ship's cold metal railing. "Climb up, Mei Lien."

She looked at him in horror. She'd always obeyed him without question. But this? "I can't." She pressed a hand to where her heart pounded in her chest and felt the coin purse under her bindings. "Please!"

His face hardened. "Do not disappoint me, Daughter. Do it. Now!"

His tone made her fear recede long enough for her to hear her own voice of reason. It told her Father was right. She had no other choice.

Shaking, she climbed up on the railing to sit at the top, her hands holding tight to the wet metal bar. Beneath her right palm, she felt a pockmark where someone had painted over an old chip. She wondered if that was the last thing she'd touch before death.

Before Mei Lien could say another word, Father placed his palms at the small of her back and pushed her off the steamship.

"*Bàba!*" she screamed, the words echoing as she fell. Her breath left her as she hit the bitterly cold water. Icy fingers dragged her into the void below.

Somehow she found the strength to fight. Kicking and clawing at the water, she dragged herself upward, her lungs on fire.

As her head broke through the surface, she dragged in lungfuls of air between racking coughs. When she managed to wipe the water from her eyes with her fingers, she saw the ship passing dangerously close. Father stood at the railing but his back was to her, as if he hadn't just cruelly pushed his only child to what could be her death.

A wave splashed over her face, and she felt herself sinking again. This time her limbs felt stiff and her muscles were starting to cramp in the near-freezing water. Instinct took over, making her feet kick as she dragged her body away from the ship with her arms, as Father had taught her all those years ago. She shut off her mind and swam, with no idea of what she might be heading toward.

Mei Lien's head pounded from the cold. With each kick, her limbs ached to rest, to give in to the pull from below that promised ease and warmth.

She looked one last time toward the ship, but it was little more than a distant blur of light growing smaller.

Her family was gone from her. Her life was gone from her. If she gave in to the pull of the water, what would it matter?

She stopped trying to fight and let herself fall into the water's frigid grasp, willing it to carry her to the spirit world. She even saw death coming. It rose out of the water as a huge, black sea monster, one glaring yellow eye boring into her aching head. Just as the monster grabbed her, she felt the void take over her mind.

She welcomed it.

# Chapter One

*Sunday, May 27—present day*
*San Juan Islands, Washington*

I nara Erickson stood at the ferry's side rail with her sister and watched as the wake from their ship splashed against Decatur Island as they passed. A blast of cold air wrapped around her, filling her nose with hints of sunbaked cedar, damp moss, and tangy salt. Immediately her mind took her ahead in her journey, to the family estate and all she'd left behind there years before.

She wasn't ready to face the memories yet, so she pushed them away and, in an attempt to ignore the shaky, melting feeling in her core, turned her attention to her older sister, Olivia. "Liv, are you warm enough? We can go inside if you want. Get a cup of coffee."

The wind tugged a strand of long blond hair from Olivia's bun. She tucked it behind her ear and lifted her face to the unseasonable sun shining down on them. "God, no, this is heaven." Despite her words, she pulled her jacket tighter around herself and hunched her shoulders against the biting cold air off the water.

"Thanks for coming with me today. You sure Adam's okay with the kids?"

Olivia opened her eyes and shot Inara a glance that told her she wasn't worrying about her family today. "They're fine. I'm happy you asked me to come with you. I can't believe it's been nine years since we've been there."

Inara nodded and watched as a pod of porpoises raced alongside the ferry, their black bodies arching in and out of the sun-splashed waves. "I should have come to see Aunt Dahlia before she died, but..." She shrugged, at a loss for the right words. "I don't know. It was too hard, I guess."

At that, Olivia put her arm around Inara's shoulders and squeezed. "Me too... It was easier to move forward."

Inara swallowed and would have said more, but a rowdy group of kids burst out of the ferry's side door. One of them, a boy about ten years old, pointed to a porpoise and exclaimed, "Look! A killer whale!"

Inara grinned with her sister. As kids, when they'd come to Orcas Island every summer, they'd feel so superior about their knowledge of the islands' flora and fauna. They'd laugh at all the tourists, like these kids, who expected to see orca whales along the ferry route. The locals knew the whales tended to stay west of San Juan Island in Haro Strait.

"Those sure are small whales." A shorter, female version of the boy put her fists on her hips. "Are you sure that's a killer whale?"

Her brother scoffed as only brothers can do. "I'm not stupid."

Just then Olivia nudged Inara's elbow and pointed to a channel marker where a fat harbor seal rested on the rusting metal.

It was like time had not passed here at all, Inara realized. Just as the ferry slipped between the islands, she was slipping into the life she'd left behind—and that felt surprisingly comfortable. The only difference was that today she counted her sister as a friend, while years ago, they couldn't quite bridge the eight-year age gap between them.

Inara's cell phone buzzed in her jacket, and she pulled it out to answer the call, thankful the kids were moving to the front of the boat, leaving the side deck quiet. "It's Nate," she told Olivia before putting the phone to her ear. "Hey, big brother, guess where Liv and I are right now."

"Portland?"

"No, closer." She had to shout over the noise of the ferry's engines.

"Vancouver?"

"No. We're on the ferry to Orcas."

Silence. Then Nate cleared his throat. "You okay?"

"Yeah," she answered, even though she wasn't sure that was true. Leave it to Nate to understand how hard it was for her to come back here for the first time. "Olivia is keeping me distracted."

"Good. Hey, I've got a question for both of you. I'm here with Dad, and we're nailing down a date for our dedication of the Duncan Campbell Memorial Park. Since the mayor will be out of town the week before, we're thinking October sixth. Does that work for you?"

Duncan Campbell was their great-great-great-grandfather on their mother's side of the family, and the man who had single-handedly launched the maritime trade industry in Seattle. He'd emigrated from Scotland in the late 1800s to what had been little more than a muddy logging town and built an international shipping company from practically nothing. Because of him, Seattle was known as a major port for trade. If not for Duncan Campbell, Seattle might never have been put on the map and Seattleites knew it, having named buildings after him and devoted a whole section to him at the Museum of History and Industry. His success had allowed Duncan to build the family's island estate, Rothesay, named after his hometown in Scotland.

"Is this when Duncan's statue will be revealed?" she asked. A year before, her dad had commissioned a bronze sculpture for prominent placement in the new public park the company was building on the waterfront near the cruise terminal. Inara's dad ran the company Duncan founded, Premier Maritime Group, or PMG as it was known, after taking over from her mother's father more than a decade ago. He'd had great success of his own since expanding the company to include cruise lines serving Alaska, Mexico, and the Caribbean.

"Yes. So, the sixth?"

"Hang on." She moved her phone away from her ear to pull up her schedule and fill in Olivia on the plans. Olivia nodded. "We're both good with the sixth," Inara told her brother.

A loud beep sounded over the ferry speakers, followed by the announcement that passengers disembarking on Orcas Island should return to their vehicles.

"I gotta go," Inara told Nate, turning with Olivia toward the door that led inside.

"Wait. Dad wants to know if you want him to call his real estate agent and get the paperwork going."

Inara smiled to herself. "Tell him I've got it handled, but thanks." Her dad made no secret of his relief that she was selling the estate that none of them wanted.

"Good luck today. Let me know how it goes."

"I will." She hung up, and she and Olivia made their way down the green metal stairs to the car deck and the old BMW she'd owned since graduating from high school. Through the windshield she watched Orcas Island draw nearer, her heart beating faster with each passing second. Sweat pooled between her breasts.

At fifty-seven total square miles, Orcas was the largest of the islands in the San Juan archipelago in the northwest corner of Washington State, though not the most populated, at only five thousand year-round residents. The ferry dock at Orcas Village was at the bottom of the left arm of the horseshoe-shaped island that bent around the body of water called East Sound. This meant Inara would have to drive up through the bend, where the town of Eastsound—named after the water—was located, and then a quarter of the distance down the right arm to get to Rothesay. On that drive, she'd pass the accident site.

This was a mistake. She should have arranged for someone else to come and inspect the property and box up her Aunt Dahlia's ninety-seven years' worth of personal possessions. With one phone call Inara could have had a real estate agent on the job, and she'd be home in Seattle, at peace today. She had enough going on, what with her new job starting in a couple of weeks.

Olivia must have seen her panic. "Inara, it's okay. I'm here and we'll face this together. Don't be scared."

Inara felt like a kid about to get a vaccination on Olivia's exam table, but she had to admit that the soothing voice helped. She looked at her sister. "Aren't you freaked out at all? You haven't been back either."

Olivia nodded. "A little." She looked out the front window as the brake lights on the car in front of them came on, indicating it was time to turn their own car on and drive off the ferry. "Tell me about your new job. Fresh out of grad school in March and about to start a career with Starbucks. I bet you're excited, huh?"

Inara went along with her sister's ploy to distract her as she carefully maneuvered off the ferry and onto the island. "Yeah, I guess. I'll be on the global supply chain operations team. Did I tell you they might send me to Italy within the first three months?"

"So why do you only 'guess' you're excited?"

Of course her sister had caught her slip. Inara shot Olivia a look of frustration, then gave in and admitted, "I know it's a great opportunity, and Dad is so proud of me for getting it and all…" She struggled to find the right words. "I'm just not sure it's the right job for me."

"So do it for a few years, then find something else. Dad will understand."

"Yeah," Inara agreed, not so sure. As they continued chatting about the job, Inara found herself distracted by memories.

Orcas Road looked exactly as it always had, with sunshine spearing through the trees, leaving dappled shadows flickering on her windshield. Through the forest she spied occasional glimpses of beach shacks tucked beside million-dollar mansions. Dirt driveways were often the only indicator of a dwelling behind the trees. She rolled down the window and drew in the scent that her mind had forgotten but her soul had held on to—sun-warmed dirt, blooming blackberry bushes, briny salt water. As she breathed it in, she felt something inside of her shift, like a puzzle piece sliding into its niche.

She was still breathing deeply when she crested the rise and came upon the corner where their mom had been killed. The moment she saw it, every bit of air in her lungs was sucked out, leaving her gasping.

"Just keep going," Olivia murmured. "You're okay."

Inara had been fifteen when their mother died in a car accident on this corner. The police said there must have been something on the road, like a deer or raccoon, and that her mom had swerved to avoid it and lost control. But Inara knew her mom was a hypervigilant driver who never would have lost control of her car if she hadn't already been upset and distracted by the argument she and Inara had just had.

Olivia didn't understand. Not fully. She'd been twenty-three, already married, and doing her residency when it had happened. She hadn't been at Rothesay when the local sheriff had pulled in with lights flashing and a rain-soaked hat held to his chest in sympathy.

Inara slowed down, way below the forty-mile-an-hour speed limit, and focused on breathing while trying to avoid looking at anything but the pavement in front of her.

But then her gaze darted to the side of the road.

No sign of trauma remained on the huge cedar. Blackberry vines and wildflowers grew abundant and pristine, as though nothing bad had ever happened here. As though a car hadn't slammed into the tree, flinging her mother's mangled body against the rough bark.

Someone behind her honked, and she realized she'd come to a complete stop in the middle of the road. Flustered, she lifted her hand in a wave of apology and carefully navigated around the corner, picking up speed. A black SUV tore around her and sped away. Her fingers cramped on the steering wheel.

"Maybe you should pull over."

Without answering, Inara did as her sister suggested, easing to a stop at the next gravel pullout. Then she closed her eyes and rested her forehead on the steering wheel. After that horrible day, she'd gone back to Seattle with her dad and tried to be a normal teenager, but everything had changed. Normal teenagers didn't cause their mothers' deaths.

Nate too had been off at college, leaving just Inara and her dad at home, two ships with broken propellers drifting on the currents of life, unable to find their way to shore. So she'd lashed herself to her dad and his dreams for her. After high school she'd plunged into pursuing a business degree to make him happy, even though she would rather have done something else, like anthropology or history.

"I know it's hard, but you've made it this far." Olivia was rubbing Inara's back and speaking softly, like she did to her three-year-old daughter after a meltdown. "Want me to drive?"

It helped, Inara realized. Her sister's voice gave her something to grab on to so she could pull herself from the abyss she might have sunk into if she'd been here alone. She took one more deep breath, then lifted her gaze out the windshield, relieved to find the road no longer seemed impassable. She could keep going. She'd come this far, as Liv had said, and she would continue, not because she had inherited a house she had to deal with, but because it was time to face her past and move forward. "I'm okay now."

She guided her car back onto the road and glanced one last

time at the corner in her rearview mirror before resolutely focusing forward.

Forward was Rothesay. And forward was making all the necessary decisions about the crumbling estate that Dahlia had left to her. Inara had been so surprised at the reading of the will, and yet it kind of made sense. Although Dahlia was really her mother's great-aunt, Inara and Dahlia seemed more closely related. Of the three siblings in their generation, Inara had been the one who'd loved the island the most and the one who'd spent every waking moment with Dahlia. But what didn't make sense was the next part of the will, Dahlia's expressed wishes that the estate be converted to a bed-and-breakfast so that Rothesay would once again be filled with joy and life.

Really? A bed-and-breakfast? Of course she wanted to give Dahlia her final wish, but Inara had her own career to launch now that she finally had her master's degree. She was sure Dahlia would understand that she needed the proceeds from the sale of the property to pay off student loans much more than she needed to run a bed-and-breakfast to satisfy someone else's dream. The first payment on those loans was due in September. Only a few months away.

Too bad she couldn't keep the estate to use as a vacation home like her family had done during her childhood. Dahlia had lived there year-round with her partner, Nancy, and had offered full use of the manor and grounds to the entire family, just as her parents and grandparents had done before her. It was where they'd all gathered for holidays and where Inara and her siblings had spent every summer while their parents worked in Seattle. Her mom had always taken the month of July off to spend with them on the island, and most weekends too. When she arrived every Friday night, they'd all gather on the beach around a bonfire.

Keeping Rothesay as a family vacation home made sense, but a bed-and-breakfast? Crazy.

Inara and Olivia had taken the early ferry, so it was not yet nine when they reached the twin stone pillars marking the entry to Rothesay. Inara turned onto the curving, forest-lined driveway, both sisters straining for their first glimpse of the manor. When she saw it, Inara gasped.

Everything looked desolate. Neglected. She'd wanted to feel her mom and Aunt Dahlia here, but the property felt lifeless. Her throat closed up and she felt cold, despite the morning sunshine flooding the grounds. She parked in front of what had once been a showpiece fountain but was now dry and black with mold. "It got to be too much for Dahlia to keep up, I guess."

"Yeah," Olivia agreed as she climbed from the car. "We should have come and helped her instead of believing her phone calls saying that she was doing fine."

Inara didn't realize Dahlia and Nancy were a couple until she was an adult. It wasn't something the family discussed, but it was certainly the reason Dahlia's father had hidden her away on the island, safe from tongue-wagging society in 1930s Seattle. But then, Dahlia had loved the island and wanted to be here as badly as her father had wanted her hidden.

Inara got out and went around the car to stand next to Olivia and consider the home they'd taken for granted all their lives. The sound of songbirds in the surrounding forest slowly soothed the ache inside, and she was finally able to see through the disappointment clouding her vision. She was surprised to see fresh grass clippings scattered along the edge of the asphalt driveway.

No one should have been here in the month since Dahlia died. Who could possibly have mowed the grass?

"Let's go inside." Olivia started toward the double front doors.

Inara hesitated a minute more as she studied the main house again. This time she felt a familiar thrill skitter through her body. If she squinted, she could look past the peeling paint and sagging porch to see the heart of the place, the magic and promise of adventure.

A spurt of adrenaline kicked her feet into gear, and she followed her sister toward the manor. She was a little kid again, arriving for summer vacation and eager to do everything at once, but she made herself approach slowly so she could take it all in.

The Colonial Revival–style main house stood a stately three stories tall, complete with white pillars along the wide front porch and curving steps welcoming visitors inside. From each of the front corners curved two-story galleries connecting the main house to the matching smaller buildings facing one another. The entire structure formed a wide U with the driveway and fountain in the middle.

On her left was the garage, and above it, the billiards and smoking room. On the right was Dahlia's house, the original house built on this property. Duncan Campbell had updated it to seamlessly blend with the rest of the manor when it was built, including adding pillars to the tiny front porch. Dahlia should still be sitting on that porch with her steaming mug of tea.

Pain pierced Inara's heart. She should have realized long ago how important Aunt Dahlia was to her. She should have figured out a way to spend time with her, no matter how difficult it was to be on the island. Dahlia had taken care of her and her siblings every summer. And Dahlia had held her all through that terrible night after her mom died.

But long before then, Dahlia had been like a special treasure, more important to Inara than any of her grandparents. Dahlia had let her tag along as she weeded the garden or gathered berries in the forest. She built bedsheet forts for Inara on rainy days, wove wildflower tiaras on sunny ones, and baked cookies and cakes in between, flipping a coin to see which of them got to lick the beaters. Inara was sure Dahlia had cheated to keep the chocolate ones for herself.

Had Dahlia known how much Inara loved her? Inara had left the island after the accident and had never come back. Damn, she hadn't even come last spring when Nancy died. She'd told herself that Dahlia would understand it was too hard for her to come.

And yet, here she was.

When Dahlia passed away last month, Inara's dad had arranged for her body to be taken to Seattle where they'd had a service and burial in the family plot. But being here again at Rothesay, feeling the magic of the islands come over her, Inara wondered if they'd made a mistake.

They should have buried her here on the island she'd loved, in the public cemetery next to the woman she'd happily grown old with, or somewhere on Rothesay land.

Inara took a deep breath and turned, raising her gaze to the towering, evergreen-covered mountain behind her, trying to shake the pressure in her chest by thinking of something other than Dahlia. From where she stood, the trees blocked her view of the neighbor's property across the road, making her feel like nothing separated her from the steep slope of Mount Constitution that seemed to rise from the water of East Sound behind her.

One of these days she'd drive to the observation tower on top of the mountain like they used to do as kids. But today she found she preferred the feeling of being cradled at its base, safe from everything and everyone else. Like it was just her, the mountain, the water, and the forest, where things like student loans and new jobs didn't exist.

Again she felt that stirring in her belly. The stirring of Orcas magic. Today, even with memories of all that was lost clouding her heart, she felt it.

The longer she was here, the more she felt like a snake shedding its skin, like something tight and constricting was falling off her. For nine years she'd focused on her studies and her goals for the future, and now that her future was upon her, she wanted only to sink into the comfort of the past. Of this island. This place that felt more like home to her than her father's house in Seattle.

What *would* the estate be like as a bed-and-breakfast?

She shook her head and joined Olivia at the double front door, where she pulled the key out of her purse and fit it into the lock. It took some jiggling, but finally the tumblers fell into place and the lock clicked.

With a gentle shove, the door swung open, and together the sisters stepped onto the stained oak entry landing between the first and second floors. Even in the dim light coming from the open door behind them and the fanlight above it, Inara could see down the steps to the great hall that ran to the curtained back doors. Despite the dust covering everything, the scars and scratches in the wood showed through, evidence that the stairs and floors would need refinishing.

"Race you for the corner bedroom?" Olivia teased, without moving toward the steps.

Inara laughed at the reminder of their childhood, felt for the panel of light switches next to the door, and turned each one on. As the lights along the upper balconies came on, she lifted her gaze to the row of bedroom doors on the right side. "I'm sleeping in Dahlia's house tonight, and seeing all this dust, I bet you're going to want to as well."

Making quick time, she and Olivia swept through the main hall, pulling back drapes, opening French doors to let in air and sun, and whipping dustcovers off furniture to reveal antiques they'd never appreciated as kids.

"Now *this* is Rothesay," Olivia said with her hands on her hips as they surveyed the long hall, its floor covered by two piles of dusty sheets.

"Much better," Inara agreed, but then her gaze flicked upward. "Except for one thing." She sprinted up the stairs and continued down the long balcony until she came to the back of the house and the open sitting area where the ladies of the house would take afternoon tea and while away the hours knitting and gossiping. She tugged open the drapes covering the sitting room windows and then felt her breath catch.

The view was unbelievable. From the back terrace stretched a wide green lawn—freshly mowed like the front by some mystery caretaker—followed by a strip of native forest growth separating the lawn from rocks that dropped sharply into the sound. The water sparkled between the firs, cedars, and madronas, and it pulled at her, making her want to forget her inspection and go sit on the black rocks on the beach where the water, ripe with kelp, would lap just out of reach. There, every sense would be filled to the brim, and for once, she'd be alive.

*Where did that thought come from?* She hadn't been dead these past years, just busy getting an education, making something of herself.

Shaking her head, she turned away from the windows, promising herself time at the water before they caught the ferry home tomorrow.

Ignoring the dustcovers on the sitting room furniture, Inara crossed to the balcony railing and looked down on the great hall. Olivia had disappeared, but several of the doors off the main hall were open, leading her to assume her sister was investigating the first floor.

She could almost hear her family's laughter echoing through the house, her mother's voice calling her to grab her purse because they were going to kayak to Eastsound for lunch. Olivia's teenage voice protesting the venture. Nate's begging for one more minute on the phone with his girlfriend.

Within a few months, Inara would hand over the estate keys to its new owner and then she'd walk away forever. Immediately on the heels of that thought came a sense of panic that surprised her. Why did she care? She'd done just fine without this place for a long time.

But she'd always known it was here, waiting for her. She wanted the kids she'd have someday to know the joy of summers at Rothesay. Her siblings' kids had been missing out, but they were young and had plenty of summers left to spend here. If she sold the property, she'd be depriving the next generation of its birthright.

But she had to sell. She had no choice. She had to be a responsible adult and unload this place on someone who would put it to good use. Besides, she'd be busy with her new job. She didn't have time to maintain a property she'd hardly ever get to see.

Inara headed back down the stairs to find her sister and get to work inspecting the manor and listing everything needed to fix it up before putting it on the market.

Three hours later, she unlocked the door leading into Dahlia's kitchen. "You should bring the kids up here before it sells," she told her sister as they stepped inside, but then she stopped short. The room settled around her, flashing her to the past while simultaneously stabbing her heart with Dahlia's absence. "Oh my…"

"It's like Dahlia and Nancy just stepped out a moment ago," Olivia whispered.

*Seattle Times* newspapers overflowed from a wicker basket on the Formica countertop, and a stack of dog-eared novels graced the kitchen table. Next to the sink sat a fat, white tea mug with a lip-shaped pink stain on the rim. Dahlia's pink. The one in the gold tube she always had with her. The same pink that matched the streak of pink she'd colored into her hair the summer Inara turned twelve. In all the years since, Inara still hadn't met another eighty-year-old with the spirit to match her hair to her lipstick. The sight made Inara's eyes sting and she had to turn away.

The stairs to the second floor started in the kitchen. A pair of fuzzy yellow slippers waited on the bottom step for their owner, holding down a corner of the worn carpet runner that had once been tacked onto the steps but was now curling up from the bottom.

Family lore told of how Duncan Campbell had purchased the property before the turn of the twentieth century and lived in this part of the house, which the previous owner had built, while adding on the rest of the manor where he eventually entertained guests with grand parties.

Other tales, shared only in private, told of the oddballs in the family. Like Duncan's wife. She'd lived here year-round even though her husband spent much of his time in Seattle running the shipping company. She—Gretna, if Inara remembered correctly—had been diagnosed with a nervous constitution and preferred to live her days in the peace of the island, disturbed only by her husband's many parties.

Each generation brought another oddball, including Inara's favorite—Dahlia. Being a fiercely independent young woman uninterested in finding a husband or obtaining an education, Dahlia had jumped at the chance to move to the island in her early twenties to become the estate's caretaker and live her life as she chose. After that, as far as Inara knew, Dahlia had rarely left the island.

Standing in Dahlia's house now, away from her father's expectations, Inara realized this was the only place where she'd ever felt encouraged to be herself. She had the somewhat uncomfortable realization that with Dahlia gone, she was the next one. The next family oddball.

How else could Inara explain the totally crazy thought that had been niggling at her mind since she'd stepped out of her car? She kind of wanted to stay here. She wanted to turn her back on a job most people would kill for and spend every day dabbling with paint and plaster and everything else she and Olivia had just listed that was required to put the estate back together.

A laugh escaped her before she even felt it coming, surprising her by echoing through the room.

Olivia stuck her head in from the adjoining living room. "What's so funny?"

Inara laughed again as she reached for a pink-and-purple shawl Dahlia had left hanging by the back door and wrapped it around herself. "How do I look? Like a woman who could run a bed-and-breakfast?"

A bark of shocked laughter burst out of her sister, sending them both into a fit of giggles. "You're not serious."

Inara tilted her head to the side and considered. "What if I am? Dahlia left me that binder with all the plans and projections. Blueprints even. I think the hardest part would be telling Dad I was turning Starbucks down."

Nodding in agreement, Olivia came fully into the room. "But how would you pay for renovations? I know I wasn't the only one noting all the work that needs doing in the manor just to make it livable. And you still owe on your student loans."

Inara considered. "Maybe I could take the job for a few years and work on the estate on weekends and holidays." God, that sounded exhausting.

Olivia nodded, but her expression clearly showed she wasn't convinced. Then, like the levelheaded big sister she was, she simply shrugged. "Well, you don't have to decide right this minute. Let's check out the rest of the house."

Agreeing, Inara turned to the CD player on the counter and hit the Play button. Neither of them expected the screaming guitars of classic Aerosmith to fill the house, which made them stare at each other in shock before dissolving into laughter so deep Inara's stomach was aching by the time they recovered enough to get to work. With a swipe at a tear, she pulled the notebook she'd been using to list repairs out of her back pocket and shook her head. Aerosmith. Man, she missed Dahlia.

Notepads in hand and dancing to the music, they took stock of the little house and met back in the kitchen an hour later, both starving.

"I guess we should drive into town for lunch," Olivia muttered as she stared into the empty refrigerator. "Some neighbor must have cleaned this out after Dahlia died."

Inara stuck her head into the pantry. Peanuts, packets of

oatmeal, olive oil, balsamic vinegar. "How do saltine crackers and tea sound?"

"Good enough for now," Olivia answered, reaching for the teapot and filling it at the sink.

With their feet up on chairs, they sat at the round kitchen table and dug into the crackers.

"I could live here and hire crews to get the manor in shape," Inara mused.

Olivia narrowed her eyes. "You're really considering this, aren't you? What about Starbucks?"

She'd be crazy to turn Starbucks down. The job was exactly what she'd been working so hard for in school over the last seven years.

But not once in all those years, and not even when she'd gotten the job offer, had Inara felt this alive and full of ideas of what might be. Not until she set foot on the estate again had she realized she'd been asleep all these years. Only in coming here had she woken up. She didn't want to go to sleep again. "I don't think I've really thought about what I want for a long time," she finally answered, unsure of what to say.

"But now you want to open a bed-and-breakfast?"

"No." A bubbling feeling started in her gut and made her sit up straighter as a vision filled her mind. "Not a bed-and-breakfast. A boutique hotel. I could make this *the* vacation destination for the entire Pacific Northwest."

Olivia was nodding and seemed to be considering. Then, over the music still coming from the CD player, they heard a distinctive ringtone coming from upstairs. Olivia jumped up. "Dang, I must have left my phone in Dahlia's room." She took off at a run up the stairs but didn't make it past the first step when her toe caught on the curling carpet runner. She fell hard, her shins banging the edge of the next step. "Ow!"

Inara jumped up. "Oh my God, are you okay?"

Olivia twisted around so she was sitting on the stairs, her

hands holding her injured shins and her eyes shooting daggers at her sister. "If you're going to live here, you need to take care of that death trap."

Inara had been hovering over her sister, inspecting her bruises, but now she fell still and met her sister's gaze. "You think I should do it?" They both knew she wasn't referring to fixing the carpet runner.

Olivia grabbed Inara's hand and squeezed. "I think you should do whatever will make you happy. You never liked coffee much anyway." She paused, then cleared her throat as she released Inara's hand and went back to rubbing her shin. "It won't be easy convincing Dad, though. He seemed thrilled to think we could all forget about this place for good."

Inara nodded, instantly sobering. "I know." She didn't want to think about that right now. She scowled at the curling carpet runner. "I really should do something about that."

As Olivia continued upstairs to retrieve her phone, Inara grabbed hold of the curled-up corner and tugged with all her strength. With only one side still secured to the bottom step, it didn't take much to free the carpet. The portion of the step beneath the carpet was made of a golden hardwood, marred with what looked like years of scuffs and scratches.

She shifted her hold and gave another tug on the runner. The second tread gave her more trouble. She straddled the step with one foot braced on the bottom step and the other on the third and gave a hard yank on the carpet just as Olivia came back down the steps. The runner gave just enough to encourage her to keep trying.

"I'll find a claw hammer," Olivia offered, stepping around her.

Not wanting to wait, Inara gathered her strength and pulled again. This time the carpet jerked loose with a popping sound. When she looked down, she saw it wasn't only the runner that had come free. In her hands she held the entire stair tread, still connected to the carpet. Where the second step should be was nothing but a dark hole.

"Should've waited." Olivia turned back to the cabinet and her hunt for a hammer.

Sighing, Inara started to replace the tread, intending to leave the runner for someone else to deal with, when something in the hole caught her eye. "There's something in there."

"Probably a mouse nest."

Inara shivered at the thought. "Forget the hammer. I need a flashlight. And rubber gloves." No way was she going to stick her bare hands into a mouse hole. Olivia returned a moment later with both, which she silently handed to Inara with a "you're crazy" look toward the hole.

Inara slipped on the gloves, then braced her knees on the bottom step and pointed the flashlight into the hole.

Under a coating of dirt and cobwebs and, yes, mouse droppings—yuck—lay a bundle of some sort. Definitely man-made. Not rodent.

But the mouse responsible for the droppings could still be there.

Afraid to reach in, yet unable to walk away from the hidden bundle without knowing what it was, Inara held her breath and slowly reached inside the hole with a gloved hand.

The bundle felt soft. And surprisingly lightweight.

"What is it?" She could feel Olivia breathing on the back of her head.

"Watch out." Quickly Inara grabbed the bundle and pulled it from its hiding place. Then, still thinking of mice, she held it away from her body and turned toward the table as Olivia dropped the stair tread back into place with a bang.

With her free hand Inara grabbed a stack of newspapers from the basket on the counter and spread them over the kitchen table before setting the filthy bundle on top.

Whatever was inside had been wrapped in a cloth and tied with brown twine. The whole thing was square-shaped and no bigger than a cantaloupe. She reached for the twine and tugged. It slipped out of her gloved fingers without budging loose from its knot.

"Here." Olivia handed her a carving knife from the block on the counter.

Soon Inara had the twine cut off and the stained oilcloth unwrapped.

Inside was yellowed blue-checkered fabric. Surely this wasn't all there was. "Who would tie up and hide an old piece of fabric?"

"Maybe it's wrapped around something more valuable, like a jeweled necklace." Olivia moved to stand so close that Inara could smell her sister's coconut body lotion.

"Or maybe it's a purse full of gold, or a diary full of juicy secrets." Inara met Olivia's excited gaze and knew they were both thinking of the treasure hunts Aunt Dahlia had dreamed up for them as kids.

"Open it," Olivia urged.

Inara reached out to do just that but stopped when she saw the dirty gloves still on her hands. "Hold it for now, but wait. Don't open it."

Olivia reverently took the gingham cloth bundle out of the dirty oilcloth. Hurrying, Inara balled up the oilcloth and newspapers and threw them all in the garbage can under the sink, along with the gloves. Then she washed her hands and rushed back to the table where her sister relinquished their treasure to her.

Carefully, Inara pulled the cotton back, unfolding each crease until the cloth was spread open on the table. "It's a man's work shirt."

"Where would Dahlia have gotten a man's work shirt?"

Then they saw what the shirt had been protecting.

It wasn't gold, jewels, or secrets, but Inara had no doubt this was a true treasure. Folded into a square as big as one of her hands was a piece of blue silk embroidered with colorful threads in intricate patterns.

Slowly, being careful with the fragile fabric, she lifted it from the work shirt and unfolded it.

Once she had the silk completely unfolded, all she could do was stare in wonder. Olivia too seemed speechless.

It was a sleeve. Not a whole garment, but a single long sleeve with a funny-shaped cuff. The entire thing had been cut from whatever it had once been attached to. But, intriguingly, every inch of the sleeve was intricately embroidered with richly colored threads, creating pictures as detailed as if they were paintings.

Inara knew nothing of textiles or sewing, but even she could tell this sleeve was not merely a piece of clothing, but a work of art.

"What do you think it is?" she asked her sister, not really expecting an answer. She squinted at it, holding it at different angles to try to make sense of what the pictures depicted and what kind of garment the sleeve could be from.

"Why would Dahlia hide an old sleeve under her stairs?" Olivia leaned closer to get a better look. Inara shifted so she wasn't blocking the light and could see the pictures better.

The scene created in the stitches seemed to center around a large steamship floating on turbulent seas. People, or maybe they were sea creatures like mermaids, swam all around the ship.

Away from the steamer, farther down the sleeve, she saw a male figure standing in a tiny boat, holding up a yellow light.

"Maybe it wasn't Dahlia who hid it, but someone before her," Inara mused. "Duncan Campbell sailed to Asia often. Maybe it was his."

It definitely had an Asian look to it. Like Japanese or Chinese paintings she'd seen in museums. She could even make out what looked to be characters from an Asian language woven into the scene.

"Maybe it's valuable, especially if we can find the rest of the garment hidden here somewhere."

"Valuable or not, why cut the sleeve off and hide it under the stairs? It doesn't make sense." Inara dropped onto a chair and stared at the sleeve. "And what am I supposed to do with it?"

Olivia sat on the chair next to her and tilted her head. "I guess it's yours now, so you get to decide."

Inara stared at the ship on the sleeve. As intriguing as it was, something about it told her she should just stash the sleeve back under the stairs and forget about it.

# Chapter Two

*Sunday, February 7, 1886—before dawn*
*Seattle, Washington Territory*

I n this town full of gambling, alcohol, and opium, the banging and shouting that woke Liu Mei Lien seemed no different from any other night. She rolled over in the tiny bed she shared with Grandmother and pulled the scratchy gray blanket up to her neck to ward off the damp cold that never seemed to go away this time of year. Just as she was drifting off again, a man's voice yelled in Chinese directly below her window, "They are coming!"

Grumbling, though quietly so she did not wake Grandmother, Mei Lien eased from the bed and pulled aside the burlap sack that served as their curtain. Through drifting fog she peered down to the muddy street below.

Three men wearing *samfu*, the traditional Chinese hip-length, side-fastening jackets over loose trousers, ran uphill away from the docks, their long dark queues trailing from black skullcaps. One man tripped and the other two pulled him up without stopping, their faces turned to look over their shoulders, eyes wide, faces tight.

Mei Lien shook her head. When would those Yeung brothers learn not to cheat at cards? They were forever running from trouble and asking Father or Mr. Chin to cover their debts.

Letting the curtain drop back into place, she decided she might as well get dressed and start the day. She reached for the length of cotton she wore daily to flatten her chest and, with quick fingers, wrapped it tightly around her gooseflesh-covered body, tucking the ends securely under.

At seventeen she was older than her mother had been when she'd married Father and only one year younger than when she'd died in childbirth. Mei Lien knew Father had been thinking for some time of arranging her marriage, but she had no interest in that. She loved helping him run his store in the mornings and spending afternoons embroidering with Grandmother. She never wanted to leave them.

Now fully awake, she was eager to stoke the fire in the stove downstairs and warm up with morning tea. Still moving as quietly as she could, she shoved her cold-stiffened legs into cotton pants, *fu*, and threw on the jacket, *sam*, and cap that convinced everyone on the streets of Seattle she was a boy. As a boy, she could move freely about town, helping Father deliver orders from his store. As a boy, she wasn't bothered by the lonely Chinese bachelors or curious white men. This freedom was how she'd learned to speak English, and how she gathered news and gossip to bring home to share with Grandmother, who still fretted that Mei Lien wasn't being a good Chinese girl.

As she shoved her feet into her flat-soled shoes, she tied a scrap of red string around the end of her queue, which trailed down her back to her waist. The string was the only feminine convention she allowed herself, but she knew no one would question it, definitely not now. Red was the color of good luck. She, like all of Seattle's Chinese residents, had been quietly celebrating the Chinese New Year all week, with signs of double happiness posted outside doorways and red candles lit to honor ancestors and chase away demons. Three nights ago she'd sat with Grandmother at their window and cheered as the Yeung brothers set off firecrackers late into the night.

Still shivering, she rushed down the steep stairs to the room behind Father's store and the welcome warmth of the stove. The stove door creaked as she opened it, and she knew the sound would signal to Father it was morning. Quickly, she shoved split logs into the belly of the stove, set the waiting kettle on the burner, and then moved to light candles and incense at their family altar, where she whispered words of respect to her ancestors. Today marked the third day of the New Year, the Year of the Dog, and today was the day Father had promised she could have one of the preserved plums he'd ordered for the festivities but that remained unsold.

Her mouth watered as she thought of the sweet, chewy plum. Maybe, if she hurried through her chores, Father would give it to her before they opened the store for the day.

First chore, the morning meal. She moved about the small room, gathering the jar of preserved cabbage and onions she would mix with the rice and broth left over from supper last night. Just as she was spooning the mixture into a pan on the hot stove top, pounding noises echoed from the store out front, followed immediately by anxious shouts that reminded her of the three brothers running frightened up the street. She froze to listen but couldn't make out the words, or even if they were in English or Chinese, but the tone was enough to make her grip the wooden spoon handle tightly as she held her breath and strained to hear more.

Through the thin wooden walls, she could hear what sounded like a great commotion coming closer, the cries urgent, angry even.

And then she knew.

But she didn't want to know. No. It couldn't be happening. Not here. Not now.

With the rice spoon still clutched in her hand, she eased open the door connecting their living quarters to the darkened store. Through the glass windows overlooking Washington Street, she saw a crowd of white men carrying guns and what looked to be heavy sticks. A few carried lanterns, but the lightening sky illuminated the mob clearly. As she watched, one of the men, wearing a businessman's black suit and hat, broke from the mob and came to the locked door. His black eyes seemed to be staring right at her under the name of the shop painted on the glass. Cold fear sliced through her, causing her body to jerk. The handle of the spoon dug into her palm,

"Pack up, Chink!" the man yelled at her. "Today you're going back to China!"

"Mei Lien! Come away from there." Father grabbed her arm and pulled her out of the doorway enough to close it and block out the sight of the mob and the man outside.

"The rumors were true, *Bàba*," she cried, as she turned to face him and saw he was still wearing his sleeping clothes. "They are driving us out of town!"

"Hush, Daughter." He held her shoulders in his warm palms and looked into her eyes from a breath away. "Do not show them your fear. As long as we are together, we will be fine."

He released her then with a small shove toward the stairs. "Go wake Grandmother and get her dressed. Pack whatever you can. I don't know if we'll be back."

She was going to protest but he'd already disappeared into the tiny back room where he slept. With her stomach squeezing painfully, she climbed the stairs and kneeled beside Grandmother's side of the bed.

"*Nǎinai*, wake up. We must prepare to leave." Mei Lien shook her grandmother's shoulder, knowing the older woman's hearing had been failing steadily over the last months. She repeated her words in Chinese, since Grandmother had never learned English, and kept shaking her gently.

"I must tell my maid to hurry," Grandmother cried, jerking upright. "Mother does not like to be kept waiting on market day." Her eyes were as clouded as her words were confused.

Mei Lien, used to Grandmother's nightly dreams of life back home in China, patted her on the shoulder and turned to open the chest beside the bed where Grandmother's clothing was stored. But just then she heard her father's cry from the store below, followed by a crash and a bang.

She threw the first garment she touched onto the bed, then raced down the stairs, her feet suddenly clumsy. When she reached the door to the store, she stumbled to a halt. Father knelt on the floor at the feet of two white men. A sack of rice had been split and was spilled all around him. The taller man grasped a rifle across his chest, while the short fat one wielded a stick of wood painted black—it looked like a piece of trim from around the store windows.

Both men wore the dark suits and hats so common of white men, though the short one in front looked like he hadn't changed in days, so wrinkled and stained was his jacket. Both had a crazed look in their eyes that caused all the saliva in Mei Lien's mouth to dry up. Her gaze shifted to the store's front door. Shattered glass littered the floor. Splintered wood framed the opening where the men had kicked the door in. The area around the dead bolt still held fast into the wall.

"Please no hurt family," Father pleaded in fractured English, his body curved into itself and his head lowered. Mei Lien had never seen her father act so scared or so weak. Her stomach convulsed and she had to swallow hard to keep down the bile.

In spite of the danger to them both, she scurried to him, careful to keep her eyes downcast the whole time. She grabbed his arm. "*Bàba*, get up."

Father's head jerked toward her, his eyes wide with horror, and she knew she should have stayed upstairs. He stumbled to his feet and together they took several steps back. She still held his arm. He shifted his body in front of hers.

The man with the club slapped it against his palm and spit onto the floor, leaving an ugly brown mark where only yesterday Mei Lien had scrubbed it clean. "All you Orientals are leaving on the one o'clock steamer this afternoon. It's back to China for you."

"But this is our home," Mei Lien protested without thinking. She'd been born in Seattle. She knew no other life. "We don't want to leave." Father patted her hand but said nothing.

The fat one looked back at his friend. Wide smiles that didn't reach their eyes spread across both of their faces before the short one turned back to face Mei Lien and her father. "That don't rightly matter, now, does it? A vote's been cast. No one wants you Chinks here takin' jobs and money from us Americans." He took a step toward them, and Mei Lien felt her father stiffen. "I'm thinking I can't trust you to get your asses on that boat, so's I'd better take you there myself."

His hand snagged Mei Lien's arm before she or her father saw it coming. "Let go of me!" she shouted, but his grip tightened as he yanked her away from her father and gave her a shove toward the door.

"Get going, Chink."

"Wait!" Father was suddenly in front of her, his own body between her and the men. "We go. Please get our things and old mother. She no walk."

"*Bàba!*" Mei Lien hissed in Chinese into his ear. "Why should we go? There's nothing in China for us. You've said so yourself many times."

Father turned his head to look at her, his eyes commanding her to obey. "My son," he said in English, used to their charade when strangers were about. "We are given no choice. Go collect your things and help *Nǎinai*. I'll gather what I can."

"You've got five minutes. Not a second more. Any Chinaman left on shore when the steamer departs will be shot." As if to emphasize the man's words, the sound of gunfire erupted from up the street outside.

While the white men hurried to look out the window, Father pushed her toward the stairs with an urgent directive whispered in Chinese. "They're looking for an excuse to kill us. Don't give them one. Collect everything you can of value. Hurry!"

His words made Mei Lien stumble. How could this be happening? How could these men barge in here and force them to sail "home" to a country where Mei Lien had never been? A country her father had bid farewell to with no intention of returning?

She found Grandmother sitting on the bed, her eyes wide in her small, pale face. She'd managed to dress herself in her finest *mang ao* worn over the matching red and pleated skirt she'd worn on her wedding day. The clothing looked baggy on her frail body. As though she knew they were about to embark on a journey, she'd even squeezed her tiny bound feet into her best black embroidered shoes.

Seeing the fear etched on Grandmother's creased face made Mei Lien's heart dip, but she didn't take time to comfort her. She grabbed her market bag from the chair next to the bed and started throwing in clothing, her hairbrush, and the lucky money she'd received just three days ago. As soon as the bag was full, she grabbed Grandmother's embroidery bag and dumped all of the floss, needles, and half-finished purses onto the floor. Into it she shoved some of Grandmother's clothing, her antique hairpin, and the pocket money she kept in a pouch wedged behind their shared washstand. Finally, she faced Grandmother.

"*Nǎinai*, we must leave," she said. "The *Bok Guey* are forcing us to sail to China today. *Bàba* is waiting downstairs."

Grandmother's eyes lit up at the mention of China, then quickly clouded again. "Don't forget my face powder, Mei Lien. I mustn't be seen without my face powder."

Mei Lien gently but quickly brushed the white powder over Grandmother's paper-thin skin and touched a dab of rouge to her cheeks and bottom lip before dropping the containers into the embroidery bag. "Your *mang ao* is beautiful, *Năinai*," Mei Lien said as she tied the bag closed. "The dragons and phoenixes will surely protect us on our journey."

Grandmother smiled wide and lifted her chin high. She had told Mei Lien often how the red silk of the jacket brought good luck and boasted how the eight dragons were a sign of her late husband's official rank. The silver pheasant badge on the front had become worn and faded, but the stitching, done in Grandmother's own hand, was so fine one had to look closely to see the design had not been painted on. Mei Lien hoped the ornate jacket wouldn't bring them undue notice today.

Father appeared in the doorway with the taller white man behind him. "It is time to go," he said, his voice sounding stiff.

Mei Lien nodded. "Yes, *Bàba*. Can you carry our things? I'll get *Năinai*." Grandmother needed to be carried wherever she went because her deformed feet prevented her from putting much weight on them. Mei Lien was used to carrying her around the apartment on her back, which was usually all that was required since Grandmother had not left their home in years. Even though she was physically small, carrying her three blocks to the docks was going to be difficult.

With Grandmother on her back, Mei Lien followed the men down the stairs, where the smell of burning cabbage made her eyes water. Candle flames danced on the family altar, lighting the tintype picture of the mother she'd never known in a way that made her seem to be looking directly at Mei Lien. "*Bàba*, the pictures," she murmured, reminding him to stash them with their belongings, which he did, shoving them into Grandmother's bag. Resigned to leaving the rest of their belongings behind, they turned toward the store out front.

They found the shorter white devil in the store filling his pockets with tins of opium and tobacco. Mei Lien ignored him as she passed, her shoes crunching over broken glass. When she emerged out of the shadowed interior of the store onto the wooden sidewalk, Mei Lien instinctively shuffled sideways, pressing herself and Grandmother, weighing heavily on her back, against the glass front of Father's store.

The crowd that had gathered on the street looked like something out of a bad dream, unconnected to the outside world and enshrouded by drifting fog and daylight filtered through a gray, drizzling sky. Pale-faced men in black and brown suits and hats hovered around and over the smaller Chinese men, who wore the same gray loose jacket and pants as Mei Lien and her father. Grandmother's jacket surely stood out as the only spot of color on this dreadful morning, though Mei Lien could not see more than the sleeves wrapped around her neck. She huddled against the building, suddenly afraid of the unprovoked hatred she felt from the crowd.

Even in the cold, the air hung thick with the acrid stench from the tide flats and the backed-up sewer pipe that leaked into the street. An occasional gust of salt air carrying the scent of tar from the docks did little to ease the stench. Down the street, as far as the fog allowed her to see, Chinese men were being herded along like cattle by rows of angry white men brandishing guns and sticks.

"I'll get us out of this," Father whispered in Chinese as he paused beside her on the plank walkway. "Stay close."

His words gave her the courage she needed to step with him into the flow of people in the dirt street. Her foot landed in horse manure, and she felt herself start to slip. With Grandmother's weight throwing her off, it was impossible to stop her fall.

But just then, two strong hands grabbed her and held her upright, with Grandmother still clinging safely to her back. Mei Lien lifted her gaze to see who had helped her and found it was the youngest of the Yeung brothers. She smiled her thanks, but he just frowned and turned away, prodded by the end of a rifle.

That same rifle dug into her side. "Get moving, boy."

Given no other choice, Mei Lien obeyed. With the muscles in her legs and back burning, and the more devastating fire of fear searing her chest, she started downhill toward the water with the rest of the Chinese being dragged from their homes.

"My son, over here!" Father's call came from the alley between his store and the laundry next door. He would never use her name outside their home, but she recognized his voice.

As quickly as she could under her burden and with the white devils herding everyone along, she made her way to the alley, where she found Father with his back pressed against the damp wood siding, his eyes darting behind her.

"Quickly, this way." He pushed away from the wall and headed deeper into the alley, leading them, she hoped, to safety and a chance to stay in this land.

"You there. Stop!"

The shout made them quicken their steps. Mei Lien dug deep inside herself for the strength to move, even though Grandmother's weight made her feel like she was trying to run in a dream where her legs would not work. She pushed on, hearing footsteps behind them. Getting closer.

All she saw then was a blur of darkness passing beside her and her father dropping to the mud. Mei Lien lurched to a stop before she tripped over him and the white man who was grabbing him, pulling him up with fists as large as Father's entire face.

"Where d'you think yer goin'?" The man didn't wait for an answer before he slammed his fist into Father's cheek, making his head snap back with a crack. The man's black mustache twitched over a smile that made the cold fog sink deep into Mei Lien's bones.

"*Bok Guey*! Let him go!" Grandmother let loose a tirade against the white devil, though he wouldn't understand her words. Mei Lien started to slide Grandmother off her back so she could help Father, but Grandmother squeezed her neck tighter, choking her. "No, Mei Lien. He will hit you too," she warned.

Knowing she was right, Mei Lien boosted Grandmother higher on her back, then dragged in a lungful of much-needed air.

Father was the gentlest person Mei Lien knew. He never raised his voice to her or the young men who came into his store on payday making demands and behaving like pigs. He'd never been in a fistfight in his life. To see him being beaten and dishonored hurt Mei Lien more than if she was the one receiving the punches. She couldn't stand here and watch. She had to do something.

Bending over at the waist to balance Grandmother on her back, Mei Lien grabbed the man's arm before he could slam his fist into Father's bloodied face again. "Please, sir," she pleaded in her best English. "Please stop hitting him. We will go to the ship with the others. We won't cause any more trouble."

Just then the crack of a gunshot echoed through the alley. Horror coursed through Mei Lien as she looked toward Father, searching him for signs of a bullet hole. His injuries appeared to be from the beating, not a gun, and he still breathed. Grandmother continued to yell in her ear, so she must have remained unharmed. Mei Lien closed her eyes in relief as she let out a shaky breath.

When she opened them again, she saw the white man still holding Father's jacket twisted in his bloodied fists, though he was looking past Mei Lien toward Washington Street where the gunshot came from. Whatever he saw made his mouth twitch into a smirk, but she didn't turn to see what caused it. She had to get them out of this alley alive.

"Please," she said again. "We will go."

When his black eyes landed on her, she saw hatred so pure it made her legs tremble. She drew herself as tall as Grandmother's weight allowed, hoping that would hide the terror that sizzled through her.

With a growl of disgust, the man threw Father to the ground and stood up, dusting his meaty hands off as a slow smile again spread across his face. "Damn right you will, boy." He kicked Father. "Now git, before I change my mind."

Mei Lien did her best to help Father stand. One eye was swollen shut, and blood ran down his face from his nose and a cut on his cheek. Anger welled up in her, burning away her fear. He'd done nothing wrong. None of them were doing anything wrong. Their only crime was being Chinese, something the white people in America considered lower than farm animals. No matter that the Chinese had built their railroads, chopped their lumber, and canned their salmon. The Chinese had worked just as hard, if not harder, than any white man on this soil, but now they were being kicked out. Unwanted. Unclean. A nuisance.

"Son, we must go." Father's voice held a warning, and she knew he must have seen the anger raging inside her. She didn't trust her voice for fear of unleashing her anger on the white man and causing him to hurt Father even more. Or kill him. Sobered by that thought, she just nodded and fell into step beside Father as he limped back to the street.

When they reached the wooden walkway again, she jerked to a stop and had to fight to remain standing as her legs threatened to crumble beneath her. Lying sprawled in the mud in front of them was the youngest Yeung brother, the one who had helped her. The back of his head had been shot off, leaving a gaping, bloody wound she knew would haunt her every time she closed her eyes. His sightless eyes stared into the alley she'd just come from. The other Chinese passing by them looked away.

"Get on with you," the mustached man ordered, prodding her from behind.

Father pulled on her arm, and finally her feet cooperated, though she felt an unbearable weight crushing her body, a weight that she knew was more than just Grandmother. Together they stepped around the body and into the street toward the wagon that would carry them to the ship.

# Chapter Three

*Sunday, May 27—present day*
*Rothesay Estate, Orcas Island*

O livia went upstairs to call home, but Inara was still studying the embroidered sleeve when she heard the sound of a car engine outside. That was when she remembered they'd left the main house doors wide open. Anyone could walk right in.

She rewrapped the sleeve in the blue-checkered cotton and left it on the kitchen table, hurrying through the sitting room to push the lace curtain aside and peer out.

A banged-up green pickup truck with tools in the back sat parked next to her car. A big man with rust-colored short hair, wearing a Carhartt jacket, strode toward the main house doors.

Despite a niggling feeling of unease, Inara slipped outside and called, "Hello? Can I help you?" She wasn't about to let this stranger walk right into her family's manor.

The man swung around to face her, his weathered eyes narrowed. "Who are you?"

She lifted her chin. "Inara Erickson. The owner of Rothesay. Who are you?" She purposely matched the man's confrontational tone.

Like sun coming from behind clouds, the man's face lit up with a grin. He closed the distance between them and stuck out his hand. "Sorry, thought you were a nosy tourist or a squatter or something. Tom Gardner. My wife and I live across the road."

She shook his hand, then let it go and took a step back.

He didn't seem to notice the intentional distance as he stuck his hands in his pockets. "We got in the habit of helping Dahlia and Nancy out with the place. They mentioned you often, you know. Anyway, now that they're...gone..." He paused and cleared his throat. "Now that they're gone, we've kept on, wondering what's going to happen to it."

At the sight of this big man fighting emotion at the mention of losing Dahlia, Inara's defenses dropped and she smiled. "Good to meet you. Was it you who mowed the grass?"

Tom nodded. His ruddy face turned back toward the main house. "So, what are you going to do with this place?"

Inara followed his gaze and saw it as he must—a neglected money pit. "I came here to see what needs doing to get it on the market."

"You're selling? What about the B and B?"

Her gaze shot back to Tom. "You know about that?" Inara had only found out about Dahlia's plans a couple of weeks ago when the lawyer handed her the packet of materials Dahlia had pulled together.

He smiled and jerked his chin toward his truck. "Forgot to mention I'm a builder. Dahlia was relentless with her questions." He paused, then added more quietly, "She was one smart lady."

Before Inara could respond, Tom went on as though emotion hadn't just roughened his voice. "So, you're not going to do it? The B and B?"

Inara looked back at the house and tried to imagine the inn Dahlia had created in her plans. Her mind grabbed hold of the images and took them further, as it had been doing since she'd arrived. She could see her boutique hotel as clearly as if she'd been creating the vision all her life. "You know, I think I have a better idea. A boutique hotel."

"What's that?"

She still stared at the house, seeing her hotel. "Think elegance, impeccable service, privacy, modern amenities, and personalized attention."

"Sounds like something my wife would like."

Inara blinked and saw the house as it was now and all the work she was going to have to do. She turned back to Tom. "Now I just need to figure out how I'm going to pull it off."

Worry threatened to completely erase her vision. This was going to be more than a full-time job. It would be a whole life change. And it meant she'd have to walk away from the Starbucks offer. Was that really what she wanted to do?

It also was going to take a lot of money she didn't have. She glanced around at the potholed driveway and moss-covered fountain, thinking of the long list of items that needed attention and knowing there would be lots more she hadn't yet thought of. Then, on top of all that, rooms would need to be reconfigured, bathrooms added, and utilities updated.

"I wonder what renovations are going to cost," she murmured to herself.

"I can help you with that," Tom said.

She squinted at him. "How?"

"I'm the best contractor in the islands, maybe on the mainland too." He kicked at a rock on the pavement. "If you're looking to get started soon, I have time on my schedule. Lost the bid on a job I was counting on."

Inara felt a smile stretch across her face. Of course, she'd check his references, but something told her Dahlia had planned this all along. "Want to come in for tea and to discuss plans? You can meet my sister too."

Tom glanced toward the sun before shaking his head. "Wish I could, but I've got a crew across the island that I need to check on before quittin' time. I just came home to pick something up, and that's when I saw you over here."

"How about you give me your contact information and I'll call you later this week?"

Tom pulled a well-used pad of paper and a carpenter's pencil from his back pocket. After scribbling his info on the top sheet, he tore it off and handed it to her. Soon he was in his truck and heading out the driveway with one quick honk and a wave out his window.

Inara waved back, then looked down at the paper he'd given her, thrilled to have someone who wanted to help her.

A cool breeze fluttered the paper and caused her to shiver, making her realize how fast time was flying. She should grab Liv and head into town for dinner before it got dark. They planned to stay the night and catch an early ferry tomorrow to beat the Memorial Day holiday crowds later in the day.

Knowing she'd want to walk through the manor in the morning, she dashed through the house, turning off lights and locking the doors.

All the while, her heart raced with anticipation as she envisioned what might be.

Back in Dahlia's house, she grabbed her keys off the kitchen table and called up the stairs, "Liv, you ready to head into town?"

"Be right down!"

While she waited, Inara unwrapped the embroidered sleeve again and was struck anew by the bold details in the pictures. It had to be significant if for no other reason than because someone had hidden it under the stairs. It could be her hobby, she decided. In between working on the hotel renovations, she could research where the sleeve had come from, who had made it, who had hidden it, and why.

This was going to be a fascinating summer.

Up before the sun, Inara wrapped herself in a blanket and settled on the front porch with hot tea and her laptop. As the forest woke around her, she dumped all the hotel ideas firing in her brain into several spreadsheets.

When she finally had everything down and felt a semblance of control over the project, she raised her arms overhead to stretch. Halfway up, she froze.

Just across the driveway a deer was nibbling on a bush. Inara watched, silent and unmoving, until the deer wandered away. Seeing the deer felt like a sign that being here was the right decision.

Fully awake now, she went back inside to refill her tea and see if Olivia was up yet. She wasn't. As Inara headed back to the porch, her gaze caught on the sleeve still lying on the kitchen table. Grabbing it, she went back to the porch and her laptop and searched for the word *embroidery*. Quickly she realized the term was too vague. Next she tried *Asian embroidery*. This yielded more promising results. Soon she was lost in her reading and barely noticed as her tea got cold.

The pictures and descriptions she found confirmed her suspicion that the sleeve was Asian, though from which specific country she couldn't be sure.

Careful to keep the sleeve away from the layer of dust coating the porch furniture, she unfolded it to get another look and compare it to the embroidered clothing shown on the screen.

The sleeves on some Chinese garments had a similar style, but the embroidered design was totally different. Japanese kimonos had much fuller sleeves, again with different designs. She found significant differences in embroidered Korean, Vietnamese, and Indian robes, gowns, and jackets.

She was getting nowhere, and she was wasting time.

Still, she couldn't just stash the sleeve away and forget about it. She pulled up a new search window and kept looking.

"Wow, I forgot how gorgeous mornings are here."

Inara greeted her sister and only then noticed the spear of sun coming over Mount Constitution and bouncing off the dew droplets coating the cut grass at the bottom of the porch steps. Immediately she was back to being a kid, waking up early to go kayaking with her mom. Her mom used to tell her that she loved the morning best because even the wind was still asleep, which kept the water smooth as glass.

There was no better place to watch the world wake up than from on the water. Inara had felt so special being the one her mom took with her in the two-person kayak. She also loved the almond croissants her mom would buy from the bakery in town where they'd stop for breakfast.

Inara looked in the direction of the water, even though she couldn't see it with the manor house in the way. "Want to take the kayaks out before we head home?"

Olivia dropped onto the padded love seat next to her, narrowly missing the sleeve. "Not really," Olivia answered as she scrubbed her palms over her face. "I slept longer than I meant to, and Adam's already called to see what time I'll be home."

"Think we can make the 8:50 ferry?"

Olivia glanced at her watch, then jumped to her feet. "Only if I hurry."

As Olivia ran back inside, Inara took quick stock of what needed doing before she headed out and decided that, since she planned to return soon, all she really needed was to grab her overnight bag. She still had time for more sleeve research as she waited for Olivia to shower.

This time she typed *Asian symbolism* into the search engine, thinking of the unfamiliar pictures and characters in the embroidery. Most of the results had to do with the actual Chinese or Japanese symbols in the written languages. She scrolled down and started seeing more promising options. After browsing a few sites, she stumbled onto one that seemed more academic.

It was a paper explaining how certain symbols in the Chinese culture denoted social standing, provided protection or good fortune, or represented a moral message. After typing the author's name—Daniel Chin—into the search bar, she found he was a professor at the University of Washington–Seattle, her alma mater.

Perfect. He was local, and she'd bet he could tell her something about her sleeve.

She scribbled his contact information onto her notepad. Then, with a glance at the clock, she realized it was almost time to head for the ferry.

"Liv! You ready?" she called into the house through the open door. There was no reply, so she took that to mean she had a couple extra minutes. That was all she needed.

She quickly typed an email to the professor, telling him about the sleeve, describing the design embroidered on it, and asking if he could shed some light on it for her. She finished with a request for him to get back to her as soon as possible and listed her cell phone number. At the last minute, she decided to snap a picture of the sleeve and attach it to the email. *That ought to snag his attention.*

Then she closed her laptop and gathered her things to go inside. "Olivia, time to go!"

She'd come back later this week to get started on the manor house renovations, she decided. That way she could meet with Tom and get the ball rolling.

And then a new thought struck, making her hands fall momentarily still. Dad. He wasn't going to be happy about her plans. He'd been proud of her, bragging to everyone who'd listen about his daughter following his footsteps into international business.

A hotel could be considered international business. Right? She'd have guests from all over the world, after all.

The thought did little to comfort her as she climbed the stairs to get her bag—and Olivia. She'd have to get her dad on board tonight. Get it over with quickly.

The sun was hanging low over the Olympic Mountains as she let herself into her father's house where she'd been living for the two years since he'd had his heart attack. After dropping her bag off in her room, she went in search of him and found him in his den on the computer.

"It's Memorial Day, Dad. A holiday. Take a break."

His gray-blue eyes lit up when he saw her, and a wry grin split his mouth. "Not in Shanghai, Nara-girl."

She knew he was in the process of negotiating a business buyout that would expand the cruise ship side of the company into Southeast Asia, so she wasn't surprised he was working. She was surprised, however, when he got up from his desk and came to sit with her on the leather sofa in front of the fireplace.

"Was it as bad as you thought?" he asked.

She paused, trying to figure out what to tell him. "It wasn't too bad. The estate could use some work."

"What about you?" He cleared his throat. "Are you okay?"

His compassion caught her off guard. She'd expected him to avoid the emotional side of her visit to the island. He hadn't been back to the island since the accident either, but he never talked about that kind of thing. She knew he loved her, but their conversations usually revolved around safe topics like the company, her new job, and their family.

"It was rough," she admitted, rubbing her fingers. "Olivia helped a lot. But when I got to Rothesay, it felt so good to be back, like I belong there. In fact, I'm heading up again in a couple days. You should come this weekend."

"I'm proud of you, honey." He put his hands on his knees like he was getting ready to stand up. "I'm sure the new owner is going to love it just as much."

She noticed he didn't reply to her suggestion, but she let it go and placed a hand on his arm to keep him from leaving. "Actually, I want to talk to you about that. Got a minute?"

He leaned back against the cushion. "What's up?"

She shifted to face him. "Dahlia was a genius, Dad. When I looked at Rothesay with her plans in mind, I could totally see it. Remember that hotel we stayed in outside Bordeaux the summer I was fourteen?"

"Yes. What about it?"

"Remember how you liked the personal service we got from the staff and how they had wine and cheese every evening in the library?" She was trying hard to set the stage before springing her idea on him.

"Your mom loved that." He sounded suspicious.

Time to jump in with both feet. "I want to do that with Rothesay. I want to turn it into a boutique hotel."

He shook his head but didn't say anything. The look on his face told her what was going through his mind. Before he could reject the idea, she kept talking.

"Liv and I went through the whole place, and it's perfect. I even got a lead on a builder for the renovations. I have to talk with him first, of course, but I'm hoping to have the place ready for guests by next summer."

The more she talked, the more excited she felt. "There's something special about Rothesay, Dad. I love it there. I'd forgotten how much, but it felt like home. This could be an amazing opportunity, you know? The islands are becoming more and more popular as a vacation destination, and my hotel would give tourists a place to stay unlike anything else on the island. It'll be a place where guests want to return every year. Even you'll want to stay there."

"What about your job?" He asked like she was a little girl who wanted to head to the mall with her friends instead of doing chores.

She swallowed and looked down at her lap. "I'm going to turn it down."

His palms slapped his thighs so hard she jumped. "The hell you are! Do you know how many strings I pulled to get you that interview? You can't just throw it away to play innkeeper on an island in the middle of nowhere!"

All the air in the room was suddenly sucked away. She'd been certain she'd gotten the job based on her own merit. "No," she choked. "I didn't know you pulled strings."

He shot her an exasperated look. "I did what any father would have done, and you should be grateful for it."

She stared at a scar on the leather seat as she calmed herself. She had to stay focused on the real issue here, she told herself. "I appreciate all you did for me, Dad. I really do. But I feel so alive at Rothesay. I've got so many ideas for renovations and am excited to run the hotel—"

"What do you know about hotel management? Nothing."

"That's not entirely true. I did that work-study at the Rome Cavalieri and loved it."

"Two weeks does not provide work experience."

*Ouch.* She deliberately lowered her tone and changed her tactic. "I think Aunt Dahlia left the estate to me because she knew I belonged there and she knew I was the person to give it new life. I want to do this. Far more than I want to work with Starbucks coffee suppliers."

He was silent for a long time. "How would you pay for it? Even without your student loan debt, you wouldn't have the money."

She closed her eyes and went in for the kill before she lost her nerve. "You, Dad. I want you to be my financial partner on this. Think about it. You know all about tourism with your cruise lines. A boutique hotel on Orcas Island would be the perfect investment for a man like you."

"Inara." He shook his head.

"Mom would have loved the idea. Rothesay was her family's legacy, and it would break her heart if we sold it." She held herself very still as she waited for his next words, knowing she might have pushed too far.

His shoulders slumped, and his gaze turned to the framed picture of his late wife above the mantel. Instead of acknowledging Inara's claim about her, though, he stuck to business matters. "I can't make such a risky investment right now, with the buyout and all. You know this."

"Just a personal loan, then," she said before he could say no. "A loan that covers renovations and personal expenses, all of which I'll pay back with interest once we open."

"And if it doesn't work? If you never go in the black?"

"I still own the estate." She hated what she was about to say. "Use it as collateral. If the hotel doesn't work out, I'll sell it to pay back your loan."

His phone started ringing, and he quickly got to his feet and crossed to his desk to answer. "I've got to take this," he told her. Inara listened as he put the caller on hold. Then he pressed his lips together and seemed to be considering. When he raised his gaze to her, she saw a spark in his eye.

"Can I help it that I want my daughter happy? Let's iron out the details later, but I'll give you the loan on the condition that you give me a full monthly accounting of every penny spent. Agreed?"

She dashed to him and threw her arms around him. "Thank you! You won't regret this. I promise."

He hugged her back with the arm not holding the phone. "I reserve the right to call in the loan at any time if I don't like what's happening. You'd have to sell the estate right away," he warned. "Is that something you're willing to risk?"

It wasn't going to come to that, she decided. The Rothesay Hotel would be opening next summer; she was sure of it. "Yes. Thanks, Dad."

"Don't thank me, yet, Nara-girl. Let's see how your renovations go."

# Chapter Four

Are you comfortable, *Năinai*?" Mei Lien asked again, even though Grandmother had assured her over and over that she was well. They both knew the question was pointless. When they'd boarded the *Prince of the Pacific*, they'd been told the steerage berths were full and all that remained were first-class berths on the upper deck. They were then ordered to pay twelve dollars each for their tickets, which, of course, they paid for fear of what the alternative might be. They would be arriving in China with little money to start their new life. But as Father had reminded her, at least they'd be alive and they'd have each other.

After settling into their cabin and tending to Father's wounds, Mei Lien had stood at the open door, stopping any crew member who passed to ask for food. No one helped them. From the white-uniformed boys whose jobs seemed to be keeping everything clean and shining to the blue-uniformed officers barking orders, they all ignored her equally. Once the ship left the dock after four o'clock, well past the scheduled sailing time, she'd finally worked up the courage to venture belowdecks herself.

She'd found a loaf of dry bread in the pantry, which she'd hidden under her jacket and taken to her family. Still, they were hungry.

"I'm fine," Grandmother answered Mei Lien's latest inquiry from where she sat propped against the cabin wall on the double bed. "Just tired. You should rest too." She scooted down until she was lying beside Father, who was asleep. There was no bed for Mei Lien, which was just as well since she wasn't interested in sleep.

She leaned over Father again, worried that he was sleeping so long. The skin around his eye and along the entire side of his face was swollen and purple. She'd tended his cuts as well as she could, but blood still seeped into the cloth wedged under his cheek. Though he hadn't complained, the fact that he'd fallen asleep almost immediately after eating his bread proved to Mei Lien that his injuries were probably more severe than he'd allowed her to see.

Exhausted from worry and fear, she dropped onto the single chair and let her head fall back against the wall. She could feel the rumbling of the engines as the steamer chugged through Puget Sound, heading away from Seattle and her home. Through the single round window, she saw the last hint of light splashing red on the island they were passing. It was nearly nightfall, and she could not ignore the truth any longer. She'd never see her home again. They were going to China.

A low moan sounded from the bed. Mei Lien jumped up from the chair to lean over its two occupants. A quick glance confirmed Grandmother had fallen into a peaceful sleep, but Father's battered head was jerking back and forth.

"Shh, *Bàba*, you are safe," she murmured to him as she lay her hand on the uninjured side of his head, where the shaved area met the midnight-black queue that twisted under his back. Seeing him so hurt scared her. She wouldn't know what to do if she lost him. All her life her two companions had been Father and Grandmother.

White children had been kept from playing with her by their mothers and nannies, and she'd rarely known slant-eyed children like herself. Most Chinese in Seattle were bachelors who'd come to work and send money home to China. Only a handful of Chinese families lived in Seattle—and none had children Mei Lien's age. Grandmother had taught her everything she needed to know about Chinese culture and caring for the home and family. Working in Father's store had taught her how to speak, read, and write in English, as well as all she knew about American culture. Her family was her whole life. She needed Father to be well.

He moaned in his sleep. She had to do something, anything, to ease his pain.

Then it came to her. She'd heard that all of the Chinese people in Seattle had been loaded onto the steamship. Jong Li had to be on board somewhere.

"*Bàba*, I'm getting you some help. I'll return as fast as I can," she whispered to him. Then she moved quickly to the door, slipping into the cold evening air intent on finding the herbalist who tended all of Seattle's sick and injured Chinese. She'd find him, she decided, if she had to search every corner of the ship.

She started forward, past the wooden lifeboats covered in canvas, toward the stairs she'd used earlier when she'd gone in search of food. But before she reached the stairwell, a door opened several yards in front of her and two uniformed stewards emerged. An idea came to her, one that might be better than searching for Jong Li.

The young men seemed to be deep in discussion and did not notice her, but remembering she appeared to be a boy and could do such things, Mei Lien stepped right into their path, forcing them to stop and notice.

"Please, sirs," she begged in her best English with appropriately downcast eyes. "My father is injured and needs assistance. Is there a doctor on this ship?" She peeked up to see their reaction.

Neither man seemed moved by her plea. The freckle-faced one turned his head toward the railing and pretended she wasn't speaking to him. The other cleared his throat but did not say anything. She repeated her request louder.

They still ignored her, this time pushing past her and continuing on with their discussion as if she'd not spoken.

Water droplets from the sea splashed her face as she watched the young men walk away from her, but she didn't take notice of the freezing cold water. Her skin felt inflamed by the fury she felt shooting through her.

From the moment she'd woken this morning, she'd been subjected to the cruel treatment of white men who were convinced they were superior. She'd heard plenty of stories of the beatings, hangings, shootings, and cruel injustices the white man had inflicted on the Chinese from California to Wyoming so she'd allowed them to force her from her home. She'd boarded this ship. She'd even paid the fare she didn't want to pay for passage to a country she did not want to go to. But it should not matter that she was Chinese and the men walking away from her were not. They were all human, and that, at the most basic level, entitled Father to receive help.

Without realizing what she was doing, she marched up behind the pair and tapped the red-haired one on the shoulder. "Excuse me. My father needs a doctor. Now. Where can I find him?"

The two men gaped at her, then their gazes met and they burst out laughing. "I don't think Doc is available," the tall, dark-haired one said with a nudge to his friend.

"Just go below with the other Orientals. It's warmer there," the one she'd tapped told her. His eyes were friendlier, and in them, she saw a flash of what looked like shame.

"I'd be happy to go where it is warm, as soon as my father sees the doctor."

Instead of answering, the older rude one straightened his spine, then grabbed his friend's arm. "Come on, Ralph. We've got orders."

Ralph hesitated. "I'm sorry," he said to her in a low voice. "We were told not to interfere—" Before he could finish whatever he was about to say, his friend succeeded in dragging him away.

Mei Lien wished she really was a boy. If she was, she could march after those two and interfere in their precious rounds with a fist to the jaw. That seemed to be the only thing white men listened to.

She spun around and headed back toward the stairs, back to her original plan of finding Jong Li. But then her attention was caught by the door ahead marked *Pilot House*, its window lit from the other side. That was where the man in charge could be found, no doubt. Maybe she could convince him to help Father. They'd paid their way, after all.

Without a care for what might happen to her, she marched up to the door and lifted her hand to yank it open. But a voice from inside made her stop before the door budged.

"Are you certain about dumping the cargo, sir?" the voice asked in a hushed tone that led Mei Lien to believe its owner did not wish to be overheard.

"Och, of course, Cap'n," answered another voice, this one heavy with a foreign accent Mei Lien had never before heard, with a lilt at the end of the words and a heavier sound to the vowels that made it hard to pick them apart from one another. "I can't afford to have this filth on my ship. No self-respecting man would knowingly sleep on the same berth where a dirty Oriental has lain. The sooner we can rid ourselves of them, the better. How much longer until we can dump?"

"We've got to get out of the straits first," the captain answered. "We don't want the currents littering the sound's beaches with bodies."

"Right ye are, Cap'n. But the sooner we lighten the load, the better."

A chill that had nothing to do with the icy wind slid through Mei Lien's body, freezing her in place. Dump the cargo...bodies...

She and all the other Seattle Chinese were the cargo.

The truth hit her like a physical punch. She reeled back from the metal door, her hand still hanging in the air as though about to grasp the handle.

They weren't going to China.

They weren't going anywhere but to the bottom of the sea.

No. She had it wrong. She must have it wrong. People didn't dump whole ships full of people into the ocean. Even the *Bok Guey*, the white devil, couldn't commit mass murder just because he didn't like the Chinese.

But it had already happened, hadn't it? Pockets of Chinese all along the coast had been killed over the last twenty years, especially since the passing of the Chinese Exclusion Act four years ago. Why was this so unbelievable?

Trembling, she backed farther away from the door and the evil on the other side.

Before this night was through, she and her family would be killed. The truth was too horrible for her mind to fully understand.

She thought of Grandmother, asleep in the cabin. Though stubborn and strict about proper behavior, Grandmother was her strength. She was the only mother Mei Lien had ever known. Grandmother was the one who had taught her to read and write in Chinese. She'd taught her to cook, clean, and care for their home. She'd taught her how to embroider the fine coin purses they sold at Father's store, which earned the family enough to buy a whole chicken every Sunday. It was Grandmother who'd decided Mei Lien should dress as a boy when she'd started filling out and drawing attention from men about town.

And Father! Father, who had brought his pregnant wife and mother to America where he planned to be a successful merchant and raise strong sons. Instead, he'd lost his wife and raised a daughter, but he'd never once complained and he'd always made Mei Lien feel cherished. He called her his thousand pieces of gold. Even though she hadn't known many other Chinese children in Seattle, she'd always known it was rare for a daughter to feel important to her father. Knowing that such a strong, honorable man was about to meet his end—and there was nothing she could do to stop it—made Mei Lien feel as if her bones had left her body.

Weakly, she stumbled to the railing just before her stomach repeatedly heaved what little contents it had. Through tears, she watched the bile and saliva that dripped from her mouth catch on the wind and fall to the swirling black waters below. Her hands slipped along the metal railing from the sweat coating her palms, despite the winter cold.

A noise caught her attention, and Mei Lien turned in time to see the door to the pilot house start to open. She quickly threw herself into the shadows next to a lifeboat, squeezing her body into the tightest ball she could form, holding her breath.

The same two voices emerged, discussing nautical miles and water currents. Mei Lien grasped the rope tied to the lifeboat with both hands and willed herself not to make a sound, despite her convulsing stomach and shaking breath.

She would not confront them. She would not lose her honor and beg for her family's lives. These weren't men, but demons. Demons didn't listen to reason.

As they passed her hiding place, she turned to look at the men who would end her life. Both were surprisingly young, only a decade or so older than her seventeen years. One was difficult to see because he had his jacket collar lifted and his captain's hat pulled low over his eyes. The other was the one she was most interested in. The one with the odd accent. The one the captain answered to. He was to blame.

He walked with the gait of a man who knew he held power. The lanterns on deck cast enough light to show his features in great detail, even though she could only see him from the side. He wore no hat, and his short red hair parted down the center of his head and ended above his ears. Matching eyebrows slashed in straight lines over eyes that looked dead, even as he laughed at something the captain said. A straight nose ended above moving thin lips, though the roaring in her head kept her from hearing what they said.

She'd rarely had cause to despise another human, but her hatred for this one burned hot. Again she wished she was a boy because then she'd have the strength to grab him and throw him over the side of the steamship before he could do the same to her family and all the innocent others below.

As soon as they were out of sight, Mei Lien ran toward her family's cabin.

"My son, what is it?"

She jerked her head up and saw Father leaning weakly against the open door to their cabin as though he'd come searching for her but did not have the strength to venture far. The worry on his face cut through Mei Lien's anger like an arrow point.

Her footsteps faltered. She closed her eyes and drew a deep breath. She had to tell Father. He might think of a way to save them. Maybe since he'd sailed on a steamship before, he'd know a place where they could hide until the ship docked.

She hurried to him, wishing she could crawl into his lap as she'd done as a child and know that he'd protect her from all evil. Instead she raised a hand and lightly stroked the uninjured side of his face as she looked into his eyes and saw the pain he would never admit to feeling. "I hate that you are hurt."

He leaned into her touch for a moment, causing Mei Lien's heart to ache even more. This gentle, brave soul did not deserve the fate that awaited him. He, more than anyone, did not deserve this.

"Tell me, Daughter. What puts that expression on your face?"

Mei Lien closed her eyes, holding on to this moment before she spoke the words that would change everything. Right now they were a family caring for one another. After she told him what she knew, they would be a family fighting to survive, or crying at their inability to choose their own fate.

Tears fell before she could stop them, so she squeezed her eyes shut tighter. "Forgive me, *Bàba*. I must tell you something unspeakable."

She felt him stiffen under her palm and she opened her eyes. As though filled with renewed energy, he glanced at his sleeping mother behind him, then drew the door closed.

"Did someone hurt you? A man?" He ran his hands over her head and down her arms as his eyes searched for signs of injury. Even in the dim light cast by the deck lamps, she could see that all color had drained from his skin except where the bruises were.

She wanted to guide him back to his bed but knew he would not allow it. She shook her head in answer to his question. "No, it's not that."

"Tell me." Despite his pallor, his voice sounded as strong as always, and that gave Mei Lien the push she needed.

She looked behind her and to each side. Even though they appeared to be alone on the damp, shadowed deck, she leaned closer to her father. "I heard the captain and his superior talking. They aren't taking us to China."

"Then where? Victoria? San Francisco?"

She shook her head. "They aren't delivering us anywhere. I heard them talk of dumping the cargo where the currents won't wash bodies up on beaches."

His eyes widened until Mei Lien could see the full brown circles rimmed with white. He shook his head hard, despite the pain it must have caused him. "No. No, you must be wrong."

"*Bàba*, think about it." She grabbed his hands, willing him to believe her. "Just last fall three Chinese were killed after being attacked for no crime other than working at the hop farm in Squak Valley where the white men wanted jobs. Over these last months, Chinese have been driven out of Tacoma and all the local mines for the same reason. They don't want us here. Why would they waste time or money shipping us all the way to China? To them it's no different than shipping garbage."

Father's gaze darted over her shoulder, and she turned in time to see the captain coming along the deck from the rear of the ship toward them, alone this time.

She felt her body cringe as he passed without a glance. They watched, silent, until he disappeared into the pilot house.

"What do we do?" she whispered to Father, eager to set whatever plan he might create into action.

He turned his face to look at her, and something in his eyes made her chest feel like it was being crushed. "*Bàba?*"

In a voice so low she had to strain to hear him over the sound of the engines and water slapping the ship, he asked, "You are certain, Mei Lien? You know our fate?"

She wished she was wrong. "Yes, *Bàba*. What do we do?" she asked again.

Instead of answering, he looked at the black water rushing past them and seemed to be considering. Then, without a word, he turned and went into the cabin where he grabbed the bags he'd earlier dropped onto the floor.

Mei Lien stood just inside the door and watched with growing dread as he pulled his money purse out of his own bag, then opened Grandmother's bag. The fact that he would dare to look through his mother's things, dishonoring her privacy, told Mei Lien she wasn't going to like what was about to happen.

When he finished his task, Father held his own embroidered money purse in his hands. They shook as he reached toward her, placing the pouch in her hands. "Hide this in the bindings you have about your chest so it is not lost. Hurry, do it now!"

Without question, Mei Lien snapped to obey. As fast as she could move with fingers stiff with cold and fear, she unfastened her outer jacket and slid the pouch into the neck opening of the shirt she wore beneath. Then she wedged it into the bindings that hid evidence of her femininity. When she finished refastening her coat, she faced Father again, trusting him completely. "What do we do next?"

He looked at her for a long time, a jumble of unspoken thoughts and emotions marring his features. Then he raised a calloused palm to each side of her face and met her gaze. "Daughter, live happy and love deep. This is my wish for you." Then, before Mei Lien could question why he was saying this to her, he let go of her and stepped back. "You must go now before it is too late."

Go? "Where are we going, *Bàba*? Do you know where we can hide?"

A dark shadow fell over his face. "Your grandmother and I are going to be with your mother and my father. Our fate has led us here, and we will accept this when the time comes. For you, my daughter, I do not accept this as your fate. Hurry!" He ushered her back through the door and outside to the railing overlooking the black water.

Mei Lien didn't understand. "What are you saying? Where am I to go?"

Father turned to face the water and gestured with his chin. "There. See that black mass over there? It is an island. Possibly the last before we reach open sea. You can swim there, Mei Lien. You are a strong swimmer. I taught you in the lake five summers past, remember?"

The very thought of jumping into the inky, swirling foam below made her feel like she was about to lose control of her bowels. "I can't. No, *Bàba*, I can't do it." She shook her head as she stepped away from the railing and the terrifying blackness beyond.

"Daughter, look at me." Father grasped her arms and put his bleeding face right into hers. "You don't have a choice. If you want to live, you must jump." He looked across the water, then turned back to face her again. "We will be past the island soon. You must go now."

She shook her head. "I can't. I can't."

"You will." He pulled her to him and crushed her in his arms. "May the ancestors watch over you."

Mei Lien felt the steamship shudder beneath her feet and wondered if the quaking of her own body had caused it.

"You don't have a choice," Father hissed. Before she knew what was happening, he'd prodded her to the ship's cold metal railing. "Climb up, Mei Lien."

# Chapter Five

*Thursday, May 31—present day*
*Downtown Seattle*

"Hey, Zoé, is my dad available?" Inara said into her phone's Bluetooth as she navigated downtown Seattle traffic. She was heading back to the island with her car packed to the ceiling, but had just realized she'd forgotten all week to ask her dad about the sleeve. Packing and making arrangements to start work on the hotel had filled her every waking minute. Yesterday she'd finally met with her hiring manager at Starbucks to let him know she was turning down the job. It had been a quick and uncomfortable meeting, but difficult as it was, Inara felt she was doing the right thing for herself.

Which was terrifying. What if she was making a huge mistake?

"No, sorry, Inara," answered her father's executive assistant. "He told me not to disturb him for any reason during his meeting with the Yŏu Yì executives. They're at a critical stage of negotiations."

"Oh, right. I forgot they were in town. Well, I'll just catch him later then." After hanging up, Inara glanced at the clock and saw she was making good time. Barring traffic or ferry delays, she'd be on the island well before dinnertime. She couldn't wait.

The sleeve was still on her mind, though, as she merged onto I-5 north from the Olive Way ramp. She hadn't heard back on the email she'd sent to that professor. The University of Washington, where he worked, was just across the bridge. She could stop in quickly and talk to him in person. And then she could get back on the road, forget about the sleeve once and for all, and concentrate solely on the hotel.

Yes, that was what she'd do. She put on her right turn signal and eased onto the off-ramp to the University District. Hopefully the professor wasn't on vacation for the summer.

As soon as she found parking on campus, she pulled out her phone and pulled up the UW website to find where the professor's office was located. Ten minutes later, she knocked on a wooden door labeled *Daniel Chin, PhD, China Studies*.

No answer.

She knocked again and then noticed the schedule posted on the wall next to the door. Apparently, Professor Chin could be found in Bagley Hall teaching History of Modern China. The class ended at twelve twenty.

Checking her phone for the time, she realized that waiting for the class to end would make her miss the ferry she was hoping for. It was worth it, she decided, to have the mystery out of her mind. She headed back outside.

She was well acquainted with the campus and Bagley Hall, where she'd taken several classes over the years. She headed in that direction and soon found herself by Drumheller Fountain with the breathtaking view behind it of Mount Rainier in the distance. Like any local, she took a moment to appreciate the view of the mountain when it was out from behind the clouds, and then she continued into the hushed stone building beyond.

She peeked inside the first classroom and saw the teacher was a woman. The next room, the auditorium, was packed with students listening to the Asian man at the front, who surely must have been Professor Chin. In all her years on campus, she'd never run across this particular professor. This one glimpse showed her she might have missed out by focusing her graduate study on Europe.

He was young for a professor, probably in his early thirties, but clearly an expert on his topic. He caught the audience's attention with interesting facts and visuals on the screens behind him, but the passion in his voice cemented each person's focus on him.

She slipped into a seat three rows down, scooting past two girls hunched over laptops taking notes. They both shot her a scowl as she passed. After settling into the seat, she looked around and noticed the room was almost entirely filled with women.

"So what do you think that meant to the Han when the Manchu took over the country?" The professor sounded like he was about to reveal a juicy secret, and she found herself leaning forward, waiting for what he'd say next.

In the next ten minutes, she learned more about Chinese history than she'd ever known. Energy sizzled from the professor, electrifying the whole room, so that even the normally half-asleep students in the back sat up straight and listened. Professor Chin made his lecture sound like Hollywood gossip.

As soon as the lecture ended, the room erupted into commotion. Inara waited in her seat as students gathered their things and streamed out. A knot of girls converged on the stage around the professor, asking questions as he gathered his things, unhooked his laptop from the projector, and slid it into a bag he slung over his shoulder. As the group of girls moved toward the stairs, with the professor in the middle, Inara got to her feet to intercept him before he reached the door.

"Excuse me, Professor Chin. May I have a moment of your time?"

His hazel-colored eyes paused on her face for a fraction of a second, then returned to the girl next to him. "Britta, why don't you email my assistant and set up an appointment during office hours? I'll be able to explain it to you in more detail then." Then he raised his gaze to encompass all the females around him, Inara included. "The same goes for all of you. Make an appointment, and I'll be happy to answer your questions. But for now I've got to run to a meeting."

He pushed out of the knot and made it as far as the fountain outside before Inara caught up to him. "Professor Chin, I just need a moment."

He stopped to face her and even smiled at her, revealing straight white teeth, but she saw the tightness around his eyes that showed he was irritated. "I'm sorry, Ms....?"

"Inara Erickson." She stuck out her hand and he shook it.

Before she could explain who she was and what she wanted, he was already turning away. "Office hours are from two to four. Come to my office then."

She rushed to catch up as he hurried across the brick path. "Professor Chin, I'm not a student. I found an embroidered sleeve that I'm hoping you can tell me more about, or at least lead me to someone who can help. I emailed you a picture."

He stopped so suddenly that she was two steps ahead of him before she noticed and turned back. "Ms. Erickson, of course. Forgive me. I saw your email but haven't had a chance to reply yet. That's a fascinating specimen you have."

She couldn't help the glow of satisfaction that spread through her—as immature as it was—that she'd managed to catch his interest. "I have it with me." She patted her shoulder bag.

He glanced at his wristwatch. "I can be a little late to my meeting, I suppose. Let's go to my office."

Once in his artifact-cluttered office, he pushed aside a pile of books to clear a space on his desk and laid out a plain white cloth. Inara unwrapped the blue-checkered cotton and held the sleeve out to him. "I found it under the stairs in my family's estate on Orcas Island. I have no idea where it came from or how long it's been there."

Professor Chin's eyes didn't leave the sleeve as he put on a pair of white cotton gloves. "It would be a good idea not to handle the sleeve too much. The oils on our hands could degrade the fragile stitching."

Inara bit back a smile, drawn to his sexy nerdiness in spite of herself. "I'll keep that in mind, Professor."

"Call me Daniel." Finally, his gaze left the sleeve and he smiled at her, revealing a single dimple next to his mouth. "You're not a student after all."

She let her smile widen. "And you can call me Inara."

"Is that a family name?" Something flashed in his eyes, but he dropped his gaze back to the sleeve before she could figure out what it was. He carefully lifted the sleeve from her and laid it on the waiting cloth-covered desk.

Flustered, she crossed her arms. "No, actually, it's an Arabic name. My mother worked with a woman from Lebanon when she was pregnant with me who told her the name means illuminate or shining."

"It's beautiful."

This time she knew what it was she'd seen in his eyes, because now his gaze lingered on her face with the unmistakable gleam of interest. She felt her breathing quicken in response but forced a smile to ease the tension arcing between them. "Thank you."

He blinked, then turned abruptly to snatch up a magnifying glass from the shelf above the desk and bend over the sleeve. For several long minutes he studied the embroidery silently.

"This is incredible," he finally said with such enthusiasm she wondered if she'd imagined what had just happened between them. "I've never seen such intricate embroidery detail on such a scale. The technique looks to be random stitch embroidery, which was developed in the 1920s and '30s. What that means is that the lines of thread cross one another and are added layer by layer, from very thin to very dense, so that the end effect is like an oil painting. See here…" He pointed to where the water splashed against the ship's hull. "The hallmark of random stitch embroidery is that individual stitches vary in length, direction, color, and thread weight. It's anything but random, but if you compare it to traditional embroidery, the stitches appear chaotic."

He shifted the sleeve and stood upright as though looking at the entire thing rather than at the details. "What confuses me is that although the stitching leads me to think this was created in the 1920s, the cut of the sleeve hints at the Qing Dynasty of China, which ended in 1912. Also, the designs themselves are highly unusual."

"What do you mean?" She stepped next to him and peered at the sleeve, trying to see what he described.

"Well, it's not like any Chinese embroidery I've ever seen, yet it's clearly Chinese with some of these symbols." He pointed to the wrist section. "See, here is what seems to be a sword stitched into the trees of the forest. The sword is an attribute of one of the Eight Taoist Immortals.

"And here," he went on, moving the magnifying glass to the left, "is clearly a lotus flower, even though it's blending into the swirls of the water. The lotus is arguably the most popular of Buddhist symbols."

He paused. She waited, feeling her own excitement grow, and wondered if there was more.

There was. "With this horse-hoof cuff, the sleeve appears to have been cut from a Chinese dragon robe, but the design's all wrong."

"Wrong how?"

"During the Qing Dynasty, Imperial officials wore a dragon robe, or *ch'i-fu*, for all occasions except the most formal. These robes usually had a rank badge on the chest and twelve dragons embroidered on the robe in specific locations, like one on each shoulder. As you can see, there are no dragons on this sleeve at all. Plus, the elaborate ornamentation on dragon robes usually ended above the elbow, with a plain design filling the forearm down to the cuff, which was just as elaborate as the body of the robe. This sleeve doesn't follow that pattern at all."

"What does that mean?"

"I don't know. I've never seen embroidered designs like this except on silk room panels, but even then never with this complicated detail and never with this intricate technique. Usually embroideries depict nature or a scene from a Chinese fable—"

He stopped suddenly, as though he'd just thought of something. "It's almost as if…"

"Almost as if what?"

His eyes were wide when he looked at her and his voice deepened. "It's almost as if this embroidery is telling a story, but one I've never heard before. And, believe me, I'm familiar with Chinese stories."

His voice drew her in, made her wish he would tell her those stories. Captivated, it took her a moment to realize they were standing close enough to touch.

She stepped to her left to put some space between them. "I can't believe how much you can tell just from a quick look at it."

He grinned. "Oh, I've only begun, Ms.—er, Inara." He cleared his throat. "Would you consider leaving the sleeve with me? I can offer you insurance and a small stipend for loaning the sleeve to the university, and I will personally promise it is treated with the respect it deserves. We can specify an exact return date, if you so choose."

A small stipend. Money she could use toward her hotel. "Do you think the sleeve is valuable?"

"I really can't say at this time," he hedged. "It would certainly be worth more if you had the garment it was cut from."

"About that," she said as he carefully rewrapped the sleeve. "Why would anyone cut the sleeve from the robe and then hide it?"

"I'm sure they had a good reason. I'd love the chance to figure it out."

She thought about his offer. Clearly, he felt passionate about the sleeve, and, also clearly, she would have her hands full with the hotel and wouldn't have time to research it herself. What was the worst that could happen? "Sure, you can hold on to it."

"Excellent! I'll take good care of it for you, and I'll stay in touch on my research. I promise." He carefully wrapped the sleeve in the cotton cloth and locked it in a desk drawer. Then he filled out a receipt and handed it to her to sign, with a glance at his watch. "I'm sorry, but I really have to get to that meeting."

"And I have a ferry to catch." She walked with him out of the building where they shook hands. His professional demeanor convinced her she'd imagined the interest she'd thought she'd seen in his office.

"It was nice to meet you, Inara. I'll be in touch about the sleeve."

"Thank you. I appreciate it." She watched him turn and walk away before pivoting on her heel to head to her car and the soon-to-be boutique hotel waiting for her on the island.

After the hour and a half drive to Anacortes, she ended up missing the first ferry and had to wait in line for the next one, which meant she didn't get to Rothesay until after nine that night. The sun had set, but the island was still cloaked in that blue-black moment before dark that felt in equal parts like a quiet sigh and a pounding heart. As she carried bags inside Dahlia's house, she felt the night falling around her and realized she hadn't considered whether she'd be safe out here. On an abandoned estate. Completely alone. Surrounded by ten acres of spooky forest.

With the doors locked, she went upstairs and opened the bedroom window. A humming sound like traffic on the freeway filled her ears, and it took her a while to realize it was the sound of the breeze blowing through the evergreens. Every few moments a birdcall broke the dark stillness—an owl hoot from the woods, a loon off the water. Being all alone out here would make anyone afraid, and yet the night sounds eased her fear. She was safe here, as safe as she'd once been in her mother's arms.

Even though those arms were so suddenly taken from her.

She left the window open to the night breeze and readied for bed. Tom would be here early tomorrow morning to get started. She couldn't wait.

As she drifted to sleep listening to the night sounds, she found herself thinking about the professor and wondering when he'd call.

Purely for his information on the sleeve, of course.

# Chapter Six

S omething was wrong.

Perhaps it was the smell of wet wool and chimney smoke that first alerted Mei Lien to the fact that she wasn't in her own bed lying next to Grandmother. Or perhaps it was nothing more than the hollow, cold ache in her chest that erupted into a fit of coughing and yanked her from the warm comfort of sleep. Whatever it was, even before she opened her eyes, she knew she didn't want to face what awaited her.

When her coughing eased, she kept her eyes squeezed tightly shut, holding on to the dream she'd been having of swimming with Father in Lake Union. How happy they'd been that day!

A shuffle. A cleared throat.

A male-sounding throat.

Father's image disappeared and her eyes flew open.

She lay on a straw tick mattress that was pushed into the corner of a dim log cabin. Standing over her like a monster about to devour her was a huge white man with matted brown hair covering his face.

Her memory flooded back. The last thing she'd seen was the sea monster grabbing for her. How had she come to be here? She yelped as she pushed up and scurried backward until her back hit the rough log wall. When she couldn't go any farther, she grabbed the pillow to use as a shield in front of her, ready to swing it at him, if necessary, and get away. The door. Where was the door?

"I'm glad to see you're awake. I was worried you wouldn't make it."

Instead of clawing at her, the monster-man remained unmoving beside the bed. His gentle, caring words were so at odds with his appearance that it took a long moment for her to understand their meaning. Not a monster. Only a man.

A white man.

She studied him, the pillow still clutched in her arms.

He had dark hair that fell unbound to his chin, where more hair hid his mouth. He wore brown pants and a blue-checkered shirt that buttoned up the front. One hand hung by his side; the other held a tin drinking mug with steam curling from it. He cleared his throat again, bringing her eyes back to his face. He stared at her just as she was staring at him. He had eyes that normally she would have thought kind. Now she knew not to trust them.

The man's gaze slid away from her as though he was uncomfortable looking at her. Because she was Chinese, she thought, knowing Father would admonish her for meeting the man's gaze in the first place.

"I don't know if you can understand me or not, but here's some coffee." He shoved the mug toward her. "It'll warm you up."

Mei Lien had never tasted coffee, but the cold ache in her chest craved warmth. She took the mug, being careful not to touch his fingers, and sniffed the liquid as the man walked away. It didn't smell earthy, like the tea she always drank. This was stronger, pungent. Warm. Taking the tiniest of sips, she sampled the liquid and then cringed. It tasted of burnt ashes. But as the coffee slid down her throat, it soothed the raw aching there. She took another sip. It would do.

She drank all of the foul-tasting liquid, letting the warmth fill her as she watched the man move around what she could see of the adjoining room. The cabin was no more than a box divided in the middle by a stone fireplace open to both sides. From where she sat on the bed, Mei Lien could see straight into the main room to the worktable shoved into the opposite corner. Hanging above the worktable were three shelves overloaded with various cookery tools and tins.

She leaned forward onto her knees, straining to see more of the room, looking for the man's wife or other family members.

Just then the man appeared again from around the fireplace, carrying a plate heaped with food. She hurriedly returned to her place against the wall, still holding the coffee cup. The smell of warm food made her stomach growl. She grabbed the pillow again with her free hand and pressed it to her stomach, hoping it would block the noise, unwilling to let this stranger hear her weakness. She hid her face behind the mug as she drained the contents in one last gulp.

"This is for you." The man unceremoniously set the plate on the bed in front of her drawn-up legs and shuffled back as if he wanted distance between them too. "I don't know if you like fried ham and potatoes with dried apples, but it's hot and it'll fill your belly, which I'm sure needs fillin' after these two days you've been asleep."

Two days? But that meant by now Father and Grandmother were...

She couldn't finish the thought. Surely Father had found a way to escape his fate. Surely she had been mistaken in the first place and they were safely on their way to their home country.

Father must be so worried about her! She would need to find a way to get word to him in China that she'd survived the water and was now... Where was she?

"I see by your reaction that you understand me some," the man said as he pulled a low stool over to the bedside and sat down a moment later with his own plate of food. He dug into it without waiting for her to eat. "The name's Joseph McElroy. I saw you fall from the steamer as I was making my way back from Victoria. You're lucky we was running late, or else no one would have been there to save you. What's your name?"

The question caught her off guard. No white man had ever asked her name, and all Chinese men she'd met had simply called her *nánhái*, meaning *boy*, since she'd always dressed like one outside her home. She was comfortable in men's trousers and jackets and, in fact, didn't own anything else. "Liu Mei Lien."

"Good to meet you, Liu. You can call me Joseph."

She was used to white men making this mistake. "Liu is my family name. Mei Lien is my given name."

He looked confused, but instead of saying anything, he only nodded and kept eating.

She looked down at her own plate of food and, in doing so, saw she was wearing only a long cotton shirt that she'd never seen before. Even the cloth wrap she always wore tight around her chest was missing.

She set the empty mug beside her plate on the bed and used both hands to feel along her body anyway, just to be sure. Sure enough, her own clothes were gone. As was Father's coin purse!

"My...my clothes?" She hated asking him, hated having to trust this man who might decide to throw her into the ocean or beat her for no other reason than because she was Chinese.

Her next thought chilled her worse than the water had. This man had undressed her. He knew she was not a boy. Grandmother had warned her plenty of times what men did to unguarded women.

The man had smiled at her question, but as he watched her, that smile dropped and he moved quickly, setting his plate on the bed next to hers as he got to his feet. "Don't be scared. I won't hurt you." He reached for something on a chest of drawers she had not noticed at the end of the bed. "I had to remove your wet things and get you warm or you would have died. But they are all here. See?"

He held up a pile of her clothing. Lying on top was Father's embroidered purse. Seeing it brought to mind the image of Father stuffing the purse with all of their money and shoving it at her. She wished Father was with her now. He would know what to do. He would protect her from this strange white man.

Through tears, she lurched toward him and grabbed the bundle. She let the clothes drop to the bed as she clutched the purse and brought it up to her face. With eyes closed she inhaled deeply, trying to smell Father, to feel him close to her.

But all she smelled was the salty tang of the sea. Father's scent had been washed away as surely as he had been.

She pressed the purse against her eyes and dropped to her side, her face buried in the bedding, no longer caring what the man might do to her.

Why had this happened to her family? Why couldn't they have been left alone to tend Father's store and live in peace? They'd done nothing wrong. Nothing. And now Father was gone. Grandmother was gone.

She should be gone too. Her body on the bottom of the sea. Her spirit with the ancestors.

She must have fallen asleep again, because the next time she opened her eyes, the cabin was brighter. Pale light filtered through the paper-covered window over the bed. Her plate and mug were gone, and the clothing had been moved to the end of the bed. The man must have tucked her back under the covers because she lay on the pillow, warm. She still clung to Father's purse.

What was the man's name? He'd told her but she hadn't cared at the time. James? John? It was one of those white man's names she'd heard often. Joe? Joseph. That was it. Joseph.

"Mister Joseph?" she called, not really wanting him to come

to her but wanting to see where he was before she got up. When there was no reply, she threw back the blankets and sat up. A fit of coughing erupted, forcing her to stop. The burning in her chest and throat ignited into fire with every cough, the flames licking upward to her head, making it ache. Is this how Father had felt after being beaten?

Once the coughing subsided enough, she pushed through her pain to her feet and had to steady herself with one hand on the wall next to her. When her legs finally cooperated, she shuffled to the other room to see for herself if she was alone in the cabin.

The room was dominated by a scarred square table with four chairs. In front of this side of the fireplace was a long wooden bench, on which lay a canvas bag bulging with whatever it contained.

No Joseph. She had the cabin to herself.

She returned to the bedroom and, as quickly as her weak muscles allowed, dragged off the borrowed shirt and slipped into her own clothes. The effort exhausted her so that she had to sit on the bed and draw careful breaths to keep from setting off another fit of coughing. She hated feeling this helpless, hated knowing she needed help from the strange white devil whose cabin she slept in.

Eventually she managed to dress fully with the exception of her shoes, which she could not find.

Just as she returned to the main room in search of food, the outside door opened and Joseph walked in, carrying an armful of firewood. Mei Lien froze.

He stood in the open doorway staring back at her. "You're up," he said finally, as he closed the door and kneeled to stack the wood on the hearth, his eyes avoiding hers. "Ready for that food now?"

She nodded and looked around, wondering what had happened to the plate he'd offered earlier.

"Sit down. I'll get it for you."

She eased into the chair he indicated at the table and watched as he wrapped a cloth around the long handle of a pot nestled in the ashes at the corner of the fireplace. He left the pot sitting on the stone hearth as he got to his feet and took a tin plate from the shelves along the wall.

"I'm happy to see you up and about," he told her as he scooped food from the pot and slid the plate of ham and potatoes in front of her. "I need to get the mail delivered to the islanders but I've been afraid to leave you for that long."

She waited to see if he would fill a plate for himself. When he didn't, she gave in to her hunger and grabbed a piece of ham with her fingers, shoving it into her mouth. The salty meat melted on her tongue, making the back of her mouth ache with a sudden flood of saliva. It was wonderful.

A fork clattered onto the table next to her plate. "Here," he grunted as he passed her on his way back to the hearth, where he squatted and started scraping at the bottom of the pot with a metal spatula. "You see," he continued as though his story had been uninterrupted, "I got awarded the mail contract this year, and until today, meaning you no disrespect, I've never been late in delivering to the good people of Orcas Island. They count on me and it's a good way for me to know folks. One day I'll be a council member, maybe even mayor."

She didn't understand all the words he used, but one word stood out. The strange-sounding word seemed to be important. She swallowed the bite of dry potatoes she'd been chewing before asking, "What is Orcas? That is the name of this place?"

A smile broke through the thick hair on his face and his eyes widened, revealing their green color, like the trees that lined the ridge above Seattle. "I knew I hadn't imagined your voice earlier." He scraped the last of the burned bits of food into the fire and set the pot on the hearth before looking back at her. "That's right. Orcas Island. We're in the San Juan Island archipelago, part of Washington Territory but close to British Columbia. I've lived here six years, by way of Indiana. I'll bring my bride here someday. As soon as I meet her."

He was not married! That made everything so much worse. She was an unchaperoned Chinese female with a single white man. Sure, he said he wouldn't hurt her, but she'd heard how white men lusted after foreign-looking girls like her. She'd have to be very careful until she got away.

Joseph must have also been thinking of her leaving because he tilted his head to the side as he looked at her. "Where were you headed on that steamer before you fell off?"

When she didn't immediately answer, he sat on the bench next to the canvas bag she'd noticed earlier and leaned his elbows on his knees. "'Cause I'll do my best to help you get to where you're goin', but I gotta know where that is."

As Mei Lien stared back at him, her fork—such a strange tool that they stocked in Father's store but never used at home—lying limp in her hand, she realized two things. One, this man had no idea what had happened in Seattle. And two, she wasn't going to be the one to tell him.

"I was bound for China," she told him since he wouldn't stop staring at her.

"Is that where you're from? China?"

She shook her head and stared down at her plate. "I have only known Seattle. I don't want to go to China." It was the closest she'd get to telling him the truth.

"Do you have family?"

Her last image of Father standing at the ship's rail came to mind, and she had to squeeze her eyes closed to keep the tears inside. She didn't trust her voice so she just shook her head in answer.

He seemed to think this over. After a long moment he asked, "So where do you want to go? You can't stay here."

She kept her eyes down. "I know. Thank you for saving me and for…" She hesitated, wondering what words to use. "For this," she finally said, nodding to the food in front of her.

"You're welcome." He cleared his throat, as she realized was his habit, and got to his feet. He looped the mailbag across his body. "I've got to get going. Make yourself at home while I'm gone. If you want to wash up, the spring is across the yard over by the bluff and the tub is hanging outside the door."

He pulled a hat from a nail by the door and slipped it on. "I won't be back for supper, so help yourself to what you find in the root cellar or milk house. Oh, and if you go down to the water, be careful. It gets deep right quick."

As he pulled open the cabin door, a gust of cold wind carried in the spicy scent of cedar and musky soil. It smelled to her like Seattle, only cleaner. Through the open doorway she spied a small clearing surrounded by tall trees and a huge brown barn peeking through the forest from a short distance away. Stacked next to the barn was enough fresh lumber to build a large structure.

"One more thing," he said as he looked back at her. "Although I don't expect anyone to stop by, it, uh, might be best if no one sees you, if they do. Stop by, that is." His eyes slid sideways, showing his discomfort even more than his shuffling feet already had. "But if you need help, my neighbor, Duncan Campbell, lives over the ridge. He travels a lot, but his wife and elderly father will be there. They're good people."

Mei Lien nodded, knowing she'd rather die than ask white folk for anything.

Relief washed over his face as Joseph raised a palm in the air, she supposed as a way of saying good-bye. Then he closed the door behind him and was gone.

Mei Lien sat unmoving for several long minutes, thinking. Where was she to go? Surely not back to Seattle where they'd either put her on the next steamer to her watery grave or kill her outright there on the street. China? She quickly rejected that idea. She may look like she'd belong, but she'd be foreign there. Washington Territory was all she'd ever known. There had to be somewhere else, somewhere in the territory where she could find work and be safe.

She ate a bite of potatoes and chewed as she studied her

clothing. She'd have to remain a boy. No one would hire a lone Chinese woman for any kind of respectable work.

As a boy, she'd have more options. She could work as a house servant or in a cannery. She could even be a cook.

With that decided, she finished her meal and set out to explore Joseph's property, stopping often to rest when a coughing fit overtook her and constantly listening for the sound of people coming through the trees. No one did.

Joseph must have returned after Mei Lien fell asleep, for when she woke the next morning, she found a pair of boots in her size beside the bed. He wasn't in the cabin so she shoved her freezing feet into the boots and hurriedly finished dressing before she lost the opportunity for privacy.

Then, unable to sit and do nothing, she went about her routine as she'd done at home in Seattle. She swept the floor with the straw broom leaning in the corner and then prepared the morning meal. By the time Joseph wandered in from wherever he'd been, she had steamed root vegetables and bacon hot and ready. He didn't say a word, but his silence—and the appreciation in his eyes as he sat down at the table—reminded her of her father and made her start to like him.

Despite herself, she was no longer afraid of him.

And so began the pattern of their days. They found themselves settling into a strange yet comfortable arrangement of sharing meals, chores, and the quiet moments at the end of the day. She helped him measure, cut, and hammer the lumber she'd spied that first day and that he was slowly building into a proper house for his future family. The only chore she refused to help him with was butchering animals for their food. The scene reminded her too much of how Yeung Lum's head had looked after he was shot.

Hours became days; days turned into a week. Her cough cleared and images of that night plagued her mostly in her sleep instead of all the time. The relative remoteness of the property gave Mei Lien a sense of security, real or imagined. Surprisingly, she often found herself laughing at Joseph's funny stories.

The trees surrounding the farm held her in their embrace, protecting her from the horrors of the outside world, just as Grandmother's arms had done for her as a child.

And then, on her eighth day on the farm, just as she hung the dishcloth on the peg on the wall and turned to tell Joseph good night, it happened. She hadn't heard him come up behind her, but when he reached for the milk pail on the shelf just as she turned, their bodies met. It was a moment so quickly ended that it wasn't until later, as she lay in bed in the quiet cabin, that she realized why touching him had flustered her so. Touching Joseph was nothing like touching Father. Her body had startled onto a feeling she'd never experienced before, and she found herself wanting to feel it again. Her skin had felt open and alive, reaching for him.

After that she felt nervous around him, although not in fear. She wondered if he had also felt that awakening in his body that she had in hers, but it wasn't something she would ask. They talked about the farm and his plans for it, but they never talked about why she dressed as a boy or how she came to be sharing his cabin. Even though he had undressed her the night he found her in the water, the only way Mei Lien knew for sure that Joseph was aware of her gender was the fact that he gave her his bed to sleep in while he slept in the barn, and he always knocked before entering the cabin. If she were really a boy, no doubt she'd be the one sleeping on the floor.

She knew she would need to leave sooner rather than later, and the thought saddened her. Joseph had been with her from the moment when she'd lost everything. On the day when she would leave his farm, she'd lose that final link to her old life. She would be alone in the world.

Joseph did not seem to be in a hurry to send her on her way, though. He questioned her about her life and her family, but when she didn't answer right away, he kept on talking as if the question didn't still hang between them. She was unable to answer most of his questions because of the terror and overwhelming pain they caused her. But she didn't answer one of his questions because she didn't know how.

"Why do you go to the water every night at dusk?"

She'd blinked and turned away.

Starting on that first day when she woke in the cabin and Joseph went off to deliver his mail, Mei Lien had found herself drawn to the water as the daylight faded and the world around her turned blue and then black. But even when the colors couldn't be seen in the cold, pounding rain, as was often the case, she'd go to the water anyway, where she'd carefully stand so the lapping waves would not touch her. She'd stare at the water, knowing Father and Grandmother had not made it to China but were somewhere below the shifting surface. She'd pray to every god and ancestor she'd ever heard of that they were no longer hurt or scared. Sometimes she prayed for them to take her with them.

On the third night, as she'd searched the dark water for a vision, a sign, anything, a black head had popped up and stared right back at her. She'd cried out, thinking it was the sea monster she'd seen the night Father pushed her from the boat, that it had come back to eat her.

But then the black head dipped back below the water and she saw a curving, sleek body follow suit. Not the body of a sea monster, but a seal, like the ones that stunk up the beach on Elliott Bay in Seattle.

After that Mei Lien started watching for other sea creatures, wondering if the seal—or perhaps that orange sea star or the leaping salmon—was Father watching over her. Or if the seagull crying into the wind was really Grandmother admonishing her.

Being near the water, even though it had nearly killed her and had most likely killed her family, made her feel closer to them. And so she returned, night after night.

But she couldn't tell this to Joseph. It was difficult, having her body yearn to reach for him even as her mind pulled her away.

One night, Mei Lien quietly cleaned her dinner plate and returned it to the cabin shelf before reaching for the warm coat Joseph had loaned her. Night was falling and it was time to go to the water. Tonight was different, though. Tonight was the first full moon of the New Year. In Seattle they would have celebrated the Lantern Festival by going to the water, where they'd release boats glowing with candles to give light to all spirits in the underworld, but most especially in remembrance of those who perished by drowning. Father's own father had died of drowning when he'd been caught in a battle during the Taiping Rebellion and had fallen into the Yangtze, so this was a special tradition in her family.

And now Mei Lien had more family who had died by drowning. Father and Grandmother would need the light of the lanterns she'd made out of tree bark and had hidden in the barn.

Just as she was reaching for the door handle, a loud knocking sounded from the other side. She snatched back her hand as her gaze flew to Joseph. His lips pressed into a grim line as he got to his feet. Under his breath he said, "Go to the bedroom. Stay out of sight unless I call for you."

The knock sounded again as she obeyed, slipping silently around the fireplace to the bedroom side where she pressed her back against the warm stones and tried not to breathe.

"Duncan!" she heard Joseph exclaim as he opened the door. "I didn't know you were back. How was the voyage?"

"Good, thank ye," the visitor replied. Something about the man's voice pricked at Mei Lien's memory, and she closed her eyes to listen.

"I jes' returned today. Took the train up from San Francisco while my captain sails on ta the Orient. Got a business to run here, ye ken?" Arrogance filled the man's voice and Mei Lien wondered why Joseph considered him a friend. He went on, "Came home ta find the missus and my pa havena' plowed the field. Do ye think you could give me a hand tomorra?"

Memories slammed into Mei Lien, stealing the muscles from her legs and making her sink to the floor even as her mind screamed to run away. That voice. She knew that voice, the drawn-out vowels, the clipped consonants. It was the voice of certain death.

And now she knew Death's name—Duncan Campbell, Joseph's neighbor.

She wasn't safe here, wouldn't be safe anywhere.

She rested her forehead on the rough wood planks of the floor and willed herself to be silent as she listened to the men.

A chair creaked. "Didja hear the Orientals were run out o' Seattle? About time, if you ask me. I told you we were doing the right thing when we ran them off our island last year."

Joseph cleared his throat. "No, can't say that I did hear that. Hey, I've made good progress on the new house. Care to see it?" Boots clunked, floorboards creaked. Soon the door slammed shut behind the men, taking Campbell's hateful words with him.

Mei Lien didn't move. She deliberately took small, shallow breaths. Until Joseph returned and assured her he'd watched the man leave the property, she was going to stay hidden. The thought of what the devil Campbell would do to her if he saw her was too frightening to let enter her mind, so she pushed it away.

But fear grabbed hold of her nonetheless, and her mind screamed with the realization that she had been rescued from death at that man's hand by his very neighbor. Fate could not be so cruel as to spare her life only to toss her carelessly to the same end just days later.

But what if Joseph knew more about her situation than he'd

let on? That would explain why he never pressed her for answers about that night—because he already knew all about it. He could be helping Campbell. Hadn't they just said they ran the Chinese off this island themselves?

And she'd let herself come to trust him. And worse, she yearned for his touch!

She'd let her guard down too easily. Too quickly.

From the moment she'd woken in his cabin, Joseph had been there, caring for her, making her feel safe. But now she knew the truth.

She was not safe.

She was completely alone.

The water. The water called to her. It would help her know what to do next.

Suddenly frantic to get to the shoreline, she sat up and managed to climb to her feet. Silently, shaking, she tiptoed to the cabin door. Being careful to make no noise, she pressed her thumb on the latch and pulled the door open a mere crack.

She neither saw nor heard the men. Slowly she eased the door open wide enough to slip through and just as quietly closed it behind her. Then she set off at a run through the trees to where the water called, louder now.

This time she didn't stop safely at the edge. She splashed in to her calves, ignoring the stab of sharp rocks against the side of her leg when her boot slipped. She needed to feel the water and learn from it. Only now, as she stood in the freezing wet, did she look up and realize it was a clear night. The clearest it had been since that night on the steamer.

The moon hung low in the sky, big and full and round, shining down on her. It perched atop the mountain on the other side of the long body of water that bordered Joseph's property and shone its beam straight to her on the surface of the water like a roadway. Joseph had shown her a map of the island, so she knew this long inlet was called East Sound. If one were to go left from this property by boat, one would reach other islands, more waterways, and then finally open water.

But it wasn't open water beckoning to her. It was the moon.

All around her the night held still, watching the moon. Watching Mei Lien, who felt outside of her own body. Questions about her fate pummeled her.

Answers didn't come, but memories did. In the moon road on the water, Mei Lien saw her Father laughing with her as he taught her mah-jongg at the rickety table in front of his store. She watched Grandmother's wrinkled hands patiently guiding her own through short, precise black stitches on red silk, the smell of ginger and onions scenting the air. She smiled when she saw Father standing behind the counter at his store, appearing to her so tall and powerful as customers asked him for advice and chatted with him, comforted by the use of their own language in what to them was a strange and hostile land.

The memories rolled together, coming faster and faster, then pausing on one image only to flash forward again, pulling her in, soothing her.

The water had taken everyone from her. It should take her too. In the water she'd be with her family again. She'd be away from this lonely ache and living fear that gnawed at her every breath. The water waged a battle and tonight she'd let it win.

Mei Lien wrapped her memories around her body and, ignoring the cold and her trembling limbs, stepped deeper into the water. Step by step she walked until she stood neck deep, her body jerking with uncontrollable spasms even while she felt numb. With her foot stretched forward, she searched for the next step. But instead of rocks, she found only open water. This was it.

"I'm coming, Father," she whispered as she moved forward and deliberately fought the urge to hold her breath.

The cold water slithered around her and over her head, tugged on her clothing, and pulled her down. She didn't struggle. She didn't kick or wave her arms. With her eyes wide open, she sank.

Her lungs ached for breath. She fought the urge as long as she possibly could and then her lungs spasmed, forcing her mouth to open and the water to pour in where air should go. Blackness snaked through her vision and wrapped around her head. She welcomed it, gave herself over to its warm tentacles. She let go.

The next thing she knew, her head broke through the surface of the water and her body heaved, pushing out the salty water between racking coughs. A lingering tentacle from the water monster gripped her stomach, but instead of pulling her into the depths, it squeezed the water from her lungs. Her chest burned; her throat burned; her body shivered and jerked.

She felt her knee bang painfully into a rock and realized she was being dragged to shore. Only then did she realize it wasn't death's tentacles that had grabbed her, but Joseph's arms. Joseph had somehow seen her go into the water, and now he was dragging her out. Again. Saving her from her destiny, keeping her from the fate that had been chosen for her.

He laid her on the rock and shell beach. "Mei Lien, talk to me. Breathe!" He pounded her back.

Her stomach heaved, and she jerked to the side to let its contents empty onto the beach. Water surged from her lungs. She kept coughing until she could once again draw in breath without choking.

The air felt glorious to her lungs but biting to her skin. She shivered, still coughing and spitting out salt water.

"What were you doing out there? You could have drowned." His huge hands pushed hair out of her face and traced down her limbs, checking to see if she was hurt. The trail of warmth his hands left in their wake brought Mei Lien back into her body from wherever the moon had pulled her.

She sat up and wrapped her arms around herself. The moon still beckoned her into the water but the roadway was fading, pulling away from her, rejected. Rejecting. "You should have let me be."

"What?" His hands dropped from her body.

"You should have let the water take me."

He responded with silence, which she took to mean he was thinking it over. The thought that he'd stand idly by and let her die stabbed into her chest so thoroughly she was unable to hold back a moan, only now realizing that a small part of her had believed he cared for her.

But obviously she was wrong. Harnessing her pain, she spit out, "The water is my destiny and you've taken me from that destiny twice now. Don't interfere again." Before she could think any further about her decision or how wonderful the air felt filling her chest again, she stood up and marched to the water. "*Zài jiàn*, Joseph."

She stomped in until she was knee deep. Her feet and legs were bruised from the rocks, but soon she would cease feeling that pain, or any pain.

He grabbed her arm and spun her to face him. In the moonlight she saw his face clearly and in it, buried under all that awful hair, she saw something surprising. Fear.

"Why do you want to kill yourself?" He shook her. "Tell me!"

She very calmly met his frantic gaze. "Two weeks ago my family and I were forced from our home by white men and put onto a ship. They said they were sending us to China, but then I—" She broke off, remembering the devil Campbell, remembering he was Joseph's friend.

Remembering she couldn't trust anyone. Her head pounded as she searched the trees. "Where is he? Where's he hiding?"

"The man here earlier? My friend Duncan Campbell? What's he got to do with this?"

"Where is he?" she asked again, searching the darkness.

"Campbell's gone. He went home."

She nodded, believing him for no reason she could identify. Her fear eased enough that when he tugged on her arm, she let him lead her out of the water until they were standing once again on the sharp shells and rocks that made up the beach. Her eyes, however, stayed fixed on the trees, where she knew Campbell could appear at any moment.

Joseph pulled Mei Lien to his chest and wrapped his thick arms around her, his hands briskly rubbing her back and arms for warmth. Tired, she melted into him, drawn by the safety he gave her that she knew she shouldn't trust but did anyway.

"Do you know the man who came to the cabin tonight?" Joseph's voice sounded loudly against her ear, drowning out the soughing of the trees and the lapping water.

She nodded against his shoulder.

"Did he hurt you?"

Campbell had never touched her, as she knew Joseph must be thinking, yet he'd hurt her. Hurt her more than a soul could bear.

When she didn't answer, Joseph asked another question. "How do you know it was him? It's dark tonight, and when he came to the cabin you were in the other room—"

She pushed out of his arms. "I'm certain. His voice gives him away."

Joseph nodded, his hands hanging limply at his sides. "I reckon you're right about that."

Mei Lien turned to face the water and saw the moon had risen high overhead.

"What did he do to you?" Joseph's question was as hushed as the forest around them, yet it sent a fresh stab of fear through her, as though remembering that night would bring Campbell back. "He's my friend. I need to know what he did."

"I can't." She stepped toward the water, knowing it would take away her pain.

"Don't go into the water, Mei Lien," his gentle voice implored from right beside her, though he did not touch her. Her feet stopped. "Let me help you. We'll find a place for you to go where you are safe. I promise. I don't want you hurt. No more."

She couldn't say why, but she believed him. No other white

man had shown himself to have good in him, but somehow she believed this one did. She turned her head to look at him and saw confirmation of his kindness in his eyes. He reached for her hand and gently squeezed it.

Still holding his hand, she turned back to look at the water once more, searching for the visions she'd seen earlier that had lured her. All she saw was empty moonlight dancing on the shifting black surface. Whatever spirits had been here earlier had gone. The water didn't want her anymore.

A shiver racked her body as the night breeze picked up and pushed through her wet clothes straight to her bones. Her lungs felt inflamed, causing another coughing fit to overtake her. When it was over, she felt drained. Joseph's fire beckoned now.

She took a step toward the trees but stopped to face him again. "Thank you, Joseph," she said, hoping he understood all that she thanked him for.

He squeezed her hand. "You're welcome, Mei Lien."

# Chapter Seven

*Thursday, March 4, 1886*
*East Sound, Orcas Island, Washington Territory*

M ei Lien's cold fingers numbly gripped the sides of the wooden rowboat that Joseph propelled through the waters of East Sound with long pulls on the oars. She stared straight ahead to the channel that would lead them to Orcas Village and the steamer that would carry her to her new life. The thought of stepping onto another steamer sent her belly slamming against her spine. She blinked and refused to think about it, preferring instead to focus on Port Townsend, her destination.

Every night since Joseph pulled her from the water they'd talked about where she should live, where she could work, how she could be safe.

Although she knew she'd never feel safe again.

"You won't find work on Orcas or any of the San Juan Islands, even dressed as a boy," Joseph had told her. "Last year the folks hereabouts drove all Chinese off the island and passed a resolution barring the hiring of Chinese."

Mei Lien hadn't been surprised. She'd read the newspapers Joseph brought home. It was happening all over the country. With the railroads stretching coast to coast and towns as far-flung as Seattle acquiring a sheen of polish, white folks no longer wanted to share their money or their land with the Chinese whose sweat had made it all happen. "Where can I go?" she'd asked him. Joseph had just shaken his head and poked at the fire, the lines on his face etched deep.

But one morning, after picking up mail at Orcas Village, he returned with a huge grin. "Things aren't as bad as we thought, Mei Lien. Come." They shut themselves inside the cabin and Joseph told her the gossip he'd overheard from passengers disembarking from the steamer SS *Dauntless*, which had tied up next to the mail steamer.

"It seems the incident in Seattle caused all Chinese people to flee that city, but they say a new Chinese laundry and a dry goods store owned by a Chinese man opened in the last week and no one is bothering him." He leaned closer to Mei Lien. "Do you know what this means? You can return to Seattle to make a living."

Excitement came and went so fast it left an ache in Mei Lien's head.

She didn't want to return to Seattle, didn't want to live there without Father and Grandmother. Alone. Afraid.

"No," she told Joseph in a voice that didn't sound like her own. He didn't know that she was one of the people driven from the city, and he certainly didn't know that everyone else driven out that day now lay at the bottom of the sea. Seattle would never feel safe to her.

More days passed and then Joseph came to her while she milked the cow as he'd taught her. "It's time for my monthly trip to Port Townsend for supplies. I go Thursday. You should come with me."

"Don't be fooling me, Joseph." She got to her feet. "I can't be seen with you. You'd be shunned. And then what would that future wife of yours think?" She smiled to show she was teasing him. He'd told her all about his plans to find a perfect Christian woman to marry and give him as many babies as possible to help him run the farm, all of them growing up to become respected members of the island community. Though she liked seeing the joy his plans brought him, she couldn't help but think that, with Father gone, she'd lost her opportunity to find a husband for herself. She'd lost her chance to raise children. Her future held nothing but long, lonely years of hard work.

Joseph had laid his palm on her shoulder, sending an increasingly familiar jab of awareness down her body. "No one will look at me twice if they think you're my servant. My male servant. Especially in Port Townsend. I've been asking around. The anti-Chinese unrest isn't as rampant there." His hand dropped and he took her place on the milking stool. "We'll take Beecher's mail steamer when we go. He was the one who helped me pull you from the water that first night, and he dropped us off on my beach instead of at Orcas Village. Otherwise you'd probably have died. He promised he wouldn't say a word. We can trust him."

She patted the cow's long face and thought it over. "What's in Port Townsend for me?"

"By all accounts, a strong Chinese community exists there. Maybe you could stay, make a life for yourself."

"Will I see you again?"

He nodded but kept his gaze on the cow's teats. "You can bet on it."

And so, the plan was decided and here they were, three weeks after they'd met, on their way to Port Townsend and the rest of her life. The devil Campbell's rocky property was already behind them, and she'd seen no sign of him or anyone else. Joseph still did not know the story of what Campbell had done, yet he'd rowed past Campbell's shoreline as fast as his strength allowed, his watchful gaze darting between her and the land. Mei Lien knew she owed him an explanation but hadn't yet been able to find the courage required to relive that night.

Joseph maneuvered them out of East Sound and along the southern shore of Orcas Island, keeping close to land and away from the whitecaps that frosted Harney Channel. In every direction she saw numerous other islands, all blanketed with fog that wove through the green cedars and firs and the occasional bare limbs of alder, oak, or red madrona. Sharp, black rocks jutted from deep, black water reflecting the oppressive gray sky overhead.

"Almost there," Joseph said as he strained on the oars. "Pull your hat lower."

She did as he ordered, remembering to hunch her shoulders like a boy to complete their deception.

"Remember," he told her in a low voice, "people will expect me to treat you like my servant. If I'm harsh, don't take it to heart."

The fact that he cared about her feelings warmed her body. She peered at him from under the brim of the white man's hat he'd given her. "All Chinese are treated like servants. I'm used to it."

The bottom of the boat scraped against pebbles and Joseph jumped out, tying up to a tree on the beach. Without waiting for assistance, for no servant would expect it, Mei Lien jumped out as Joseph had done, ignoring the freezing cold water that grabbed at her feet, and reached back into the rowboat for the satchel of items Joseph insisted she take—extra clothing, a blanket, biscuits wrapped in oilcloth, and two apples he'd stored in the root cellar from his fall harvest. Her father's coin purse was again safely against her heart beneath the bolt of clean cloth Joseph had awkwardly given to her to bind her breasts.

Soon they were aboard the small mail steamer *Hope* and heading away from Orcas Village and the crowd of people waiting for the passenger steamer to Seattle, which apparently had a schedule but never kept to it, according to Joseph.

"Saw the revenue cutter on my way over from Whatcom," said the captain whom Joseph had introduced as Herbert

Beecher. He glanced back at Mei Lien as if to be sure she was paying attention. As he did, his long, gray mustache bent against his shoulder. "You'll want to stay hidden if he comes sniffing around during our passage. I assume you don't have papers?"

His eyes, heavily shadowed by charcoal gray brows, squinted as if in bright sun even though the day was overcast.

Mei Lien looked at Joseph. "Papers?"

Joseph stood against the cramped wheelhouse wall with his arms crossed. His eyes shifted with concern from the water spread before them to her, then back again. "Smuggling from Canada is common in these parts. Wool from Victoria passed off as raised in the islands sells for four times the cost. Same goes for liquor. But ever since the Exclusion Act passed four years ago, a whole new smuggling trade has sprung up." He gave her a sad smile. "For fifty dollars a head, smugglers are bringing in boatloads of Chinese and dumping them on mainland beaches to find their own way from there. The Chinese pay it—if they get there alive, that is."

"Now, Joseph, don't go spreading rumors," warned Captain Beecher from where he stood manning the controls. "You'll scare the boy."

"You're right, Herbert. They are just rumors," Joseph conceded as he sat down next to Mei Lien on the cabin's single bench. "But folks say they've heard tell if the cutter comes too close, the smugglers dump their goods overboard, human or not."

Mei Lien shivered, wrapped her coat tighter around herself, and spent the rest of the voyage looking over her shoulder.

She was exhausted by the time they reached the bustling dock in Port Townsend two hours later, but she knew the hard part was just beginning. As they stepped off the *Hope*, Mei Lien heard Captain Beecher's quiet advice to Joseph. "If he needs papers, go see the Baron."

Joseph thanked the captain, then turned to lead Mei Lien into town. "Follow close behind me," he told her in a low voice. "If we get separated and I don't notice, call for me—Mr. McElroy, not Joseph. Worst case, backtrack and we'll meet in front of this building here, the Zee Tai Company. Got it?"

She nodded. "Got it."

He frowned. "Lower your voice."

"Got it," she practically whispered.

His mouth twitched. "No, I mean, sound more like a boy."

"Oh!" She bit back a laugh, then cleared her throat. "Got it," she said as low as she could make her voice go.

"Good enough." Joseph spun on his heel and started toward the main street of town, turning only once to see that she followed.

She managed to keep up, but barely. Port Townsend was alive with activity. At least a dozen sailing vessels, steamers, and tugs were lined up at the docks, loading and unloading. Countless smaller craft, like canoes and rowboats, were rafted together and tied in the spaces between. Once she and Joseph reached the bustling main road, Water Street, Mei Lien saw it was crawling with bearded men moving purposefully along, as well as women in severe black dresses carrying baskets and holding small children's hands. Pedestrians had to carefully maneuver around horses and carriages. Vendors called out their wares from store stoops and open stands, showing no signs of retreating inside even though drizzle had started falling from the dark mass of clouds overhead.

If she dared close her eyes, Mei Lien thought she might feel as if she were back home in Seattle, on her way to the vegetable peddler or to deliver paper-wrapped parcels for Father.

But she didn't dare close her eyes or she'd lose Joseph. She quickened her pace to keep up. Without him, she wouldn't know where to go or what to do. She needed him.

At the thought, her feet stumbled on the boardwalk and a man passing by cringed as though afraid she would grab him.

She needed Joseph. The idea was the most ridiculous thought that had ever entered her mind, yet it was true. In the short time they'd known one another, she'd come to rely on his company and friendship. She felt safe with him, liked him even. He was all she had.

But she could not let herself feel this way because after today she would never see him again. He planned to rush off and find his Christian wife, and she'd be left here to live with people with slanted eyes like herself. It was the way of things.

They arrived at a store three times the size of Father's, and Mei Lien had no trouble assuming the subdued role of servant. She felt as if the dark clouds overhead had settled into her heart.

"Velcome, velcome, good sir!" came a booming voice from the back of the store. The strange accent forced Mei Lien to concentrate hard on the words. Just as she got it sorted out in her mind, a rotund man wearing a fancy blue suit swept forward and placed his palms on both sides of Joseph's face, his own split wide in a smile. "I vas hoping you come back to my store. I order twice as many potato seeds, jes' for you."

Joseph laughed and extricated himself from the man. "Thank you, Baron. But I only need the amount I ordered, as well as these items." From his coat pocket he pulled a carefully written list, which he handed to the Baron. "I'll need all this delivered to the dock first thing tomorrow morning." He paused and glanced around as if to see who was listening. His gaze settled on Mei Lien for a moment, and he gave a small nod. "And one more thing. It involves obtaining some needed paperwork."

Mei Lien squirmed as both men scrutinized her. She ached to raise her chin and meet the Baron's gaze head-on, but she forced herself to play her role. She quickly dropped her chin to her chest and hunched her shoulders again, assuming the position of the unseen servant.

The two men spoke in low tones before the Baron excused himself to go into a back room. Joseph muttered to her that they would wait and so they did, pretending to inspect the spices and grains lined up in large barrels under the counter. Five minutes later the Baron returned. "Here is vat you need, Mr. McElroy. Pay for it ven effer yous feel like it."

Joseph took the small package and thanked the Baron, promising to pay in the morning when he paid for the rest of his order. He then led Mei Lien from the store.

"Don't believe a word he says about paying whenever I feel like it," he told her as they headed down the sidewalk with her two steps behind. "He can get quite demanding if payment isn't given in a timely manner. Here, put these in a safe place."

Mei Lien took the package from him. "Papers?"

He nodded. "Papers. You'll need them before long, no doubt. Excuse me." He stopped a passing hollow-eyed Chinese man carrying two baskets heaped with squash and mushrooms. "Where is the Chinatown?"

The man replied in Toisanese that he didn't speak English. Mei Lien stepped forward before either man lost patience, as she'd seen happen numerous times in Seattle. "Please forgive us for keeping you from your important work," she said to him in his native language. "I wonder if there is an area of this fine town where our countrymen gather to live and work. Is there such a place? Perhaps up the bluff?"

He came alive then, rattling off street names and business names, his chin pointing the way since his hands were both full. Mei Lien thanked him with a small bow, then let him go on his way. "He says it's here in downtown. On top of the bluff is where the rich white folks build their palaces."

Joseph's eyebrows drew together as he squinted south down Water Street, then north. "The only Chinese establishment I've ever noticed is the Zee Tai Company. Come, let's start there."

They made it no more than one block before they noticed people running excitedly toward the beach north of town. Two men rushed from a saloon, nearly knocking Mei Lien down in their hurry to jump into a friend's waiting carriage and then they too took off to the north.

"Probably nothing more than an expected ship coming into port," Joseph guessed, leading her onward.

But then a group of young men her age raced past and Mei Lien caught the words "dead body."

The feeling of the water demon's tentacles wrapping around her flashed into her mind, bringing a sense of foreboding. She stopped in the center of the sidewalk and grasped Joseph's sleeve with trembling fingers. "We need to go to the beach."

The line between his brows deepened. "You wanna see the ship?"

She shook her head, her feeling of unease growing. "Joseph, we need to go now. They said a body has been found on the beach at Point Hudson."

"The authorities will take care of it. It's no concern of ours."

She stepped closer to him and lifted her eyes to his, not caring if anyone watching thought her behavior inappropriate. "You don't understand. The men on Campbell's steamship, they worried about bodies washing ashore. I think that's what happened."

Horror filled his gaze as he realized she was referring to the night he'd found her. His mouth dropped open as if he were going to say something, but instead he grabbed her hand and started pushing past people and horses, heading for the beach north of town.

Mei Lien hurried to keep up, fighting to keep hold of her satchel and Joseph's fingers at the same time, the whole while whispering prayers to the ancestors that she was wrong in her suspicion of what they'd find.

The wooden sidewalk soon gave way to dirt and then the graveled beach that ran under the high bluff. Ahead, where the beach widened, a large crowd including women and small children had gathered around what Mei Lien knew must be the body, blocking her view of it. She let Joseph tug her along the beach, though each step felt harder and harder to take.

Her breath came in shaking gasps, and she knew it was from

more than just the physical exertion. She should turn around and run away, she told herself. Run away now. But just then someone moved and she caught a glimpse of bright red cloth.

Everything inside her stopped.

No. It couldn't be.

Joseph tugged on her hand. With a look of concern, he tugged again, harder. Stiffly, she forced her feet to move.

The wind chose that moment to shift, and the smell it carried made her already shaking stomach heave. She let go of Joseph's hand to cover her mouth and nose.

"It looks like her feet were eaten by crabs!" a young boy's voice cried out in fascination.

Mei Lien froze. Red jacket. Female. Deformed feet.

Slowly, afraid to move too fast, for surely she would break if she did, Mei Lien pushed through the crowd until she could fully see the body.

She lay on her back, her arms and legs splayed as though rough waves had picked her up and thrown her here on the beach like seaweed. Her beautiful red jacket with embroidered green and gold dragons and blue phoenixes hung limply over her torso, the fabric ripped in places and muddied. The red skirt Mei Lien knew should be there was missing. Long black trousers, typically worn under the skirt, twisted around frail-looking legs and were pulled up to the knees, revealing naked tiny feet that had been wrapped tightly and not allowed to grow since childhood, the misshapen toes bent under so far they almost touched her heels. Most of the skin was gone, revealing putrid flesh and bone.

Mei Lien finally let her gaze lift to the face. Grandmother stared unseeing at the gray sky. Raindrops splashed in the sockets where her eyes should be and on her matted white hair and swollen face where the flesh had been torn off in chunks by sea animals that had mistaken her for food.

Pain erupted inside of Mei Lien. It came from so deep she had no choice but to let it come out of her or it would have torn her to shreds. It burst forth as a wail and dragged Mei Lien to her knees beside her grandmother's body. After that she didn't know what she said or did for a long time because she was lost in the black hole of her grief.

Time did not matter. The people watching her and talking about her did not matter. She wanted nothing more than to be back in their house in Seattle that awful morning this all started. She would lift Grandmother onto her back and pull Father with her as she ran and hid in the woods before the white devil came to take them away and murder them. Grandmother did not deserve this end.

And if this had happened to Grandmother, Mei Lien knew the same or worse had happened to Father. A rolling pain in her chest brought up another wail of grief that she could not contain.

The very last of her hope fizzled out like an ember left in the rain.

Her stomach twisted, then violently heaved, sending its contents upward. She turned just in time, emptying her stomach onto the rocks near Grandmother's feet.

When nothing was left and the cramps had lessened, she fell limply onto the cold, wet rocks, knowing this was the last time she'd be near Grandmother. She would never again hear her breathing in bed beside her. Nor would she ever again hear her father's voice calling to her, calling her *my son*, which he always made sound like an endearment.

She did not feel the stones or the rain or the biting wind, nor even the stares of the people around her as she lay prone beside her grandmother's rotting body. With eyes squeezed shut, she clung to every memory she could summon of their happy life in Seattle. She wrapped images and moments around herself, burrowing inside what used to be and what still should be.

She stayed that way until no tears were left inside her. Until nothing was left inside her. Until her memories had caught up to the present and refused to soften. Only then did the rest of her surroundings start to come back into focus.

"Let me pass, sir! I can help him calm down. He'll go to sleep and stop making such a scene."

Mei Lien turned her head to see the owner of the voice she knew was talking about her. A tall man so thin and pale that he reminded her of a sail mast was trying to push past Joseph and get to her. He held a black medical bag in one hand and a white handkerchief in the other, which he repeatedly dabbed against his nose.

"I'll take care of him," Joseph replied in a voice brooking no arguments. "He's my servant. No one is to touch him, and if you are here to take possession of the body, you'll do so with as much respect as you would any citizen of Port Townsend. Do you understand?"

The tiniest flicker of warmth lit Mei Lien upon hearing Joseph's words. He was standing up to this man because of her. No one but Father had ever fought for her before.

She ignored their conversation after that, knowing Joseph would protect her and make arrangements for Grandmother's body. Only now did she notice the crowd had dispersed, no doubt driven off by Joseph, or no longer interested in a lowly Chinese body. She was glad. This moment, her last with Grandmother, was a time for privacy.

She pushed to her knees and took a deep breath to steady herself for what needed to be done. Then, trying not to think about what could happen to a body that had been in the water for so long, she gently pulled Grandmother's pant legs out from under her and tugged them down until they covered her feet. Grandmother would have hated how undignified she looked to all those people who had found her.

After another deep breath taken through the fabric of her own sleeve because of the smell, she reached out her fingers to smooth Grandmother's hair. The moment she touched the puffy soft skull, she cringed in horror. Grandmother's scalp felt like it might slip right off her bones if Mei Lien pressed too hard. Shuddering, Mei Lien made certain to be gentle as she completed the task, even though every muscle in her body strained to turn away.

"Mei Lien." Joseph was there beside her, talking so softly she knew the doctor could not hear him. He laid his hand on her back and upper arm, urging her to stand. "It's time to go. Come. The doctor will see her properly buried. I've made certain of it."

Mei Lien looked at Grandmother one last time, seeing her as she'd been the last day they spent together embroidering. Grandmother had insisted that Mei Lien needed to start preparing for her someday wedding, so they'd been working on the slippers traditionally given to the groom's parents. Grandmother had told her stories of her own wedding and marriage, and her face had seemed to grow younger with the telling, her eyes clearer, her smile softer. That was the image, Mei Lien decided, that she would keep with her. Not this one before her now.

"Good-bye, Grandmother," she whispered in Chinese. "I will honor you all the days of my life."

She allowed Joseph to pull her to her feet and she turned away, heading back toward town. She did not look back at Grandmother's body because she was holding so tightly to the picture in her mind of Grandmother in life.

"Come," Joseph said once they were back on bustling Water Street. "We'll stop here for a warm meal before we do anything else." He pulled open a heavy door and held it for her to precede him inside.

He must have forgotten to pretend she was his servant, she mused, though she was too tired to remind him. With a nod she walked inside—but jerked to a stop when the buzz of conversation ceased. She raised her eyes to find every face in the room staring at her.

Joseph bumped into her back. Then she felt his body stiffen as he too noticed the attention they'd drawn.

The building seemed to be a boarding house and this, its dining room. Scores of tables lined up across the room, almost all filled with pale-faced men, some with their wives. She saw two Indian women, squaws they called them in Seattle, eating at a table with two white men and their three small children. Even the squaws stared at her.

"Excuse me, sir. Can I help you?" A matronly woman approached, wiping her hands on her starched apron, her question aimed at Joseph.

"Yes, ma'am." Joseph pulled his hat from his head but Mei Lien kept her own on, knowing it helped her disguise. "We'd like some supper, please."

The woman pursed her lips as her eyebrows jutted into her hairline. She looked Mei Lien over from her feet to the top of her head. "By 'we' do you mean you have another companion arriving shortly?"

"No, ma'am. It's just myself and my servant here."

The woman's expression turned to stone. "I'd be happy to offer you supper, but your servant will have to eat in the kitchen."

Mei Lien was too tired to feel anything but acceptance of her situation. She simply turned and walked back through the door they'd come in. She wasn't hungry anyway. When Joseph didn't follow her immediately, she stopped and waited for him on the street corner, watching carefully for him and worried what would happen to her if they got separated before he'd helped her find a place to live and work.

Finally Joseph emerged from the boarding house, and Mei Lien knew he'd had words with the woman inside. His face was reddened and his hat crumpled as he plopped it back onto his head. He didn't say a word about it to her as he gave her a small smile and led her across the street and along the boardwalk.

They tried one more dining establishment and even a saloon

before Joseph gave up and went into the next restaurant alone. She waited outside with her back pressed against the wood siding, her hat brim hiding her face from passersby.

When Joseph emerged with two meals wrapped in paper, she shoved off the wall and fell into step beside him, neither of them speaking. Silently they trudged through puddles across the town and up the steep stairs that climbed the bluff. At the top Mei Lien stopped to catch her breath and found the landscape looked nothing like she'd expected. For miles, all but the occasional clump of trees had been cut down. Dotted here and there were grand houses and gardens, all linked by freshly graveled roads.

Without a word, Joseph nudged her with his elbow and she fell into step with him again, walking until they came to a wide, muddy field away from houses or businesses or judging eyes. Out of the rain, under cover of a lone fir tree amid a bramble of blackberry vines, they found a patch of ground dry enough to sit on and eat their lunch of dry biscuits and tasteless ham.

This town was going to take an awful lot of getting used to, Mei Lien thought as she ate in silence. The townspeople may not have driven the Chinese community out, but they sure didn't welcome its people. What was she going to do to support herself, and where would she live?

Where had that doctor taken Grandmother's body?

Where was Father?

The questions swirled through Mei Lien's mind until her head hurt and she couldn't force another bite past her lips. Setting the rest of her meal aside, she turned her gaze to the water. From this vantage point she could see clear across the water to the land on the other side and far down the sound leading toward Seattle. This town felt so isolated that, if not for the tiny tugboat heading that direction, she might have believed no other cities lay farther down the waterway.

If only she could crawl into her bed next to Grandmother in their upstairs bedroom in Seattle and forget any of this had happened.

# Chapter Eight

*Thursday, July 5—present day*
*Rothesay Estate, Orcas Island*

Inara had been at work on the hotel for a month now, and she was thrilled with the progress they'd made so far. She still couldn't believe her luck in finding Tom that first day. He was a big man with a booming laugh and a brain that seemed to work twice as fast as everyone else's. He had a way with the crews, making everyone want to do their best work.

At their first work meeting, he'd instantly understood her vision for the hotel and the changes she wanted to make to Aunt Dahlia's plans. He'd returned four days later with permits in hand, updated plans from the architect, an itemized breakdown of costs, and a crew of ten guys to start working. When anything new came up, he had a smartphone packed with contacts for all the crews and subcontractors they needed.

For the first two weeks, Inara had hung around the construction site all day answering questions and making sure the work was being done according to plan. It hadn't taken long to realize she was in the way. Tom had it all under control.

After that, she'd fallen into a routine of stopping at the main house in the morning to check in with Tom and again in the afternoon before the crews left for the day. The hours in between she spent in Dahlia's house, or rather, *her* house—she'd have to remember to call it that now—getting quotes and placing orders for things like paint and professional-grade kitchen appliances, and adding to her growing list of items still to be ordered, like shower tiles and doorknobs. In the pockets of time left at the end of the day, she read through the pile of books she'd ordered on hotel management.

She loved it. Every minute of it. She even loved the line of pickup trucks in her driveway and the country music battling the eighties hits coming from different areas of the manor. Nothing could ruin her fun, not even the unexpected costs that kept springing up, like the totally new, industrial-strength furnace that had to be installed in the cellar under the kitchen.

The blood in her veins raced from the minute she woke until long into the night when she'd finally worn herself out enough to sleep. She felt alive. Each day was another day of rediscovering that she was finally doing what she'd waited her whole life to do—without even knowing what she'd been waiting for. With the hotel, she felt she was finally living the life her mom had wanted for her. Only a small part of her felt guilty for turning her back so easily on her career in international business. Her dad still brought it up every time they talked, asking if she wished she was at Starbucks headquarters right now. Her answer was always no.

But it made her worry. Her father may have given his blessing to this project, but his disappointment in her made the possibility very real that he might snatch away her funding at any moment, without warning. Because of that, she'd spent the better part of two days looking into other options such as a home equity loan, a small business loan, a personal loan from the local bank...but she didn't qualify for any of them. She couldn't get around the fact that she already owed thousands on her student loans, and at the moment, she had zero income. She was stuck relying on her dad.

It hurt that he was so clearly disappointed in her, but she was holding on to the fact that he was going to be blown away by what she accomplished here. Once he saw it, he'd understand.

For some reason, being back here on the island made her feel closer to her mom, which was weird since she'd become a bona fide daddy's girl over the years since the accident. It was almost as though the nine years had melted away and her mom had just gone on one of her business trips, like she'd turn up any day to pitch in with Inara on the hotel. Of course, her mom would have turned the place into an orphanage or something, but still she'd be proud of Inara.

Every day was filled with decisions she had to make. She first filtered those decisions through Aunt Dahlia's original plans and then she'd think of what her mom would have liked. A part of her felt like she was doing this for her mom, as though by bringing life back to the estate and sharing it with people, she could undo her hateful words to her mother. Undo the pain that her mom had died with.

If only.

Her mom would have been intrigued by the sleeve too. She'd traveled the world in her too-short life and might have been able to help Inara figure out the sleeve's history. Not that Inara was doing any work on it. The hotel consumed all of her time so she'd been leaving the sleeve research purely to Daniel, who sent her entertaining weekly emails with small updates, though he hadn't discovered anything of note yet. Still, she looked forward to his friendly banter and funny stories from the university.

Other than his emails, she hadn't thought much about the sleeve until yesterday when something happened to change that. Today she couldn't think of anything else.

Yesterday had been Independence Day, and she'd decided to take a floatplane flight to Seattle her dad had offered so she could spend the holiday with her family, as was their tradition. They typically spent the day at her father's house in the Magnolia neighborhood with a barbecue, followed by a sunset cruise on her father's yacht on Lake Union where they anchored in the middle of the lake to watch the fireworks show.

Logistically the day had gone like it always did, but something had felt off and at first she wasn't sure what it was.

It had started at lunch, when she was sitting at the patio table with her siblings and their spouses while the kids played on the grass. Her dad had gone for an early round of golf and Inara hadn't yet seen him. She'd had to reassure Nate, not for the first time, that she wasn't making a mistake in committing herself to the huge project and life-changing career that was the hotel.

The more she told them about her plans, the more her brother seemed to come around, or at least back off. Olivia helped by getting excited by everything Inara told them. When her dad came home and joined them, he'd expressed surprise at the extent to which she was going ahead with the renovations, but when he didn't object to anything, Inara took that as support.

And then she'd told them about the sleeve, describing it in detail and showing the pictures she'd taken with her phone. They were all fascinated by the mystery the sleeve presented and surprised that no one had found it hidden away in Dahlia's house all those years.

Everyone was fascinated, that is, except her dad who had scoffed, "It sounds like garbage left by some Chinese servant. Throw it away."

His reaction had seemed overly heated, which made Inara wonder if he knew more than he was letting on. But what he'd said about the possibility of a Chinese servant wouldn't leave her.

Sitting at Dahlia's—er, her—kitchen table with her laptop a day later, Inara thought again of the possibility that a Chinese servant had once lived at Rothesay. Maybe that was who'd hidden the sleeve.

She closed the expense sheet she'd been working on and opened a browser to see what she could find about former residents of the house and if they'd had any Chinese servants. The best place to start, she decided, would be with census records.

She found the right site and started her search by entering Dahlia's name and the Rothesay address in the search field for the 1940 census, the most recent year available because of privacy laws.

The record that came up showed the residents as Dahlia Campbell, age twenty-five, and a handful of Caucasian servants. No Chinese.

Both the 1930 and 1920 censuses listed only servants as residents, none of them Chinese, but Inara wasn't surprised. The tradition Duncan Campbell started—living in Seattle and using Rothesay for lavish house parties—must have been going strong until his death in 1932 and probably observed still longer by the rest of the family.

Inara sat back from the computer. Daniel had told her that the sleeve was embroidered sometime in the 1920s or '30s, so it made sense that the sleeve was hidden under her stairs about the same time or soon after. No one on the census records seemed to be the likely party, but that didn't mean a Chinese servant or guest, or even a non-Chinese, might have come and gone in a non-census year and hidden the sleeve. And there was also the possibility that the person who hid it hadn't created the embroidery. Maybe someone bought it, or even stole it, from someone else.

There were too many unknowns and the census records were too vague. What she needed was something more specific about Rothesay's history and the people who passed through its doors.

Before she talked herself out of it, she picked up her phone and dialed her dad, managing to catch him in his office.

"Question," she said after a quick hello. "Do you know of any family diaries or journals or records of any kind that tell more Rothesay history?" She was about to mention the sleeve when she remembered he'd already told her to throw it away and concentrate on the hotel. Instead, she lied. "I'm hoping to find descriptions of the original structure and decor for my renovations."

"Not that I know of. If there were any, they're gone now." His voice sounded distracted, which she knew was to her advantage. Otherwise he might see through her lie. "I told Dahlia years ago to get rid of all the old stuff lying around. I know I don't have anything here."

"Oh, okay." She thought of the boxes she'd spied in Dahlia's attic on that first day she and Olivia were here. Now she was in a hurry to get off the phone. "I'll let you get back to work. Thanks, Dad."

By the time she clicked the off button, she'd already grabbed a flashlight and was halfway up the stairs, stepping carefully over the loose second tread and curling runner.

The attic was tiny and layered with at least two decades of dust. It wasn't really an attic, but a small area under the eaves that had been converted for storage by some not-too-distant relative. At least, she didn't think they'd had fold-down attic ladders when the house was built.

Wedging herself between stacks of boxes, she started digging through them one by one. Tax records, bank records, receipts for everything from shoes to a new stove to the old Pontiac Dahlia used to drive. There was even a letter and photo from the local artist Dahlia had hired to paint a giant purple dahlia on the side of the car. In the photo, a younger Dahlia stood beaming and pointing to the work of art. Inara could still hear Nancy muttering about the ugly piece of junk, but Dahlia had loved it.

She found pictures of Dahlia and Nancy on vacation in New York, wearing Statue of Liberty crowns, as well as baby pictures of Inara and her siblings, and some of their mother. One box held records from when electricity and plumbing were added to the buildings, so Inara set that one aside to give to Tom, thinking it might come in handy.

Despite all she found, nothing shed light on who might be responsible for the sleeve.

Her phone buzzed in her sweatshirt pocket, and Inara answered while flipping through old phone records.

"Inara, it's Tom. I've been knocking on your door for the last five minutes. Are you home?"

"Oh, I totally forgot! I'll be right down." Inara threw the papers back in the box and put the lid back on. Then she climbed down the ladder and rushed downstairs to the front door to let in her builder. "Tom, I'm so sorry. Time got away from me."

She led him into the kitchen where she motioned toward the stairs. "I appreciate you doing this. I've been tripping over that thing since the day I arrived."

He set down his toolbox and stood back with his hands on his hips as he surveyed the job ahead of him. "No problem. Shouldn't take long to rip it up and cart the rug out of here. You say the second tread got pulled off?"

"Yeah, but don't fix that yet." She explained about the step and what she found underneath, promising to show him the sleeve when she had it back from Daniel. "Dahlia or Nancy never happened to mention it to you, did they?"

"Nope." Tom grabbed a clawed hammer out of his toolbox and hunkered down on his knees on the bottom step. "Would surprise me if they even knew about it."

As Tom got to work on the carpet runner, Inara returned to her laptop on the kitchen table and the financials she'd been working on before getting sidetracked with the census research. A few minutes later, Tom grunted and she looked over to see him squinting at the nails he held in his palm.

"What is it?"

"When you told me the second step had a lot more nails than all the others, I figured they'd have been added by later residents. But these all look exactly alike. And old."

She got up to see. The nails in his calloused hand were thick and squared before they tapered to a point. They looked nothing like nails she'd ever seen. "What are you saying?"

Tom handed her the nails so she could inspect them further, then he sat on the bottom step and rested his arms on his wide-spread knees. "You can get a good idea about the age of a house by the nails used in the construction. You also get an idea about the owner, or at least the builder, of a house." He jerked his head as if motioning toward the manor house. "All the nails in the big house are wire nails with the exception of any used in masonry, as one would expect. Masonry requires cut nails, like those you're holding, for their extra holding power.

"The person who built the manor house used all the latest materials and construction methods available around 1900, and that meant wire nails, which became widely available in the 1890s and are what we still use today. Everything before then was built using cut nails like you hold there." He paused as a wide grin split his face. "You know, I think I just solved part of your mystery. To find who hid that sleeve, you'll have to look to someone living here before the manor house was built. Early 1890s at the latest."

Inara felt dumbstruck. And confused. How would a sleeve embroidered after 1920 have been hidden in 1890?

She needed to talk to Daniel. Maybe he'd been wrong about that date.

As Tom went back to work, she wandered into the front room to make her call. Unfortunately, Daniel didn't pick up the phone and she had to leave a message. Then, knowing she wouldn't be able to concentrate on financials now, she decided to go back to her census research at the kitchen table, being care-ful to stay out of Tom's way as he worked on the stairs.

Thinking of what Tom told her, she clicked the link for the 1890 census, but the message that came up informed her that nearly all the records for that year had been destroyed in 1921 in a fire at the Commerce Department building in Washington, DC.

"Dang it." She typed in the info to bring up the 1880 records, just in case, but the search results said no records were available for that year. "Hey, Tom?"

The squeaking sound of nails being pried out of wood paused. "Yeah?"

"Know anything about census records?"

"My wife researched her genealogy last year. Why?"

"Why would there be no records available for this place in 1880?"

Tom came down the stairs holding his baseball cap in one hand while wiping sweat off his forehead. "Depends. Could mean the census takers didn't make it to the island, or no one was living on the property at that time. Washington was just a territory, you know, not a state."

Inara considered. When Duncan Campbell purchased the property, it had a small house and an old cabin already on it. Someone had lived here before her family. But who? And when? "What about records on the property and buildings? Like when they were built or added onto and who previous owners were. Where would I find something like that?"

"Oh, that's easy. Check the San Juan County website, though you might just want to call over there. Not everything is online yet." He reached into his toolbox and came up with a water bottle. "Start by tracing the transfer of deed for the property to see who owned it." He took a long drink from his water, and when he finished, he looked at her and smiled. "Need help?"

He sat next to her at the table and guided her through the county website. "Bingo," he said, leaning back with a self-satisfied expression.

Inara looked back at the screen. There, listed with Rothesay's address, was the name of an owner she'd never heard before. "Joseph McElroy? When did he own the property?"

Tom studied the information. "It looks like he bought the

land in 1880 and moved into the house he built in 1887 with his wife, Mei Lien."

Inara drew in a breath so fast she choked on her own saliva. When she could talk again, she asked, "Mei Lien? That's a Chinese name, right?"

Tom gave her a funny look. "Probably."

"And she was his wife?" Inara thought about that for a moment. Mei Lien had to be the person who'd hidden the embroidery, and probably even created it. She had to be. Who else, in the entire life of the house, could have been responsible? No one. She had been the only resident with any real connection to Chinese culture, which the embroiderer obviously had because of the symbols Daniel found. "What else can you find about her?"

Tom shrugged and got to his feet. "Heck if I know. Call my wife. She loves this kind of stuff." He paused, still holding his water bottle. "On second thought, call my friend Kira over in the county clerk's office. She helps me out all the time when I need something for my building sites."

He took his ever-present notepad and carpenter's pencil out of his pocket and jotted down the number, which he handed to her. "She'll be able to give you all the construction history of the house, if you're interested."

Inara felt like hugging him, but she held back. "What about things like tax records, marriage records, births, deaths? That kind of stuff."

He just nodded and started up the stairs to where he'd left off on the carpet. "Kira will know."

Not wanting to waste a second, Inara took her phone into the sitting room and dialed Kira, who answered on the third ring. Inara explained why she was calling and the information she was trying to find. "Can you help me?"

"No problem," the friendly voice on the line answered. "It's slow here today anyway. Give me all the info you know, as well as your number and email address. I'll call you if I find anything."

After hanging up, Inara hugged her phone to her chest. This was becoming a lot of work to track down what might turn out to be nothing important. She knew she should be focusing her time on fixing up the hotel, not on chasing after clues to a hundred-year-old mystery.

But these had been real people. Real people who built her house and lived their lives in the same rooms where she lived today. And amazingly, the first woman to live in her house had been the Chinese wife of one of the first island settlers. And he was, presumably, white since his name seemed Scottish or Irish. Then again, the name might not mean a thing, and he could have been black or Asian or of some other descent. Still, the possibility that they'd had an interracial marriage back when those arrangements were frowned upon opened up all kinds of questions. She had to tell Daniel.

When he didn't answer this time either, she left another message. "Daniel, it's Inara Erickson again. I tracked down the name of a Chinese woman who lived in my house. It was Mei Lien. I don't know her maiden name, but she was married to Joseph McElroy. Call me."

She'd just hung up when someone knocked on her front door. Opening it, she found a man with a tool belt slung around his hips, squinting at her. "Can I help you?"

"Is, uh, Tom here? We have a problem with a delivery."

She turned to call for Tom just as he appeared in the kitchen doorway. "What kind of problem?"

"Pink toilets."

At first Inara had no idea what he was talking about. And then she remembered that the guest toilets, all sixteen of them, were scheduled to be delivered today. "What do you mean pink?"

"The toilets are pink," the younger man explained as though she hadn't heard him the first time.

Tom looked at her. "Is that what you wanted?"

"Of course not. They should be white." Was this a sign that

she needed to stay focused rather than worrying about a scrap from someone's old robe?

Tom jerked his head toward the door. "Come on. I have a feeling I'm going to need you to sort this one out."

When they stepped outside, Inara saw a huge delivery truck parked with the back of its trailer angled toward the manor's front door and a metal ramp stretching from the trailer onto the porch. Sitting on the porch were four large, unopened boxes. In front of the wide entry doors sat a rose-pink toilet with the packing materials scattered around it.

"What's going on, Josh?" Tom asked the man supervising the unloading.

"This guy"—Josh jerked his thumb toward the driver—"says his order calls for pink toilets, not white. He refuses to take them back unless his supervisor tells him to."

Inara looked around. "Where's his supervisor?"

The driver, a college kid wearing a ripped T-shirt and a blue Seahawks baseball cap, answered, "At the warehouse. In Renton."

She pulled her phone from her pocket and handed it to him. "Call. I'll talk to him."

The kid did as she ordered and soon handed the phone back to her. "His name's Carlos."

Inara took the phone and held it to her ear, trying her best to keep her frustration out of her voice. "Hi, Carlos, this is Inara Erickson from Rothesay. I'm the person who ordered and paid for sixteen white toilets, not pink."

"I apologize for the mix-up, Ms. Erickson. Let me pull up your order." She could hear the sound of typing as she waited.

"Here it is," Carlos finally said. "It looks like you did order sixteen of the white toilets on June 18, but it was changed first thing this morning to pink. You're lucky you caught us before the truck was loaded at the warehouse."

Inara looked at Tom. "Did you call the company this morning?" He shook his head.

"No one called to change the order, Carlos. Someone must have made a mistake."

"No, ma'am, it's not a mistake. It says here a Mr. Erickson called at eight changing the order to tulip pink."

All of the commotion around her faded as his words sunk in. Mr. Erickson. She knew two Mr. Ericksons, and only one of them had the nerve to do this to her. "Regardless of what the order says," she told Carlos, trying hard to keep anger out of her voice, "we will be returning this shipment to you and will expect the original order of sixteen white toilets delivered by next week. No, wait. By Monday. Understand?"

Tom stepped toward her upon hearing this. "That puts us behind schedule."

She covered the mouthpiece of her phone. "Sorry. You got any ideas? We're not installing pink toilets."

He shook his head and turned back to the delivery driver.

"It will cost you," Carlos said, bringing her attention back to the phone call.

"I realize that. I don't have a choice." After ending the call and confirming that everyone understood the toilets were returning to the supplier's warehouse, Inara turned her back on the construction chaos and headed for the path through the woods that led past a crumbling old cabin to the beach. Despite the drizzle, she needed quiet with no interruptions for the phone call she planned to make next, and the beach was the perfect place for that.

Beaches like this one were scattered through the islands. Most of the islands' edges were sharp rocks that jutted out of the dark water like walls. Where there were beaches, they were short, covered with driftwood and kelp, and often unreachable except from the water.

Her beach was long, curving almost the entire length of the little inlet they called Rothesay Bay, which nestled between two high bluffs on the east side of the sound. The beach itself was covered with black and gray stones and white shells and dotted here and there with sharper, larger black rocks. The bank behind the beach sloped gently into the shrubs and trees of the forest, the boundary marked by driftwood tossed ashore by storms. At high tide the beach was no more than ten feet deep, but at low tide it stretched a good thirty, revealing bigger, barnacle-crusted boulders.

Those same rocks were a hazard to private yachts—the largest vessels to venture up East Sound—but didn't interfere with kayaks or small boats. Only a few feet farther out, the bottom dropped off steeply, leaving a deep-water inlet where even her father's yacht could anchor. No boats were here now, though. The beach was secluded and peaceful, and the perfect place for being alone.

Even though the rain was more of a mist, she ducked under the branches of a tall fir that grew at the edge of the beach. She dropped her bag beside a dry boulder, then sat on it to make her call.

"Dad, it's me," she said the moment her father came on the line. "I know what you did with the toilets."

"You're welcome," he said, surprising her.

"What do you mean, 'you're welcome'? You've cost me a week and a lot of money. They're pink!"

His sigh echoed through the line. "Inara, pink is more historically accurate for when Rothesay was in its heyday. And they're cheaper. I did you a favor."

Inara shook her head in disgust even though her dad couldn't see her. "I'm not going for historical accuracy, Dad. And you gave me control of the project, remember? That means you butt out."

"My money is paying for it all."

"Dad, I know, and I appreciate it. And I will pay you back." She took a deep breath to calm down before she said something she'd regret. "I need to do this my way. Do you understand that? Can you trust me to do what's right for this place?"

It took a moment but when he finally answered he sounded placating, and not at all convincing. "Sure, Nara-girl. I'll butt out. Sorry about the toilets." After a short pause, he surprised her by saying, "I'm glad you called. Good news. I forgot to tell you earlier that I ran into Aaron. You know, the HR manager at Starbucks. He agreed to hold your job open through September."

Shock hit her like a physical blow. "My job? Starbucks? Dad, I turned it down. I meant it. You're wasting their time if you told them to wait for me."

"Inara, you're making a mistake burning this bridge. Don't walk away from this opportunity."

She shook her head, even though he couldn't see her, and tried not to let the hurt banging around in her chest consume her. "Dad, I'm sorry you don't believe in me or my hotel, but it's what I'm doing now. It makes me happy. I won't be taking the Starbucks job. Ever."

He made a noncommittal sound, then was silent for several moments. "Are you coming home this weekend?" he asked, changing the subject.

"What?" Was she missing something? "No. Dad, you know I'm busy with the hotel this summer. I can't afford to take a day off."

"You were here yesterday."

"That's because it was a federal holiday. My crews weren't working." Just then a beep sounded, telling her she had another incoming call. "I gotta go, Dad. I'll call again soon."

She said good-bye and then, relieved, clicked over. "Hello?"

"Inara, it's Daniel." The warmth of his voice soothed her, and she was able to draw a deep breath of the rain-cleansed forest air.

Then she remembered Mei Lien. Excitement flashed through her, propelling her to her feet. "You got my message? Can you believe I found her?"

His deep chuckle sent a surprising shiver of awareness along her limbs. "It was exactly the information we needed."

She paced the beach along the water's edge, mindless of the drizzle. "It is her, right? The woman who made the embroidery?"

"It's got to be, especially with the information I dug up."

She stopped walking to stare unseeing across the water. "What'd you find?"

"Because of the random stitch embroidery, I thought the sleeve was made sometime after 1920, but you're saying Mei Lien lived in that house only until 1895 at the latest, right?"

"Right. When my great-great-great-grandfather bought the place."

"Well, the Wing Luke has in its collection three embroidered Chinese purses confirmed as having been purchased from a store in Seattle's original Chinatown sometime before the Great Fire of 1889."

"Hold on, what's the Wing Luke?"

"Officially it's the Wing Luke Museum of the Asian Pacific American Experience. It's a Smithsonian-affiliated museum in Seattle's International District. I'm on the board of directors."

"Okay. So what do three purses have to do with the sleeve?"

"The technique on the sleeve is so similar to the purses that I decided to compare them and asked Yong Su, an expert in the field of East Asian textile arts, to give me her opinion. She concurs. They were most likely created by the same hand."

"So this is confirmation that the sleeve was made earlier than we thought. Are you saying that Mei Lien McElroy lived in Seattle either before or after she lived on Orcas?"

"It looks that way. Though we know it probably wasn't after 1889 because no evidence exists of her work after the fire. But there's more. After I got your message an hour ago with Mei Lien's name, I did some searching and found a Liu Mei Lien listed as clerk and translator in a store in Chinatown owned by Liu Huang Fu, probably her father since Chinese women didn't traditionally take their husband's family name. There's no record of what happened to either of them. I thought maybe they left Seattle after the fire, but it seems Mei Lien left Seattle before the fire."

"How do you know that?" The raindrops were getting fatter so she moved back under cover of the tree.

"Because I found her marriage license to Joseph McElroy. They were married in Port Townsend. I don't know how they met or how or when she moved to the town, but they were married there on March 4, 1886. Orcas Island is listed as their residence."

Inara couldn't sit still on her rock, but the rain, falling harder now, kept her under the tree. She moved restlessly within the small dry circle. "Daniel, we're getting there. We're finding her!"

He laughed. "We are. And I've got some ideas about the picture on the sleeve, but I want to talk to you about that in person. Can we meet soon?"

Remembering the toilets, Inara groaned. "I can't leave the island right now. We had a delivery fiasco today, and after I hang up with you, I'm going to meet with my builder to see how we can shift schedules around and not have this time wasted." She thought for a moment. "Maybe I can come down for a day next week, but I'm not sure."

"What if I come to you?"

"To Orcas? You'd do that?"

"Sure. I have all weekend free. I'll shoot for the first ferry Saturday morning."

"You don't have to go so far out of your way. Why don't I check my schedule and come up with a plan for next week?"

"Inara, it will be my pleasure to come see you." His voice deepened when he said it, sending her nerves dancing.

*Cool it, Inara. This is only a business meeting.* "Saturday it is, then." At least he couldn't see the dopey smile that was surely on her face.

She gave him directions to Rothesay, then hung up.

*Oh God, I have a crush on him,* she realized as she stared at the rain falling in sheets now. She decided to wait it out a little longer under the tree. The only constant in Pacific Northwest weather was that it constantly changed.

So she had a crush on the professor. Big deal. She didn't have to do anything about it, that was for sure. And she certainly didn't need anything distracting her from the hotel.

She crossed her arms over her chest. She'd play it cool and keep things professional. That was all he probably wanted anyway. He was coming here not to see her, but to see where she'd found the sleeve. Yes, that had to be it.

She played their conversation over again in her mind and paused on the information he'd discovered. Liu Mei Lien had worked in her father's store when Seattle had been little more than a logging town. This was back when Duncan Campbell was just starting his business. They might have run into one another on the street and not even known they'd both end up on Orcas Island.

How had Mei Lien ended up here? And why did she embroider the sleeve, then stick it under the stairs? Was the rest of the garment hidden somewhere else in the house?

Just then the shiny spotted head of a harbor seal popped up from the water and seemed to look right at her. Inara held her breath, not wanting to move and scare her away.

The seal didn't move. She just floated there, staring right at Inara as though she was as fascinated by Inara as Inara was with her. Finally, after several long minutes, the seal turned and dove beneath the black water.

Inara waited, but the seal didn't resurface.

The water was like her sleeve mystery, she decided. It seemed so pure and uncomplicated on the surface, yet below were all kinds of secrets.

The sleeve knew something. It knew something about Mei Lien's life that Inara had yet to discover, and it had something to do with Rothesay. Which meant it had to do with her family and herself. She knew Daniel would find out what that was. And who knew? Maybe it would be something compelling she could use in the hotel marketing materials.

Funny how a few months could completely change a life,

she mused as she stared at the water, its surface dimpled by rain. She'd become a landowner, a soon-to-be-hotel owner, and she was chasing down answers to a mysterious embroidered sleeve with the help of a very intriguing professor.

Dahlia had been right to force her to come back.

# Chapter Nine

*Saturday, July 7—present day*
*Rothesay Estate, Orcas Island*

T he man who climbed out of the green Volvo looked only vaguely like the suit-wearing professor she'd met a month ago. He was even more attractive than she remembered. Today his black hair was mussed just enough to make her want to slide her fingers through it. He wore a snug, long-sleeved black Henley over jeans and black boots.

"Inara, this place is beautiful."

She stepped off the porch and met him with a handshake. *Keep it professional,* she reminded herself. "Thank you. I appreciate you making the trip up here. How long was the ferry wait?"

His lips spread into a smile that shot directly to her stomach. No wonder his class was full of girls.

"An hour," he answered, his warm gaze on her. "Not too long."

"Want a tour?" she offered on impulse, needing to move and put a layer of professionalism back between them before things got too sticky. "I'm turning the manor into a boutique hotel that I hope to have open by next summer."

His eyebrows shot up. "Impressive. I'd love a tour. You sure you got time?"

"I'll make the time." She led him up the front steps and through the main doors, all the while explaining the history of the house and pointing out the changes Tom's crews were in the process of making. Forty-five minutes later, they were in Dahlia's kitchen, peering into the hole where she'd found the sleeve.

"It's amazing the sleeve was preserved as well as it was, considering it sat in there for a hundred years." Daniel shook his head as he shined the flashlight she handed him into the hole. "I wonder why the mice didn't eat through it."

"That's exactly what I wondered. Disgusting, isn't it?" Inara's hip bumped against his, and suddenly she wasn't thinking about the sleeve or mice.

He was still bent over, looking under the stairs, but he glanced her way and smiled in a way that made her suck in her breath. To hide her reaction, she jumped to her feet and busied herself by filling the teakettle and placing it on the stove. "You brought the sleeve today, right?"

He stood up and clicked the flashlight off. "The purses I mentioned too. I'll go get them."

While he ran out to his car, she fit the step back into place, then washed her hands, made tea, and placed some store-bought cookies on a plate, wondering all the while if he felt the sparks between them too or if she was imagining them. When he returned carrying two flat black boxes and with a duffel bag slung over his shoulder, she grabbed the cookie plate off the table and slid it onto the counter out of the way. "The table is clean if you want to lay them out."

"Thanks. I want to show you the purses first. You'll see what I mean about them being similar to the sleeve." He set the boxes on a chair and pulled a cotton cloth from the duffel bag. After spreading the cloth over the table, he pulled out two pairs of white cotton gloves and handed her a pair before slipping on his own.

"Contrary to what one might think, these purses weren't used by women, but by men who attached them to their belts to carry money, fans, tobacco, opium, spectacles, even chopsticks." He opened the top box and pulled out three silk purses of different shapes and colors, each with embroidery decorating the front and back. Two had tassels hanging off the sides. He laid each on the cloth. "We believe purses this ornamental were purchased by men here in the United States to send money or gifts to relatives in China."

He lifted the red one and handed it to her. "This design is much more traditional than that on the sleeve, but if you look closely, you'll notice the same random-stitch embroidery in the background. I'd been under the belief that random stitch wasn't invented until much later, but these purses and your sleeve are proving otherwise."

She studied the purse and was taken aback by a symbol she recognized. "Is that a swastika?"

Daniel nodded. "Don't worry. It has nothing to do with Hitler. The swastika is an auspicious symbol used since antiquity by many of the world's cultures. It means good luck or good fortune. Nothing evil about it."

"Oh." She set the purse down and lightly touched the narrow blue one. "These are amazing. You say they were sold in Seattle before the Great Fire?" The fire of 1889 destroyed most of Seattle's business district and led city leaders to create a new plan that included brick buildings that wouldn't burn, as well as the regrading of streets to minimize the steep hills early residents had to climb.

"At a Chinese store on Washington between Third and Fourth. A man named Huang Fu Liu—or, since Chinese naming conventions place the family name before the given name, Liu Huang Fu—owned it and lived above the shop in a tiny apartment. Immigration documents show he arrived in Seattle in the spring of 1868 with his wife and mother. Vital records show a daughter was born in August of that year and the wife died soon after."

He picked up the blue purse and handed it to her as he kept talking. "What's interesting is that all mentions my research team have found of that store in newspaper ads and settler journals say the owner had a son."

Inara studied the blue embroidered purse, not sure what she was supposed to be looking for in the embroidery. "You have a research team?"

"Yeah. I pulled together some grad students to help me with this project. Hope that's okay with you?" He cocked his head to the side, sending a lock of black hair over one eye.

The sleeve really was a big deal, she realized. "Why are you doing all this? It's not like I'm paying you."

A thoughtful smile spread across his face. "It's grabbed hold of me like nothing has in a long time," he admitted with a toss of his head to move the lock of hair away. "I come from a family very proud of the fact that we can trace our history back centuries into ancient China. Add that to the fact that I spent a lot of time at the Wing Luke as a kid. Before he died, my dad worked there and often let me tag along. I grew up surrounded by history. It turned me into an Asian history buff. Your sleeve is an enigma I need to decipher. I plan to keep working on it until we know the whole story, or as long as you'll let me."

She nodded, her mind going back to what he'd said earlier. "Okay, so if accounts say the store owner had a son, do you think the birth records were wrong?"

He shook his head. "I don't know. The records could have been right, and for some reason, the family lied and presented the baby as being male. Or, they could have been wrong."

"Why would someone say their baby girl is a boy?"

Daniel crossed his arms. "Historically, and occasionally still today, a male heir has been preferred to carry on the family name because they can physically do more labor and because it is a son's responsibility to care for his parents in old age. Once married, a daughter becomes part of her husband's family and no longer part of her parents'. Maybe the father didn't like the idea of one day losing his daughter when he'd just lost his wife. Also, we need to consider that Seattle in 1868 was a rough town populated largely by fishermen, loggers, and trappers. If it were me, I'd be worried about my daughter's safety in a place like that."

"So they lied to keep her safe?"

Daniel just shrugged. "Maybe. Or maybe the baby really was a boy."

Inara carefully laid the purse back on the cloth. "So we don't know. But am I understanding you correctly that the person who made the purses that were sold in the Chinatown store is the same person who made my sleeve? And because the baby's name was Mei Lien and we know Mei Lien McElroy lived here as Joseph's wife, it was probably the same person?"

Their hands bumped as they both reached for the third purse, which made them freeze. In his eyes she saw she wasn't the only one feeling the attraction between them. It quickened her pulse, and though she tried, she couldn't look away.

"Yes," he answered with a slight hitch in his voice. "I do believe so." He blinked, breaking their eye contact, and picked up the gold purse. "Yong Su agrees with me. And Mei Lien was not a common name. The fact that it shows up both places we found this embroidery is not a coincidence."

Inara let that sink in. "So now what we need to figure out," she said, studiously avoiding looking at Daniel to keep her pulse in check, "is why she made a robe and then cut off its sleeve. And where's the rest of the robe?"

"Maybe the subject of the embroidery can tell us. I'll get out the sleeve." Daniel carefully wrapped up the purses and returned them to the flat box, which he then placed beneath the other flat box. Opening the second box, he reverently lifted out the sleeve. He laid it, and the tissue paper it rested on, over the cotton fabric. "Yong Su agreed with me that the embroidery is telling a story."

He stepped to the side in a clear invitation for her to lean over the sleeve. "Look here, where the sky seems to be covered in dark swirls that signify fog or night." He pointed. "Right there. That's the Chinese symbol for lie or lying, telling a fib. I didn't even see it until Yong Su showed me."

He was talking faster now. "And look here, on the ship's hull, there is this symbol that we believe shows markings on the ship, if it existed, but hidden in the stitching there's something about dumping cargo. Plus, there are demon figures in the water with the human bodies and walking on the decks. It's common in Chinese mythology for serpents or evil spirits to be in the water, but walking like a man on a ship?" He shook his head. "Highly unusual."

Inara stopped listening to him as her attention caught on the markings on the ship's hull. She knew those markings. Not the hidden ones, but the apparent markings. The ones that had probably been painted on the actual ship.

She knew the symbol, recognized the stylized *C* and *L*. It wasn't the name of the ship, but the name of the shipping company.

It was Duncan Campbell's ship. Premier Maritime Group, the company her dad had taken over from her mother's father when he retired, used to be called Campbell Lines—CL.

Her own family's ship was depicted in this work of art!

She opened her mouth to tell Daniel when her gaze landed on the demons and the dead bodies. She swallowed and did not say a word. Mei Lien wouldn't have created these horrifying images on Duncan Campbell's ship without a good reason.

A tremor shook Inara's body.

*What does this mean?* She didn't know, but it couldn't be good.

Maybe there was more to Duncan Campbell than family lore and history books depicted.

"Why do you think Mei Lien embroidered this steamship?" Her voice sounded shaky to her own ears so she smiled, hoping that would keep Daniel from noticing.

He was too caught up in the story on the sleeve to give her more than a quick glance before flipping the sleeve over to the other side where the picture continued. "I think something important happened to her on this boat. We know she went from Seattle to Port Townsend and Orcas Island. Perhaps it was on this ship that she met her husband, Joseph. Maybe it was an abusive relationship, which would explain the demons. But I think it's something else."

"Why do you say that?"

"Well, look at this. On the bow of the ship are the English letters *POP*."

"Pop? What does that mean?"

"There was an ocean steamship named the *Prince of the Pacific*, *POP*, that holds an important place in Seattle history." Here he pulled out a chair and sat down. He then slipped off his gloves and ran both hands through his hair as though he'd just awakened. "On the morning of February 7, 1886, all the Chinese living in Seattle, about three hundred fifty people, were rounded up and forced onto the *Prince of the Pacific*, which sailed that afternoon for San Francisco."

Sensing this was going to be a long story, Inara also pulled out a chair and sat. "Why were they forced?"

"It was during the era of the Chinese Exclusion Act of 1882, which was an immigration law banning Chinese from the United States except in very small numbers and allowing in no laborers at all. But the prejudice went much further." He had a distant look in his eyes, as though his soul could remember the pain even though he hadn't personally lived through it. "All up and down the West Coast, Americans of European descent— white Americans—tried, often successfully and usually brutally, to force all Chinese out of their communities."

He propped one ankle on the opposite knee and fiddled with the gloves in his hand. "White culture viewed the Chinese, including those born on American soil, as temporary sojourners draining their country of resources. Once the railroads were built, Chinese laborers looked to settle and find new jobs. Combine that with the recession of the 1880s and white men worrying about losing jobs to hardworking, low-pay Chinese, and you're sitting on dynamite."

She sat forward. "So they decided to force the Chinese to leave the country even if they didn't want to go? How could they do that?"

He shrugged. "They just did."

She looked at the sleeve, at the demons forcing the Chinese out of the city they called home, and felt shame. "They should be teaching this in school. We should know about what was done."

But then her gaze landed on the water. It was dark, swirling with vortexes and half-hidden demons and what looked to be snakes. But there were also bodies. Dozens of bodies floating in the water, some with mouths open as if screaming, others obviously limp and lifeless.

And in the middle, right where the inside of the elbow would be in the sleeve, was one female figure with arms and legs splayed and, strangely, a smile on her face.

"See here?" Daniel went on, pointing to characters on the sleeve, unaware of the turmoil filling Inara. "Here above this woman are the Chinese characters for father and grandmother. I don't know why they are in the water."

Whatever it all meant, it made her feel sad. "Did the ship reach San Francisco?"

"Yes. Then it went on to China from there." Daniel clapped his hands together, startling her. "I think we need a break. Can I take you to lunch? I hear there's a great new restaurant in Eastsound."

Inara swallowed hard and forced herself to look away from the sleeve. She mustered a smile. "That would be nice. Just give me a minute."

She escaped to her bedroom upstairs, feeling unsettled. Whatever story Mei Lien was telling on the sleeve, Inara knew it was sad and had something to do with Duncan Campbell, their family hero.

She stared out the window toward the main house—the legacy left to her by that hero.

She shook her head and forced on a smile to improve her mood. She was being silly, letting embroidery affect her like this. Whatever story the sleeve was telling, it couldn't be that bad. Right?

*Why did I agree to this?* Inara asked herself not for the first time as the hostess at the New Leaf Cafe led them to their table half an hour later. The tiles she'd finally decided upon for the guest room showers needed to be ordered, and she had to make a final decision on whether to enlarge the restaurant space, thereby closing off the great hall at one end. Tom's crew would be ready to start on it Monday morning if they'd finished framing the new walls that would turn the upstairs sitting room into a guest room. Really, her time was better spent at work.

But then again, what harm was there in a quick lunch with an attractive man?

"How did you hear about this place?" she asked as the hostess left them with their menus.

"My mom told me about it, actually. She's the owner and executive chef at Toisan in Seattle and Bellevue. She once worked with the chef who started this restaurant."

Inara dropped her menu. "Your mom owns Toisan?"

He just grinned.

"Remind me to never cook for you. Can't compete." Why did she just say that? Hoping he didn't notice the implication of any future relationship between them, she went on. "The food at Toisan is amazing. My family eats there all the time."

"Then you've probably seen my mother. She practically lives at the restaurants."

The waiter appeared to take their drink orders. Once he left, Inara said, "Tell me more about your family."

Daniel's features softened in a way that told her he loved his family very much. "It's just Mom, my grandmother who lives with my mom, and my sister, Cassie. My extended family lives out of the area."

A family of females could indicate he had a softer side to him, like her own brother, Nate. "Tell me about Cassie. Are you close?"

"She's a pain in the ass, but I love her." His eyes gleamed. "She's younger than me by four years and works as an attorney. Family law."

"Impressive." She scanned the menu but kept the conversation going. "You mentioned your grandmother lives with your mother?"

He nodded as he set his menu aside. "Yeah, on Beacon Hill, in the house where I grew up. She knows everything there is to know about every Chin who ever lived. She's better than Ancestry.com."

The waiter arrived with their wine and to take their orders. When he left, Daniel tilted his glass toward her. "Your turn. Tell me about your family."

She took a moment to sip her wine and reach for a breadstick from the basket as she decided how much was safe to tell him. Until she knew more, she wasn't ready to admit that the ship on the sleeve belonged to her family. However, not many people knew PMG used to be called Campbell Lines, so she'd be safe telling him a little history. "Well, my dad runs Premier Maritime Group, shipping and cruise lines. He took over from my mother's father, and he's now grooming my big brother, Nathan, to take the reins from him someday. My sister, Olivia, is a doctor. Both of my siblings are married with adorable kids." She bit into the breadstick.

"And your mom?"

She stalled by chewing slowly. She never liked talking about her mother to people who hadn't known her. Usually she brushed the question aside and talked about something else, but Daniel sat waiting for her answer like he had all the time in the world.

She washed the bread down with more wine. "She died when I was fifteen. Right here on Orcas, in fact. Car accident."

His lips pressed together in sympathy, but then he surprised her. Instead of awkward words of condolence, he said, "I lost my dad eight years ago. Cancer."

So he understood. "I'm sorry." Now she was the one with the lame condolence.

"I still think of him every day." He tilted his head to the side. "Tell me about her. Your mom."

A surprising urge to open up to him came over her, but she knew the risk. Mom, and everything that was tied to her memory, was too deeply woven into her soul to be treated like any old conversation topic with someone she barely knew.

But Daniel did seem genuinely interested. And he'd get it, at least partly. Maybe that was enough.

"Well." She wiped her palms on the napkin spread across her lap as she sorted how to begin. "Everything she did was done big. She ran the philanthropic side of PMG and was constantly on the go, raising funds to help orphaned children in South Korea or land-mine victims in Rwanda. She often picked up newly arrived refugees from the airport herself to help them get settled in the United States. That kind of thing. And yet, at home, she made me feel like my siblings and I were her whole world."

"She sounds amazing."

"She was." She looked down at the blue candle between them. "Losing her tore me apart. If it wasn't for my father, I don't know what would have happened to me. He kept me focused in school and was a big influence on my decision to go into international business."

"Did you work for PMG?"

"No. He wanted me to, but I always knew I had to do my own thing. Dad says I'm too independent."

"Independence isn't a bad thing."

"You're right," she agreed. "Although the few times I've exerted my independence, Dad wouldn't have agreed with that statement." She laughed to lighten the mood. "That's hardly ever an issue, though. Since what happened the night Mom died, I try not to argue with Dad more than necessary. But he's been pushing my buttons lately." *Like with pink toilets.*

Daniel leaned his forearms on the linen tablecloth. "What happened the night your mom died?"

*Change the subject.* But when she opened her mouth, the words that came weren't the ones she'd intended. "We fought the night she died." How did he keep getting her to do that?

She gulped her wine, then realized Daniel wasn't staring at her in horror. More like pity. She didn't know which was worse. She looked out the window at the flower box and sighed. "Mom was heading back to Seattle to meet a family resettling here from Somalia and wanted me to go with her and help. I wanted to stay on the island because the boy I had a crush on was having a party the next night. We got into it as only mothers and teenage daughters can. I screamed into her face that I hated her, and at that moment I meant it. She told me I was selfish, and I was, and then she walked out without saying another word and drove away."

She paused for breath. "'I hate you' were the last words she heard from me."

His warm hand covered hers and squeezed, sending shivers of awareness through her. "I'm sure she knew you didn't mean it."

Inara looked at his hand and noticed the white half-moons on his fingernails. "I shouldn't have said it, and I have to accept responsibility for the fact that my mother was the safest driver I knew and I upset her enough that night to distract her. They think a deer or something probably ran onto the road and her car skidded out of control on the wet pavement, but I was with her a handful of times before when that happened and she handled it fine. The only thing different that night was our fight."

Daniel's thumb was rubbing the back of her hand. She couldn't seem to tear her eyes away, as though it wasn't her own hand she saw in his.

Suddenly uncomfortable with how much she'd revealed to him, she drew back her hand and occupied it with her wineglass. "Whew!" She pasted on a bright smile. "Let's change the subject. Are you single?"

He didn't play along with her, though. Instead, he tilted his head to the side like he was trying to figure her out, but then a slow grin made its way across his face and a single dimple appeared in his left cheek. "I like you, Inara Erickson."

So this was how he wanted to play. She tilted her own head, copying him. "I like you too, Daniel Chin."

Their server appeared with their lunch, and the subject turned to less personal topics, though awareness of each other vibrated through them unabated.

Later, as Daniel drove her back to Rothesay, he said, "I'm sure you need to get back to work. But if not, I'm going to spend a few hours digging through archives at the Orcas Island Historical Museum before heading to the ferry. Care to join me?"

His invitation was tempting, if only to spend more time with him. "I wish I could, but you're right; I do need to get back."

"I'll let you know if I find anything interesting." They drove in silence until they pulled up in front of her house, where he parked but made no move to get out of the car. He shifted in the driver's seat to face her. "I am, by the way."

She was reaching for the door handle but stopped to look at him. "You are what?"

His eyes danced. "Single."

She felt a smile tug at her lips and couldn't help but give in to it. "Good to know."

"Can I take you to dinner the next time you're in Seattle?"

It would be so easy to fall for this guy, but the timing was horrible. "I'm not looking for a relationship right now."

"Me neither, yet here we are." His dimple flashed, drawing her gaze to his mouth.

Yes indeed, here they were. Heck, the next time she was in Seattle could be months away. What would be the harm in agreeing to one dinner? "I'd like that."

He shifted closer, instantly heating the air between them.

She swallowed, and even though she tried to stop it, her tongue slipped out to wet her lips.

Daniel leaned closer, so close she could smell the spice of his cologne. Time slowed down. Her focus narrowed so that nothing else existed but the two of them and the sound of their breathing. Her gaze traced his slightly parted lips, and she wanted nothing more than to taste them.

When his mouth was mere inches from her own, something in her brain clicked and she pulled away, at the same time fumbling for the door handle and pushing it open.

"Th-thank you for lunch." She didn't look at him as she got to her feet, then reached back to grab her purse from the car floor.

"You're welcome."

She could tell by his voice that he was smiling, but she still couldn't look at him. She was about to slam the car door shut and escape when she remembered the sleeve and purses inside the house. "Wait a second," she said, finally meeting his amused gaze. "I'll run inside and get your boxes."

"Nah," he said, leaning across the center console. The look in his eyes teased her for being a chicken, but all he did was smile and say, "You can bring them when you come to town. I'm going to have my team focus on Mei Lien and Joseph for a while. Try to figure out their story."

"Okay." She stepped back, her hand on the door ready to

close it, but she lingered, feeling awkward, like she should explain herself but not knowing what to say. "Have a safe drive."

His dimple flashed. "See you soon, I hope."

She shut the car door and backed away, waving and hoping her smile didn't look dopey, because as much as she knew she should keep things professional between them, she really did like him.

She didn't wait for Daniel to clear the drive before she turned and headed to the manor. Time for some good, old-fashioned hard work to clear her head.

Early the next morning, before Tom's crews usually showed up, Inara was awakened by the sound of a car driving in, its brakes squealing as it stopped in front of the house.

She groggily got up to peer through the upstairs sitting room windows to the driveway out front.

A white sedan was parked near the fountain. A plump woman with short blond hair stood at the open trunk, her eye gazing through the viewfinder of a camera pointed toward the manor. As Inara watched, she lowered the camera, walked a few feet closer to the fountain, and lifted the camera back to her eye again.

*What in the world?* Inara went back to the bedroom and threw on her clothes from the previous day before slipping downstairs and out the front door.

"Excuse me. Can I help you with something?"

The woman glanced her way, paused, then snapped one more shot of the main house before facing her fully. She stuck out her hand. "Good morning. You must be Ms. Erickson. I hope I'm not disturbing you. I wanted to get some photos before your construction crews get here. I'm Lacey Gray, with Luxe Real Estate in Seattle. Your father asked me to take a look at the property and provide a market analysis so you could see what you could get for this place. It's amazing, by the way. I like what you're doing with it."

Inara couldn't have moved if she wanted to. "Market analysis?"

Lacey's smile was brighter than the sun spearing over Mount Constitution. "I'd love a tour, if you have the time, both inside and out. From what I can tell so far, we could slant the listing toward private buyers as well as commercial." She shot another picture of the garage wing.

Inara still couldn't move. Or speak.

"Of course, in this economy, it might take a while to find a buyer, but don't worry; we're the best." Lacey kept talking and snapping pictures, unaware of Inara's inner horror.

He'd done it again, she realized. Her father wasn't taking her seriously, and he was trying to steamroller her into doing what he thought best. And clearly he thought she should sell.

What was going on in his mind? Was Starbucks such a great job that he couldn't accept her turning it down? Or was it more personal? Was he trying to protect her from the failure he thought inevitable?

*Was it inevitable?*

No. Of course not. Her dad had no business putting these doubts in her head.

And then she remembered the pink toilets. He'd probably known exactly what he was doing when he changed the order, and she sure as hell no longer believed he had been trying to help. He'd only been throwing up roadblocks to make her back down on her own. And when she didn't, it pissed him off enough to up his game.

She loved her father, but this ruthless business side of him was more than she could take.

Without another word to Lacey, Inara stormed back inside and headed straight for her cell phone, intending to call her father and give him a piece of her mind.

But before the call connected she stopped and clicked her phone off.

No, over the phone would have no effect on him. She needed to meet with him in person, like the business professional she was, and force him to see her vision. If he didn't come to believe in this project as much as she did, he would withdraw his funding and leave her without any options.

On her way to pack a bag, she glanced at the black storage boxes on the kitchen table. Inside one of them was the embroidered sleeve with a sad tale that had something to do with her family. If only she knew what.

This would also be the perfect time to dig further into what might have happened on the *Prince of the Pacific*. Yes, earlier than expected, she was headed for Seattle.

# Chapter Ten

*Thursday, March 4, 1886*
*Port Townsend, Washington Territory*

S he was family?" Joseph's voice cut into her thoughts.

Mei Lien nodded, knowing to whom he referred, though she kept her eyes on the water. "My grandmother."

"What happened, Mei Lien? Will you tell me?"

She knew he wasn't asking about what happened to Grandmother, but to all of them. And, though she thought of refusing him, the words started spilling out like they'd been pent up behind a dam.

"It was early," she began. "So early the sun had not yet risen when I was awakened by the sound of shouting. I wasn't concerned since such noises were common at night, what with the saloons and brothels just a block away."

She closed her eyes as the memories washed over her and described what happened for Joseph as best as she could. "I knew they were there to drive us out just like they'd done to the Chinese people in Tacoma last November."

"My sister wrote to me about what happened in Tacoma," Joseph said, startling Mei Lien. He had his legs stretched out in front of him and was leaning on one arm. The pose appeared casual but the fist resting on his lap was clenched. "She lives there. Such a nasty business that was, what with the beatings and everything burned to ashes."

Mei Lien drew her legs up, rested her chin on her knees, and watched water drip from a branch as she talked. "Because we'd heard stories from people driven out of Tacoma, we knew to be scared that morning. But we weren't as scared as we should have been."

She continued the story, telling him everything that had happened that morning and leaving nothing out. Occasionally Joseph would set his hand on hers for comfort, or grumble in disgust at the things he heard, but she didn't stop. Now that she was telling him, she couldn't stop until he knew everything.

"What was the name of the ship?" Joseph interrupted.

She'd never forget the name; it was so burned into her memory. "The *Prince of the Pacific*. Why?"

Joseph's face reddened until he was nearly purple. His chest rose and fell rapidly, and then, all at once, he was on his feet in front of her. "The *Prince of the Pacific* is Campbell's ship. No wonder you're afraid of him." Suddenly he grabbed her and pulled her up and against his chest, where she could hear his heart pounding. "Oh, Mei Lien." He drew in a long, slow breath, and then quietly he asked, "What did that bastard do to you?"

She didn't answer right away, so overcome was she at the sensation of being held against his body, safely wrapped in his arms.

"Mei Lien?"

Taking a deep breath, she stepped away from him to think clearly and finish her story. Back on the ground with her legs curled to the side, she continued—and this time Joseph didn't interrupt until the story was finished. "And then I woke up in your cabin."

"I wish you would have thrown him overboard."

Mei Lien blinked. She'd been so caught up in her story that

she hadn't noticed Joseph pacing in front of her, fury coming from him so ferociously that she imagined she could see it fill the space under their tree with red heat. "Joseph?"

He stopped to face her with his fists clenched at his sides. "I can't believe I've lived all these years next door to a man capable of such cruelty. Mei Lien, you must believe me. If I had known what he would do, I would have stopped him. I should have stopped him."

She got to her feet again and grabbed his hands, holding tight. "You did not know, Joseph. I don't blame you."

He blew out a breath and freed one hand to cup it behind her head, bringing her forehead gently against his own. "I'm sorry, Mei Lien. So sorry."

She closed her eyes and let herself enjoy the feeling of Joseph holding her, caring for her.

Joseph didn't speak for a long time, though the emotions flitting across his face told her he was reviewing all she'd just told him. When he did speak, the tightly controlled anger in his voice made the hair on the back of her neck stand up. "He has to pay for what he's done."

Mei Lien would not argue, nor would she fight a losing battle. "It is done. Let it go."

"Campbell and all the men responsible should be brought to justice."

"No, you mustn't say a word to anyone." Mei Lien forced her limbs to move until she faced him squarely. "No one will believe you. We don't have proof Grandmother was thrown overboard. They'd say she jumped as I did, but didn't have the strength to survive."

Joseph cocked his head to the side. "Could that be what actually happened?"

Mei Lien understood he still held hope that his friend wasn't completely guilty of all this cruelty. "No," she answered him, forcing her voice to remain even. "Grandmother had bound feet and couldn't walk. She was incapable of climbing over the ship's railing. Someone would have had to lift her over it."

"Forgive me, but could your father have done it?"

The thought shocked Mei Lien into silence. She supposed Father could have lifted his own mother and pushed her to her death in an attempt to save her as he'd done to Mei Lien. It was possible.

But no, it wasn't likely. Father knew how weak Grandmother was and how cold the waters were. He had known as surely as Mei Lien that Grandmother would not have been able to swim to shore. If he'd pushed her over the side, it was to save her from an even crueler end at the hands of the white men, and in that case, the blame still lay with the white men. With Campbell.

She didn't want to talk about Grandmother's death anymore. It made her feel cold and sick inside, and right now they had other things to worry about. She started to wrap up the remains of their lunch. "We'd best hurry if I'm to find a job and a place to live by nightfall."

Joseph nodded absently as he helped her. When everything was packed away, he didn't start heading back to town as she expected. Instead he turned to her, his hand gentle on her upper arm. "Mei Lien," he said now, his chin set stubbornly. "Let me protect you. I'll keep you safe."

"How would you do that, Joseph?"

"You'll be safe if you're my wife." His thumb stroked her shoulder. "We should marry."

## Chapter Eleven

*Thursday, March 4, 1886*
*Port Townsend, Washington Territory*

Marry.

The word was so unexpected that Mei Lien had to repeat it over and over in her mind before she understood him. "Marry?" She shook her head. "Don't be *shă*, foolish, Joseph. That's impossible. Come, we must go."

She stepped past him, intending to lead him back to town, when he grabbed her arm.

"I'm serious, Mei Lien." He had a challenging light in his eyes. "I know I'm not the kind of man you expected to marry. I don't have the right religion or customs, and I don't know all your words, but I can protect you and keep you safe. I can give you a good life."

He was serious. He really thought they should wed. She shifted the satchel on her shoulder and managed to shrug off his hold and move past him this time. "I can't let you do that, Joseph. You have a good life on your island, and soon you'll find your Christian bride to start a family with. You don't need me, nor do you really want me."

"You're wrong." His voice held a command but his words were what made her stop walking, though she kept her back to him. "I do need you and want you, Mei Lien."

Now she spun around. "What for?"

He remained where she'd left him under the dripping boughs of the tree, his hands hanging limply at his sides. "In these last weeks that we've been sharing my cabin, I've come to long for the sound of your voice when I return home at night. My body craves the feel of yours next to mine as we work in the fields. I find myself wondering if your skin is really as soft as I remember it from the night I undressed you after pulling you from the water. When I think of my children, I picture them with your black hair and brown eyes."

She'd had no idea he felt this way. She'd been certain she was the only one to feel something when they were together. For what seemed like several minutes all she could do was stare at him. His words seemed to shock him as much as they did her because his face flamed into a color she'd never before seen on a man. He kept his gaze locked on her, but the way he fidgeted with his hat in his hands revealed his true unease.

"What about the good white woman who would be by your side in the community?" she finally managed, resisting the pull of his words. "What happens if you meet her someday but are stuck with me?"

He stepped to her then, out in the open, and took both her hands in his own. His forgotten hat dropped to the muddy ground. "I can't imagine any white woman more beautiful or more perfect for me than you already are. I don't want some woman I don't even know. I want you. Will you marry me, Mei Lien?"

"What about people who will shun you once they know you're married to me? You'll be laughed at. You won't become a town council member and certainly not mayor." The way he'd described those jobs to her had told her how important they were to him.

Surely she had him convinced to forget the idea now.

But he shook his head. "I don't care what anyone thinks. After spending these weeks with you, I've come to see people and situations differently. A civic life isn't so grand when the people I'm serving climb over others to serve themselves. You are all I need."

When she didn't respond, he squeezed her hands. "What do you say?"

She tried to tug her hands away but he wouldn't let her. Frustrated, she said the only thing left she could say to stop them both from making this mistake. "But, Joseph, I don't love you."

Even as she said the words, she recognized the absurdity of someone like her saying them. If she was still in Seattle, she would be facing an arranged marriage with the concept of love not considered. Did she even know how love would feel?

His mouth twisted. "That's all right. Maybe someday you will."

"You don't love me either."

"I wouldn't be so sure if I were you."

Suddenly his lips were on hers. At first she felt detached, as if she was watching from a distance. But then the softness of his lips, the warmth of his breath against her cheek, the pull of his hands on her shoulders narrowed her attention until all she knew was Joseph. His lips tasted salty, like the ham he'd eaten, but underneath was a taste she could not identify. As she opened her mouth and tilted her head to better fit his, she realized the flavor was Joseph. Simply Joseph. And she wanted more. Craved more.

His lips moved to her cheek and over to her neck. She closed her eyes and let her head fall back, completely forgetting they were standing in an open field where anyone could see them. Something hot and wet slid up her neck to her earlobe, and she gasped at the delicious tremors it set off in her body. Never had she known that a tongue could be used for such a purpose.

"Now try to tell me we wouldn't be good together," Joseph whispered into her ear between kisses.

She immediately grasped the challenge and promise in his words and felt her body respond with a flood of warmth that pooled low in her stomach. She needed to think. She stepped back to put distance between them and realized she was shaking, though she wasn't cold.

Joseph's lips looked swollen and his eyes were half-closed, as if he'd just woken from a long night of sleep. She put her fingertips to her own lips to see if they were just as swollen. They were.

Slowly a lazy smile spread across his face and shot straight into her knees, weakening them. The sensation was entirely uncomfortable but she liked it.

She wanted to say yes, wanted to wrap the safety he represented around her and never emerge from it. She wanted him to kiss her again.

With shaking breath she let her gaze wander down his body and wondered how it would feel to let him touch her as a husband touches a wife. She'd heard about these things when she was a boy among men in Seattle.

Joseph's large, calloused palms should feel rough against her skin, but they were warm and gentle. He reminded her of Father in that way. They were both caring men who deeply loved family. And marriage or not, she and Joseph were already family.

But he was so big. Bigger than Father. Bigger than Yeung Lum, or any Chinese man she'd known. Surely he would hurt her.

Then again, maybe not. She'd seen him cradle a wild rabbit in his arms, then set it free when they could have eaten it for dinner. She'd felt his gentleness in the way he'd stood behind her with his hands wrapped around each of hers, teaching her how to hold the hoe when working the fields. Just now he'd held her so gently she'd felt cherished. He may be big, but he would not hurt her. He wasn't like the other white men.

As Joseph stared back at her with his kind green eyes, the redness of his lips paling as he patiently awaited her answer, she thought about his cabin and property, the place across the meadow where he'd already started building a proper house, as he called it. It was nothing but a frame right now, but he worked on it every spare minute he found, and by the end of summer he planned to move in. She could move in with him and live in a house grander than any place she'd ever lived. She could see herself in that house, cooking Joseph's dinner in the kitchen that filled the entire back of the first floor. She saw herself tending the garden that would grow in the plot outside the back door. She could even see herself helping with the farm animals in the barn or going with him when he caught fish from the sound or hunted deer on the mountain behind the farm.

Perhaps more surprising, she could see herself on the porch next to Joseph as they grew old. She could see herself lying beside him under his bed quilt. Their children would have his patience and her spirit. His green eyes and her black hair.

They would have a good life. Joseph was right in that, she knew. But would she ever grow to love him? She might come close, but she'd felt that part of herself shrivel up and die the moment she'd seen Grandmother's body on the beach. She'd loved only two people in her life, Father and Grandmother, and having them ripped from her tore away the part of herself that had been attached to them. She wasn't sure there was enough left inside her that was capable of love. Her heart had been ground under the boot heel of that white devil Campbell. She gasped. "Campbell!"

"Where?" Joseph pulled her to him, his arm wrapping protectively around her back as his gaze searched the field around them.

"No, he's not here." She stepped out of his hold. "I...I just remembered that he lives near you. Once he knows I'm there, he'll want to kill me because I know what he did. I would spend every day of my life hiding from him and wondering when he'll strike next. I'll never feel safe."

"I'll be there. I'll keep you safe."

She shook her head and wrapped her arms around herself. "You can't. You can't be by my side every minute of every day. You have fields and orchards to tend, supplies to purchase, crops to sell. Mail to deliver."

"Campbell stays in Seattle most of the time. He's on the island only a few days every couple months. Besides, on the steamship he thought you were a boy, right?"

Mei Lien nodded slowly.

"Well then," Joseph continued. "I'll take you back to the island as a woman, my bride from Port Townsend. No one will ever connect you to Campbell's boat."

She hadn't thought of that. But, still… "Campbell and others like him will hate me on sight for no other reason than because I look different. The fact that he won't know I was on his ship doesn't protect me from him."

She saw the knowledge in Joseph's eyes as he realized the truth of her words. To save him the trouble of retracting his proposal, she changed the subject. "I'm hoping to find a position as a houseboy," she said as she started across the field toward the nearest house without waiting to see if he followed. "Or maybe a cook would be better. Something that will let me hide for the most part in one room."

His hand on her arm stopped her from marching away. When she spun back to look at him, she saw his brow had become furrowed.

"I'll protect you from Campbell and anyone else who wants to cause you harm." His voice hitched, causing him to pause and press his lips together before continuing. "I promise I'll keep you safe. Just please, say you'll be my wife."

She could say that look of vulnerability did it, or the way he nearly begged her, or even her lack of options. But she knew the real reason she gave in was because of the fire he'd ignited in her body. She yearned to know where it led, and she knew only Joseph could show her. She'd never felt so alive and so full of power—a sensation quite foreign to her but entirely welcome.

Suddenly shy, she looked down at the dirt. "Yes. I'll marry you."

Joseph's finger lifted her chin so they were standing face-to-face. In that moment the world around her came into focus, as if they were subjects of one of the photographs she'd seen propped in the window of the Occidental Hotel in Seattle. The rest of the world felt frozen in time and only the two of them were present, captured in a scene that would forever be imprinted on her mind.

Joseph's smile started slowly and spread across his face until it seemed to light him up from inside. It started an answering glow inside herself, and she felt her own smile widen as Joseph picked her up and swung her around with a whoop. In that moment she forgot all that had happened to lead her here. She closed her eyes and thrilled at the sensation of being held.

When Joseph set her back on her feet, he landed a kiss on her lips again that ended as quickly as it started. Then, stopping only long enough to gather up their belongings, he nearly dragged her back to town.

It took more than an hour to settle the details. Joseph paid the Baron to help them find a wedding officiant—a Tacoma ship's captain waiting for his cargo to be off-loaded who had no qualms about marrying a white man and a Chinese woman, for the right price—as well as a plain gold band from the Baron's store and a dress and shoes for Mei Lien.

She'd tried to refuse the dress since she preferred to wear trousers and a jacket, but Joseph reminded her she needed to dress like a woman to keep Campbell from recognizing her. And then he'd laid his palm against her cheek and told her she deserved to look and feel beautiful on her wedding day. Even though this dress wasn't her idea of beauty, she'd accepted the garment and allowed herself to be whisked away to prepare for the ceremony two doors down from the Baron's store. No reputable hotel or private home would allow Mei Lien entrance, but the Baron found reluctant help at the brothel.

Even now, standing before a full-length mirror in one of the upstairs bedrooms, with her hair done up in a feminine bun and wearing layers of petticoats and the starched black silk dress with a bustle at the back, she still did not feel beautiful. She felt ridiculous wearing this clothing with the linen undergarments and tight whalebone corset. Never in her life had she worn anything like this, and she never wanted to again if it meant feeling this confined and exposed all at once. How did a woman do a day's work all trussed up like this?

"I don't see why we should be fussing over one such as her."

Mei Lien darted a look at the complaining prostitute lounging on the bed that took up most of the space in the small room. She was a harsh-looking woman with red, stringy hair and too much rouge on cheeks that sagged with age. A green silk robe hung loosely off one shoulder that was covered with freckles.

"Hush, Pearl. Because we're getting paid to and that's all the reason we need." The younger woman, who'd said her name was Sapphire, stood behind Mei Lien, carefully fastening the row of tiny buttons along her spine. She met Mei Lien's gaze in the mirror and smiled, revealing a missing front tooth. "Don't pay her no mind. She's just jealous."

"Jealous of a smelly Chink?" With a sound of disgust, Pearl bounced to her feet and disappeared through the bedroom door.

"There. All done." Sapphire stepped back and planted her hands on her hips. Then she tilted her head sideways. "Maybe we should powder your skin so it's not so dark."

Mei Lien ignored the woman as she stared at herself in the mirror and saw the effect the dress had on her figure. She crossed her arms over her body as a shield. Was she really expected to go out in public where people, where Joseph, would see her…her breasts sticking out from her chest like this? She might as well be naked for how noticeable the two bumps on her front appeared. And her waist! It looked unnaturally small, which made her chest appear that much bigger. Sapphire had even said something about how Mei Lien's husband would be able to fit his hands completely around her waist, which was a ridiculous notion.

"The Baron says it's time," Pearl mumbled from the doorway before disappearing again.

Mei Lien closed her eyes and imagined herself wearing the *sam* and *fu* she always wore and instantly felt the tension ease from her body. She preferred men's clothing, but she knew that from today forward what she preferred would come second to her husband's wishes. And he wanted her to wear dresses. Plus, dresses would help hide her from Campbell.

With a sigh, Mei Lien opened her eyes and forced her arms down by her sides. Then she followed Sapphire down the stairs to the brothel's front parlor, where Joseph waited with the Baron and the captain. When he saw her, Joseph's eyes widened with a look of surprise and admiration. He shot her a warm smile that eased some of her tension.

Without a word, Mei Lien took her place beside Joseph and kept her head bowed so he would not see the embarrassment on her face. This wasn't the wedding day she'd always thought of having. Despite the handmade doilies on the furniture and imported lace curtains on the windows, this was still a brothel. She should be arriving at her new husband's parents' house riding in a brightly painted sedan chair and wearing a red silk *hung kwa*. Rather than being surrounded by ladies of the night and merchants here to make a buck, she and her husband should be surrounded by family and friends.

As the captain started speaking, Mei Lien pushed away her negative thoughts. It was time now to bid farewell to her past and look ahead to her new future with hope. If not for her own sake, then for Joseph's.

When prompted, she repeated the words the captain spoke. She smiled at Joseph as he made his pledge to her, and she tried all the while to believe this union would lead to happiness.

When it was over and the captain announced they were man

and wife, Joseph lightly kissed her on the lips, which caused the ladies in the room to hoot and shout out bawdy encouragement. Joseph ignored them and grinned down at her. "I'm pleased to meet you, Mrs. McElroy."

Mrs. McElroy. The name felt so odd directed at her. In her culture, women did not change their names to match their husband's. For Joseph, she smiled. "Thank you."

He squeezed her hand. "You look beautiful, Mei Lien."

She felt heat climb up her neck. To hide the surprising longing his words breathed to life in her, and the accompanying embarrassment, she turned her eyes away.

Soon they were on the street again, hurrying to catch a steamer bound for home since even the Baron could not secure them respectable lodging for their wedding night, and the sun was setting fast. As they reached the docks and the waiting stack of supplies the Baron charged Joseph extra to expedite, Mei Lien felt her gaze stray past the gaslit streets to the north of town and the darkening beach where Grandmother's body had been found. The tide had come in, completely covering the rocks where she had lain.

All trace of Grandmother was gone and Mei Lien knew her life before that horrible night was gone forever too. She would never again touch, smell, see, or hear anything from that time. It was gone forever.

A low, burning anger settled into her stomach as she stared at the water-covered beach. Silently she promised her family she would never forget what had been done to them.

Someday, somehow, she would make sure the truth was told. She would tell the story, or she would die trying.

# Chapter Twelve

*Monday, July 9—present day*
*PMG Headquarters, Seattle*

Inara pulled out another file drawer to sort through the dusty records in the basement of Premier Maritime Group, looking for anything from 1886. She'd been at it an hour already and had only forty-five minutes left before the meeting she'd scheduled with her father.

She could have confronted her father at home yesterday when she got into town, but she wanted their meeting to be on a professional level. She hadn't told him she was here, in fact, and had stayed last night in her sister's guest room even though Olivia and her family were vacationing in Hawaii. First thing this morning Inara had called her father's assistant, Zoé, to schedule the meeting.

And then she'd come straight to PMG, where the security guard knew her and didn't blink an eye when she told him she needed to do research in the company archives.

Hopefully soon, she'd find what she was looking for and she'd know whether this heaviness weighing her down had merit or not. For all she knew, Mei Lien had embroidered the *Prince of the Pacific* on her sleeve as a coincidence and its being there was of no significance.

But still, she had to know.

With only ten minutes left, she found a file with handwritten logs from the *Prince of the Pacific* dated February 7, 1886, the date Daniel said the Chinese were driven out of Seattle. Duncan Campbell, owner, was listed as the person in charge of the sailing; the captain was second-in-command.

Three hundred forty-seven people, all Chinese, had boarded in Seattle, their passage paid at a discounted rate, some by the Chinese themselves, some by the citizens of Seattle willing to do anything to rid their city of an entire ethnicity.

The next entry was dated one day later in Astoria, Oregon. Although nothing was unloaded there, the *Prince* took on two hundred seventy-six passengers, their belongings, and nine hundred tons of canned salmon bound for San Francisco.

There was no way all of that could have fit on board with the more than three hundred passengers already there.

She looked closer at the ink scratchings. Nothing had been unloaded when the ship docked in Astoria and no other stops were recorded prior. Where were all the Chinese people? They couldn't have just disappeared.

And then she knew.

And with the knowledge came a wave of nausea so great she broke out in a sweat and had to sit down right there on the dusty cement floor.

They'd been dumped overboard. By her great-great-great-grandfather.

She pushed the palms of her hands to the sides of her head as horror and shame consumed her. Her thoughts whirled. If the ship had docked somewhere to unload the passengers, the log would have noted that. Plus, an influx of Chinese into any community at that time would have caused a stir. The fact that no logical explanation for their disappearance was noted on the log proved that the company wanted no record of it. Something illegal and inhumane had occurred.

The pictures on the sleeve weren't metaphors or exaggerations as Daniel had assumed. The pictures depicted the actual event in which Duncan Campbell and his employees had murdered hundreds of innocent people by dumping them off his ship. These people had disappeared, and no one in her family had thought to question it in all the years since.

She knew if she dug into the incident, she'd find evidence showing the citizens of Seattle had believed the Chinese made it safely to San Francisco or China. That is, if they thought about the Chinese people at all. The families and friends of the Chinese killed had probably been too afraid to question why their loved ones were never heard from again. Or they too had assumed that those on the ship had moved to California and had gotten on with their lives.

But Mei Lien had known the truth. And she'd used her embroidery to tell the world what happened. Oh God, had she been thrown overboard too? And somehow survived? Is that how she ended up on Orcas?

The alarm on Inara's cell phone chimed loudly through the dusty basement, startling her. It was time for her meeting with Dad. Good. He'd know what to do about all this. Hurrying, she stashed the file in her shoulder bag and climbed to her feet, sliding the file drawer shut before heading to the elevators.

In less than four minutes, she was on the top floor of the building, standing in front of her father's desk with a view of Elliott Bay sparkling sixty-seven floors below in patches of sun poking through breaks in the clouds.

Charles Erickson looked happy to see her. "I thought you weren't coming home for a while," he said, planting his hands on his desk and pushing to his feet. She held up a hand, stopping him from rounding the desk to give her a hug. He sat back down with a questioning look.

She got right to it. "Back when the company was first getting started, did we ever carry people, especially Chinese, from Seattle to San Francisco?"

He held himself strangely still. "Of course. We carried whatever needed to get from one place to another."

She hesitated, afraid of how her news would affect him. He was going to be as devastated by the information as she was.

"Dad," she started gently, "there was one voyage in particular that has me concerned. On February 7, 1886, the *Prince of the Pacific* left port with a full manifest of passengers. Chinese passengers."

He pressed his palms onto the polished top of his desk. "Go on."

She swallowed. "The Chinese passengers never made it anywhere. It's like they disappeared. The next port the ship went to was Astoria, and not one passenger disembarked. Yet they loaded more, plus freight."

Her dad got to his feet and turned his back to her as he gazed out at Elliott Bay, where a PMG container ship was being tugged to the dock at Harbor Island. A twinge of regret sliced through her. Maybe she shouldn't burden him with this.

But he had to know. "I…I think Duncan Campbell murdered them."

He bowed his head, making her wish she could pull the words back into herself.

Just as she opened her mouth to say she was wrong, it was a misunderstanding, he said, "I knew you poking around that place was a mistake."

She closed her mouth and stared at her father. The words made no sense. As she struggled to comprehend, Zoé buzzed the intercom. "Mr. Erickson, the driver just called. He's picked up the Yŏu Yì Cruises team from the airport and expects to be here within twenty minutes."

Her father stepped to the desk and hit a button. "Thanks, Zoé. Tell me as soon as they arrive." After disconnecting, he shoved his hands in his pants pockets and looked at Inara across the wide desk. "Your grandmother told your mother about the incident, how Duncan referred to it as 'dumping the worthless ballast.' He knew not to talk about it in public, but privately he was proud of what he did. Claimed to have saved his ship from ruin, had he let filthy Orientals stay aboard. Afterward, he turned into Astoria for a regularly scheduled pickup of passengers and freight, and no one was the wiser."

Her attention caught on his first sentence. "Mom knew?"

He nodded. "And she worked every day of her life trying to make up for it."

Her throat constricted and she sank into one of the chairs facing the desk. Her parents had known all along, and they'd let her and all of Seattle worship Duncan Campbell as the great founding father when really he'd been a racist murderer. She'd written reports on him in school and proudly watched the annual school production in which Duncan was a key character. If she'd known, she...she... She dropped her chin to her chest. She didn't know what she would have done. Maybe nothing, like her parents.

"Why, Dad?" She didn't know if she was asking why Duncan did it, or why her parents hadn't told her the truth before now. Maybe she was asking both.

"Things were very different then. People didn't understand about other cultures and ethnicities. All they saw was that the Chinese weren't like anything they were used to, and that scared them. Fear drives people to do horrible things."

"But most people don't murder innocent families out of fear." Inara closed her eyes and drew in a deep breath, willing herself to calm down. She still couldn't make sense of the fact that her parents had known all this time.

"When you started talking about the Chinese sleeve you found, I knew it must be connected in some way to those people, to what Duncan did." His voice dropped an octave. "You should get rid of it, Inara. Burn it."

Her eyes flew open. "And keep lying about our family and how wonderful we all are like you've done for so long?" She got to her feet to pace, keeping her distance from her dad. "Should I stand in front of the media in a couple months and dedicate the Duncan Campbell Park to the people of Seattle knowing that he murdered hundreds? No. I can't do that. I won't."

"You have to, Inara. The truth would do more damage than it's worth."

She stopped pacing. "Seriously, Dad? Don't you think the damage was done a century ago, and you and Mom and Grandpa and everyone else just made it worse by lying about it?"

He sat wearily in his leather chair, his face pale. "You sound like your mother. She thought the truth should be told too, but she understood the damage it would do to our company and our family. That's when she started giving so much of her time and our money to charities. Her life's mission became trying to undo some of the harm done by her great-great-grandfather."

"I didn't know that." It explained why she'd worked so hard.

"No one did, honey."

Inara had so much to think about that she felt overwhelmed by it all. She took her father's place at the window and stared down at the water below, wondering what it had been like that day Mei Lien and her family were loaded onto a steamer, never to return. Guilt burned her soul. Inara may not have been alive at the time, but she felt responsible for what had happened. Like her mom, she wanted to find a way to make it better. To absolve her family shame.

"Did it help Mom? The charity work?"

"Some." Her dad didn't elaborate, but Inara knew her mom must have died with the guilt still weighing heavily on her.

"A Chinese woman lived in Dahlia's house before Campbell bought it. Did you know that?" She could tell by the widening of her father's eyes that he didn't. "Her name was Mei Lien, and she was married to a man named Joseph McElroy. She's the one who made the sleeve. She knew what Duncan did that night, but we don't know how she's connected or how she ended up on the island. Do you?"

"No. And we'll probably never know, but you have to give this thing up. Stop researching it and let the secrets stay buried. You've got enough on your plate with the hotel." He stood up and leaned his hands on his desk. "Think of your brother, who's down the hall preparing to meet with Chinese businessmen who are selling us their company, entrusting us with their assets, staff, and reputation. Someday Nathan will take over from me. Do you want to hurt his future? And your sister's? No one will want to take their kids to her clinic if they know the truth. You have to keep it quiet, Inara."

The censure in his voice stabbed into her but she pushed it away. "Yeah, I know," she hedged. "You've got to get to your meeting so I'll get out of your hair now."

She returned to the chair to gather her things. The anger that had been burning her up just a moment ago now fizzled into a dragging sadness. The secret may have been kept this long, but she knew the sleeve was going to change that, no matter how much her dad wanted to keep the incident buried.

Unless she did as he asked and stopped researching the sleeve and Mei Lien. Told Daniel to stop his research too. Burned the sleeve.

"I'm serious, Inara. If word about this gets out, I'm going to have to pull your funding." His face was turning red and he looked sweaty.

She knew that getting this worked up wasn't good for his heart, but she had to ask, "You would really do that to me?"

"If you insist on hurting the rest of us, I'll have no choice."

All she could do was stare at the carpet and consider her options. But, of course, she really didn't have any. She was defeated. "I won't let the truth get out. And you're right. I need my focus to be on the hotel."

His brow smoothed, but as he sat down in his chair, his hand slipped into his coat pocket and drew out a tiny vial of pills. She could tell he was trying to hide the nitroglycerin tablet from her as he slid it under his tongue, but she saw and it worried her.

"You okay, Dad?"

"I'm fine, just fine." He pushed to his feet and reached for his suit jacket.

"When was the last time you saw Dr. Kozlowski?"

He had his jacket on now and was heading for the door. "Just a couple weeks ago, and I got a clean bill of health. Don't worry. Let me see you out."

Inara held up her hand, remembering just in time the other reason she was there. "Wait, I'm not done."

Dad had been reaching for the door handle, but he stopped at her words and turned back to her with a sigh. "What?" He sounded exhausted.

"Luxe Realty? Really?"

She saw guilt flash over his face as he stuck his hands in his pockets. Wordlessly he returned to his desk, where he leaned against the polished oak and crossed his arms over his barrel chest. "All I asked her to do was a market analysis. That way we'll know what the property is worth when the time comes."

With his complexion looking stronger now, she had no qualms about arguing. "When the time comes? So you're just expecting me to fail?"

"I worry about you, sweetheart. You don't have enough real-world experience to successfully manage this project, and you won't let me bring on someone who does."

"Because I can do this, Dad. It's important I do it my way."

"But you're spending a lot of my money, and I'm not sure I'll see a return on my investment." He shifted, crossing one ankle over the other. "Normally I'd let you feel your way, but this time the stakes are higher. I'm trying to save you from a disaster that could take you, literally, the rest of your life to dig out from."

He didn't think she would succeed. God, the truth hurt. She sank into the chair behind her, grateful it was there.

Her dad had always supported her, always made her believe she could do anything she set her mind to. His belief in her had pulled her through every challenge she'd ever faced. If he didn't believe she could succeed with the hotel, was it because she couldn't? Was she fooling herself?

As she sat there staring at her father, she realized she'd expected him to back down, apologize, give her what she wanted.

*God. Grow up, Inara.* Acid burned her throat.

"Why pink toilets?" She had to know.

His only movement was raising his eyebrows. "I provided the needed catalyst to get you to shut down the project. You're overqualified to live on that godforsaken island and be an innkeeper. Think of where you could go in a career with a global company like Starbucks. Which, incidentally, still has a job waiting for you. Or I could put feelers out to see who else is hiring."

Just as she'd suspected. She didn't know whether to laugh or cry or shout at him. She opened her mouth, but then closed it again without making a sound. She wasn't going to accept the Starbucks job—or any other job he found. She was going to build her hotel, and she was going to run it, and it was going to be the best damn boutique hotel in the region.

She belonged on that island, and she belonged in the hotel business. It may have been Aunt Dahlia's original dream, but it was completely her own now. This was what she wanted to do with the rest of her life. She was sure of it.

But she didn't have the capital to see the project through, and with her student loans and lack of income at the moment, she wouldn't be able to get a loan from anyone but her dad. Without him, she'd fail. "Why'd you give me the loan in the first place?"

His eyes softened. "I can't help it. I want you to be happy. But I don't believe the island is where you belong."

"Come up and see it. You'll understand then."

At that moment the door opened and her brother, Nate, walked in with a huge smile for her. "Zoé told me you were here. Everything okay?"

She gave him a distracted hug and tried to smile. "Yeah, I'm fine. Just having a chat with Dad."

"Anything I can do to help?" He was next in line to run the business. Of course he was prepared to help with any problem, financial or otherwise. She wouldn't ask him for a loan, though. His wife Jennifer's clothing boutique was still getting off the ground, and they had two boys to put through college.

"Thanks, Nate, but I'm good. Really. It's good to see you."

He stared at her a minute, clearly not believing her, then squeezed her shoulder. "You too." Then he turned to their father and shifted back into business mode. "The Yǒu Yì execs just pulled up downstairs. Be ready in five minutes." And then to Inara, "They're just about ready to sign off on the buyout. Cross your fingers they accept our offer today."

She held up her hand, fingers crossed. "Done."

"I'll see you in there, Nate." Her dad hadn't moved since Nate came in.

She and her father were both silent as Nate left. The minute the door clicked shut behind him, the pressure in Inara's chest grew. "Will you look at my concepts? I have some drawings with me, and the financials. I'm just getting started, but you'll be able to get a good feel for everything." She knew she was grasping.

When he didn't respond, she pulled back her shoulders and tried again. "Well then, let's make our business deal even more formal. How about if I sign over part ownership of the estate to you, so you not only will be paid back for your loan with interest, but you'll get a cut of all future profits from the hotel or"—she took a deep breath—" profits from the sale of the estate if that's what it comes down to."

She swore she saw a flash of interest in his eyes. "I know this isn't what you envisioned for me, but I promise you, everything I learned in graduate school I will put to use at the hotel. It's challenging in ways that make me feel alive and happy. The hotel, every complicated aspect of it, is exactly what I'm meant to do with my life, and when you see it, you'll agree."

"You're playing with a lot of money, Inara." He sounded tired.

"It's not a game." Getting an idea, she went back to her chair and grabbed her cell from her bag and pulled up her schedule. "At the end of this first phase of the renovation, which we're targeting for Labor Day weekend, why don't you come up and inspect the place? See it with your own eyes and decide at that time if you'll continue as my business partner or back out. If you back out, I'll pay you back in full at that time, even if that means putting the estate on the market." She swallowed. "Until then, you give me an honest chance. What do you say?"

He didn't say anything, just lifted his graying eyebrows and looked at her like she was still a teenager asking to stay out past curfew. She chewed her lip.

Finally he shook his head, sending her heart crashing to the floor. "I'm not going to take equity," he said, surprising her. "We'll keep to our original loan agreement. But I do like the idea of Labor Day being a decision date. You have until September. My decision at that time stands."

"And you'll stop meddling with my orders and tell the real estate agent to go away?"

"Yes." The smile he gave her was the one that always made her feel like his special little girl.

She smiled back. "You're going to love it. I promise."

When he opened his arms to her, she stepped into his embrace. Then, knowing he had to get to his meeting, she gathered her things and said good-bye.

She'd driven six blocks feeling high on the success of her meeting before she remembered the first half of the conversation. Had she really agreed to stop researching the sleeve?

If she didn't, her dad might take away her funding, despite agreeing not to do anything until Labor Day.

She couldn't risk it. She had to let the sleeve go. And she'd have to figure out how to explain her sudden change of heart to Daniel.

Without the sleeve she wouldn't have a good excuse to see him again, which made her feel even more depressed. But if she kept seeing him, she'd have to lie to him about all she knew of the murders, about there even being murders. He didn't know any of that, and as a college professor and history buff, he'd want the truth revealed to the whole world.

As it should be. But not at her family's expense.

She had no choice but to tell Daniel they were finished.

# Chapter Thirteen

Sunday, August 8, 1886
McElroy Farm, Orcas Island

M ei Lien woke early and rolled out of bed, being extra careful not to wake Joseph, who had arrived home late the night before after meeting the mail steamer at Orcas Village. She didn't understand why the steamer couldn't come up into East Sound, which would be much less distance for Joseph to travel, but he just smiled and shrugged when she asked him about it.

She tiptoed out of the bedroom and closed the door softly behind her before hurrying down the stairs to the kitchen below and on into the sitting room where she'd left her surprise in her sewing basket.

A thrill went through her as she looked at her surroundings. They'd moved into the new house last week after spending every spare minute since their wedding working together to finish it. She loved living here. The house felt solid and grand, with more rooms than they could use. "We'll fill them with children, then," Joseph had teased her. She'd secretly been pleased that he wanted children, for she did too. Very much.

She smiled now as she looked up at the sitting room windows framed by curtains that she'd sewn herself out of flour sacks. Each had an embroidered red dragon along the bottom edge, which would bring her and Joseph good fortune and happiness. Grandmother would be proud of her for the fine work she'd done.

Still smiling, she reached into her sewing basket and pulled out the surprise she'd finished last night. She spread Joseph's new mailbag over her lap and carefully studied the design she'd embroidered on the strong canvas. Instead of traditional Chinese symbols, she'd decided to embroider a scene from her husband's world. On the bag was the same imposing mountain that stretched into the sky behind their farm—Mount Constitution was what Joseph called it. Stretching along the bottom was an expanse of blue water—East Sound. And in between mountain and water she'd embroidered his farm, complete with their new house half-hidden behind tall evergreen trees.

Because she'd been unable to resist, she'd added small symbols to help Joseph on his journeys delivering mail. Along the side of the house was a vine for protection. Hidden in the water were goldfish, never to be found in the actual waters of East Sound, but on the mailbag to bring Joseph wealth and prosperity. On the mountain, hidden behind the trees, lay a tiger for the courage and bravery Joseph sometimes needed on his journey and was sure to need in the coming days as more and more islanders learned of their marriage.

But Mei Lien's favorite secret symbol was the mushrooms she'd embroidered throughout the forest to represent virility, for she'd decided it was time they start that family Joseph had teased her about.

"Mei Lien?"

She jerked at the sound of Joseph's voice coming from the kitchen, then shoved the mailbag into her sewing basket.

"What have you got there?" Joseph asked, filling the small sitting room with his large frame. Coming to her, he crouched beside her sewing basket and, with the corner of his mouth tugging upward, tapped the bag she hadn't been able to hide completely. "What's this?"

She smiled at her husband, aware as always how fortunate she was to be with this man. "It's a surprise."

With a tilt of his head, he pulled the bag out of the basket and held it up. "A mailbag?"

Suddenly shy, she stared at her lap. "Yes. It's your farm."

"I can see that. It's beautiful." He pulled her to her feet and into his arms, the mailbag crushed between them. "You are very talented. And I am honored."

She giggled as he strapped the bag across his chest and strutted around the sitting room modeling it for her, wearing only his trousers and undershirt.

He'd surprised her on their wedding night by shaving off his beard and mustache, and he'd shaved every morning since. She had never told him she liked his kisses better without his hair tickling her face, but he'd somehow known. She'd grown to love the feel of his smooth jaw against her neck as he nuzzled her in the morning before heading out to do chores.

That smooth face was smiling at her now. "I have a surprise for you this morning too."

She smiled back. "You do?"

"We're taking the day off, Mrs. McElroy. We're going to hike up the mountain to see the view from the top. You'll be able to see the snowcapped mountains on the mainland." He bit the inside of his cheek, a sure sign that he wasn't entirely sure she would like his surprise.

She wasn't sure she did, but she didn't want to disappoint him. "Let me cook breakfast before we go." She headed to the kitchen, twisting her long hair on top of her head as she went. "I'll make extra biscuits we can pack with us. Oh, and can you pick some blackberries from out back? I'll add them into lemonade I'll make with those lemons you brought from Victoria last week—" She broke off with a squeal as Joseph looped his arm around her waist and pulled her back against his chest.

"So you like the idea of a hike?" he asked against her neck with the nuzzle she loved so much. "You won't mind all the steamer tourists? Or the islanders?"

She hadn't left their farm in the five months since they'd returned from Port Townsend. Whenever a neighbor stopped by to see Joseph, she'd hidden in the cabin or barn or down by the water, wherever she could disappear until they were gone. Joseph was good at hurrying people on their way.

She knew she couldn't hide here forever, though, and a leisurely day spent with her husband sounded too good to resist. "I'll be fine. Really. Now let me go so I can feed you!"

Golden sunlight warmed them as Mei Lien and Joseph stood hand in hand on the top of Mount Constitution, tired after the long hike. Sweat pooled under Mei Lien's breasts and in the middle of her back, and she yearned for the cool, loose cloth of the men's clothes she used to wear. Women's dresses were hot and they restricted her movements, but she could see the pleasure Joseph took in seeing her dress like the women of his culture, so she continued to do so without complaint. She rarely exerted herself as much as today, anyway. She was sure she'd be used to the dresses before too long.

But now she focused on the view. Below them spread the other islands in the San Juan archipelago, separated by water so deeply blue it hurt Mei Lien's heart to see it. From this vantage she could see the Canadian islands to the north, Whatcom on the mainland to the east, and the Olympic Peninsula to the southwest. Two snowcapped mountains towered over the mainland—Baker to the north and Rainier to the south. From here, Mount Rainier looked smaller than it had from Seattle, where, on a clear day, the mountain seemed to hover just beyond reach of the city. Seeing it for the first time since she'd left Seattle reminded Mei Lien of the life she'd had there. Of the people she'd lost.

She turned away from Seattle as surely as she turned away from the life she'd been forced to leave behind. Facing west, she saw past the other islands to the water of the Strait of Juan de Fuca, through which the steamship had carried Father and Grandmother to their deaths. It had happened somewhere out there in that expanse of blue that stretched so far it disappeared into the white haze of the horizon. Was Father's body beneath that peaceful surface, being lobbed around by the currents and tides? Or had he washed ashore somewhere like Grandmother, his body treated cruelly by animals or, worse, humans?

"Nice breeze, isn't it?" Joseph asked, cutting into her thoughts.

The breeze did bring relief from the August heat. "Wonderful," she told him, smiling to hide her melancholy. "Ready for our picnic?"

They settled on the blanket Mei Lien had packed in the hamper Joseph had lugged up the mountain. Between bites of carrots and cucumbers from the garden, canned salmon and the biscuits from breakfast, Joseph told her the story of the last time he'd climbed this mountain, the first month he'd lived on Orcas. A tourist from Tacoma had offered to pay Joseph to act as his guide up the mountain, and Joseph, not wanting to miss an opportunity to make a buck, had agreed without telling the man he'd never been up it himself.

"I practically had to run to stay far enough ahead of him to scout the route before leading him anywhere. The path wasn't as well-worn then as it is today." He shook his head as he laughed. "That was the most exhausting twenty dollars I've ever made."

Mei Lien laughed too and felt the ache inside her release a bit. Her memories of her family were always with her, as was the fear that her time here was only borrowed until Campbell or someone like him sent her away, but for the most part she was happy now. She watched her husband as he told her another story, his hands and entire body getting into the telling, and wished her father could have met him. Father would have loved Joseph, despite his not being Chinese.

And then a new realization caused a thundering in her head that drowned out her husband's words.

She loved this man.

For all he'd given her and given up for himself, and for the tenderness and joy he'd brought to her shattered life—she loved him.

Tucking the realization away, she turned her attention back to his story, feeling joy in a way she'd been certain she would never feel again.

When the remains of their picnic were packed away, Joseph held out a hand to her. "Time for the easy part. Going down the mountain."

Laughing, they headed down the path playing a game of who could find the most tree branches growing in the shapes of letters of the alphabet.

They were on the letter *M* when they first heard voices echoing through the forest.

"Someone's coming." So far they hadn't encountered anyone, and she'd forgotten it was a possibility. She'd forgotten to be watchful and ready to hide or flee. Her feet refused to move another step as terror flooded through her. "Someone's coming, Joseph!"

"Sweetheart, it's all right," Joseph reassured her with a pat on her hand as he urged her along. "They're just hikers out for the day like us. No one to worry about, I'm certain."

She allowed him to tug her down the path, even though her feet didn't want to cooperate. She kept her hand in his, holding tight for reassurance.

*Joseph won't let anything happen to me. Joseph will keep me safe.* She let the words repeat over and over in her mind, knowing the truth of them but unable to grasp the comfort they should have brought.

"Well, lookee here. If it ain't the postman himself!"

Mei Lien's feet stopped moving again, and she held her breath as two men and their wives rounded the bend and came into view a short distance down the trail. One woman wore a gown of deep blue that reminded Mei Lien of the water she'd seen from the mountain. Over her shoulder the woman carried a lacy parasol that seemed better suited for a stroll on a cobblestoned street than a hike in the forest.

The other woman wore a dress as black as the scowl she directed toward Mei Lien. Her flawless but sour face was pulled tight by the severity of the bun she wore at the back of her head below a hat with lace and feathers sticking from it.

Mei Lien suddenly felt self-conscious of her own appearance. In honor of the special outing she'd chosen to wear the dress Joseph had purchased for her in Port Townsend on their wedding day. It had never fit well, even though Mei Lien had hemmed the bottom. Standing next to these two white women for whom gowns like this were made, Mei Lien felt out of place and silly. Maybe she should return to dressing like a man and be comfortable.

"Mr. and Mrs. Honeycutt, good to see you again," Joseph was saying as he shook the men's hands and tipped his hat to the women, leaving Mei Lien standing alone. "Mr. Talmidge, I take it this is your lovely wife?"

The foursome greeted Joseph with warm smiles before turning curious and guarded eyes to Mei Lien. "And who, Mr. McElroy, do we have here?" asked the woman in the blue dress.

Joseph returned to Mei Lien's side and drew her against him with an arm around her shoulders. "This is my dear wife, Mrs. McElroy," he said with such pride in his voice that Mei Lien felt the sting of tears hit the backs of her eyes. "Perhaps you heard I got married this spring."

The two couples shuffled their feet and looked out of the

corners of their eyes at one another. The one Joseph called Mr. Talmidge raised his eyebrows as his wife pursed her lips so tightly she looked like the puffer fish Father had hung from the store ceiling two years ago. Mr. Honeycutt cleared his throat and said, "Well then. I can see why you've been keeping her hidden on your farm all these months."

Mei Lien clenched her back teeth together and stared at the ground.

The two women giggled behind gloved hands.

"Now see here," Joseph barked as he stepped in front of Mei Lien as though to protect her from attack. "That is my wife you speak of, sir."

Mrs. Talmidge sniffed. "We don't like her kind on our island."

Mrs. Honeycutt twirled her parasol. "Perhaps you are unfamiliar with the laws and constitutions set forth by the Orcas Island Anti-Chinese Association and signed by residents?"

"Oh, quite the opposite, Mrs. Honeycutt. I am very familiar with the laws that bar any of us from hiring a Chinese person as a worker. Perhaps you are unfamiliar with the fact that a wife is not a servant?"

The parasol stopped twirling as the woman gasped and backed up several steps until her fancy blue dress rubbed against a fallen log. Mei Lien hoped ants from the log crawled up her skirts.

"Now, McElroy," Mr. Honeycutt said as he stepped forward, his palms raised in surrender. "Don't be getting riled up. The missus didn't mean anything. We're just surprised is all. I mean, I've heard grumblings, but I didn't believe them."

Joseph's fists clenched and he dropped the pretense of civility from his voice. "What grumblings?"

Mr. Talmidge removed his bowler hat and wiped his brow with the back of his hand. "How do we know you aren't sending money—money the good people of Orcas have paid you as our postman—to her people in China instead of reinvesting it in our economy? Or worse, how do we know you aren't going to bring her whole family here to muddy our society with their filthy ways? I don't know about you, Honeycutt, but I'm glad I don't live near McElroy or I'd be worried about my land value."

Mei Lien felt anger burn through her so hot that it was all she could do to remain where she was, several steps away from the horrid people. Oh, she could show him filthy ways, all right. Starting with a clump of dirt between his beady little eyes!

"You should be ashamed of your ignorance and prejudice." Joseph turned his back on the two couples and returned to her with a look of concern that helped straighten her spine again. With his back to the others, he said, "When you are ready to apologize, we'll be at the farm."

He took Mei Lien's arm and led her off the path and around a tree to get past the people who wouldn't lower themselves to move out of the way for one such as her.

Mei Lien and Joseph had taken no more than three steps down the path when Mr. Honeycutt's voice cut through the silence. "I'll be petitioning the postmaster general to relieve you of your duties. I, for one, don't want my mail coming through your possession before reaching me."

The other three murmured agreement.

Joseph's footsteps faltered and his hand twitched in hers, but he didn't say anything. Neither of them spoke the whole way down the mountain.

As they reached the farm and entered the cool sanctuary of their new home, Mei Lien worried what Joseph must be thinking and feeling. This wasn't like him to be so stoic. From the moment she'd first woken in his cabin, he'd been a talker. She hadn't known he was capable of this deep silence.

"Joseph," she started as he sat at the kitchen table with a glass of water in his hand. "For your sake, I'm sorry I look so different from the other women on the island. I am proud to be Chinese, but I wish I could change myself for you. You don't deserve the things they said." She stopped pacing beside him. "Please, say something."

He set his glass on the table and turned to take each of her hands in his, drawing her to him until she was sitting on his lap. "Ah, May," he said, using the nickname he'd taken to calling her. "I don't care one whit what those idiots say or do to me. I care that they hurt you and judge you without getting to know you. It is I who must apologize to you. Don't ever change for them or for me or for anyone. Do you promise?"

Ducking her head, she curled into his chest. The sound of his heartbeat soothed her.

"Promise?" Joseph repeated.

She looked up to reply but was suddenly overcome with fear. By loving Joseph she'd opened herself up to pain again. And there was nothing she could do now to protect herself.

"I promise I won't change, Joseph," she finally answered him. "But it is I who am sorry. If I wasn't here, those people wouldn't treat you so cruelly." She pushed to her feet and started putting away their picnic supplies, intent on keeping busy in hopes her frantic mind would quiet.

"Maybe we should move. Go someplace where people are more tolerant of differences."

Mei Lien's hands stilled as she looked at her husband to see if he was joking. He wasn't smiling. "Joseph, you can't be serious. You love this farm. We just moved into the house you spent all year building."

"None of it matters if you aren't happy."

"But where would we go?"

He shook his head and looked past her to the east window and the view of the apple orchard outside. "I don't know. How about Tacoma? My sister and her family live there."

"The same Tacoma that drove three hundred and fifty Chinese from town last November and burned their stores and homes to the ground?"

"Well then, how about Victoria?"

She shook her head. Chinese were driven out of there too.

"South to San Francisco?"

She pulled out the chair next to him and sat down, wringing one of the picnic napkins in her hands. "Would we really be treated any better in those places? Americans and Canadians alike are afraid of the Chinese. We look different, sound different. We even think differently. It won't matter where we go because no one in America will want me as a neighbor."

He rubbed both hands over his face. "You're right, of course. And I'm damned ashamed to be American right now." His hands dropped with a slap onto his lap. "So what do we do?"

Mei Lien got to her feet again and grabbed her largest bowl from the shelf. "We do what my father taught me to do. We work hard and we stay out of everyone's way." She headed for the back door. "For now, I'm going to pick more blackberries and make you a cobbler for supper."

She left Joseph sitting at the kitchen table worrying, as she headed to the wild vines along the back of their property. She and her husband were very different in one important way. He liked to think and talk about everything that could go wrong and every option he had to solve problems. She had learned young that worry and thought didn't accomplish much when there was work to be done.

And so she worked, picking blackberries in the hot sun until her fingers were stained purple, and her hands and arms were covered with bloody scratches from the thorns. When thoughts of the people they'd met on the mountain intruded, she pushed them away and thought about the cobbler she would make or the jam she'd make tomorrow or the child she and Joseph would create together.

She had become very good at avoiding the thoughts she didn't want to face.

Three days later, Joseph was gone delivering the weekly mail—no one had shown up to tell him he couldn't—and Mei Lien was spending the afternoon working in her kitchen garden. She'd picked the ripened tomatoes from the vines and harvested the lettuce and peas. They all lay jumbled in the basket next to her as she knelt to tend the beans. If Joseph returned home in time for dinner tonight, she'd make him a fresh salad to go with the steamed fish with preserved olives she planned to make.

She was so lost in her work she didn't hear the birds stop chirping. Only when she heard the unmistakable sound of a boot scraping over rocks did she realize she was no longer alone.

She jumped to her feet and twisted around in one motion, her gardening trowel still in her hand. When she saw the man walking through the potato patch toward her, her only thought was to run inside and lock the door. With her free hand she lifted her skirt and took off.

"Och, there's no need ta be afraid!" called Campbell. "I mean ye no harm. Jes' bein' neighborly and stopping to say hello."

Upon hearing his words, Mei Lien realized two things that made her stop running. One, Campbell had no idea she knew him. And two, this was her chance to make sure he never came around here again.

She breathed deeply, silently praying to her ancestors for courage, and turned around with as genuine a smile as she could muster. "Forgive me. You startled me is all. You say you're our neighbor?"

He stepped over rows of vegetables to reach her. "The name's Duncan Campbell. I live down that way with me wife and son and me aging pa." Upon reaching her side he tipped his hat and flashed his teeth, though she noticed the smile didn't reach his eyes. She yearned to shrink away from his intense gaze, but she held her ground.

"Pleased to meet you, Mr. Campbell." The name felt wrong in her mouth, like spoiled milk she wanted to spit out. "What can I do for you?"

He slid his wide-brimmed black hat from atop his head and squinted past her to the house, then across the meadow toward the barn. "Is Joseph around? I'd like ta pay him my respects since I'm here."

A buzzing started in her head but she ignored it. "No, my husband is delivering the mail. I'll tell him you called."

Campbell put his hat back on and propped both hands on his hips, pushing his jacket back in the process. Hanging at his waist was a deadly looking pistol. "Ye do that, ma'am." He started to turn away, then stopped. "Oh, and give him a message for me. My wife has a hankerin' to plant an apricot orchard, and wouldn't you know, our land is hemmed in by rocky buttes. Tell Joseph I'd like ta do us both a favor and buy his farm, seeing as how the talk in town is none too friendly toward ye, iffin ye know what I mean. Joseph will be relieved ta know he has a willing buyer living right next door who'll make him an honest offer."

"We aren't going anywhere, Mr. Campbell."

He did not move, but something about him changed so that he appeared larger and more ominous. "If ye know what's good for ye, Chink, ye will go." He spoke so low she wondered if she'd heard him correctly. "And if that husband o' yours has any brains, which evidence before me tells me he doesna, he'll take my offer and leave before the choice is taken from ye."

She raised her chin to look him in the eye, despite everything in her telling her to back down, look at the ground, and run away. "No one can force us off our property. As for you, Mr. Campbell, it's time you left."

His eyes narrowed and moisture flew from his nostrils as he stared her down. She did her best not to blink.

"Watch your back, Chink." Then, with a haughty sniff, he turned and marched back the way he'd come, this time trampling her vegetables without care.

He hadn't recognized her. He had no idea she'd been on his steamship that night. Joseph's plan had worked.

But he hated her all the same. All the islanders hated her, but Campbell wanted to hurt her. She saw it in his eyes.

Mei Lien watched him until he disappeared into the trees. Then, shaking, she dropped the trowel she only then realized she still held and ran inside the house where she locked the doors for the first time ever and dropped to her knees in the corner where no one would see her through the windows.

Sweat ran down her back and her hands shook. *Campbell can't hurt me here*, she told herself. Then, because that wasn't working, she said it aloud to the empty room: "Campbell can't hurt me. Campbell can't hurt me. Campbell can't hurt me…"

Over and over again she repeated it. With her arms wrapped around her knees, she rocked back and forth to the mantra her words had become. Rocking, rocking, hiding in the corner as shadows lengthened across the room, listening for footsteps outside, imagining she heard Father's voice telling her to be brave.

She wasn't brave. She wasn't strong. She couldn't stand up to Campbell or force him to leave her alone. If he wanted to evict her from the island, he could do it. She knew very well how capable he was of making her disappear.

The thought sent a fresh wave of terror through her body. She curled tighter into herself and laid her head on the cool floor.

Later, after what could have been hours or minutes, she saw herself as if from above, standing over her pitiful, weeping form. The image filled her with shame.

Enough! She sat up, forcing her spine to straighten and her chin to lift, even though it physically hurt her chest to do so. Nothing would be accomplished by lying here, a victim.

Besides, the sun was setting. With Joseph gone, she could spend more time than usual tonight with Father's and Grandmother's spirits at the water.

Her decision made and her legs only wobbling a little, Mei Lien made her way to the kitchen, where she went about gathering supplies to take with her to the water. Two apples.

Cold rice she'd wrap in alder leaves as Grandmother had taught her—since the bamboo that tradition called for did not grow here—and tied with five strings, one each of red, blue, white, yellow, and black to represent the five elements. Water dragons would be afraid of this amulet and leave the packets alone for Father's and Grandmother's spirits. Then she took two candle stubs and matches and loaded everything into a basket. On her way to the shore, she pried off two large pieces of Douglas fir bark that were rounded and long like canoes and added these to the basket as well.

At the water's edge she stood silent and still, listening to the sounds of the air and water. Sometimes when she was there, a steamer on the way to Eastsound Village would pass by, or a settler on his way to the town would pass in a rowboat. At these times she would hide behind the ferns and salal and Oregon grape bushes and wait until she was alone with the water once more.

Alone with the spirits who reminded her who she was and where she'd come from.

Tonight the water was empty. Colors were already fading into blue with the setting sun, and the water had blackened except for the silvery surface, which was flat as glass. In the air she smelled damp moss, even now in midsummer, and the woodsy scent blowing from trees that had baked all day in the sun and now soughed with relief. It was the kind of night Father had loved in Seattle, when he and Mei Lien would walk to one of the nearby lakes where they would fish and discuss the day's business before walking back home in the dark, taking the long route to avoid the white parts of town.

Mei Lien let herself become immersed in the memory as she lit the candles and placed them carefully in the center of each bark boat. To each she added an apple and a rice packet and wished she had incense to complete the offering. As she set the boats afloat, she gently pushed them away from shore, where the currents would take them. They would light the way for the spirits of her family and all others who had perished with them.

And then she did what she did every night. She looked for signs of their spirits around her. She'd seen them in the loons, crows, and sea otters, and once in the water itself. Tonight she was rewarded by the flight of a blue heron that swooped low over the bay and then came to perch on a boulder jutting out of the water just offshore. It looked at her with wise, dark eyes before opening its beak and letting out a lonely cry as it took flight again, heading in the direction of the setting sun.

"Mei Lien!"

*Father? I hear you, Father,* she answered in her mind, knowing his spirit didn't need her voice.

"Mei Lien! Catch the rope!"

She jerked and snapped to attention. It wasn't Father's spirit calling to her but Joseph in his rowboat, ready to throw her a coiled rope so she could pull him ashore.

She reached out and caught the rope for him while keeping her face averted. She was horrified she'd been so wrapped up in watching the heron that she'd missed seeing Joseph round the bluff and enter the bay. It could have been anyone and she hadn't been paying attention.

But that was not why she wouldn't look at her husband. What made her turn away was the realization that he'd witnessed her in her most private moment. He often offered to accompany her to the shore in the evening, but she'd always turned him down, preferring those moments of solitude and private communion with her family. Joseph might have been her only family, but he wasn't a part of that.

He didn't say anything about the offerings floating toward the middle of the sound, though she saw him looking at them as he pulled the rowboat out of the water.

"I made it from here to Orcas Village to pick up the mail load and back again to Olga before they confronted me," he told her, referring to the small settlement southward down the sound where he always started his delivery rounds. He wrapped the rope around a tree and worked on tying knots to keep it secure as he went on with his story. "The Honeycutts and Talmidges were there, as well as half a dozen other families. Told me James Tulloch would be taking over the route from now on. I gave him the mail and rowed away without a word. Felt good too."

"But you love your mail route. I just made you the new bag."

He yanked hard on the rope to tighten the knots, then dropped the end onto the beach and turned toward her, wiping his hands together. "The mail route was never about power to me. It was about getting to know my neighbors and doing a service for the community. The moment they decided to punish me for loving a person they don't approve of was the moment my service ended. I don't care to know people like that, and I can find other ways to serve my community."

She stepped into his welcoming hug. "You're earlier than I expected, but still you're home late for having not completed your route."

Joseph released her and went to the rowboat to gather his things. "I would have been home earlier, but Campbell hailed me from the shore. You know I try to stay away from him, knowing what I now know, but at that moment I decided the old saying is correct. 'One must keep friends close, but enemies closer.'" With a hand on her back, he guided her through the forest back to the house in the clearing beyond. She noticed he still carried the mailbag she'd made, but it was empty now.

"He told me he'd heard I'd lost the mail carrier position. Then he said if things got too rough for us, he'd offer me a fair price for our land."

Mei Lien stiffened. "He told me the same thing earlier today. He's up to something."

Joseph stopped in front of the porch steps. "He was here?"

She nodded and, afraid he'd see her fear, kept her head low as she bent to pull weeds from the flower bed. "Introduced himself and was friendly until he learned you weren't here. He promised he was going to drive me away. Then he left."

Joseph squeezed her shoulders. "I won't let him hurt you, May. And I won't let him drive us off our land. I told him so."

Joseph went upstairs to change his clothes and Mei Lien followed him as far as the kitchen where she stood staring out the window to the garden, trying to calm her shaking nerves as the day's events played through her mind again.

Of one thing she was certain—she hadn't seen the last of Campbell. But at least now she wouldn't be alone so often.

# Chapter Fourteen

*Monday, July 9—present day*
*South Lake Union, Seattle*

Inara waited for Daniel at Chandler's Crabhouse on Lake Union. It would be their first official date, and their last.

And then she'd return to Orcas and put this miserable day—and the sleeve and Daniel—behind her.

After leaving her father's office, she'd driven randomly around the city for hours, thinking about her mother, the sleeve, Mei Lien, and all the people killed. Telling the truth would bring shame on her family and dishonor all the good work her mother had done. But keeping the secret was dishonoring all those who had died and their families.

Part of her believed Daniel had the right to know the true reason why she wouldn't be seeing him any longer. The other part reminded her she'd promised her dad she'd keep the story secret.

She had no idea what she was going to say.

"Sorry I'm late. Traffic." Daniel leaned down to kiss her cheek, his touch jump-starting her already frazzled nerves. This was going to be harder than she'd thought.

If only she could have kept this thing between them going and seen where it led.

"No problem. You're not that late." She smiled as she lectured herself about just getting through this and leaving. The sooner, the better. "I hope your mom forgives you for canceling your plans with them tonight."

He just shrugged. "I'll stop by later. They'll be okay. I was surprised you came down today."

"I hadn't planned on it, but something came up and I had to meet with my dad." She decided to tell him half of it as she worked up her nerve for what she'd come here to say. "He ambushed me with a real estate agent trying to convince me to sell the estate."

His eyes widened. "You're not going to, are you?"

"I talked him into holding off until Labor Day. If the hotel doesn't impress him by then, he'll call in my loan and I'll be forced to sell."

"Well, that's something. At the rate you're going, in two months no one will be able to walk away from the project. Not even your dad. I wouldn't worry if I were you."

Warmth flowed through her at his words, and she wanted to lean into him and feel strengthened by his presence. Instead she sat up straighter and looked down at her lap. "Thanks."

*Now or never, Inara.* She took a breath, but right as she opened her mouth, Daniel spoke.

"I have news." The corner of his mouth twitched upward as he placed both arms on the table and leaned toward her. "I found the 1890 census. They had a son."

Inara blinked as her mind struggled to keep up. "Who? Mei Lien and Joseph?"

He nodded and she could tell it was killing him to rein in his excitement. It stirred an answering thrill inside her. But she was confused. "Wasn't the 1890 census lost in a fire?"

"The federal census was, but not the state records."

The truth sank in. Mei Lien and her husband had had a child. A son. A boy who had probably gone on to have a family of his own. Suddenly the stakes were higher. "This means there could be a descendant of Mei Lien's somewhere who could tell us what happened to her."

He nodded and reached for his menu, though he didn't glance at it. "The son's name was Yan-Tao McElroy. In 1890, he was listed as being two years old, so we looked into birth records and found a Washington Territory birth certificate for Yan-Tao Kenneth McElroy, born July 27, 1887."

"A year and a half after they got married." She did the math in her head. "That means he must have been about seven when my family bought the property. How can we figure out where the McElroys went?"

Daniel dropped his menu back on the table. "I already have my graduate students researching it. They're looking through old newspaper records and other settlers' diaries that have been donated to the university, the state archives, the Orcas Island Historical Museum, or the Orcas Island Library in Eastsound. I also have them searching the 1900 census records of surrounding communities to see if the McElroys pop up anywhere, as well as interviewing anyone in the region with the last name McElroy."

She nodded, impressed that he was covering so many bases. They would find Mei Lien's descendants and possibly learn more about her than the embroidery was telling them. "I wish Mei Lien had left a diary along with the sleeve. Then there wouldn't be so many unanswered questions."

And then she remembered why she'd come here tonight—to stop Daniel from doing any further research. They were supposed to forget all about Mei Lien.

But how could they, especially now that they knew there might be descendants still alive who could tell them more about Mei Lien and what happened to her?

Daniel turned his attention to his menu, so she did the same, though she didn't see any of the words printed on it. Would it be so bad to keep researching what happened to Mei Lien and her family? Everything they'd be looking at was well after 1886 and should in no way lead anyone to discover the truth about the murders.

But Inara had promised her dad she'd forget about the sleeve.

Which she'd do. But if they shifted focus to what happened after the story depicted on the sleeve, she'd be okay, right? She could put the sleeve away and keep her promise, yet still find out what happened to Mei Lien and her family.

She could still see Daniel.

He set his menu aside and smiled at her across the table. "I'm glad you came here tonight."

She made a quick decision and set her own menu aside. "Me too."

Casually, like he did it all the time, he reached across the table and snagged her hand. "Tell me more about your hotel. I can't wait to see it when everything starts to come together."

"You're welcome to visit and see our progress any time." His thumb was drawing circles on the back of her hand, making it hard to focus. "They'll be putting up drywall this week."

"Sounds exciting." He paused. "How about this weekend?"

She searched his face to see if he was kidding, but he just stared at her with those hazel eyes that made her want to sink into them. "Um, sure. You can even stay in my guest room."

His eyes darkened. "I'd like that."

She was too flustered to think up a response so she stayed silent.

"Can I answer any questions about the menu, or are you ready to order?"

The sudden appearance of the server made them spring apart. Inara felt her face flame as she picked up her menu and stammered out her order. Once the server disappeared, she reached for the glass of wine she didn't remember ordering and sipped it to keep her hands busy.

"Are you staying with your father tonight?"

She shook her head. "No. There's an eleven o'clock ferry I plan to be on."

He glanced at his watch and shot her a grin. "Plenty of time."

Over dinner they didn't talk about the sleeve or Mei Lien, and Inara was happy about that. She hated keeping what she knew from Daniel, and it was easier to push it all out of her mind for an hour and just be normal.

They talked more about their families and where they went to school (she at UW, he at UCLA with graduate work in Beijing), how he wanted to try stand-up paddleboarding but had a terrible sense of balance, and how she had a weakness for chocolate.

Inara was reluctant to leave when it was time to hit the road. Daniel walked her to her car, and there in the parking lot, tinged pink by the setting sun, his palm found the center of her back and gently pulled her toward him so they were face-to-face. His eyes stayed locked with hers as he slowly bent his head, his mouth drawing closer and closer. Finally she could take it no more and she closed her eyes, giving in to what she only now realized she'd been waiting for all evening.

His hands pulled her body tighter against him and she wrapped her arms around his neck, marveling at the perfection of their fit. She tilted her head to deepen the kiss, savoring the moment, the taste of him, the delicious sense that nothing mattered but the two of them. Not their families, not the sleeve, not her hotel.

She completely lost track of time. When they paused for breath, Daniel rested his forehead against hers and said, "I've wanted to do that since I first saw you."

She smiled and kissed him again.

The sound of a nearby car beeping as its owner unlocked it reminded them where they were, and they reluctantly stepped apart. "I'm so glad you came into town today," Daniel said as a lock of his hair fell over one eye.

She gently brushed it back. "Are you really going to come to the island next weekend?"

He glanced at the couple getting into the car two spaces over and jammed his hands into his pants pockets. "Yes," he answered simply.

She smiled. "Good."

Much later, as she was sitting in her parked car on the ferry, she received a text from Daniel that made her laugh out loud:

Are you really going to make me stay in the guest room?

She replied:

Let's decide when you get here.

He arrived on Friday afternoon and stayed until Sunday.
He didn't use the guest room.

# Chapter Fifteen

*Wednesday, July 27, 1887*
*McElroy Farm, Orcas Island*

M ei Lien slowly opened her eyes to see sunlight streaming in through her west-facing bedroom window. The heat in the room told her she should have been up hours ago, but she was glad for the rest. She didn't want to get up just yet, so she was careful not to move and cause her swollen belly to put pressure on the part of her that would necessitate a visit with the chamber pot. Instead, she let her thoughts drift.

The winter had been a hard one. Not because of the weather—it only snowed around the time of the New Year on Joseph's calendar and stuck on the ground for two weeks. Otherwise, it was just cold and gray and wet. No, it was hard because of the mental strain. Since the day the islanders forced Joseph to hand over his mailbag last summer and Duncan Campbell had threatened her, Mei Lien had felt hunted and watched.

She did not like to leave the farm, but when she did, to go into Eastsound Village for supplies or to Port Townsend or Victoria for larger purchases, she always stayed by Joseph's side. They both heard the whispers and insults. They both noticed how people crossed the street or left a shop to avoid them. Most refused to speak directly to Mei Lien, preferring to ignore her and pretend Joseph was alone—if they spoke to him at all.

She knew she was the reason Joseph was no longer invited to supper at neighbors' houses or on hunting or fishing trips with friends. He no longer had any friends.

Folks did occasionally stop by the house to see Joseph, away from the eyes of other islanders. But always, she noticed, it was because they wanted something from him. An extra pair of hands to thresh the wheat. Joseph's mare to pull their plow. His strength to help raise their new barn walls. His beach to land their rented barge loaded with building materials.

He always helped.

Not once in the past year—and she had kept track—had anyone stopped to offer them help, food, or a kind word. Not once had anyone shared a smile with her. Always they ignored her as though she wasn't Joseph's wife, but his dog or, probably more accurately, his pig in the mud.

She could handle being ignored, but she was tired of the way her husband was taken advantage of and mistreated for the crime of marrying her. What did it matter to anyone else what she looked like or where her ancestors were born? As long as she was a hardworking, caring wife to Joseph, what could they possibly have to complain about?

When she voiced her thoughts to Joseph, he just shook his head and gave her a sad little smile. "What people think don't matter none," he told her. "I'm happy and I hope you're happy. You are, aren't you?"

"Yes, I'm happy," she agreed.

"Well then, we don't need anyone else."

And so they continued on, tending their farm and tending their deepening relationship. But still she worried that he yearned for what might have been, had she not come into his life.

Just as she sometimes wondered what might have been had none of this happened.

Would she still be embroidering purses with Grandmother and helping Father in the store? Or would Father have arranged her marriage to a Chinese man, a proper merchant like himself or someone like Yeung Lum? Would she still be wearing men's breeches, or skirts and aprons like Grandmother? Would she have adopted the white woman's dress as she'd done here?

Why was she wasting her morning lying in bed thinking about things that did not matter or could not be changed?

Resigned, Mei Lien rolled to her side and pushed her weary body up to sitting. Her constantly swollen feet hung over the side of the bed. She paused as she always did to rub her huge belly, waiting for movement inside.

Joseph's son—she was sure the baby would be a boy—would be born soon, and they were ready to meet him. Joseph had built a cradle that now waited at her side of the bed. A pile of clean cloths was stacked on the kitchen counter downstairs, and she kept their largest pot of water on the stove, filled and ready to bring to a boil. She'd visited the herbalist in Port Townsend months ago and purchased herbs to help with the labor and others to help her heal afterward. She'd traded him four embroidered purses she'd made over the winter to pay for the herbs so Joseph wouldn't have to hand over any of his dwindling cash.

Without neighbors willing to help with the harvest last fall, Joseph had had no choice but to leave apples and pears to rot on the trees. The rest of the crop he'd taken to sell in Port Townsend had filled only half a barge.

But this year would be different, she decided as she finally pushed to her feet, leading with her belly. It would have to be different if they expected to survive.

Just as she stood up, a sharp pain arced through her back and wrapped around to her stomach. She bent over with one hand propped on the wall in front of her and the other rubbing her belly to ease the ache away.

Aches, pains, twinges, pulls...such was her life now. She used the chamber pot, dressed, and waddled down the stairs to start breakfast. Just as she reached the kitchen, Joseph came in through the back door, carrying a full milking bucket.

"Mail came," he said as he set the bucket in the sink.

"This early?"

He removed his gloves as he raised an eyebrow at her. "The morning's nearly over, May. I thought you could use the extra sleep."

She went to the back door to look up to the sky and judge the time for herself. Sure enough, the sun had already cleared Mount Constitution and would soon reach its highest point overhead. "You should have woken me. I've got hundreds of things to do today."

She quickened her steps, moving around the kitchen to prepare breakfast while Joseph settled himself at the table to sort through the mail he pulled from his back pocket. Frying bacon proved to be nearly impossible without her belly getting splattered with grease. Then, when she went to pull the biscuits from the oven, she tried to bend at the waist but felt the baby's weight shift her off balance. Trying again, she bent her knees and just about had the pan in her towel-wrapped hand when Joseph intervened.

"Come. Sit. I'll finish breakfast." He guided her to a chair and pressed on her shoulders until she gave in and sat down.

"I can't sit here and do nothing." Being fussed over irritated her. She'd never been fussed over in her life, and she was perfectly capable of taking care of herself and her husband. "I don't need you to do my chores."

He turned from the stove with a fork in his hand and his teeth biting a smile. "I know you don't mean to sound ungrateful so I'll ignore it. And you will rest. That's my child you're carrying."

"How could I forget? This baby won't stop moving around

when I'm trying to sleep, and when awake, my body won't do what I want it to. Oh!" The stab of pain hit her spine again.

"What? Is it time?" Joseph was suddenly beside her, crouching to lay a hand on her belly. His eyes were huge as they looked from her belly to her face and back again. "What do I do?"

The pain disappeared as fast as it hit. She shook her head at her husband as she rubbed her belly. "No, it isn't time. I'm just sore from lying in bed so long."

He gave her a look that said he didn't believe her, but he returned to the stove anyway. "If you insist on doing something, you can read me that letter there from my sister."

His sister's letters were full of boasts about her perfect twin daughters and how her husband was building what was reputed to be the greatest ship of all time in his shipyard in Tacoma. Mei Lien had never met the woman and she was glad, since Elizabeth would no doubt be in person just as she was in her letters— arrogant, bragging, belittling Joseph, and completely ignoring the fact that Mei Lien existed.

She picked up the letter from the stack on the table and unfolded the rose-scented paper. Elizabeth's handwriting was small and tight with occasional flourishes, as though she felt particularly fancy about certain words. Slowly, Mei Lien started to read, interpreting some of the scratches as best she could. "*Dearest Joseph. I trust this letter finds you as well as we are here in town.*" She paused in reading and looked up. "Why does she act as though Tacoma is the only town around?"

Joseph shrugged. "It's the center of her world, so to her it is the only town around."

She shook her head but went back to reading. "*Marcus has taken on a new partner and so is finally able to take time off from work. I informed him I'd like to visit my brother and meet his wife, so that is what we are doing. We will arrive on the morning steamer August twelfth and will stay through the weekend.*" With nausea lying heavy in her throat, Mei Lien paused to calculate the date in her mind.

"Joseph! That's only two weeks away! The baby should be here by then. It's too much to have your family here as well. You'll have to write her back today and tell her not to come for another month or so." She paused. "Does she know we're expecting?"

"Yes, she knows. I told her in my letter months ago." He slid her plate in front of her and turned back to the stove to fill his own. "Why can't she come? She could be a big help to you."

Mei Lien stared at her food. "Possibly. Or she could cause more work when I'll have my hands full as it is." She picked up the biscuit Joseph had slathered with the wild strawberry jam she'd made last month and took a huge bite. With the letter lying beside her plate, Mei Lien leaned forward and continued reading. "*We hear your little island is becoming quite popular amongst Seattleites, so we simply must be the first from Tacoma to know if reports are exaggerated.*"

Joseph grunted at that as he sat down across from her with his own breakfast. "Sounds like she expects to be shown around like a tourist."

Mei Lien lowered her chin. "Please promise you'll write to her and tell her not to come yet. After harvest would be best, unless they plan to help with it."

Joseph carefully chewed his bacon, then washed it down with a cup of milk dipped from the bucket still sitting in the sink. "I'll write to her."

"Thank you."

As they finished their breakfast, they went through the rest of the mail together. Among the bills was one from the Baron sounding quite irritated that Joseph had not yet paid for the goods he'd procured three months ago, despite the fact that the Baron had said over and over again, "You pay ven effer yous feel like it."

"Can we pay him?" Mei Lien asked as she shoved her body up from the table to make her way gingerly to the sink to wash their plates.

"Yes. Some. Not all."

Soon the fruit trees would be ready to pick, but Mei Lien would be busy with the baby. They might need to find another source of income. Soon.

"Do you think Elizabeth and Marcus could be convinced to help with harvest?"

Joseph laughed. "And get her hands dirty?"

Mei Lien grimaced and then turned her attention to cleaning the kitchen. As soon as she finished, she turned toward the door. "Did you take care of all the animals this morning too?" she asked her husband. He nodded. "What about the garden? Have you checked to see if the deer or rabbits got through the fence last night?"

"It's fine." He stood up and put his hands on her upper arms, stopping her from going out the back door to start her chores. "Wait. There's something else."

What more could there be, other than debts that needed paying and their only source of income needing tending? "What, Joseph? I'm already behind today."

His lips pressed together as the corners of his mouth twitched upward. He was up to something.

"Wait here," he said, both his hands on her shoulders as if to plant her in place in the middle of the kitchen floor. "I'll be right back."

He rushed to the back door and stopped to look back to ensure she hadn't moved. She just raised her eyebrows at him.

With a grin, he opened the door and stepped onto the porch, where her laundry tub and clothes wringer stood propped against the house waiting for her. Joseph left the door hanging open as he disappeared around the corner for a moment, then quickly reappeared with a brown paper-wrapped parcel in his hands.

His smile filled his whole face as he walked toward her with the package in both hands stretched out in front of him like an offering. "This is for you," he told her as he kicked the door shut behind him. "For you and the baby."

Mei Lien couldn't imagine what he might have ordered for her that came wrapped in paper. "Joseph, what is it? How did you pay for it?"

A scowl flashed across his face at the question but then was gone, replaced with his excited smile again. "That doesn't matter. Open it."

Mei Lien took the package from him and instantly felt the sides give, indicating that whatever was inside was soft.

Setting the package on the table, she carefully cut the waxed strings with a kitchen knife and pulled back the paper, knowing she'd think of something to use the paper for later. Nothing was wasted in their home.

The moment she peeled back the final layer, she gasped.

Inside the package was the richest blue silk she'd ever seen, finer than any Father had sold in his store. It was woven tight with threads so fine it felt as soft as water as she ran her fingers over it. Instantly an image flashed in her mind of a scene she could embroider on its delicate surface. Father's store on Washington Street, Father standing in the open doorway. Grandmother in the window above, her own embroidery in her hands. "It's beautiful," she breathed, not sure if she meant the silk itself or the image she knew she'd create on it.

"That's not all. Look under the fabric."

Curious, Mei Lien lifted the bundle of cloth and found a package of embroidery needles and what must have been twenty different colors of silk embroidery floss. Lucky red, rich gold, midnight black, sea blue, cloud white, earth brown, and shades she could not identify because they balanced between two colors, dyed by hands with talent and a lifetime of experience.

"How did you know?" she asked her husband, only realizing she was crying because his image was blurred as she tried to look at him.

He shook his head. "I didn't. I knew you were good with a

needle after I saw the mailbag you made for me, and I see the way you pull at your gowns like you aren't comfortable in them—"

"I'm uncomfortable because of the baby," she interrupted. "My gowns are fine." She didn't want him to know she just couldn't get used to them. How she felt smaller every day that she dressed in white women's confining, drab clothing. How she felt she was losing herself and her history.

He went on as if she hadn't spoken. "And then I saw you looking at the silks in Port Townsend when we were there buying your herbs. I wanted to buy them for you then, but that was right after Preacher Gray stopped by and guilted me into donating to the new church."

"I still think you should have told him no."

"I wish I had." They both knew they'd never set foot in the new Episcopal church in Eastsound. "Especially after I saw you with those silks." He ran a finger over the blue cloth. "You really like it?"

"I do. I love it."

"Will you make yourself a dress or something you can be proud to wear?"

She looked at him closely. He avoided meeting her gaze and kept his eyes downcast to where the fabric and floss lay spread before them. He must know, she realized. Despite her best pretense, he'd known how she hated dressing like a white woman.

"Yes," she answered finally. "A gown for myself and something for the baby as well." She turned now and stepped into his arms. Her belly kept them from getting as close as she'd like, but by turning sideways she was able to lay her cheek against his heart. The familiar thump she heard made her own heart squeeze painfully. This wasn't a man she would have chosen for herself if life had turned out differently, but she loved him with every fiber of her being. One day she might be brave enough to tell him so.

A pain stabbed at her back, then shot into her belly and down her thighs. She caught her breath and pulled away from Joseph to bend over, hands on her knees.

"May?" Joseph's hand rested on her back; a tremble betrayed his fear.

As the pain eased, she forced a laugh to reassure him and smooth the crevasses around his eyes and mouth. "It was nothing. Just a matter of having to lean over this great belly to hug you. I'm sure it won't be the last time this baby stops us from showing affection."

He laughed with her.

The ache had settled low in her belly and the baby chose that moment to roll over, jamming a foot or elbow into the very spot that was tender. She hid her grimace of pain by turning to the table to carefully fold the silk and threads into the paper again. "I'm going to put these away in my sewing chest and then I'd better get to work. You too, Mr. McElroy."

Her teasing had its intended effect. He laughed as he gave her a quick kiss on the cheek, then headed back outside. Once she was alone, she carefully lowered herself into a chair and rubbed her belly. "Are you coming today, little one?" she said quietly to the empty room. "Is that what's happening?"

Each time she thought of facing childbirth without a midwife to guide her, she felt the air being sucked out of her lungs, as it was now. Her throat burned. She would be alone with no one but Joseph to bring their child into the world. At best, they would welcome a healthy child. At worst, this day would be her last.

She'd been praying to the ancestors for months that her child would not be left here without her. A slant-eyed, black-haired child needed his mother to help him through this pale world.

The pains came and went all day. After dinner, when Mei Lien hadn't felt one for several hours, she left Joseph in the sitting room with the farm ledgers while she went down to the water for her nightly visit with her family's spirits.

It was still full light out. At least another hour would pass before the sun set into the sea on the other side of the island. She loved nights like this, when the warmth of the day still lingered in the leaves and berries, filling the air with sweet scents that made her draw deeply into her lungs with her eyes closed, savoring every nuance to pull forth from her memory on cold winter nights.

The nearer she came to the water, the more the smells changed. Near the house she smelled the dry, sunshine scents of grass and baking soil, but beside the water everything smelled more alive. Here she detected the damp, pungent odors of mushrooms growing on the forest floor where the sun rarely reached, and the briny seaweed and algae strewn like paint on the beach rocks.

The bay at this hour before sunset almost always turned glassy, as though an invisible hand had switched off the wind and directed the animals and currents to rest, leaving a mirrorlike surface to reflect the blue sky above streaked with orange and pink. It made her wish she could open her arms and soak it all into the tiniest of pores in her skin.

Mei Lien eased her sore body onto her favorite boulder and thought of Father and Grandmother. Their faces were losing definition in her mind. Time was smoothing their rough edges just as the invisible hand smoothed the water. She'd lived the past year and a half with only white faces to look upon. Occasionally in Port Townsend or Victoria she would see another Asian face, but they almost always turned away from her upon seeing Joseph beside her.

If not for the silvered mirror Joseph had bought for her, she would not remember the slant of her eyes, the slash of black eyebrows under black hair, her smooth round face. She was forgetting. She was becoming one of them. But in her own reflection she saw Father and Grandmother. Soon she would be able to look at her child and see her family and remember.

Maybe then she could stop searching the water every night, trying to feel whole but always returning home fractured.

"Shouldn't you be scrubbing something?"

Mei Lien jerked at the sound of the voice. Not ten feet offshore sat the devil Campbell in his rowboat filled with what looked like crates of nails, tools, and seed packets. She'd been too lost in her thoughts and hadn't heard him coming. She should have been more alert.

She'd been so stupid! So stupid to put herself and her child in danger like this.

Fear filled her mouth and kept her from replying to his question. As fast as she could, she pushed up off the rock to make her way to the path at the far end of the beach that would lead to home and Joseph. Safety.

*Faster, Mei Lien!* She picked her way carefully over the rocks. If only she could run. But the belly, the pains, the aches in her hips and legs—the best she could do was shuffle at a pace akin to walking. If he had a mind to hurt her, now would be his opportunity.

*Go!* Her mind urged. *Ignore the ache. Ignore the pains.* She was halfway to the forest path when her foot slipped on an unsteady rock and jammed hard into another sharp rock covered in dried barnacles. The pain shot up her leg and curled itself into her belly like a snake about to spring.

That was when her belly clamped tight and sent the pain right back down her legs with such intensity she had to stop and bend over, her hands cradling her stomach. She could not move until it eased.

"You shouldn't be down here all alone, Mrs. McElroy," Campbell taunted, coming closer, though she didn't have the strength to turn and look at him.

All she could do was focus on filling her lungs with air and sending the pain out with her exhaled breath.

"Come now, is that any way to treat your neighbor? By ignoring him?"

She heard splashing now and knew he'd rowed to shore and was coming toward her. She pushed through her pain to force her feet to move forward. One agonizing step at a time she headed toward the trail.

But Campbell caught up to her. It was his boots she saw first, standing on the rocks beside her.

"Are you ill?" Revulsion filled his voice and she knew then he wasn't going to touch her. She thanked her swollen body for that.

"What do you want?" she managed as the iron fist clamping onto her insides eased enough for her to get the words out.

"I want your land." His boot kicked at a rock, sending it rolling to hit her foot. "I don't know how you did it, but you poisoned Joseph against me so he won't talk to me. Get your husband ta take my offer. Settle elsewhere. Somewhere your kind is wanted."

She moaned through the pain gripping her body, only half listening to him.

He backed up so that she no longer saw his boots. "Ye tell Joseph I made a fair offer. Tell him to take it before it's too late."

"Tell him yourself," she managed between pants.

"Oh, I would, if you hadn't turned him against me."

The fist inside clamped tighter and twisted, bringing her to her knees with a shameful cry. Her whole body, including the muscles in her face, tightened. She breathed through the pain, focusing on the moment she hoped was coming when it would ease and she could find her way home to Joseph. Just then a gush of warm liquid ran down her thighs. She hated that Campbell witnessed something so private, but she could do nothing about it. She could only breathe through the pain.

She didn't hear Campbell's boots crunch over the shells and barnacles or splash back to his boat. She didn't hear his oars row away. But when the pain lessened and she could look up and focus on her surroundings, he was gone. No trace of his visit remained and she wondered if she'd imagined him there at all. Or maybe it was his devil spirit preying on her.

"May!"

She turned to see Joseph running across the beach to her. Only then did she realize she was on her hands and knees on the rocks, tears soaking her face.

Before Joseph reached her, another pain grabbed her. She squeezed her eyes shut and tried to focus on her breath again, but the pain was too demanding and all she could do was suffer and hope she survived.

"Let me get you to the house," she heard Joseph say as if from a long distance.

She felt his hands on her back, trying to shift her and lift her. "Don't touch me!" she hissed, knowing if he moved her right now she might tear completely apart. "Wait." *Breathe. Breathe.*

Finally the pain lessened and she looked up at her husband. "I can move now, but I don't think I can walk."

Immediately the fear she'd seen on his face vanished. His eyes narrowed and his jaw hardened, then he nodded. He looked ready to face anything at that moment and his enemy was her pain. For the first time Mei Lien felt her own fear lessen. She wasn't alone. Joseph would fight through this with her. He would help her.

As he lifted her against his chest, she wrapped her arms around his neck. "I'm sorry I'm so heavy."

"Sweetheart, you're tiny even with the babe in your belly. Don't worry; we'll be home in no time."

She closed her eyes and let her head rest against her husband's shoulder, dreading the next pain she knew would come soon.

It came just as they left the cool of the forest and entered the field where shadows were creeping toward the house over tall sunbaked grasses. She cried out as the pain gripped her.

"What do I do?" Joseph asked, jostling her roughly as he quickened his steps.

"Stop. Don't move," she managed between her teeth. He immediately froze and she turned her focus inward. Breathing. Breathing. Imagining the baby moving into place, ready to be born.

"All right, go," she said as soon as the pain lessened several minutes later. She wanted to lie down right there, but she gritted her teeth and urged Joseph on. She would not lie down until she was in her own home, in her own bed. Her child would not be born in a dirty field like the animal the islanders thought her to be.

Joseph did as she said, moving quickly, each bounce and jostle sending agony through her internally bruised body. But she didn't complain. The sooner they got to the house, the sooner she could get to the business of bringing her child into the world.

As they entered through the back door into the kitchen, she heard the door slam shut behind them and then they were climbing the narrow stairs to the bedroom. She felt Joseph's arms trembling under her, but she knew she'd never make it up the stairs herself, so she let him continue while she held on tight to his neck.

Her belly started to tighten. "The pain's coming," she told her husband as she closed her eyes and prepared for it. He laid her on the bed and she rolled to her side, wrapping her arms around her belly and feeling it harden beneath her hands. Again she breathed and waited until the torture ended.

"Boil water," she said as soon as she could talk. "Linens."

As she lay there feeling bruised and battered and terrified, she unbuttoned her gown and kicked off her boots. Then she waited for Joseph to return to help her with the rest.

Soon he was by her side again and helping her undress and settle into the bed with pillows behind her and extra linens under her.

"Have you ever seen a woman give birth?" Joseph asked as

he removed the quilt from the bed and left it on the chest of drawers under the window. "Do you know what to expect?"

She shook her head. "I only know what the herbalist from Port Townsend told me." She paused as she remembered. "Oh, get the packet labeled 'before' and make a tea of it for me to drink."

He nodded and was gone again.

But the tea wasn't needed after all. The minute Joseph left the room, another pain gripped her, but this one was different. This one made her feel like she should push. "Joseph!" she called as soon as she could draw a breath.

He ran into the room and immediately the color drained from his face. "Oh my God," he said as he rushed to her. "I see the head."

"Help me. I don't know what do to!" Despite everything the herbalist told her, actually feeling her body ripped apart from the inside scared her more than anything she'd ever experienced.

"I'm here, sweetheart. I'll help. It can't be much different from a cow or sheep, right?"

She didn't appreciate the comparison but didn't have the strength to respond. Cow or not, she was glad for Joseph's help. He grabbed a towel from the stack next to the bed and talked her through as she pushed their child from her body.

Through her exhaustion she heard her child's first cry and felt her heart tug in answer.

"It's a boy!" Joseph's voice sounded husky with emotion.

She nodded. She closed her eyes to rest as Joseph wiped the baby clean. She still had her eyes closed when he laid their son on her chest, and she relished the fragile softness and heat of him. Then, she opened her eyes and looked at her baby for the first time.

His eyes were open and staring up at her, dark and deeper than the ocean. In that moment she felt something pass between herself and her son. A kind of communication that didn't need words. She'd never met him before, but at that moment she knew she'd always known him.

"Welcome, little one," she whispered in Chinese through her tight throat. With her fingertip she gently caressed the black fuzz on top of his head and examined the rest of him from his little nose to the tips of his ten toes. He was perfect.

And, from this moment on, he was forever hers to protect.

Unbidden, the image of her father's agonized face as he pushed her from the steamship filled her mind. At the time she'd believed he was in pain from his injuries. Now she knew he was feeling the pain of loving another person so much.

She would never push this child away from her.

Hours later, after Mei Lien and her son had learned to nurse and had taken a nap, which wasn't long enough for Mei Lien, all three of them were snuggled together in the bed. The baby was wrapped tight in a soft green blanket Joseph had traded a box of pears for.

"What should we call him?" Joseph asked, his gaze tender on his son.

"Yan-Tao," she told him, suddenly feeling shy that she'd never considered anything but a Chinese name for their son. "It means handsome."

Joseph nodded and ran a finger down the baby's cheek. His hand looked huge next to the baby's tiny face. "I like Yan-Tao. Can we also choose a second name for him that would help him fit in with the other kids on the island?"

She knew he meant a name that might help Yan-Tao seem more white, not Chinese. Her eyes burned and she couldn't form the words he wanted, so she just nodded, accepting what had to be.

"Do you like the name Kenneth?" His fingers moved from the baby to stroke lightly up and down Mei Lien's arm. "It was my father's name. He was a good man."

This child who would forever straddle two worlds, Chinese and white, would have the honor of being named for his white grandfather. Mei Lien felt fresh tears flood her eyes. Her son was surely blessed to be watched over by the spirits of both grandfa-thers. And he was blessed with a father who looked at him the way her own father had looked at her.

"I'll see he carries the name with honor."

# Chapter Sixteen

*Friday, August 12, 1887*
*McElroy Farm, Orcas Island*

The next weeks were a blur of caring for the baby, caring for her own healing but still very sore body, eating when she could, sleeping when she could, and crying along with Yan-Tao when she couldn't calm him.

Mei Lien longed for another woman to talk with who had experience raising a child. She'd never been around babies and felt stupid asking her husband, who'd helped with numerous younger cousins back home in Indiana and knew how to pin diapers and hold the baby's head. Shouldn't a mother know these things?

But slowly she learned and even surprised herself when her instincts guided her correctly and she was able to soothe Yan-Tao all by herself when Joseph was in the orchard. Slowly she gained confidence and strength.

But not sleeping was taking a toll on her. The baby woke crying and hungry every three hours, and Joseph could not help with feeding him. Besides, Joseph was busy picking the apples in their orchard every day and needed to sleep through the night.

At midmorning two weeks after Yan-Tao's birth, Mei Lien was mixing dough in the kitchen for the bread she should have made hours earlier. Instead she'd stayed in bed, attempting to recapture some lost sleep with Yan-Tao beside her.

He lay in the bassinet Joseph had built and placed in the kitchen where she could keep an eye on the baby as she worked. He wasn't fussing at the moment, but she knew it was just a matter of time, so she worked quickly, scraping the dough onto the countertop, then working it with her hands—shaping and kneading until it was smooth and ready to go into the pan to rise on the back of the stove.

The sound of voices drifted in through the open kitchen window and she froze. Campbell. She was sure of it. He always seemed to show up when Joseph wasn't around, and today he was out picking in the section of the orchard farthest from the house.

Willing the baby to remain silent, she wiped her flour-covered hands on a tea towel and crept to the sitting room window. Careful not to move the curtains more than necessary, she peeked through to the yard outside where the voices came from.

It was Campbell, all right, and he had another man, a woman, and two little girls with him in his wagon. Joseph would be furious to find Campbell on his property. Thus far, he'd been able to avoid the man almost entirely, and when forced into conversation, Joseph had made it clear, without explanation, that they were no longer friends. Campbell never asked Joseph for help on his farm anymore, and except for that day on the beach when Mei Lien went into labor, he'd kept his distance from both of them.

As she watched, Campbell pulled up in front of the house and jumped out. The second man also jumped to the ground and reached back up to lift the little girls down.

Campbell and the other man spoke together, their hat brims nearly touching, though Mei Lien could not make out their words. As she watched, Campbell raised his arm and pointed across the road to the orchards where she knew Joseph was working—but how did Campbell know that?

The woman, in the meantime, handed several bags down to what Mei Lien assumed were her daughters, who in turn threw them on a growing pile on the ground. The girls looked identical, from their long blond ringlets to their matching dusk-blue dresses, black stockings, and black leather boots. Their mother, a sturdy sort, had chestnut-colored hair pulled back into a severe bun topped by what Mei Lien assumed was a fashionable hat. With a look of exasperation aimed toward the men, the woman grabbed hold of a corner of her gray skirt and climbed from the wagon herself since the men were so caught up in their conversation.

"You go on into the house and get settled," said the second man to his wife. He was about the same size as Campbell, though a bit plumper. "Mr. Campbell's going to take me to find your brother in the orchard."

Brother?

Mei Lien gasped. Joseph never wrote back to tell his sister not to come!

The woman lifted her face toward the house and Mei Lien jerked back, afraid of being caught watching. What was she to do with houseguests? She barely had the energy to get through the day herself with her son, let alone cook, clean, and make conversation with people she didn't know.

She could hear footsteps on the porch now and knew she could hide no longer. Quickly, she smoothed her apron over her still swollen stomach and then brushed her hair back, tucking it behind her ears since she didn't have time to pull it into a proper knot.

The door opened without a knock and in swept the woman, followed closely by her daughters. Joseph's sister wore fine gray silk in a style that had clearly been made for her, not like the shapeless clothes Mei Lien wore. The woman held herself tall and stiff, her chin lifted so that the feather on her hat fell back rather than in front of her face. The air around her smelled of rose water, a scent Mei Lien had never cared for.

The woman's face pinched as her gaze took in the messy house. Soiled clothing lay in a heap on the floor beside the door waiting for Mei Lien to wash them, two weeks overdue. Mei Lien knew the dishes from breakfast were visible through the door to the kitchen, stacked on the counter amid the flour she had yet to clean up.

At that moment Yan-Tao woke with a cry. Mei Lien snapped into motion and bustled into the kitchen to scoop him from the bassinet. When she turned, she saw the woman had followed her. She watched as Joseph's sister took in the full mess of the kitchen and then, with lips pinched, landed her cold gaze on Mei Lien.

As the woman's eyes met hers, Mei Lien felt her breath catch. It was like looking at Joseph. The same green eyes, slightly almond shaped, but lacking Joseph's warmth and humor.

"You may inform your mistress that her guests have arrived." The words were clipped and condescending.

It took Mei Lien a moment to catch the woman's meaning. Shamed, she hid her face against Yan-Tao's cheek, then stiffened her back and forced a smile. "You must be Joseph's sister, Elizabeth. I'm so sorry. We forgot you were coming. Our son was born just two weeks ago, and Joseph's been so busy with the harvest..." Her words floated away from her.

"Well, thank heavens for that charming Mr. Campbell who gave us a ride from the steamer landing. Otherwise, who knows what would have become of us!" She sniffed as if it was Mei Lien's fault Joseph had not been waiting for his sister at the dock. Elizabeth placed her hands on her daughters' shoulders as though to keep them from coming any closer to Mei Lien.

"I am sorry," Mei Lien said again, knowing nothing she said would help. She stood dumbly as Elizabeth raked her gaze over her, revulsion darkening her features.

*Of course Elizabeth doesn't like what she sees*, Mei Lien thought, comforting herself. Her clothes and hair were a mess, and she probably had Yan-Tao's dried spit-up on her shoulder.

That, and she was Chinese.

"Please," she said as she bounced Yan-Tao against her shoulder, trying to hold off his next feeding. "Come with me. I'll show you where you will sleep so you can get settled."

"Who are you?" Elizabeth asked bluntly.

The question stopped Mei Lien. Who else could she be? She forced her smile to stay in place as she turned back to her sister-in-law. "I am Mei Lien McElroy. Joseph calls me May, and you can do the same if you choose. I'm very pleased to finally meet you because I have no family of my own anymore."

"And that?" She pointed to Yan-Tao.

Mei Lien felt her smile drop and could do nothing to stop it. Feeling the sudden need to protect her child, Mei Lien held him tighter. "This is Joseph's and my son, Ya—" She stopped, remembering her son's white name. "Kenneth. After your late father. We call him Ken."

The girls broke from their mother's grasp and crowded closer to see their cousin, remarking on his tiny nose and seashell ears, seeming not to notice his darker skin and hair, nor the rounded Chinese face pressed against her shoulder. Their mother, however, remained across the kitchen, her nose wrinkled. "He sure is...squinty," she stammered.

Squinty. Mei Lien felt the heavy burning inside that had become familiar to her since the day she'd been forced out of her home in Seattle. Of course her son had slanted eyes; he was half Chinese. No one would make her feel ashamed of that. No one. Not even family.

It was all she could do to hold back a retort. Instead she turned to the stairs to lead the woman to the room that would become Yan-Tao's when he outgrew the bassinet. She cared little if the woman actually followed.

She did follow, of course, and so did her girls.

"You and your husband can sleep here, in this bed," Mei Lien told her as she smoothed the quilt with one hand, grateful she'd cleaned the room just a few days before Yan-Tao's birth. "We don't have another bed for the girls, but I can make up a place for them on the floor with blankets and pillows."

"My children are not dogs who sleep on floors."

Mei Lien straightened and stood staring at the wall as all the blood in her body seemed to rush to her head. Her womb chose that moment to twinge, making her yearn for the chance to sit and rest, but her pride wouldn't allow it. She knew there would be many more moments like this one over the next three days.

Mei Lien turned to her guest. "We do have the cabin Joseph built when he first moved here. It's in the trees across the meadow but is close enough to come to the main house for meals and such."

Elizabeth clapped her palms together. "Then it's settled! You and Joseph will sleep there and the girls will sleep in your bed. Come, girls. Let's collect our things."

The three tromped back down the stairs, leaving Mei Lien standing in the bedroom with her mouth hanging open. She and her newborn baby had just been kicked out of their own house.

Three days, she reminded herself as she forced her feet to move. Three days and then they'd be gone. She could do this. For Joseph's sake.

Somehow that first day Elizabeth talked her brother into stopping his work at noon to guide them up the famous Mount Constitution. She wanted to see the view someone told her stretched from Canada to Oregon. Mei Lien did not have the strength to make the climb and was happy to see the lot of them go, leaving her alone for the entire afternoon to straighten the house, cook dinner, and move the belongings she and Joseph would need to the cabin.

When they returned, Mei Lien had dinner on the table. What followed set the pattern for the rest of the weekend. Elizabeth and Marcus, her husband, would sit and talk with Joseph and only direct a comment to Mei Lien when necessary. Joseph did his best to draw her into conversation or try to include her in a card game, but she knew her presence made the others uncomfortable so she politely refused and took herself off to clean the dishes or nurse Yan-Tao.

She watched carefully and saw how Marcus ignored Yan-Tao, even when the baby was in Joseph's arms right in front of him and screaming at the top of his lungs. Elizabeth at least looked at the child, though it was always with a pinched expression. She never touched him.

Their girls, however, whom Mei Lien learned were ten years old, did not seem to notice their parents' revulsion or indifference. They would sit on their knees in front of Yan-Tao, talking and cooing and giggling with each other over him and repeatedly begging to hold him.

Mei Lien ached with exhaustion made worse by the tension gripping her shoulders in her guests' presence. Elizabeth never offered to help her with chores or meals, leaving everything for Mei Lien to juggle along with the fussy baby.

But to her credit, Elizabeth loved her family and her brother. That much was obvious, and it went a long way toward making Mei Lien tolerate her presence. As Joseph talked, telling them about their life here on the island and their plans for shipping their harvest to Seattle and using the profit to expand the house and someday build a dock in their harbor, Elizabeth listened intently, staring at her brother with adoration.

At night, as they lay in the old cabin together with Yan-Tao sleeping in the bassinet beside them, Joseph told her stories of how he and Marcus had been best friends growing up in Indiana and how Elizabeth had followed them everywhere until, eventually, Marcus had asked her to marry him and they'd moved out west to Tacoma. Their letters home had convinced Joseph to make the move himself, though a chance stop in the islands convinced him this was where he wanted to settle rather than in the bustling mill town farther south.

She closed her eyes as she listened to him talk. She was so tired her head pounded from forcing herself to stay awake all evening serving dinner, then dessert, then listening to Elizabeth play the mandolin she'd brought with her. Her body ached.

Her heart ached.

She'd watched Joseph with his sister and brother-in-law and saw him smile, laugh, tell jokes, and tease his friend. She saw a side of Joseph she had not known existed, and she realized this was a part of himself he'd given up by marrying her. If he'd chosen a white bride, he would have friends and family gathered around him all the time making him laugh. Instead, his days were quiet and lonely with only her, and now their son, for company.

He deserved more.

If only she could release him from their marriage, but she knew with the certainty of one who has loved and lost that she could never let him go. She needed him more now than he'd ever need her, no matter how he might deny that. She was selfish to keep him for herself instead of setting him free to find another wife, another life. But being selfish was better than being alone.

She reached her hand under the covers until she found his hand lying at his side. She twined her fingers through his and squeezed, feeling her heart slow to a steady rhythm again as he squeezed back and she knew he was there beside her, keeping her safe.

With his quiet, strong voice still filling the tiny cabin with his stories, she fell asleep.

Mei Lien smiled even before she opened her eyes Monday morning. Today was the day Marcus and Elizabeth would go home to Tacoma and she, Joseph, and Yan-Tao would be able to settle back into their quiet life, just the way she liked it.

Joseph was already up and dressed and was lifting Yan-Tao from the bassinet. His mewling cries told them he was ready to be fed, and he was fully aware his father could not satisfy that need.

Mei Lien propped herself up against the bed pillows and reached out her arms. "Here, I'll take him." She took the baby and settled him against her breast. "What time is the steamer?"

Joseph leaned over and kissed her gently on the forehead, filling her senses with the smell of freshly washed male and wood smoke. She closed her eyes, savoring him.

"The schedule says eleven, though you know as well as I do it'll be later than that."

"Yes, but you'll have your sister there by eleven anyway, won't you?"

Joseph grinned at her as he straightened from the bed. "They won't miss today's boat. Don't worry." He turned away and had taken two steps toward the other room when he stopped and turned back. "May?"

She let her eyes travel over his lean form and, for the first time in weeks, wondered when she'd feel ready to be intimate with him again, hoping it was soon, though the ache between her legs told her it would be many days still. "Yes?"

He dipped his head. "I know these past few days have been rough on you. Thank you for, well, for everything."

Her heart rolled over and she smiled. "You're welcome."

He grinned again. "See you up at the house," he said with a wink. Then he was gone.

Mei Lien finished feeding Yan-Tao, then got them both dressed. She took a few minutes to straighten up the cabin, stripping the bed of linens and piling them by the door to wash later after everyone was gone. She piled their toiletry items in the washbasin and set this next to the pile of linens to carry back to the house later.

When everything was ready, she gathered Yan-Tao into her arms and headed toward the main house, realizing only then that she hadn't been to visit her ancestors' spirits at the water since the day Yan-Tao was born. Maybe if she finished her chores quickly enough, she could leave Yan-Tao with Joseph while she went to the water. Or maybe she should take him with her to introduce him to their ancestors.

He would need to learn about them, about where he came from. She must not let their Chinese ancestry become lost in the white world they now lived in.

As she walked, she remembered the silks Joseph had given her that were tucked away in her sewing chest. They would make a handsome jacket for her son.

And then a different idea came to her and she caught her breath at its perfection. Not a jacket, but a ceremonial robe like the ones her grandmother had told her were worn by officials in China. She could embroider images on it depicting their ancestry and family history. This embroidered robe would be Yan-Tao's link to his people, his past. He would wear it at his wedding, and on that day she would stand beside him, proud of the honorable young man he'd become.

She smiled. She'd begin work on the robe tonight, now that her evenings would be free again. Her steps quickened.

When she reached the house, she knew immediately that something was wrong. An unfamiliar mare stood hitched out front, and she heard loud voices coming from inside.

She went in through the kitchen and followed the voices to the sitting room, where she found Joseph, Marcus, Elizabeth, and a man she didn't know. Conversation ceased the moment she entered, and all eyes turned toward her.

Despite the already heavy heat, the stranger wore a full suit, vest, tie, and shirt and held a wide-brimmed hat balanced between his hands. Even the mustache on his lip looked heavy and hot as it hung over his mouth. He eyed her suspiciously.

Joseph jumped to his feet and crossed the room in three quick strides. He wrapped an arm protectively around her shoulders. "Mr. Izett, this is my *wife*, May McElroy," he said. To Mei Lien he said, "May, this is Mr. Izett. He's an immigration inspector from Roche Harbor. Says someone reported a smuggled Chinese woman living on my farm with forged papers."

Mei Lien felt a shudder move through her. Joseph told her Chinese people had been smuggled into the United States ever since the passing of the Chinese Exclusion Act, but she'd never once considered she'd be marked as one of them. "How... Who...who would do such a thing?" she stammered.

Joseph squeezed her shoulders. "Mr. Izett, as I was telling you before my wife arrived, she and I were legally wed in Port Townsend by Captain Barnes. I have the necessary paperwork upstairs. Before I met her, she was a lawful citizen of Seattle along with her father, a merchant."

"I was born in Seattle."

Izett's emotionless eyes pinned Mei Lien. "Do you have proof of this?"

Mei Lien did not know how to answer. If she gave this man her father's name, would he know she was supposed to be on the steamer reported to have arrived safely in San Francisco, though she knew otherwise? Was this man a friend of Campbell? Had he somehow learned she was on the boat that night and so sent Mr. Izett here to tie up loose ends?

"As I said, I have our marriage license and certificate upstairs. What kind of proof do you require of her origins in Seattle?"

The man pushed his hefty frame to his feet. "Where is your father now, Mrs. McElroy?"

Mei Lien's arms tightened around Yan-Tao as she looked at Joseph, hoping he would know how to answer. Joseph's face was red and the muscles in his jaw twitched as he stared at the man.

"Do you really want to know where her father is, Mr. Izett?" he growled.

Mei Lien knew she could not let Joseph say a word about the steamship that night. To do so would open her up to further danger, and now with Yan-Tao to think of, she had to be careful.

"He returned to China," she said quickly, before Joseph could continue. "Two years ago. When tensions between my people and yours were increasing. I was to go with him, but when our ship docked for supplies in Port Townsend, I found a family who hired me as a cook, and I stayed. Father was old and frail. He wanted to see his homeland before it was too late."

At her lie she felt Joseph stiffen beside her. She carefully kept her gaze averted from his. "I received one letter from him after he arrived in China," she went on. "I have not heard from him since."

"This family in Port Townsend can attest to the accuracy of your story?" Mr. Izett asked, his mustache wobbling over his mouth.

"Of course," Joseph said now, his voice gruff.

Just then, Elizabeth stood up. "Come now, Mr. Izett. My brother is an honest man who would never stoop so low as to marry an illegal Oriental."

Mei Lien wasn't sure what Elizabeth intended since Mei Lien fit half of the description. Still, she was grateful Elizabeth was trying to help.

"Do you really need my brother to dig up the paperwork you know will prove his innocence? Because if so, you're going to make us miss our steamer, in which case I will be sorely irritated."

To Mei Lien's surprise, Mr. Izett blanched at Elizabeth's words. He fiddled with his hat for several long moments before he finally spoke. "I suppose it's not necessary, seeing as how you seem like good people." He cleared his throat. "My informant must have been mistaken."

"Yes, he was." Joseph squeezed Mei Lien's shoulders one last time before gently releasing her with a nudge toward the kitchen and, she knew, out of Mr. Izett's sight.

She happily complied, going into the kitchen where she sat down on one of the kitchen chairs because her legs would no longer support her. In the sitting room she heard Joseph tell Mr. Izett he'd walk him out.

As the front door closed behind them, Elizabeth bustled into the kitchen, shaking her head. "Goodness me, it's sorry I am that Joseph has to put up with people like that."

Which he wouldn't have to do, Mei Lien knew, if not for her. She dropped her chin to hide the tears that welled in her eyes, hoping Elizabeth thought she was only tending to Yan-Tao.

Surprising her, Elizabeth snatched a baking sheet from the shelf over the stove and slapped it onto the counter. "Where do you keep the saleratus? I'm making biscuits."

Instead of answering, Mei Lien swallowed the lump in her throat. "Thank you," she managed.

Elizabeth stopped her bustling and faced Mei Lien squarely. After a long, awkward moment, she finally said, "I don't know why, but Joseph loves you. I didn't want to see him hurt." She started to turn away but then paused. "Are you illegal?"

"No."

Elizabeth nodded, then went on preparing the morning meal without comment.

Mei Lien knew she and this woman would never be friends, but they both loved Joseph, and that, she decided, was enough.

# Chapter Seventeen

*Tuesday, July 17—present day*
*Rothesay Estate, Orcas Island*

Inara flipped the switch, cutting power to the trimmer she was using on the hedges along the back patio. With her arm she wiped sweat from her forehead and stepped back to survey her work.

Right on time, mid-July, summer had finally arrived in western Washington. The rain from last week was forgotten now as flowers and grass both seemed to grow five inches overnight. The red bark of the madrona trees was peeling in earnest. A bright blue, cloudless sky reflected on the glass-like surface of East Sound, broken only by the occasional kayaker or seagull. Since the town of Eastsound no longer had a dock on its southern shoreline, the water traffic past her property was minimal. She liked it that way.

On Friday evening Inara had taken Daniel to the water to show him the beach, and she'd gone back every night since. She always felt the stresses of the day fall away as she stepped into the cool breeze and breathed in the ripe, earthy smells of the sea. Yesterday she'd discovered a bald eagle had nested in the top of a nearby tree and figured it must have babies up there, considering all the trips it made back and forth with a fish or other prey gripped in its talons. Maybe one day soon she'd get to see the babies.

Sweat soaked her shirt and trickled down her spine, making her yearn for the cool beach, but she couldn't go yet. She had too much work left to do.

Sure, she could have hired professionals to do the landscaping, leaving her days free to research the murders or order light fixtures, but a landscaping crew would have required thousands of dollars she didn't have. She was determined to convince her father the hotel was a sound investment she could handle, and considering that money was his biggest concern, she would do it as responsibly as she could. That meant making cuts to her plan. Besides, she knew a lot about yard work from her many summers helping Aunt Dahlia, so it was the most logical task for her to take on.

Satisfied the hedge looked straight and groomed, she headed toward the kitchen garden nestled in the notch between the main house and the side of her house. It was the view she looked upon every morning as she drank her tea on the back step, and today she'd start making it worth looking at. Plus, she strongly suspected she'd find some hearty veggies among the overgrown vines and weeds. Veggies that could save her money on groceries and eating out.

She set the trimmer on the grass and headed toward the garage on the other arm of the U-shaped manor to collect a wheelbarrow, shovel, and clippers. Halfway there, she spotted Tom on the porch and altered her course.

"Hey, Tom!" She waved to the contractor to get his attention.

He switched off the electric sander he was using on the porch boards and came over to lean on the railing.

"Hey, yourself. I'm gonna get my guys on to painting this wood while the weather holds. You sure you don't want me to sand down the whole thing?" He motioned to the length of the porch behind him.

They'd had to redo the section because of rot found during the inspection, but the rest of the porch was structurally sound and could last another couple years, at least. "No. The dents and grooves give it character. Just tell your guys to give it all a fresh coat of paint and it'll be perfect." She looked pointedly at the sander and sought the words she wanted to say. "Thanks for…for doing that."

When she'd returned from Seattle the previous week, she'd sat down with Tom and explained the agreement she'd made with her father and how important it was to be as frugal as possible. They'd cut costs where they could and identified tasks that Inara could do herself, like the landscaping. Tom must have decided to take on some of the labor he wouldn't normally do.

Tears stung her eyes. She knew he believed in her ability to succeed here, unlike her father, and he was helping her as a neighbor. He made her feel welcome in the small community.

Tom shrugged in his sweat-stained T-shirt. "No big deal. Oh, hey, I almost forgot. Sophie wanted me to ask you to come over for dinner tonight. You free?"

Inara smiled. "Sure. Thanks."

Though she acted casual as she waved to Tom and turned to head to the garage, she felt anything but. In Seattle she knew her neighbors, but they all pretty much kept to themselves. Orcas Island was different. Neighbors invited her for dinner; islanders chatted with her at the grocery store or post office and waved to her on the road. Her roots were sinking deeper into the island.

As she pulled open the garage doors to gather her tools, the musty scent of stale, moldy air hit her, reminding Inara just how old the estate was. But before Rothesay was built, this piece of land had been Mei Lien's yard, or maybe where her barn had stood.

Had Mei Lien felt like she belonged on the island? Did her neighbors invite her to dinner? Not likely.

The thought saddened Inara, and she made a mental note to ask Daniel when he called that night about what Mei Lien's life had probably been like. She'd been trying to learn what she could on her own about that time period and had borrowed some books from the history museum in town. In one of them she'd read about a group of islanders who called themselves the Orcas Island Anti-Chinese Association and whose sole purpose was to protect themselves from "the incursion of a race alien to us in every thing." About the time the Chinese were being driven out of Tacoma and Seattle, this group drove them off Orcas Island. Mei Lien might have been the first Chinese person to arrive on the island after that. If she was, was her Caucasian husband the only thing that kept the other islanders from forcing her off the island too?

It couldn't have been easy for Mei Lien and was probably very lonely. No wonder she had found time to embroider the sleeve so intricately.

Inara grabbed the tools she needed and returned to the garden, her mind heavy.

She was on her hands and knees in the dirt, chopping the soil around a two-foot-tall sticker weed to get to its roots, when her cell phone rang.

"Daniel! Are classes over already?" He taught all day on Tuesdays so she hadn't expected to hear from him until evening.

"Between classes actually, but I couldn't wait to call you."

Something in his voice pulled her focus away from the garden. "What's wrong?"

"We found Chinese bodies. In 1886 newspapers. Just like on the sleeve."

Pressure burned behind her eyes. "What do you mean?"

"All those bodies floating in the water next to the ship. I couldn't get them out of my mind so I looked again at newspapers from that time. Three Chinese bodies were found washed ashore within a week of each other soon after the Chinese were driven out of Seattle. One outside Port Townsend, two on Whidbey Island. I'm starting to think something pretty tragic happened."

Inara closed her eyes. Of course bodies had been found. She was surprised there hadn't been more than three. But then again, the currents were strong in the Strait of Juan de Fuca, especially in February, and plenty of animals in the water and on shore could have disposed of those that weren't washed out to sea.

"And that's not all," Daniel went on. "The shipping company records from that time period seem to be conveniently missing."

Her eyes flew open. "You went to the shipping company?"

"No, one of my research assistants did. She had a hard time tracking it down. I guess the company's name has changed or something. She figured it out and was allowed access to the archives, but she says the file was missing and they don't keep digital records going back that far."

Inara swallowed. Of course they hadn't found the file. It was sitting on her kitchen table. Daniel may have left the shipping company angle to his assistant and hadn't yet realized it was her family's company, but it was just a matter of time until he found out. She had to tell him.

"Um, Daniel?"

He'd already launched into the story told in one of the newspaper articles but stopped at her interruption. "Yeah?"

She had to do it. If she didn't, it would blow up in her face later. "The shipping company? It's my family's. Campbell Lines became Premier Maritime Group."

"Oh." He was silent a long moment. "You didn't think to tell me before now?"

She swallowed and gripped her phone tighter. "I should have as soon as I figured out the connection, but I forgot. Plus, I didn't think it was significant." She paused. "Why don't I look into it for you? I can talk to my dad and see if he knows of an accident back then."

"Okay. That'd be great. I'll stay focused on what happened to the McElroys. It's like they just vanished."

"What do you mean?"

"My team's been reading old diaries and newspapers. They've found occasional mentions of Joseph McElroy and his Chinese wife and son, usually written with scorn or outright derision. What's funny, though, is that we can't seem to find the McElroys, any of them, after 1894. We've checked ship and rail passenger lists, census records for all of Washington, Oregon, California, and British Columbia, everything."

Nothing since 1894. Her family moved into this house in January 1895. A thought irritated the back of her mind but wouldn't fully form. "What can I do to help the research?"

"Nothing. I've got a lot of help here at the university, and you've got your hands full with the hotel. I just wanted to tell you what we found."

It was all she could do to hold herself together until the call ended.

Even though he was going to focus on where the McElroys went, Daniel knew people had died. It was only a matter of time before he discovered that everyone on board was killed and her ancestor was responsible. And then what would she do?

The niggling feeling in her mind persisted. Something about Duncan Campbell moving into this house in 1895.

She'd always known the Campbell property on the island had originally been much smaller than it was today. Duncan had moved in the early 1880s from Scotland to Orcas Island, where he'd built a small cabin and a vegetable garden. He'd left his elderly father and young wife to care for it while he started and grew his business in Seattle. He saw his family very little during those first few years while he got his business off the ground, but the arrangement seemed to work for everyone involved.

The original property was still part of the Rothesay estate and lay to the south, through the forest and out of sight behind a small rise.

She decided it was time to take a walk.

Wiping dirt off her jeans, Inara headed back around the house, across the driveway, and onto the forest path. When the path curved toward the beach, she stepped into the brush and continued south, wondering why she and her siblings had never ventured over the hill when they were kids running wild through the forest.

It didn't take long, no more than ten minutes of brisk walking, before she crested the hill and came to a clearing where she saw what looked to be the stone foundation to a long-ago demolished building. This had to have been Duncan Campbell's original cabin, she decided.

It was small. Smaller than the cabin near Rothesay where Joseph and Mei Lien had lived before building the house that became Dahlia's. She stood with her back to the cabin and looked around.

The whole property sloped toward a sheer rock drop-off about one hundred feet away. No easy access to the water was visible. To her left, between the ridge she stood on and Mount Constitution, lay a small valley where an ancient fruit orchard was being reclaimed by forest. The orchard had southern exposure, which meant it must have had good sunlight, though it was small.

The rest of the clearing was devoid of trees and probably used to grow the family's food, though now it was overrun with native growth that would be forest again in another couple hundred years.

Duncan Campbell's original piece of property had sucked, Inara decided as she kicked at a rock. It was rocky, on the side of a mountain, and with difficult access to the water, not an easy homestead to get to or from. No wonder Duncan had jumped at the chance to move when the McElroy property became available.

Or maybe he'd had a hand in making it come available.

Inara started back toward home, pondering how she might

find out more. Just as she stepped back onto the forest path, she remembered Tom's friend in Friday Harbor who worked for the county. She'd bet Kira could find more specifics from the time the property had changed hands.

She pulled out her phone and scrolled through her call history until she found the right number, then waited for it to connect. When Kira came on the line, Inara explained what she needed, then disconnected. Now she had to wait.

Putting her nervous energy to good use, Inara went back to work on the weeds in Dahlia's garden, wondering again how anyone had managed to grow anything in that rocky plot south of here.

She had half the garden cleared of weeds by the time Kira called back.

"I thought I gave you the tax records a few weeks ago, but I guess not," Kira said without preamble. "Sorry about that."

"No problem," Inara told her. "What did you find?"

"Well, I couldn't find any records of a transfer of deed from Joseph McElroy to Duncan Campbell in 1894 or 1895, but that could just be because the records were lost or misplaced. I can keep looking if you want. I did find an official deed of title for Duncan Campbell in 1896. He paid taxes on the property starting in 1895."

Inara wasn't surprised that no legal transfer of deed could be found. And no doubt Duncan had paid someone off to file the paperwork later. "I appreciate this, Kira. Next time I'm in Friday Harbor, I'll buy you a cup of coffee or something."

Kira laughed. "Thanks. I'd like that, but it's not necessary."

Inara remembered the other question she'd asked Kira. "Did you find anything on the McElroy family after 1894?"

"No. They must have moved out of the county after selling to Campbell."

"I see. Thanks again, Kira."

Inara ended the call but stayed where she was, on her butt

in the dirt. Motion caught her eye, and she saw the eagle fly overhead toward her nest. She was too high for Inara to see if she was carrying food to her babies.

Where could the McElroys have gone?

That niggling thought finally came into focus: Duncan could have killed them to get the property for himself.

She hugged her knees to her chest, hating herself for thinking such a thing about her own blood. But if he'd ruthlessly murdered hundreds of others, what were three more? And if he did kill them, surely after seeing notices in the paper of bodies washing ashore, he wouldn't have tried dumping them out in the strait like the last time.

Did that mean he would have buried them on Rothesay property? Maybe down in the forest by the crumbling log cabin she and her brother and sister had used as a playhouse. Or across the road on Tom's property that had once been the Rothesay orchards. Maybe in his own orchard in the rocky soil where no one since had wanted to dig.

She had to find out. She couldn't live here and not know. She couldn't dig in the garden and wonder if she'd pull up human bones.

She had to find the truth, and somehow she had to do it before Daniel did.

# Chapter Eighteen

*Monday, October 1, 1894*
*McElroy Farm, Orcas Island*

Yan-Tao raced down the slope from the vegetable garden, his thin arms, browned from a summer spent almost entirely outdoors, pumping furiously. White teeth flashed as he laughed out loud just before he dove into the tall grass. When he came up, he was still laughing as he took off running again, oblivious to the grass and leaves clinging to his hair and clothes.

Mei Lien watched her son through the new parlor window. "New" wasn't entirely accurate, since Joseph had built the addition nearly three years ago, but she'd always think of that room as new.

The window glass, thicker in some areas than others, distorted the images outside just enough to make her have to move her head around until she found the right place to see clearly. With the exception of her son and his boundless energy, the world outside seemed to reflect how Mei Lien felt—out of focus and tired.

The grass was still green, but it had lost its luster, no doubt caused by the coating of white frost she'd found on it every morning for the past two weeks. Trees just starting to change dotted the mountain here and there with bold splashes of color on an otherwise forever green landscape. Though the colors lightened her heart, she knew it was nothing more than an illusion to distract her from the truth—soon there would be nothing left but bare branches and sleeping ground. Even the sun itself had dipped south, leaving long midday shadows over the yard.

Yan-Tao ran from the shadow cast by the barn into a patch of bright sunlight that gleamed on hair as black as oil like her own and cut short like his father's. She could hear his laughter as the black Labrador Joseph brought home for his son's fifth birthday darted past him, barking at what must have been an animal of some sort in the grass. Yan-Tao's healthy seven-year-old body twisted, jumped, ran, and dove for whatever he and the dog were trying to catch.

The years were passing too fast, she thought, not for the first time. Her baby would soon be a young man.

She and Joseph had tried to give him a sibling. Still were trying for that matter, even though they'd lost two pregnancies. Now her monthly courses had become irregular and a tender bulge pressed on her right side. She'd reached her twenty-sixth year, and she felt every one of those years in her sore legs, aching back, and swollen hands. Yet she worked all day helping Joseph bring in the crops and load them on a hired barge at their new dock so Joseph could sell them in the mainland cities.

When the farmwork was finished for the day, she turned her attention to the gift she was making for her son. Late into the night, every night, she embroidered their story onto the robe she would give to Yan-Tao when he married and started his own family.

As she thought those words—thought about Yan-Tao growing up—a sharp pain stabbed her low in the belly. She moaned under her breath and placed a warm palm over the pain, willing it away.

She couldn't wait until Yan-Tao was grown to finish the embroidery. He might have years ahead of him, but she did not. She didn't need a doctor to tell her she was dying. Her body had never been the same since Yan-Tao's birth, and she knew she must have inherited the same affliction that had taken her own mother from her before she even knew her.

She could feel the mass in her womb, growing, twisting, slowly draining her life from her.

Unlike her mother, at least Mei Lien had known her child.

Watching him now filled her with longing. Life should be different for Yan-Tao. He should live where there were other children to play with. He should be free to accompany his father on business trips. He should be treated with respect and kindness.

Since one horrible day in Eastsound Village at the statehood celebration, during which the other islanders made no effort to hide their revulsion, she and Yan-Tao had not stepped foot off their farm. Joseph did all their trading and shopping. She was happiest this way, but was Yan-Tao?

His only playmates were her and Joseph (when they could spare the time), the animals on the farm or in the forest, and his cousins, Priscilla and Penelope, Elizabeth's girls, who had visited every summer since he was born.

Mei Lien did her best during that weeklong visit every August to bite her tongue and be pleasant to Elizabeth, who still treated her like a servant. The girls, however, had turned into sweet young women who were always polite to Mei Lien and treated Yan-Tao like a little brother. For that, Mei Lien would forgive their mother almost anything.

Something in her stomach twitched and pulled, causing her to bend at the waist to relieve the pain. She breathed in and out, trying to drive the pain away but recognizing that each time it came, it was stronger. Soon it would be unbearable. She pushed at the lump in her stomach where the pain was centered and groaned. Time to sit. Time to direct her attention elsewhere.

Reluctantly she turned from the window and gingerly picked her way into the sitting room to her embroidery frame. Even though the precise and repetitive motion of embroidery had grown calluses on her fingers and made her wrists so sore that most nights she had to wrap them in cool cloths, she still loved every moment that she spent here. With each stitch she was one step closer to giving her son his heritage. With each stitch she connected with Grandmother and even her own mother and all the women of their family, lost to her forever.

She moved back the protective cotton covering and picked up the needle to make the next stitch. The section she worked on now told the story of when she and Joseph married and grew to love each other on their farm.

She shook her head. Love was such a strange emotion. She'd loved her father and grandmother with every breath in her body, and when they were taken from her, her breath was taken away too. And yet, somehow over the years she'd lived as Joseph's wife, she'd started to breathe again. Her nerves jumped with excitement when she heard his boot on the step. Her insides melted when she watched him gently guide Yan-Tao's hands holding the horse's reins, or when he tossed the boy high into the air and caught him again, their laughter mingling like music.

She loved him more with each passing day. More than she'd ever thought possible.

But still she felt the heavy dullness inside that told her she had not fully recovered the part of her soul that had died the day she saw Grandmother's body on the beach and knew she was all alone. Perhaps that dead part of her was what had settled in her womb and turned rotten. Just as surely as the devil Campbell had killed Father and Grandmother, he was now killing her.

She sat back, noting absently that her stomach pain had receded, and took a minute to stretch her neck. When she was ready, she cut the green thread she'd been using and reached for the peach-colored one she'd carefully twisted with pink to mimic the color of Joseph's skin. Before piercing the cloth, she held the thread against the fabric, testing the color against the green background that was the forest surrounding the farm.

Satisfied, she pushed the needle through and began what would become her husband's face, loving that moment of resistance before the cloth gave and the floss slid through the fabric. She pushed the needle through from the back and then repeated the motion, over and over in tiny seemingly random stitches, each with a specific purpose.

Her stomach gave another twinge but all she did to accommodate it was to hunch forward, relieving the pressure. She didn't have time to lie down. She'd wasted an hour yesterday by lying down.

Joseph's face slowly came into focus on the silk. His pink skin that he'd kept clean-shaven for her since the day they married. His intense green eyes that always seemed to be smiling at her. The strong jaw, thick eyebrows, straight nose. What had she ever done to deserve a man such as him?

Nothing.

She didn't deserve him.

But Yan-Tao deserved him. And so, for both of them, she told the story of the love they shared through her stitches. Tonight she'd tell Yan-Tao the story in words, Chinese words, so he could practice the language, and so, one day, he could look at the embroidery and remember what every symbol and picture meant.

She'd embroidered nothing on this silk that did not have meaning or purpose.

"Mama, Mama!" Yan-Tao burst through the front door and barreled into the sitting room, the dog on his heels. His round cheeks were pink and nearly bursting from his wide grin. In his thin arms he held a bundle of gray fur. "I caught a rabbit! Want to pet it?"

"Keep that thing away from my silks!" she told him, trying not to laugh for, in truth, she even loved her son's naughtiness because it showed he was happy and thriving. "I'm sure it is filthy!"

"I'll give him a bath," he said with a lift of his chin that reminded her of her father. "I'll take good care of him. I promise."

Mei Lien's hand stilled with the needle poking halfway up through the cloth. "What do you mean you'll take care of him? He is not a pet, is he?"

Yan-Tao's throat bobbed. He nodded.

"You already have a pet." She nodded to the mutt stretched on the floor at his feet. "You don't need another. Besides, a rabbit isn't a pet. It's dinner."

His mouth twisted in the way that always signaled tears were close at hand. He visibly fought the emotion with a deep breath and a swallow. His arms tightened, bringing the rabbit up to his face. "I love him, Mama. Please?"

Mei Lien looked at her son and the two animals with him and wondered if she could get out of this by telling him to speak with his father about it. She immediately rejected the idea, though, knowing Joseph would give in to anything Yan-Tao asked.

They didn't need a pet rabbit. Yan-Tao didn't need another distraction from his lessons and chores. He certainly didn't need another pet.

But what she worried about most was the simple fact that one day the rabbit would die, or be eaten by a dog or coyote, and her son's heart would break. It was a lesson he would have to learn, but not just yet if she could help it.

"No." She forced herself to resume her stitches. "But I will let you set him free outside instead of killing him for our supper, even though a rabbit stew tonight would make your father happy. You know how hungry he is after his trips to Port Townsend."

"Yes, Mother," he muttered as he turned to the front door. Without another word, he shuffled outside with the dog beside him and closed the door softly.

His palpable disappointment left a heavy pall over the room.

Mei Lien shook her head and used the fingers of her left hand to massage her right wrist. She'd done the right thing. The farm was no place for a pet rabbit.

The door opened again and she looked up, expecting to hear Yan-Tao plead for the rabbit again. Instead, he slammed the door shut behind him and raced through the parlor into the kitchen. The sound of his boots stomping loudly up the stairs rattled the lantern hanging on the wall. The click of the dog's toenails followed the whole way. A door slammed and she knew he'd gone into hiding in his room.

Several minutes later, she was again lost in her embroidery when the dog alerted her that all was not well. His whimpers carried through the ceiling from Yan-Tao's bedroom above her.

She carefully pierced the needle into the silk to hold it in place, then left it there and drew the cotton cloth over the top, protecting the entire work from dust and light.

Then, ignoring the protest from her belly, she stood and made her way to the kitchen and slowly up the stairs to the second floor where she knocked on her son's closed door. "Yan-Tao? Are you unwell?"

"No," came his muffled reply.

Mei Lien sighed and shifted to ease the pain in her stomach. "I know you're angry with me, but it's for the best that you don't take in another pet. We don't need another mouth to feed."

She waited, listening for a reply.

When none came, she continued. "Besides, you need to be careful how much you share your heart. Pets die, and if you give them your heart, well…" She searched for the right words to explain to a child what she herself didn't fully understand. "You lose yourself with them."

The door clicked open.

She nudged the door the rest of the way open and peered inside the bedroom. He'd lit the small lantern Joseph had given him and was curled up on pillows on the floor in the corner with the dog pressed against his back.

"It's all right, Mama. I don't love the rabbit."

The steely determination on his face made something in her chest feel like it had snapped and was squeezing her heart right out of her. "I'm sorry you had to let him go."

"I didn't let him go." He used his fist to swipe at his eyes.

"Where is he?"

"On the porch. You can have him to make stew for Father."

Never in her life had Mei Lien known that someone so young could exhibit more bravery than a full-grown adult. In that instant she saw a flash of the honorable man her son would someday be, and she felt a wash of emotion come over her.

Maybe she'd been too rash. Maybe she should let him keep the rabbit.

"Do you still want to keep him?" she asked, knowing the question was silly. Of course he wanted to keep the animal.

But he surprised her by shaking his head. "It's too late, Mama. He's dead."

She made the rabbit stew and Joseph's favorite biscuits to go with it, but he didn't return from his trip to Port Townsend by dinnertime. She kept the pot warm on the stove as she tucked Yan-Tao into bed and kissed him good night, thanking him again for the rabbit even though they both knew she should have let him keep it as a pet. He hadn't eaten more than two bites, and she could tell he'd had to choke those down.

A storm had blown in while they were eating, and rain pounded the house as loudly as drums. A glance out of Yan-Tao's window showed the trees thrashing madly in the wind. A branch or pinecone banged against the roof, making them both jump. "Don't fret, Son. It's just a storm. Good night."

"Where's Father?"

Mei Lien paused at his bedroom door to give him a smile she hoped would reassure him. "I'm sure he'll be here when you wake up. Go to sleep."

She closed the door and paused to rest her forehead against it with her eyes closed. *Please*, she prayed to the ancestors, *keep Joseph safe out there.*

Exhaustion rode heavily on her shoulders as she came back downstairs. Still, she put the kitchen back in order and then bundled up against the storm and made her way outside to usher the animals into their stalls in the barn for the night. The horses got handfuls of alfalfa, and the pigs, goat, cow, and sheep a cup of grain each. After filling their water troughs with buckets from the stream, she closed the barn for the night and went back to the house, all the while watching and listening for signs that her husband was returning home.

She ached to crawl into bed beside him and sleep for hours. As soon as he got home, she'd do just that.

The storm made the evening darker than usual. This was the time of night when she used to go to the water to visit Father's and Grandmother's spirits. She hadn't been back since Yan-Tao was born more than seven years ago, but tonight she felt the water pulling, felt the spirits pulling her to the water. Despite the storm, despite the rain and mud and her own exhaustion, her feet turned toward the water.

Wind whistled past her ears and forced tree branches to rub together and make eerie music. She ignored it, just as she ignored the cold rain stinging her exposed cheeks.

Her feet slipped on the muddy path, and she stopped to catch her balance against the rough bark of a cedar tree. Something made her pause there and listen, all her senses open.

Why wasn't Joseph home yet?

Nothing moved besides the shadows of the trees whipping in the wind. No lights flickered. No voices called out. No scent but wet forest filled the air. Nothing changed as she waited and watched for a signal from whatever had alerted her, because something had. Something was out there. Something had made her stop and want to go to the water for the first time in seven years. Something called to her tonight, and she didn't know what or why.

Something wasn't right.

Her family ancestors had released their grip on her when her son came into the world and she'd started the embroidery. Why would they be pulling at her tonight?

Unless it wasn't Father's or Grandmother's spirits calling to her from the water but something else. Someone else.

Heart pounding, she pivoted away from the water and hurried back to the house as fast as the storm and the pain in her stomach allowed. She wouldn't leave Yan-Tao alone for a moment longer, no matter how strongly she was pulled to the water. She could return as soon as Joseph came home.

But he was never this late. He'd left early yesterday morning and had planned to spend one night in Port Townsend and return by midday today. He sometimes even completed his business within one day and caught a steamer or private boat back home without spending the night at all. He never took two full days. Never.

Once inside and dried off, she tried to work on her embroidery but found herself making sloppy, uneven stitches, the pattern lost, so she had to pull out the threads and start over. After an hour she gave up and paced between the parlor window that looked to the water and the sitting room window that looked to the road, watching and yearning for signs of Joseph's return. All the while ignoring the water's pull.

Eventually she gave in to her tired body and lay down on the sofa, curling herself around the cold, piercing ache in her belly that was competing for attention with the burning fear in her throat. She fell asleep with the candles still burning.

The dog first alerted her that someone was in the yard. The Lab came bounding down the stairs from Yan-Tao's bedroom, barking and whining as though the devil himself were at the door. Mei Lien pushed herself off the couch, aching more than before she'd fallen asleep, and looked around.

Sun slanted through the windows to splash weakly on the knotted rug under her feet. It was morning. The storm was gone and Joseph had not returned.

The dog danced at the front door, barking at the stranger outside. He never barked at anyone but strangers, which meant it wasn't Joseph out there.

Just what she needed. A visitor.

"Is it Father?"

She turned toward her son's voice and found him standing in the kitchen doorway, fully dressed, his hair still rumpled from sleep.

She shook her head. "No, *hǔzǐ*. It's not." Moving to the window, she carefully drew back the white curtains.

Two men, white men, dismounted from their horses and tied the reins to the porch railing. The one facing her was of medium height and build and wore a dark suit. Something on his coat, probably a metal button, flashed in the early morning sunlight as he reached into his saddlebag for a canteen of water.

The other, even though he hadn't turned his head in her direction, she would know anywhere. Campbell. He carried himself like no other person Mei Lien had ever seen. Much like she imagined an emperor or king would—his head lifted to look down on his subjects, even though most were taller than him, his shoulders back and chest puffed.

The men talked in low voices so all she heard was a murmur. They didn't seem to be up to mischief, but Mei Lien knew not to trust Campbell or any man in his company.

"Stay in the kitchen," she whispered to Yan-Tao, herding him in front of her as she raced to the back door and the shotgun

Joseph kept hanging on the wall beside it. "Stay silent. Don't let them know you're here, no matter what. Got it?"

He nodded, his eyes huge above his round cheeks. "Where's Father?" he whispered.

She shook her head as she checked to see if the rifle was loaded. "I don't know. Don't worry. I'll handle these men."

Just then one of the men pounded on the door and they both jumped. With her eyes on her son's, she put a finger to her lips and raised her eyebrows. He gave a jerking nod, then scampered back to wedge himself into the corner by the stove.

Satisfied he'd stay put, she held the gun in front of her and moved silently to the front door. "Who is it?" she called in the strongest voice she could muster.

"Ma'am, it's Duncan Campbell," came the voice that made her insides shrink up. "I've got Sheriff Keppler with me. There's been an accident. Please open the door."

Her stomach dropped, as cold and heavy as the boulders in East Sound. "What do you mean 'an accident'?"

"Mrs. McElroy," said a voice that must have been the sheriff's. "It's about your husband. May we come in?"

Mei Lien jerked her gaze to the kitchen. Even though she saw no sign of her son, she knew he was there. She had to protect him from those men.

She faced the door again and drew herself up as tall as she could manage with the pull in her belly. Still clutching the shotgun, she unlocked the door and stepped outside, pulling it closed behind her.

Campbell and the sheriff stood shoulder to shoulder on her porch. The sheriff took a step back when he saw her, and she was struck by the subtle rejection. She hadn't been this close to a white person other than Joseph in five years. Those years had made her forget the many ways people let her know they hated her.

She lifted her chin and met his wary gaze with a defiant one of her own, feeling a moment of satisfaction when his drooping mustache twitched.

Dismissing him for the moment, she turned to face Campbell. The very sight of him made her clutch the rifle tighter. Campbell didn't smile, though something in his eyes seemed to be gloating. Her finger slid toward the trigger. "What do you want?"

The sheriff pulled his hat from his head and held it in front of him. As he eyed the rifle, he said, "Ma'am, can we come inside? I'm afraid we have some bad news."

That was when the truth struck her. Why else would the sheriff and Campbell be here? A trembling started in her legs and moved up her body, tugging on the pain in her stomach so that she felt sick, and then climbing into her head until she heard a buzzing noise.

She knew what they would tell her. She didn't need them coming into her home, scaring her son, all of them pretending they could be civil to each other. "Just say what you need to say and be on your way."

The two men exchanged a glance. Campbell shrugged a shoulder and rolled his eyes as if to say he couldn't care less how they handled the situation. The sheriff's head jerked in a nod before he turned back to face Mei Lien. "Ma'am, I'm sorry to inform you that the steamer your husband was on has been found lying on its side on Lopez Island. The captain's body was found inside. We searched for hours yesterday and still have men out searching this morning, but we've found no sign of your husband's or any other passengers' bodies. I'm sorry."

Mei Lien felt darkness close over her. Campbell had probably caused the accident. He was the reason her husband was missing. He was the reason the water took Joseph from her, just as he'd commanded it to take everyone else she'd ever loved.

Suddenly, and inexplicably, her fear of Campbell vanished. Gone was the nervous tension she felt around him. Gone was the physical need to lower her eyes when he drew near. Gone was the need to hide from him.

She didn't care what he might do to her. He'd done the worst thing imaginable. He'd taken first her father and her grandmother, and now he'd taken her husband.

From down that long tunnel, she heard a primal scream and knew it came from her, though she didn't feel it. Through a haze of pain, she saw herself raise the rifle and point it at Campbell's face. "You killed them!" she heard herself shout in Chinese. "You killed Joseph. You killed Father and Grandmother, and you tried to kill me. Never again, White Devil!" She pulled the trigger.

The next thing she knew, she was lying facedown on the porch, splinters jabbing into both palms as the sheriff's knee dug into her back. The black shroud that had covered her was gone, and she saw the scene around her clearly. The gun lay next to her, but then the sheriff kicked it away so that it fell off the side of the porch into the yard. Campbell spoke, but she couldn't make out the words.

She didn't care that the sheriff had pushed her, forcing her to miss. She didn't really want to kill Campbell because then she'd be just like him. She would always be better than him.

She didn't care about anything anymore. Bending her arms under her face, she rested her forehead on them and let the tears come. Silently they dripped onto the rough planks of the porch and she didn't care. She wished her whole body could melt into nothing and slide through the floorboards.

"Come on, Duncan," she heard the sheriff say. "Our job here is done."

"She tried to kill me, sheriff. You should take her into custody."

"Nah, she meant no harm. It's just grief."

Through the pounding ache of her soul, she heard the men gather up their horses' reins and mount as Campbell kept up his campaign to have her arrested. If she were a white woman, she knew, they'd have carried her inside, given her tea, called for one of their wives to come sit with her. A Chinese woman did not merit kindness.

Frankly, she was glad. All she wanted was to be left alone with her agony.

The men rode out of the yard and were gone. She lay unmoving, knowing as soon as she lifted her head she'd have to face the truth.

The door latch clicked and the hinges squeaked. She tensed. How could she have forgotten Yan-Tao? What had he heard?

"Mama?"

Quickly, she wiped her face on her sleeve and sat up with her back to her son. It took three deep breaths before she had the courage to turn around.

Her son looked physically sick. His usually round face was sagging like an old man's. His eyes were red and bruised and held shadows she knew must also be in her own.

"What did you hear?"

His chin trembled as he stepped fully out onto the porch and let the door slam shut behind him. "Father is"—he stopped and rubbed his arm across his nose—"gone?" His face crumpled and sobs tore from his small throat.

She opened her arms and he dove onto her lap, his face pressed against her chest. Loud wails erupted from his body to slice through her.

Campbell was responsible for this too. Campbell had just killed her son's childhood as surely as if he'd put a bullet in his head.

"We'll be all right, Yan-Tao," she murmured to him as she stroked his hair and rocked him in her arms. "We'll find a way. You'll see."

She kept rocking her son, comforting him as best she could as she drew comfort from the warmth of his small body on her lap. Over and over again she reassured him they would be all right.

But even as she spoke the words, she knew right down to her soul that they would never be all right again.

# Chapter Nineteen

T hought I'd find you down here."

Inara turned at the unexpected sound of Daniel's voice to see him emerge from the shade of the forest onto the beach, where she'd spent the last half hour daydreaming plans for a dock where guests could tie up their boats or launch kayaks. She just finished making a note to hunt down quotes for new kayaks and related equipment to replace the old stuff in the garage when Daniel reached her.

"You're early. I'm glad." She met him halfway. "I missed you."

"Me too." Daniel's lips found hers and she sank into his embrace.

The sound of a splash reminded her where they were. She pulled back and turned toward the water, her senses full of Daniel. "Look, she's back."

"Who?"

"The seal I told you about. The one who pops up nearly every time I'm down here. That's her." Inara watched the gray head dive under the sparkling water, then reemerge a few seconds later to look directly at them before doing it again, like a child showing off.

"How do you know it's a female?"

"I don't really, but I just have a feeling." Inara thought about that. From the first time she saw the seal here in her bay, she'd felt a kinship with it. Sisterhood.

She shrugged and stepped out of Daniel's arms to pick up the notepad she'd dropped. "As happy as I am that you're here, I have some things I need to get done before I can give you my full attention."

A sly smile spread across his face, showing his mind had gone directly to the gutter. "Then I guess I'd better let you get to it so you can finish quicker. Mind if I set up my laptop on your kitchen table?"

"Go for it. There's iced tea in the fridge and cookies that Sophie sent over this morning. I shouldn't be more than an hour or so."

"What are you working on?"

Inara hugged the notepad to her chest. "My business plan. Dad made it a requirement of the loan so I need to get it done right away. It's taking longer than I thought it would and I'd hoped the quiet of the beach would help me focus."

She looked back one last time at the seal before turning into the cool shade of the forest beside Daniel. "It doesn't help that I keep getting new ideas that require adjustments to the financials and building timeline."

"I haven't heard an idea of yours yet that isn't worth the extra work." He held her hand as they walked, the gesture natural, as if they'd been together for years. "Anything I can do to help?"

She forced herself to focus on his question, rather than the sensation of his thumb caressing her hand. "Unless you know someone who sells and installs elevators that are safe but cheap, I'm afraid not."

It was the part of the plan she was stuck on because it cost so much. She'd considered skipping elevators, but since all guest rooms were on the second and—eventually when the budget allowed for expansion—third floors, she had to make the hotel ADA compliant. Elevators would be welcome by guests and make service much more efficient for the staff, but the cost was phenomenal. She was starting to realize she'd probably need to bring on another investor even if her dad gave his approval in September.

*No*, she reminded herself, *not if, but when*. When her dad gave his approval. She had to stay positive. Of course her dad was going to approve of her work and extend the loan. He had to.

"Can I tell you what my team found now, or should I save it for later?" Daniel asked, interrupting her racing thoughts.

Her feet stopped moving and a fist squeezed her throat. *What if his team had found*—

No, she wasn't going to think it. They could have discovered anything about the sleeve or Mei Lien.

She'd been dreaming about the murdered Chinese people ever since her meeting with her dad. The dreams woke her up at night, heart pounding, lungs gasping for breath. And sometimes images of her mother's mangled car would weave into images of all the bodies in the water and she'd hear someone laughing cruelly, though she could never see who it was.

She blamed herself for her mother's death, and now she found herself with crazy thoughts that she was somehow also responsible for the lives of all those souls pushed to their deaths from the ship, responsible for Mei Lien too.

She knew there was nothing she could have done to stop the massacre because she hadn't even been alive when it happened. But the guilt and anguish still felt real.

She forced her feet forward. "What did they find?"

He stopped in front of her and grabbed both of her hands. Light fell through the leaves overhead, dappling his face with spots of sunlight and shadows. His eyes danced with whatever surprise he had for her, and she wished she could feel excitement in return. Instead she felt the slick oiliness of fear.

"I know what happened to Joseph."

"Mei Lien's husband?"

He leaned toward her. "Even though my team said they read through all the newspapers from the time, something made me take another look after finding those reports of bodies. I found him in a tiny paragraph in the *Islander* newspaper dated October 7, 1894."

"What did it say?"

"I have a printout in my car so you can read it in its entirety later, but it talks about an accident involving the steamer *Teaser* and that the search for survivors was suspended. All passengers were presumed dead and then it lists their names. Joseph McElroy is one of them."

"Not Mei Lien or Yan-Tao?"

"No mention of them. He was probably by himself. I dug further and found that particular steamer did a regular run between Port Townsend, Friday Harbor, Eastsound, and Bellingham. It got caught in a storm the night of September 30, 1894, and was found on its side on the beach on Lopez Island. The captain's body was found in the wheelhouse, but everyone else who boarded in Port Townsend that day was missing."

"You're saying Mei Lien was widowed with a young son and no means of supporting herself? What could she have possibly done to survive that?"

Daniel's eyes lost their glow and he shifted his feet. His voice was low as he answered, "I'm hoping we find out, but we may never know. There was another article on the shipwreck that says Joseph McElroy had a sister living in Tacoma. I have my team looking for her and any evidence of Mei Lien or Yan-Tao there in the years following."

Hope shot through her. "Mei Lien might have moved off the island by choice?"

Daniel's face scrunched. "What do you mean 'by choice'? She sold the property to your family, right?"

Inara realized her mistake. "Oh yes, of course. I was just

thinking it couldn't have been easy for her here by herself. But still, it was the only home she had." She hated herself for lying to him.

Daniel seemed to believe her, and together they turned toward the house.

"What do you say we take a break from talking about Mei Lien this weekend? And the sleeve and Joseph and anything connected to them?" For this one weekend, she wanted for them to be a normal couple who talked about normal things.

Out of the corner of her eye, she saw him grin. "That's all the news I have on them anyway," he agreed. "What do you have in mind to do instead?"

They tossed around ideas as they walked through the forest. The farther they got from the water, the warmer the air felt. Slowly, the salty seaweed smell was replaced by the warm scent of cedar boughs spiked with the spice of dry needles that crunched underfoot. The nearer to the house they came, the more she started picking up scents that were evidence of construction and her new life—fresh sawdust, pungent deck stain, diesel exhaust from the forklift unloading pallets of tile from a flatbed truck.

The smells anchored her again, pulling her out of the heavy dread and sadness that filled her when she thought of Mei Lien. She breathed deeply, washing the lingering shadows from her heart and mind, happy to have the hotel to occupy her.

"What do you say we start the weekend with dinner at the Inn at Ship Bay tonight?" Daniel asked as they passed the fountain. "My treat."

The Inn at Ship Bay had a restaurant in Eastsound that was written up in numerous regional and national magazines, and she was dying to try it, but with the hotel, it was way out of her budget. She squeezed his hand. "I'd love that. Thank you."

"My pleasure." He turned just as she reached up to kiss him, and her kiss landed on his lips. With a sigh she gave in to the heat that always flared instantly between them, not caring that Tom or any of the construction guys might be watching.

When the kiss ended, Daniel dropped his forehead against hers. "Or we could stay in tonight."

She playfully pushed him away. "No way." She lowered her voice and added, "But we can make it an early night."

His eyes flared as a slow grin spread across his lips. "I like the sound of that."

Inara was feeling better just being with him. The hotel was coming along fine, and they'd figure things out about Mei Lien. For now she'd just relax and enjoy Daniel because being with him felt so good.

Part of her felt horrible for keeping the truth from him when he was spending so much time researching her sleeve and getting nothing for it. Of course he deserved the truth. Especially considering their deepening relationship. But, not yet. She'd have plenty of time later to figure out how to tell him her family's secret.

# Chapter Twenty

*Thursday, August 9—present day*
*Rothesay Estate, Orcas Island*

Inara entered through the front door and paused on the landing to take it all in.

The hotel, *her hotel*, was coming together in front of her eyes. Plans that two months ago had been just that, plans, were being brought to life. From here she could see the lobby below and the new wall that had been built to separate it from the expanded restaurant space behind. Where the second floor had been open to the first-floor gallery on the far end above the restaurant, she'd closed it in to make another guest room. The result made the space feel warmer, cozier.

She could no longer stand here at the entry and see all the way through the house to the backyard and the sound behind, but that didn't diminish the experience at all. Guests would have plenty of opportunities to enjoy the view from other vantage points. With the expanded space for the restaurant, she could bring in an up-and-coming chef and turn the restaurant into just as much of a destination as the hotel itself.

That was the idea, at least.

If her father didn't kill it first.

*No*, she lectured herself, *don't go there*. She'd decided to find another investor so she wasn't entirely dependent on her father. The thought of giving up some control of the project was scary, but she knew she'd never go into business with someone she didn't trust and who didn't think like she did. She'd be careful in her choice.

Over the last week and a half she'd made countless calls to every friend and acquaintance she could think of who might be interested in going into the hotel business with her, but they'd all turned her down. She'd moved on to calling people she didn't know but had read about and admired for their business ethics, but so far she hadn't had any luck.

While her business degrees and family name gave her credibility, she didn't have a proven track record in the hospitality industry. No one was willing to take the risk.

Still, she wasn't giving up. There had to be someone out there who wanted to invest in a hotel and restaurant and had wads of cash. Someone like her who felt the magic of the islands and wanted to bring to life the vision she and Aunt Dahlia had created.

Inara lifted her gaze to the second floor where she could see the eight guest-room doors with their new brass numbers already in place. She'd hung them herself despite Tom's warning that the doors would be taken out before his crews got to work installing tiles, carpet, and new gas fireplaces.

Even so, she didn't regret the effort one bit. The hotel looked like a hotel. The sight shored up her flagging confidence.

That meant now was as good a time as any to start on phase two of her investor search. She pulled out her cell phone and dialed her brother's cell.

"I'm heading out for drinks. You have two minutes. What's up?"

"Do you think I can do this? The hotel?" She hadn't meant to lead with that, but since that's what came out, she went with it. "Because Dad doesn't."

"What do you mean 'Dad doesn't'? Of course he believes in you. Hang on, he's beeping in."

As she waited on hold, Inara headed to her own house through the library wing. Just as she locked the connecting door behind her, Nate came back on the line. "Sorry about that. He wanted to know if I was riding with him to the restaurant."

"Dad's going with you for drinks?"

"It's a celebration. The Yǒu Yì deal is finally closed. PMG is now the proud parent company of Yǒu Yì Cruise Lines, serving Southeast Asia and soon expanding to Australia."

"Are you quoting your press release?"

"Caught me."

"Well, congratulations on that. I know you've all worked hard on the buyout."

"Thanks. So, back to the reason for your call. What's up with the nerves?"

She dropped onto the sitting room couch and propped her feet on the coffee table, worn out from a full day of power washing the siding in preparation for the painters to come next week. "Oh, forget it. What I was really calling about was to see who you know who might want to go into the hotel business. Like, say, that guy from your fraternity who's a distant cousin of the Hiltons? Are you still in touch with him?"

"Alex? Yeah, but what are you planning?"

She sighed. "If Dad pulls my funding, I'm out of business. I love this place, Nate. I don't want to lose it."

She could hear a voice in the background telling him it was time to go. He came back on the line. "I'll run it by him. Was that all?"

"One more thing," she said quickly, just now getting the idea. "Will you come up on September first with Dad to see the property and all I've done on it? Bring Jennifer and the boys. Stay the long weekend."

"We'd love to come. I'll check with Jennifer to make sure we're free."

"Thanks," she said, hoping he knew she was thanking him for more than just agreeing to come.

"No problem. I really gotta go now."

"Go. Have fun." She hung up and sat with her eyes closed, promising herself just one minute more before she got up to make more cold calls.

Three more weeks. That was all she had to make this place look so amazing Dad wouldn't turn down the opportunity to go into the hotel business.

Or, another way to look at it, she had three more weeks to find an investor and business partner so she'd have no more need of her father's money.

The second option was much more appealing. She'd sooner give part ownership away to a stranger than lose the property entirely. And, if her dad eventually came around, she could tell the investor "no thanks" before they signed anything. Still, having someone on the line would make her feel so much better.

She glanced at the clock. Just half an hour left in the business day. Enough time for one more call, at least.

Determined that this would be the call that secured the hotel's and her own future, she pushed to her feet and headed to the kitchen where she'd left her notes.

She quickly flipped through her notepad until she got to her list of potential investors and, without stopping to give herself time to chicken out, she dialed the next number on the list.

By five o'clock she admitted defeat. For today.

As she was crossing out the last name on her list, her phone rang in her hand.

Thinking it was one of the investors returning her call, she pasted on a smile and answered.

"Aloha! We're back," came a voice that was definitely not an investor.

"Liv!" Smiling more sincerely, Inara went to pour herself an iced tea to take out on the porch so she could enjoy the last heat of the day as she talked to her sister. "How was Maui? Did the kids snorkel?"

They chatted about the trip and Inara's progress on the hotel as she sat on the cushioned porch swing and propped her feet on the wooden railing, enjoying the heat and fresh air. Summer in the islands was perfection.

"Oh hey, I had a message waiting when I got back from the artist we commissioned to do Duncan Campbell's statue," Olivia said. "The clay form is finished so I'm going there on Saturday to check it out, make sure it's what we had in mind before he proceeds with the wax and bronze. Want to come with?"

She'd forgotten all about the park dedication in October. Thinking of it made her feel squirmy. The last thing she wanted to do was publicly honor a man she now knew was a murderer. But how could she stop it now? "Um, sure. As it happens I'll be in town anyway. Meeting the boyfriend's family." Another thing that made her feel squirmy.

"Boyfriend? How long was I gone?"

Glad for the change of subject, Inara brought her sister up-to-date on her private life.

"I'm happy you have someone," Olivia said when Inara finished the story. "You deserve to be happy."

Something in her voice, maybe the love Inara could hear in it, reminded her of their mom. So much this summer was reminding her of her mom, and she still hadn't decided if it was cathartic or painful. Maybe both. "Thanks, Liv."

"So how's your sleeve?"

It was an abrupt change of topic, but she went with it. "Good. We've learned a few things about the woman who made it but there's still a lot we don't know."

"Like what?"

"Well, like the fact that there is a woman embroidered on the sleeve who is in the water with bodies and demons, and she's smiling. What's up with that?"

"Hmm. That is strange."

"I'm thinking she's taunting someone because she lived when everyone else died."

"Who would she be taunting?"

Oops. She had to watch herself or she'd say something she wasn't supposed to. Liv didn't know what Duncan Campbell did and she wasn't going to find out. "Oh, I don't know," Inara answered vaguely. Then, eager to end the call before she slipped again, she said, "I've gotta go, Liv. I'll call you about the statue meeting when I get into town."

She hung up before her sister could get another word in. Dropping her phone onto the table beside her, she covered her face with her hands.

God, this was getting to be too much. The secrets, the evasions, remembering who knew what and what she could and couldn't say, worrying about the future of her hotel, the emotional roller coaster from it all. It was enough to make her want to stop. Stop everything. Stop sleeve research, stop work on the hotel, stop dating the man she was lying to. Everything. It was too much.

A cry sounded overhead, and she looked up to see the mother eagle soaring toward her nest in a heartbreakingly blue sky framed by Mount Constitution on one side and the house and the huge evergreens on the others. The sight touched a place deep inside her, soothing her battered soul.

She needed this place. No matter what more they learned or what happened with the hotel, she would forever stay connected to the island. It was the only place where, despite everything, she felt whole.

# Chapter Twenty-One

*Sunday, August 12—present day*
*Beacon Hill, Seattle*

Open it," Daniel said from behind the wheel of his Volvo. His gaze left the road to meet hers, and in his eyes she saw mischief. "You're not going to believe it."

Wondering what he was up to, Inara turned to the blue file folder he'd dropped on her lap. They were on their way to his mother's house on Beacon Hill, where Inara was going to meet her, his grandmother, and his sister, Cassie. She was terrified they were making a mistake, moving too fast, but he kept telling her not to worry.

It was all she could do to keep her hands from shaking, and she had to pee. "Maybe we should save this for later."

He reached across the console and grabbed her hand. "It'll be okay, I promise. They're going to love you."

"Do you do this often? Bring women home to meet your family?"

He squeezed her hand, then released it to grab the wheel again and navigate a turn. The sun slanted through the windows and bounced off his Ray-Bans. "I admit it's a significant step in my culture to introduce someone you're dating to your family. It's often not done until, well, marriage is being discussed."

She must have made a noise, despite trying to hold in the panic his words caused, because he smiled at her teasingly. "Calm down, I don't have a ring in my pocket." He turned the radio off. "That may be how people of my culture usually do things, but my family has always been more relaxed. Cassie and I bring people home for dinner all the time."

Was that supposed to make her feel better?

"I can't wait for you to meet my mom," he went on before she could say anything. "You're a lot like her, you know. You both are absolutely fearless, and when you get knocked down, you always get back up again. She fought like hell to get to where she is, just like you're doing with the hotel."

That left her tongue-tied. She still hadn't come up with a response when Daniel continued, "I should probably warn you about my grandmother, though. She may come across as... judgmental. It's not personal. It's just her way of testing to see how serious you are about me."

And there was the nausea again. "Thanks for the warning." She studied his profile for a quiet moment. "I am, you know."

"You are what?"

"Serious about you."

His head jerked toward her, then turned back to the road. A slow grin spread across his face, deepening the lines around his mouth. Similar lines crinkled around his eye, partly visible behind his sunglasses. "Then you'll be able to handle my grandmother with no problem."

Inara dropped her chin and pretended to look at the closed folder on her lap. She hadn't known what she'd expected when she'd said that to him, but it sure as heck had been more than *you'll be able to handle Grandma.*

To hide her awkwardness, she opened the folder and found a black-and-white picture of a teenaged Chinese boy dressed in period garb like in those booths at the fair. Only, in this picture, the boy wasn't dressed like a cowboy. Instead he wore the dark pants, jacket, and bowler hat typical of working-class men of the late nineteenth century. Something about the boy seemed familiar, but she couldn't place him. "Who is this?"

He pulled to a stop at a light and looked at her like he was waiting for something. "It's Yan-Tao McElroy."

"Seriously?" Inara gasped as her gaze tore back to the photograph. The young man stood proudly, his shoulders back, his hands folded in front of his waist. His chin was lifted stubbornly, and he seemed to be staring at the photographer with a challenge in his eyes. Was it simple teenage rebellion, or was it an attitude he'd had to adopt to get through the life he'd been given?

What sort of life was that?

She looked closer. The boy was a teenager. At least thirteen. That meant he'd lived. He'd lived beyond his years on Orcas Island. Duncan didn't kill him.

Relief flooded through her, making her light-headed. "Where did you find it?"

The light turned green and Daniel accelerated through the intersection. "Remember Joseph's sister in Tacoma? We tracked down the family—Bascomb was their name—and found the woman's granddaughter still living in Tacoma. She said her mother told her stories of traveling by steamer to Orcas Island every summer where she and her twin sister played with their young Asian cousin."

Inara's heart swelled. "So they hadn't been left all alone after Joseph died."

"Well, not necessarily," Daniel hedged. He flipped on the blinker and turned onto a residential street. "The granddaughter was certain no Chinese person had ever been inside her grandmother's home. In fact, her grandfather was a member of Tacoma's Committee of Fifteen, the group responsible for driving all Chinese out of Tacoma in 1885. Some believe they were also responsible for stirring up the trouble in Seattle the following year."

"If that's true, the couple must have hated that Joseph married a Chinese woman."

Daniel nodded, his profile grim. "Exactly. Anyway, the granddaughter was told that her mother's cousin and aunt had died in the boating accident with her uncle."

"But obviously he didn't." She lifted the photograph as evidence.

Daniel said nothing until he'd pulled the car smoothly into position along the curb in front of a Craftsman bungalow with a well-tended yard. "Joseph's sister lied to her family. I thought the story sounded fishy, so I had my team look at records from local orphanages and children's homes. That's where we found him."

"Where?"

"At the Washington State Reform School in Chehalis." Silence enveloped them like a bubble as he killed the motor. "They housed juvenile delinquents and orphans ages eight to eighteen. From what I read, it seemed to be a good school. They even taught kids trades like carpentry and farming, along with regular school curriculum and Christianity."

"So he was orphaned. Does that mean Mei Lien died with Joseph?"

"I thought of that and went back and read all the reports from the accident, and I have to conclude that she didn't. I think she had a different ending."

"Something bad happened to her."

Daniel's voice was low when he answered, "Yeah, maybe."

A knock sounded on Inara's window, making her jump. She turned to find a smiling woman about her age with long, straight black hair waving to them through the glass.

"It's Cass. Come on." Daniel jumped from the car and quickly rounded it to pull his sister into a hug.

Inara had to physically shake her head to transition her thoughts to the present. She tucked Yan-Tao's picture into her bag, then got out of the car.

"Cass, I'd like you to meet Inara," Daniel said to his sister when Inara joined them. He kept his arm around Cassie's shoulders. "Inara, this is my sister, Cassie."

Inara stuck out her hand. "It's good to meet you. Your brother has told me a lot about you."

"He lies." Cassie laughed as she shook Inara's hand. "I want to hear about your hotel. Daniel says it's amazing what you've done to it in such a short time."

"That was sweet," Inara said to Daniel as she took his offered hand. Then to Cassie, "I have pictures, if you're interested. But what about you? Daniel says you're in the middle of a tough case. How's that going?"

At the mention of work, a subtle change came over Cassie, transforming her from playful sister to intimidating litigator. In contrast to the serious expression on her face, she shrugged. "My client is trying to get custody of his two kids from his ex-wife who left them alone for three hours in a hot car parked outside a dive bar. It should be cut-and-dried, but it's become messy." She shook her head and spread her lips into a wide smile. "But let's not talk about that."

She stepped between them and latched onto their arms, pulling them toward the house. "Mom and Grandma probably have their noses pressed to the glass, trying to get a look at you, Inara. Let's go put them out of their misery."

At that, the nerves in Inara's stomach started jumping twice as fast as before. Daniel must have sensed her discomfort because the moment they stepped onto the tiled entryway, his arm came around her and he pulled her tightly against him.

The house smelled of lemons and something baking. She barely had time to register the earth-toned living room before Daniel whisked her through the empty kitchen and out a sliding glass door to the backyard.

A slim black-haired woman standing at the barbecue grill with tongs in her hand turned as they came outside. She flashed a welcoming smile. "Daniel, you're here!"

She dropped the tongs onto the table and hurried over to them with her arms held out. As she pulled Daniel into a hug, Inara smelled lilies. Daniel's mother was about the same height as Inara and dressed in pressed khaki capri pants and a light-blue blouse. Her chocolate-brown eyes were curious as they landed on her. "And you must be Inara. Welcome. I'm Margaret."

As Inara shook her hand and thanked her for the dinner invitation, she couldn't help but notice how gracefully Margaret Chin moved, completely at ease with herself and everyone around her.

"Let me introduce you to my grandmother," Daniel said, leading her with a hand on her back toward a teak patio table where an older woman sat slicing lemons.

"*Năinai*, this is Inara. Inara, Vera Chin, my grandmother."

Since the tiny woman didn't budge from her seat, Inara rounded the table and held out her hand, which the white-haired woman reluctantly shook. "I'm honored to meet you."

"Hmph." With shoulders stooped, Vera turned back to the lemons.

Inara shot a glance at Daniel. He just smiled and shrugged as if to say that was how his grandmother normally acted, which did little to put her at ease. She rejoined Daniel at his side of the table and took the seat he pulled out for her. Vera's eyes shot darts at her before turning back to the lemons.

"I hope you like salmon, Inara," Margaret said to her as she joined them, tongs again in hand. "We thought about making you a traditional Chinese meal like what we serve in my restaurants, but decided instead to take advantage of the Chinook being in season."

"Love it. I haven't had any yet this year."

"You'll have to try Mom's Toisan Clay Pot Chicken sometime soon, though," Daniel said as he squeezed his mother's free hand affectionately. "Mom's is the best. It takes a whole day to make."

Eager to please, and because it was true, Inara smiled and said,

"I've had it, actually. It's excellent. My father often entertains clients at Toisan, Mrs. Chin. My whole family loves your restaurant."

"Call me Margaret, dear. Vera, those lemons are perfect. Will you dice these cucumbers too?" She turned back to Inara. "Who is your father? Maybe I know him."

Inara tensed, but tried to hide it by looking down at her lap and brushing at a nonexistent wrinkle. "He's Charles Erickson, of Premier Maritime Group."

Margaret considered the name for a moment. "Of course I know who he is, but I don't think I've met him. Didn't I just read somewhere that PMG was founded by the famous Duncan Campbell?"

Inara felt the smile on her face freeze. She really didn't want to think about Duncan tonight and worry about keeping her lies straight. "Yes. My roots run deep here in Seattle."

Then, deliberately looking at the barbecue where fragrant smoke streamed from an opening on the side, she said, "The salmon smells heavenly. How do you prepare it?"

Margaret returned to the grill and expertly flipped the salmon, causing a puff of smoke to fill the air. "I soak alder wood chips in water and place them in a foil packet on the fire so the smoke flavors the salmon, which I've brushed with garlic butter."

Inara's mouth was already watering from the aroma. "I wish you would have let me bring something to contribute to the meal."

Vera spoke for the first time. "You are a guest. You don't cook."

"Would you like some wine, Inara?" Cassie said as she came outside carrying a tray of glasses and saving Inara from having to answer grumpy grandma.

"Yes, please."

"Tell us about yourself, Inara," Margaret said as she accepted a glass from her daughter and sat down in the chair at the head of the table. "Daniel says you're renovating your family's estate in the San Juans?"

"Yes. I'm turning it into a boutique hotel."

"Which island?"

"Orcas."

"Oh, I love Orcas Island." Margaret relaxed into her chair and sipped her wine. "Kids, do you remember that time we went camping at Cascade Lake on Orcas? Daniel, I think you were about eleven and, Cassie, you were six."

Conversation turned to adventures in the San Juan Islands intermingled with questions they asked Inara about the hotel. She purposely avoided mentioning its precarious financial state and described the hotel as though there was no doubt it would open next summer. Despite her earlier nerves, she found herself relaxing and enjoying everyone, even grumpy grandma.

Later, when they were all seated around the patio table with plates full of salmon, potatoes, rolls, and three kinds of salad, Margaret lifted her wineglass. "In honor of our new friend, Inara, whom we are very happy to get to know."

Inara drank, feeling at once honored and uncomfortable, wondering if she should make some sort of toast back to her hosts. Before she could decide, Cassie spoke up. "Tell us how you two met. Wasn't it on campus?"

"Are you taking Daniel's class, Inara?" Margaret asked between bites.

"No," Daniel answered for her. "Inara came to me with a research question and we instantly hit it off, didn't we?" He squeezed her knee under the table.

She smiled at him and teased, "Yes, we did, apart from you trying to blow me off as a needy student."

Cassie's laugh filled the yard. "That doesn't surprise me. His head was probably still in dynastic China, or whatever his lecture was on that day."

Daniel looked chagrined so Inara patted his shoulder and smiled.

Margaret came to her son's rescue. "So what is it you are researching?"

She was surprised Daniel hadn't already told them. When she

sent him a questioning look, he just shrugged, so she answered Margaret. "An amazing embroidered sleeve I found hidden under the stairs on my family's property." Then she told them the story of finding the sleeve and how she found Daniel through an article he'd written.

Together she and Daniel described the sleeve and what they knew of Mei Lien.

"So she just disappeared?" Cassie asked as she stacked their empty plates. "Her husband died and her son was sent to an orphanage. No one knows where she went?"

Daniel nodded as he sat back and crossed his hands on his belly. "An islander wrote in his diary of seeing the boy leave the island with his aunt and household belongings sometime around Thanksgiving of the same year the father died. No mention was made of the mother. The diary's author said he was jubilant to see the 'dirty Oriental' go."

At the derogatory term, Daniel's family members scowled, Cassie most of all. But when Cassie spoke up, Inara realized her scowl hadn't been caused by the racist term, but by something else entirely. "You mean to tell me the aunt took him from his home and ditched him at an orphanage?" Her perfectly formed eyebrows disappeared beneath her bangs. "What kind of person does that?"

Inara cocked her head to the side, struck by the realization that she'd been so focused on Mei Lien all this time she hadn't stopped to consider how terrifying it must have been for the child. How abandoned he must have felt. And betrayed.

Nate's son, Luke—Inara's adorably ornery nephew—was the same age as Yan-Tao was when all this happened, around seven. Inara would sooner slit her own wrists than see harm come to that innocent little boy. She would never, under any circumstances, dump him at an orphanage.

Because she wanted to look at the boy's face again herself, Inara asked the group, "Want to see the picture of Yan-Tao that Daniel found?" She reached for her purse.

"It's the last evidence we've been able to find of him," Daniel said as Inara set the blue folder on the table and flipped it open. "The very next year after the picture was taken he wasn't listed in any of the school's records."

Yan-Tao looked so sad. Inara handed the picture to Margaret but looked at Daniel. "You didn't tell me that. What do you think happened to him?"

He shrugged and leaned back in his chair. "He was fourteen. In those days that was old enough to get a job and support himself. He could have gone anywhere. We're still looking."

Margaret handed the picture to Vera. "Poor kid."

Vera scowled down at the picture. "This isn't some poor kid. This is my father-in-law."

Daniel shook his head. "That's not your father-in-law, Grandmother. That's Yan-Tao McElroy."

Cassie stopped clearing dishes and moved behind her grand-mother's chair to see the photo.

Vera pursed her lips. The warning look she shot her grandson clearly said a good grandson would never correct his grand-mother. "You're wrong. This is my father-in-law, Ken Chin, as a young man. I'm certain of it."

At hearing the name, Inara froze. When she turned to Daniel, she saw he looked just as thunderstruck as she felt. Ken. Kenneth. The name was on Yan-Tao's birth certificate as his middle name. Could they possibly be the same person?

*Ridiculous*, she decided. It would be too much of a coincidence.

Slowly, Daniel's head turned toward his grandmother, his eyes huge. "Do you have a picture of your father-in-law as a young man?"

Vera's eyebrows lifted and her head tilted to the side as though she was dealing with a simpleton. She slapped the picture in her hand with the backs of her fingers. "It's right here."

Daniel's expression didn't change. "No, another picture. One we can look at to compare."

With a look of total disgust for her grandson, Vera pushed to her feet and turned to go inside the house. It was the first time Inara had seen her standing, and she realized she must be no taller than five feet. For an eighty-five-year-old woman, she moved surprisingly quickly. "Well," she snapped when she reached the glass sliding door. "Are you coming?"

They all glanced at one another, then, as one, they got to their feet to follow Vera inside. As she rounded the table toward the sliding door, Inara grabbed the photo of Yan-Tao that Vera had left on the table.

Vera led them up the stairs to the second-floor landing where open doors showed four bedrooms and a shared bathroom. Inara easily identified what had been Daniel's room by the poster of Ken Griffey Jr. and another of a flashy red corvette hanging on the walls. She was dying to go inside the room and get a better glimpse of who Daniel had been as a boy, but he was already pulling down the folding ladder that led to the attic.

"Go on," the tiny woman ordered her grandson, waving her hands impatiently. "In the chest in the corner."

"Do you need some help?" Inara called as she dubiously eyed the darkness Daniel had disappeared into. Spiders she could handle. Mice, not so much.

"Nah," Daniel's voice called down. "I found it."

They heard a creaking sound followed by a thump. A second later Daniel reappeared holding a green, cracked leather photo album. "There looks to be some interesting stuff in that chest. Is it all Ken's?"

Vera nodded as she accepted the album Daniel handed down to her. "Yes. When he passed away, we cleaned out his apartment and found the chest in his closet. I planned to go through it one day, but forgot all about it until now."

Daniel disappeared again as Vera flipped open the photo album. Without a word she turned the open album toward Inara. "See for yourself. That's the boy in your picture. I'm sure of it."

Inara took the album and peered closely at the grainy, sepia-toned photograph Vera's arthritic finger pointed to. Margaret and Cassie gathered on either side of her.

It was rough around the edges, like it had been carried around for years before finally ending up in this album. In the print she could make out a group of five Chinese men standing next to a machine of some sort that was loaded with dirt. In the background a large Victorian house teetered precariously atop what looked to be a desert butte but was clearly in Seattle because the familiar view of Elliott Bay spread out behind them with the Olympic Mountain range in the distance.

"He's the one on the left, holding the shovel," Vera told them with a harrumph as she crossed her arms. "They're working the Denny Regrade. It was his first job in America after he arrived here from China. That must have been, oh, around 1909. The same year as the Alaska-Yukon-Pacific Exposition, which he attended." Pride filled her voice. "He borrowed a suit to go and loved telling stories about the half-naked men from Polynesia and the grand exhibit from China."

The Denny Regrade was something Inara had learned about in school. After the great Seattle fire of 1889, which completely destroyed the main business part of town, the founding fathers, Duncan Campbell among them, decided the steep hills of the city needed to be lowered and the mudflats that were in the city center at that time, now Pioneer Square, needed to be filled. The regrade effectively made the city much easier to navigate. Existing buildings, like the one perched atop the butte in the picture, were either moved to other locations or destroyed.

Inara had to admit, the boy on the left looked a lot like the boy in the picture she'd brought upstairs with her.

Cassie bent over the photo, her head swiveling back and forth from it to the picture of Yan-Tao McElroy. "They look so much alike," she said with a note of disbelief in her voice as she looked up at her grandmother. "But it can't possibly be the same person. You said Great-Grandfather spent his childhood in China. In Beijing."

Vera drew herself up. "He did. He was the youngest son of a fourth-rank civil official. His connections allowed him into America during the time of the Exclusion Act as a merchant. He opened his first store not long after that picture was taken." Her eyes darted to the side. "He didn't like to talk about his past, but I learned these things from my husband who was very proud of his father."

"He could have lied," Cassie said, echoing Inara's thoughts.

Vera gasped and slammed her palms on her narrow hips, making Inara very glad she hadn't been the one to voice the thought. "Chins do not lie!"

Cassie just shrugged, unaffected by the reprimand, as she stepped back from the album and cast a curious glance up the ladder. "What's taking Daniel so long?"

"Daniel, come down here and give us your opinion," Margaret called up the stairs. She cast a worried glance between her daughter and mother-in-law before walking to the base of the ladder and looking up. "Daniel?"

Daniel's face reappeared at the dark opening. He wasn't smiling. "Come look at this stuff. It's amazing."

Margaret looked questioningly at Inara, then Cassie and Vera before turning back to Daniel. "Who? All of us?"

Daniel didn't explain. He just jerked his head in a distracted nod and disappeared again. With a shrug Cassie stepped past her mother and climbed quickly up. Margaret raised her eyebrows to Vera. "Do you want me to help you?"

Vera shook her head then shuffled over to a chair propped against the wall beside a sofa table displaying family photos. "I'll wait here. My old knees can't take the climb."

Margaret shot Inara a look that confirmed her suspicion that Vera's knees were perfectly healthy and the woman simply didn't want to climb into the attic. "Shall we?"

Inara bit back her grin and followed Margaret up the rickety ladder. In the attic she saw a pool of light coming from a bare lightbulb tacked to the rafters. Daniel and Cassie knelt beside a battered wooden trunk and were lifting items out of it and placing them on the floor around them.

"If Ken Chin and Yan-Tao McElroy were really the same person, then we might find clues to what happened to Mei Lien in all this stuff." Daniel kept pulling items out and piling them on the floor around him. "Help me look at everything."

Clothing, loose and framed pictures, a leather dog collar, an old pair of shoes, and various other trinkets whispered of untold stories. A carved wooden boat, clearly a child's toy, lay half-hidden by a worn and tattered blanket. Curious, Inara joined them on the floor and reached for the boat. It was hand-carved and varnished to be waterproof. Years of use had darkened the wood and rounded its corners. She could almost picture young Yan-Tao playing with it on her beach.

Just then Cassie gasped, drawing Inara's attention to where she pointed at the tattered blanket. Beneath the dirt and grime, Inara could make out intricate embroidery work that looked very familiar.

As Daniel lifted it, the cloth fell open from its folds to reveal more embroidery. In fact, every inch Inara could see was covered in embroidery.

In shock she looked at Daniel. "Could that be...?" She couldn't finish the question. It was too unbelievable.

Daniel gently unfolded the rest of the cloth and spread it open on the floor away from the other items and trunk. "Oh my God."

Inara couldn't speak. Too many thoughts were flying through her mind at once to allow even one of them to form into words. All she could do was stare at the intricately embroidered robe, its left sleeve missing.

The implications slammed into her, causing the attic to spin and the air in her lungs to dissipate.

Her ancestor hadn't just murdered hundreds of innocent people: he'd murdered people directly related to Daniel.

And if she told him and his family the truth now, it would destroy their relationship. His family would sue her family, ruining all of them

He'd hate her. Hate her very existence and everything she came from because her family had launched their fortune on the blood that now flowed through his veins. And worse, she'd known about the murders and had kept it from him.

But she had to protect her family and protect her mother's memory. And she had to do it at the expense of her own relationship.

She swallowed, working hard to keep the bile down that now pushed into her throat. *Deep breath. Deep breath.*

"This looks like a deed to a house," Margaret said, interrupting Inara's panic attack. "And look, Inara, it's on Orcas Island." She held the sheaf of yellowed papers out to her.

Trying to keep her hands from shaking, Inara took the papers and skimmed the legalese printed there as an invisible fist squeezed her skull. "It's my house," she croaked. No wonder the woman at the county records office hadn't found a transfer of deed to her house. The deed had been stashed with a little boy's belongings all these years. And, oh God, this was proof that Yan-Tao had become Ken Chin. And it was also proof that Rothesay didn't belong to her. It belonged to the Chin family.

"Let me see that." Cassie got to her feet and took the papers from Inara's hand. After a moment of silently reading, she looked up. "Grandfather Ken was Yan-Tao McElroy."

The three Chins started talking at once while Inara gave into the force pulling her down. She sank to her knees on the floor, unable to do anything but watch the emotions of the family before her as her own strangled her.

It was Daniel who noticed her first. He glanced at her with a laugh that immediately changed to a look of concern. "Inara, what's wrong?"

"Rothesay," was all she could manage.

It took him a moment, but she saw on his face when it clicked. "You're worried this means you'll lose Rothesay." He turned to his sister. "Cass, is this deed legal?"

She glanced from Daniel to Inara with concern before she placed a comforting hand on Inara's shoulder. "Oh, Inara, don't worry. This was the legal deed, but with adverse possession law, the property fully belongs to you now. We can't take it from you, nor would we want to."

Margaret and Daniel seconded her reassurance, but Inara couldn't help but feel she wasn't the rightful owner of Rothesay. It had always belonged to Mei Lien and still did, no matter her fate.

# Chapter Twenty-Two

*Sunday, August 12—present day*
*Chin residence, Seattle*

I wish I had the sleeve with me," Inara muttered even though she didn't mean a word she was saying.

Daniel wanted to study the robe further, so they'd all come downstairs to the Chin's dining room table, which Daniel had draped with a clean sheet from his mother's linen closet.

He shot her a grin bright with excitement. "Not to worry. I have pictures in my car." His wide-eyed gaze returned to the robe as he dug in his jeans pocket and pulled out his car keys. "Cass, go get them for me, will you? They're in the briefcase in the trunk."

Cassie grumbled but did as her brother asked, returning a short time later with Daniel's briefcase, which she set on the dining chair closest to her brother.

"I don't see why you're all so excited about this dirty thing. I would have thrown it out had I known it was there," Vera grumbled from the corner, though Inara noticed she had positioned herself where she'd see and hear everything.

Inara too wished Vera had thrown it out.

The thought made her feel like such a traitor.

"It's so filthy." Cassie leaned over the robe not touching it. "Surely he didn't wear this thing with only one sleeve? He'd have looked ridiculous."

"If his mother gave it to him, maybe he carried it around like a security blanket." Margaret rubbed Cassie's back. "Remember the one you wore to threads?"

Daniel said nothing as he popped open his briefcase and pulled out a stack of photographs and a pair of cotton gloves. He slid the gloves on and leaned over the robe, ignoring the photos for now.

"The style of the robe is just as I suspected. It's that of a Dragon robe, but without the rank badge or dragons," Daniel said, though Inara wasn't sure if he was talking to them or to himself.

She swallowed hard and forced herself to focus on the robe and not the fear raging through her.

The robe had what she'd call a Mandarin collar. The left side of the robe crossed over the right and attached under the right arm with toggles made out of braided embroidery threads. The right sleeve tapered down to a cuff that partially covered the wearer's hand. *Horse-hoof*, Daniel had called it, just like the cuff on her sleeve.

Stains and tears dotted the fabric. It was so worn and yellowed she had no idea if it had originally matched the vibrant blue silk of her sleeve, although she knew it must have.

Even through the degradation of the fabric, she could clearly see the detail of the images embroidered there. With thread that had once surely been bright with color but was now dulled and dirty, the picture on the right sleeve was of a white man holding a darker-skinned baby. Both were smiling so wide, the man's white teeth showed. Farther up, near the shoulder, the baby had grown to a young boy who stood with one hand on the head of a black dog. Both waited on the porch of a house and watched as the white man worked a horse-pulled plow.

Inara felt goose bumps prick her arms as she recognized

Dahlia's section of the house without the rest of the manor attached to it.

The boy had to be Yan-Tao, watching Joseph plow the very same plot of land where her kitchen garden now lay.

"As you can see," Daniel told them, completely caught up in his inspection, "the bottom ten inches are scenes from what must be Imperial Beijing during the time of the Qing Dynasty. See that building there? It looks like the outside of the main gate to the Forbidden City. Nothing like that existed in America at the time. If, as evidence suggests, it was Mei Lien who embroidered this robe, then we can assume this is where she documented their family history rather than personal experience, since she was born here in Seattle."

Above that section and up to the halfway point where the wearer's waist would be were scenes that were much more rural. Daniel pointed to a row of what appeared to be shacks or huts made of wood planking. "If this were to come across my desk without my knowing the history, I would swear this is depicting a rural village in China. Look at the Chinese faces on these men gathered around the table set in front of what looks to be a general store."

"What about this person?" Inara asked, pointing to a man in an American- or British-style black suit and hat walking down the opposite side of the street.

"Again, if I didn't know Mei Lien made this, I would believe he was a businessman or foreign ambassador visiting China. But it's got to be early Seattle, before paved streets and brick buildings."

"Look at these trees on the ridge up above the town." Cassie pointed higher up the robe. "I assume Seattle was nothing but forest before the city was built?"

"Think of the historical significance," Margaret breathed. "Not just for our family, but for Seattle. It's astounding."

"If that's Seattle, then up here must be Orcas Island," Inara mused aloud, then instantly regretted it. The more they learned, the closer Daniel would be to connecting the dots and knowing her family was responsible for the horror depicted on the left sleeve. She had to clench her hands into tight fists to keep from grabbing the robe and running from the house.

Daniel moved around the table to get a better look at the chest portion of the robe. "I think you're right. Look at this man. It's the same face as on the right sleeve and done with such detail that he's obviously important. He's got his arm around the Chinese woman who, if I'm not mistaken, looks familiar to me. Her face could be the same as the one on the drowning woman on Inara's sleeve."

"So that's Joseph and Mei Lien?" Margaret asked. Inara held her breath for the answer.

"I think it is."

Daniel's family grew silent as they looked for the first time at the couple who, it was starting to seem likely, were their ancestors. Inara searched the pictures for images of Rothesay.

They were everywhere. The curve of the beach and even the types of rocks and white shells. The steep rise of an evergreen tree—covered mountain rising up behind the apple orchard. Astoundingly, even the slick head of a seal sitting offshore staring at the woman alone on the beach.

And...the cabin.

There was no mistaking the cabin. It looked exactly like the one she and her siblings played around as children. The same cabin that today was being reclaimed by the forest, its roof fallen in, moss blanketing the log walls.

"Look on the shoulder there, right where the left sleeve was cut off." Margaret pointed but was careful not to touch the fragile garment. "It looks like the threads are gradually darkening, like a cloudy sky or deep water."

They all gathered close to the left side of the robe where the sleeve was missing to see what she pointed to. Just above what looked like a perfect replication of Dahlia's house, the sky indeed looked turbulent with a storm rolling in from the direction of the missing sleeve. It was also the same direction where the original Campbell property had been. That, surely, was no coincidence.

The stormy, dark sky matched what she remembered from the sleeve.

Even after finding the deed to her house, a small part of her wanted to believe it was a coincidence. But the proof was unmistakable. Daniel was a direct descendant of the people her own ancestor had murdered in cold blood.

Mei Lien—or maybe it was Yan-Tao?—had hidden the sleeve as evidence against the family responsible so that one day justice could be dealt. Now Inara had to decide what to do about it.

"Inara, could you hand me those pictures?" She jerked at hearing her name and looked up to find Daniel pointing to the stack he'd left on the table by her hip.

Could her legs carry her that far? He was only three steps away, but they were shaking uncontrollably. She must.

She swallowed hard, and then managed to do as Daniel asked with only a slight falter in her step. When Daniel's gloved fingers touched hers, she met his gaze and found a tender smile there just for her.

Her eyes smarted with tears, surprising her, so she quickly looked down at the robe, hoping Daniel would think she was just as eager as everyone else to learn more.

He flipped through the photographs until he found one he wanted and carefully set the rest aside. Blowing out a breath that revealed the nerves he must be feeling, he laid the picture on the table where the left sleeve should be.

The embroidered story transitioned seamlessly from the robe onto the photograph.

He opened his briefcase again and pulled out a magnifying glass. Without a word of explanation, he leaned over the seam between robe and photo and studied it for several minutes.

When he drew himself fully upright again, he had a look

of wonder on his face. "It matches. The cuts on both seem to match, though I'd like to compare the actual sleeve to the robe to be sure. But the jagged cuts match. It's as if someone took scissors to it and chopped off the sleeve for some reason."

"What would make someone do that?" Margaret wondered aloud, though everyone in the room knew there was no answer.

Everyone, that was, except Inara. She could hazard a very good guess why Mei Lien had chopped off that particular section and hidden it away.

Sure, she could have decided to spare her son the horror of what had happened, but Inara had a feeling it was something else entirely.

Mei Lien had known her enemy, Duncan Campbell, was about to take her house from her, however he'd managed it. Mei Lien's husband was dead and Chinese people at that time weren't allowed to own property in Washington State. Maybe Yan-Tao could have inherited the house and land since he was half-white, but how would Mei Lien have supported him to adulthood?

No, Inara's gut said Mei Lien had purposely hidden the sleeve in that house, probably for a Campbell descendant to find. She'd wanted the truth known. She'd wanted Campbell's family to suffer as her family had suffered.

Maybe not publicly, because what Campbell descendant would knowingly broadcast such damaging family secrets? But privately, the family would be torn apart.

Just as Inara was being torn apart right now.

Mei Lien hadn't known that the person who found the sleeve would be romantically involved with her very own descendant.

But she was, and if she was smart, Inara would end it now before her family was ruined. End it before Daniel learned more and was hurt by the knowledge of her lies.

But how could she end it? The Chin family had just as much of a right, if not more, than her to pursue the research even if she pulled out.

Vera, who had been silent through all of this, moved around the table to Inara's side. Inara took a deep breath and steeled herself for whatever the woman might say to her.

"I want to see where you found the sleeve. I want to come to your house."

"Vera, don't be rude," admonished Margaret, but Inara noticed it was only halfhearted.

Inara looked at Daniel and on his face she saw an eagerness shining there that made her heart twist. Swallowing hard to control the acid climbing her throat, she nodded. "I would be honored to have you come up and see the house. It once belonged to your family, after all."

"Next weekend?" Vera pressed.

Inara noticed Margaret made no reprimand this time. "Sure. Next weekend works."

At that everyone started talking at once, discussing work schedules and how to shift things around for the trip up to Orcas. Inara looked at the faces around the table. Each one held various similarities to the others and, now she knew, those features could have come from Mei Lien.

Mei Lien—the woman likely murdered by Inara's own great-great-great-grandfather.

Margaret, Cassie, and Vera had their heads together, all three talking at once about the robe, the hotel, their newfound ancestry.

When she looked across the table at Daniel, she found him looking back at her and her heart lurched. Then he smiled and his eyes filled with a tenderness that bespoke of the special bond he no doubt felt between them because of this shared history.

But there was something else there that scared her even more. It looked like love.

She looked away, ashamed.

# Chapter Twenty-Three

*Thursday, August 16—present day*
*Rothesay Estate, Orcas Island*

Over the four days since learning that Yan-Tao McElroy and Ken Chin were one and the same person, Inara had buried herself in work on the hotel. She'd come home from Seattle and immediately packaged up the sleeve and overnighted it to Daniel so he could have his team do further research on it now that they knew it belonged to his family's robe. And then she'd pushed the sleeve, Mei Lien, Yan-Tao, and even Daniel out of her mind.

She'd told herself it was because she had only two short weeks until her deadline and she had to focus solely on the hotel. In two weeks her dad would come up to inspect everything and then make his decision on whether or not he'd continue to provide funding.

Which he had to do, he had to. She hadn't found another investor. She had to stay hopeful that once her dad saw this place and all the work she'd accomplished, he'd finally believe in her and her vision. And once he did, she'd be free to finish the renovations and set a date for opening next summer.

Thinking of her dad now, only two weeks from the deadline,

she realized she needed to call him, find out if he planned to arrive on Friday of Labor Day weekend, or Saturday.

She'd use the short time between now and then, minus the two days she'd be hosting the Chin family, to finish as much as possible. There was no furniture in any of the guest rooms yet, but carpet would be installed this week, which would go a long way toward making the place feel finished.

She set the paint roller she'd been using in the main floor bathroom back into its tray and headed through the restaurant to the back patio, away from the construction noise. Out here the heat intensified, even in the shade, and she stretched toward the sun, loving the feel of it.

She settled herself on the low stone wall separating patio and grass and punched in her father's office number on her cell.

"Inara? Haven't heard from you in a while." Her father's voice sounded annoyed and distracted, which was normal for the middle of a workday. "What's up?"

"Hi, Dad." She kept her voice light. "I'm calling to see what your plans are for Labor Day weekend. I can't wait for you to see what I've done with the place."

"Labor Day weekend? What are you talking about?" The muffled sound of a hand covering the receiver echoed through the line and she knew he was talking to someone else in the room.

She waited a beat then answered his question. "That's when you're coming up to see the hotel and give me your decision on the loan, remember?" Her stomach cramped. She got up to walk along the length of the patio.

"Nara-girl, I can't. I'll be on a plane to Hong Kong that weekend."

Trying not to lose her temper, she offered, "Well, the following weekend, then. You can come then, right?"

His sigh blew through the phone, telling her exactly what she was afraid of. He wasn't coming at all.

Her whole body felt cold, even standing in the sun, so she wrapped her free arm around herself. "What's going on, Dad?"

"Look, I thought your idea to turn Rothesay into a hotel was brilliant. The work you're doing on the estate this summer will help attract bigger buyers. Hotel chains, resorts. My investment will help you get more from the property in the end."

"I don't want to sell, Dad. I want to run the hotel myself."

"What do you know about running a hotel, Inara? Nothing." He paused, then almost immediately started talking again, his tone cool. "I'm glad you had fun over the summer cleaning the place up, but it's time you get a real job."

Rage burned through her. "Like Starbucks, I suppose?"

"Exactly." He sounded pleased. "Call Lacey at Luxe and get the place listed. The sooner the better."

"I'm not selling." She didn't know how she'd do it, but she'd find an investor. Or at least a loan. Somehow.

"Inara," he snapped. "I don't have the cash to keep supporting you. I'm sorry. The Yŏu Yì deal took more cash to close than I anticipated. Even if I wanted to go into the hotel business with you, I just can't swing it right now."

She had to wait for her heart to get out of her throat before she could speak. "So, that's it?"

"Yes. That's it. I'm calling in the loan."

"Isn't there something you can do? The hotel means a lot to m—"

"Inara, no." His voice cut her off. "I've mentioned it to several associates the past couple months. I think you'll find a buyer quickly."

"Rothesay isn't for sale." She didn't bother to wait for his reply. She punched the off button on her phone and dropped her arm to her side. Unable to move, she did nothing but stand where she was, staring through the trees to the water beyond as a war between tears and rage waged in her chest.

Had he taken her seriously at all, or had he simply humored her all summer, never really intending to give her a chance? He could be lying about the Yǒu Yì deal requiring more cash than he could handle. He could be using the excuse to get her to finally sell the estate and get a job. Like Duncan Campbell, was he looking for the biggest buck?

She scrubbed at her eyes with her fists. She was being ridiculous. All the craziness of this summer was driving her crazy now. Her father loved her. He wanted the best for her. He wouldn't intentionally hurt her this way without a real reason.

But still, it hurt.

The sun was getting too hot, so she turned to go back inside but paused to look at the house.

She'd lost it. Despite the stubborn declaration she'd just made to her father, she didn't have any choice but to put the estate on the market. But not yet. Not until she at least tried one more time to find someone else to help her. Surely she'd think of something.

But, for now, she didn't have the funds to pay her construction workers. Better to tell Tom today to pull his crews out, go home.

Taking a deep breath, she started toward the French doors leading into the restaurant space to find Tom, purposely switching off the part of her that was dying inside.

Later, after the last pickup truck had disappeared through the trees toward the main road, Inara sat on the front steps of Dahlia's house feeling so drained all she could do was stare at the manor. It looked like nothing more than a ghostly shell of a hotel that could have been.

She sat there staring for so long she completely lost track of time. The sound of her cell phone ringing jerked her back to attention.

Her first instinct was to let the call go to voice mail, but then she saw it was Daniel and she realized she needed to hear his voice, hear him tell her she'd be okay.

"Mom and Grandma are so excited for this weekend; it's all they're talking about."

His voice was full of good humor and she suddenly realized

she didn't want to tell him that she'd lost her funding and was likely going to lose the property. She needed to spend some time processing it alone before she could talk with anyone else, even Daniel, about it.

"Will everyone be okay staying in my house since the hotel isn't ready? I have two guest rooms and a pullout couch downstairs."

"That sounds great. Hey, I've got some news about Ken. I mean, Yan-Tao. I still can't believe I'm related to him."

She couldn't keep the pain from her voice much longer. "I look forward to hearing all about it, but I see Tom waving to get my attention. He must need something." She swallowed, trying to ease the lump in her throat that formed with the lie. "I'll call you later, okay?"

"Okay. I've got to call my mom back to coordinate our schedules for Saturday morning." He paused. "This means a lot to my family, Inara. I hope you know that."

"It means a lot to me too. I'll talk to you later." She hung up before her voice cracked under the weight of all she wasn't saying to him.

With nothing left to do, and tired of the empty hotel staring at her, she headed for the water.

The water would soothe her. The solitude would help her figure out what to do next.

# Chapter Twenty-Four

*October 1894*
*McElroy Farm, Orcas Island*

The days that followed Joseph's death became a blur to Mei Lien. She and Yan-Tao went about their chores and did their best to help each other through the day. That first night Mei Lien was again drawn to the water, and she went, knowing Joseph's spirit would be there.

As soon as she'd reached the water, though, panic slammed into her, choking her as surely as the water demons choked her that night long ago when they tried to take her. She'd returned to the house immediately and crawled into bed next to Yan-Tao, promising herself she'd never let her son out of her sight again. She'd never leave him alone.

The next night, she took Yan-Tao with her to the water, and every night after that. The spirits called loudly, demanding she go.

Yan-Tao sat on a boulder and listened to her talk to their ancestors, and he listened to her talk to Joseph. Before long, he joined her at the water's edge. She taught him how to make an offering to the spirits so they might have food to nourish them on their journey to the afterworld. She taught him how to look for signs of Joseph in the animals, in the golden leaves that drifted on the water's surface, and in the water itself.

Together they found Joseph everywhere. He was in the horses that nickered softly to them every morning as if to comfort them in his absence. He was in the fog that drifted through the trees to wrap around their farm like a cocoon. He was in every plank and nail of the house Joseph had built for them to keep them safe and warm.

Life became a numb repetition of chores, meals, and all the tiny moments of remembering. She couldn't sleep. She'd close her eyes and feel the gaping emptiness where Joseph should be, his absence like a missing limb. Instead of battling the loneliness, she gave into it, spending hours every night embroidering her story for her son and, she realized now, for her lost husband.

She was nearly finished. Another year to work on it would be ideal, but she worried she didn't have that long. Her belly ached constantly now, the pulls and twinges fighting each other for her attention. She no longer wanted to eat and only pretended to so Yan-Tao wouldn't ask why she wasn't hungry.

With the embroidery unfinished, she'd cut the embroidered pieces off the frame while she still had the strength and had assembled them into the ceremonial robe Yan-Tao would one day wear. The left sleeve, the most difficult to create because of the story she'd chosen to reveal there, was the only piece left undone. Still, she attached it to the robe.

Weeks passed. The cold western wind swept over the island, freezing the ground and the spring so they had to bring water in every evening for the next day. Though they did their best, the two of them could not bring in all of the crops, and the carrots, squash, potatoes, even the apples on the trees were all rotting or turning black from the frost. The salted meat in the milk house was dwindling rapidly.

She went out to feed the pigs and chickens one morning and found them all dead in their pens, their spilled blood solid on the frozen ground, a sign that the killings had occurred the previous night, before the temperature dropped. She hadn't heard a thing.

The slaughter had been made to look like an animal had done it, with sharp teeth and claws rather than a neat blade, but Mei Lien saw boot prints left in the now-frozen mud. Boot prints that led to Campbell's property.

With Joseph gone, he was taking greater risks to get her land. Fear made her limbs quake, but she managed to go inside and get the shotgun. It never left her side after that.

One month after Joseph left—for she marked time not by the day she learned of his death but by the day he walked off the farm—Mei Lien was in the barn milking the cow, numbly going through the motions as always. Cold wind whistled through the cracks between the logs, reminding her that Joseph had meant to shore it up before winter set in. She'd have to find a way to do it herself. She reached under the cow to give the teat a pull when pain slammed into her.

Waves of agony shot through her body so hard and fast they left her dizzy. Pinpricks of light filled her vision, and nausea rolled through her, causing a sheen of sweat to coat her skin. With a moan, she fell against the cow, but the cow danced aside and Mei Lien felt herself falling forward with no way to stop herself.

She landed on the milk pail, knocking it over as she fell into the straw covering the dirt floor. Pain screamed through her body over and over, and Mei Lien could do nothing but ride it out. She jerked her head to the side just in time to empty her stomach onto the ground. Tears flooded her cheeks. Fear slicked over her body, racking her alternately with sweat and cold.

Her body did not feel like her own. It was ruled by some devilish tormentor. All she could do was hang on and hope she made it through.

She had to make it through. Yan-Tao needed her. She was all he had.

She clung to the image of Yan-Tao's precious face until the nausea and the shaking and the ripping feeling in her belly subsided, leaving her exhausted and aching, but alive.

Leaving the milk to soak into the ground, she started crawling to the barn doors, leaving the shotgun behind. Eventually she made it to the house where Yan-Tao was fast asleep upstairs.

It would be a long night, she knew, for she could no longer deny the truth she'd been hiding from herself. Forget defending her land from Campbell or even preserving food for winter. She had two things to focus on and two things only: one, she had to finish her embroidery; two, she had to make plans that would keep Yan-Tao safe. Soon she'd be forced to do the one thing she'd promised herself she'd never do—leave her child all alone.

She was dying.

By morning Mei Lien had a plan.

Her first thought was to pack up what belongings they could load into the wagon and catch the first transport barge to Victoria, Whatcom, or Port Townsend, where she'd find a Chinese family to adopt Yan-Tao.

She went out to the barn to hitch the horse to the wagon and bring it up to the house, where she could start loading it.

She got as far as the horse's stall when she realized the plan would never work. She couldn't even stand upright, let alone manage a horse pulling a heavy wagon. If she could get the wagon loaded in the first place, which was doubtful.

Crying with frustration and pain, she returned to the house and curled up on the sofa, where she stared at the shadows dancing on the wall from her lantern and thought of her limited options.

She had to act now. She couldn't consign Yan-Tao to the horror of finding his mother's dead body one day soon. He'd be forced to find his own way in the world, forced to defend against Campbell's manipulations. She didn't doubt for a moment what Campbell would do once word got out that she was dead. He'd be over here, claiming the property for himself, doing away with the lone survivor of the family who had lived here. Now that she thought of it, she was surprised he hadn't gotten rid of them both already and taken the property.

She would sooner take Yan-Tao to the afterworld herself than leave him in Campbell's hands.

And that was when she realized what she must do.

As soon as morning light filtered into the room, she forced herself to her feet and shuffled into the kitchen. Since she hadn't undressed last night to go to bed, she didn't have to struggle into her clothes.

"Yan-Tao, time to wake up!" she called up the stairs. As quickly as her exhausted body allowed, she put together a breakfast for Yan-Tao made up of cold rice leftover from last night's dinner mixed with a diced apple. If Joseph had made it home from Port Townsend, she'd have cinnamon to sprinkle on top, but instead she stirred in a spoonful of sugar as a special treat. "Yan-Tao!" she called again.

He clomped down the stairs, rubbing his eyes with his small fists. "*Nǐ hǎo*, Mama."

"*Nǐ hǎo, hǔzǐ*." As he plopped into his chair, she got a good look at his face and saw that it was puffy, his eyes bloodshot with dried tears pooled at the corners and streaking into his hairline. The invisible fist that usually squeezed her abdomen now squeezed her chest, bringing tears to her own eyes.

"Thinking of Father?" she asked softly, knowing the answer.

He nodded but kept his gaze on his rice.

"I think of him too. I miss him." The invisible fist climbed up her throat, choking off her words. She swallowed, but the pressure didn't ease. She squeezed her eyes shut.

"I want him to come home."

Mei Lien opened her eyes to look at her son. He was the perfect combination of herself and Joseph, with his short black hair, strong jaw, and round cheeks. All but his face had already lost the roundness of childhood, and soon he'd grow long and lanky, half boy, half man. She wouldn't be there to see it. She'd never know the kind of man he would become.

Nausea welled in her throat. She carefully swallowed and took slow, deep breaths to keep it under control, but her stomach heaved anyway, leaving her no choice but to dash to the sink and heave up the bile that was the only thing filling her stomach.

"Mama, are you sick?"

Mei Lien closed her eyes and rested her forehead on the side of the sink. Until now she'd managed to hide the worst of her symptoms from her son. "Yes, I am," she finally answered without moving.

"Go lie down, Mama. I'll take care of you." She heard his chair scrape back and knew he was coming to her, ready to take on his duty as man of the house.

If only it were that simple.

Even though her limbs trembled, she pushed herself upright and turned to face him. He stood beside her with his jaw set, shoulders back, ready to take on the load he shouldn't have to carry at such a young age. Only his eyes betrayed his fear.

*Stop thinking of that*, she scolded herself. *You must help him be strong or he will not survive.*

Throwing back her own shoulders, she raised her chin and forced a smile for her son. "Thank you for taking care of me, but I'm afraid what I have won't go away with rest." She cupped his sweet face with her hands and stared into his eyes, trying to imprint the love she felt for him onto his soul to carry him through what was to come. "I'm dying, Yan-Tao. I'm so sorry."

He shook his head, denying her words.

She nodded. "It's true."

His face crumpled in her hands, and he fell into her arms, his forehead hitting her chest painfully, but the sink behind her held her up. She wrapped her arms around him and gave into the sobs that again choked her.

Together they slid to the floor and cried at the injustice of their lives. For Joseph who should be here with them. For the knowledge that Yan-Tao's childhood was now over. No matter what happened to him, he would be forced to grow up. And he'd be all alone.

She cried for her baby, who needed a mother and father and was losing both within months of each other.

She cried for herself and all the people who had been ripped from her life.

After a long time, she felt her tears dry up and saw Yan-Tao's had as well. They stayed where they were, mother and son wrapped together for what was one of the last times, and did nothing more than breathe each other in. His scent—that boyish smell of sweat and fresh air—filled her, cutting her apart and strengthening her at the same time. "I love you, Yan-Tao," she said to the top of his head, thinking of all the times she should have said it to him before now, how she'd never said it to Joseph. "No matter what, always remember that I love you."

"I love you too, Mama," he mumbled against her chest.

With one last squeeze, she set him away from her. "We have an important errand to do now, and I can't do it without you. Go get your coat and meet me outside."

He wiped his eyes with a look of uncertainty as he stared at her face. Then, with a nod, he scooted back and pulled himself up before turning to do her bidding. At that moment, she knew he'd shed the last of the little boy he'd been.

"Six hundred. No more." Campbell sniffed, then spat onto the ground as his eyes watched her carefully.

Mei Lien held tight to Yan-Tao's hand, taking strength from his touch. They stood in Campbell's yard in front of a house that was even smaller than the cabin Joseph had lived in when they'd first met. The field and tiny orchard they'd walked through to get here were hemmed in by rocky outcroppings and thick forests that grew on a mountainside that seemed nearly vertical. No wonder he'd wanted Joseph's land so badly all these years.

Now he was going to get the land, the buildings, livestock, bay, everything.

She shook her head. "Mr. Campbell, you and I both know my farm is worth a lot more than that, and we both know I can get another buyer as soon as I put word out that I'm selling. Do you really want someone else buying what you've had your eye on all these years?"

Carefully, she kept her chin lifted and her shoulders back, refusing to let him see any sign of weakness. If he knew how sick she was, how exhausted she felt, he'd know how impossible it would be for her to find another buyer. She needed the sale today.

Campbell's mouth twisted in disgust as his eyes traveled over her and Yan-Tao but she didn't look away. He glanced over his shoulder at his cabin then toward his potato patch and she knew he was thinking of how badly he wanted her land. She kept her mouth shut, waiting for him to fill the silence.

Which he did with a heavy sigh. "Fine. I'll pay you nine hundred for everything."

She nodded, not done yet. "You'll give me the cash by Friday, and you'll allow my son and me to remain living there until the end of the year, nine weeks away. Agreed?"

His eyes narrowed, and he stepped forward. "You'd better be gone by January first, or I'm throwing you off my land."

She didn't back away, even when confronted with his violence. "We'll be gone by then, don't you worry."

"Then we have an agreement."

She stuck out her hand as she'd seen her father and Joseph

do on numerous occasions when completing a business deal. Campbell looked at it with eyebrows raised then smirked and turned away. "I'll ride over as soon as I collect the funds." Then he disappeared into the shadowed cabin, dismissing them as surely as if they'd never been there at all.

Mei Lien gave Yan-Tao's hand a squeeze. "Time to go."

Together they started the long walk home, each step painful and exhausting but necessary.

In five days, she'd have the money Yan-Tao would need to start his new life. In her mind, she checked off the first step of her plan. Now it was time to concentrate on step two.

# Chapter Twenty-Five

M ei Lien heard her sister-in-law's arrival long before she
saw Elizabeth herself—Yan-Tao's excited shout, the
dog's barking, Elizabeth's complaining.

She'd taken to lying on the sitting room sofa, sleeping when
the pain allowed and helping Yan-Tao with chores, also when the
pain allowed, which wasn't often. All other moments of the day
and night were filled with embroidery. Pain or no pain, strength
or no strength, she had to finish the embroidery. The previous
night, long after Yan-Tao had fallen asleep, she'd attached the
final sleeve to the robe. It still needed some work, but she knew
she could wait no longer.

She was fading fast. Her body was eating itself away from the
inside out. She knew this but didn't let herself dwell on it. Nor
did she let herself dwell on saying good-bye to her son. She did
what she could to prolong her moments with Yan-Tao, but with
Elizabeth's arrival, there was no prolonging what had to be done.

"Mama is inside lying down," she heard Yan-Tao tell their
guest from out in the yard. "She's sick." The last was said with

such sorrow, it forced Mei Lien to rub at the ache it caused in her chest.

"Where's your father, then? I expected him at the steamer landing." Elizabeth's critical voice grew louder, alerting Mei Lien that they were coming onto the porch and would soon be inside. She pushed herself up on shaking arms and ran her bony fingers through hair that hung limply over her shoulders.

She should have bathed before Elizabeth's arrival.

"You don't know about Father?" Yan-Tao asked as he pushed the door open and walked inside ahead of his aunt. "Father is—"

"Yan-Tao," Mei Lien interrupted. "Go make us some tea and bring those cookies you...we made." She was embarrassed to admit to Elizabeth that her seven-year-old son was doing all the cooking and baking.

"Goodness gracious, May, don't you look a sight." Elizabeth remained standing by the closed door, her coat and gloves in place as she took in Mei Lien and the room with a curl to her lip. "And what's that awful smell?"

"Smell?" She hadn't noticed a smell.

Elizabeth shook her head and rolled her eyes as if to say Mei Lien was an imbecile. Then she bustled to the window and threw it open, allowing the cold November wind to bite down on Mei Lien's tender body.

Instead of giving in to the complaint that jumped to her lips, Mei Lien drew the blanket she'd kicked off earlier around her shoulders. "Thank you for coming."

Elizabeth gave her a pinched look as she settled herself on the edge of a chair across the room from Mei Lien. "Your telegram said it was urgent, though I can't imagine what is urgent enough to make me leave my girls in the care of our housekeeper and travel in this godforsaken weather."

Mei Lien started to roll her eyes but stopped herself just in time. Elizabeth's girls were seventeen years old and plenty capable of caring for themselves and their father for a few days.

Elizabeth herself had stated in her last letter that one of them, Priscilla if she remembered correctly, would soon be getting married.

She swallowed down the burning feeling that constantly tried to creep up her throat. "I need your help, Elizabeth."

Elizabeth's already-arched eyebrows shot so high they disappeared under the brim of her black hat. "I can see that. Where is Joseph?"

Mei Lien had to look away to gather enough strength for what was required of her. That first month after Joseph's death had been such a blur she hadn't thought to notify Elizabeth. And then, when she'd realized how her own time was limited, she'd known the information might be best used to aid her in her plan for Yan-Tao.

If Elizabeth had already known her brother was dead, she wouldn't have come.

"I'm so sorry to tell you this," she began, using all her strength to keep upright, for the next few minutes were the most important of her life. "Joseph is dead. Lost in the strait during a storm last month."

Elizabeth's hands covered her mouth and she shook her head in denial, her eyes opened wide.

"I would have notified you sooner, but we were in such grief and…" She let her words drift away, knowing none were adequate.

"Here is your tea, Mama," Yan-Tao announced, carrying a tray to the small table he pulled close to Mei Lien's station on the sofa. Without her asking him to, he poured a cup and set it within her reach. Then he turned to his aunt. "How do you like your tea, Auntie Elizabeth?"

She didn't seem to hear him, so Yan-Tao repeated the question. Elizabeth blinked several times, then lowered her shaking hands to her lap. "Cream and sugar. Thank you, Kenneth."

Yan-Tao nodded, used to his aunt calling him by his white name. He stirred what was probably the last of their sugar into her tea and added milk that he'd taken from the cow just this morning. Mei Lien smiled at her son, letting him know without words that she was proud of him. If not for his great efforts, they'd have no milk. Or tea. Or anything to eat for that matter.

After he finished serving his aunt, Mei Lien held out her hand to him, and when he took it, she closed her eyes, reveling in that simple connection. "Thank you, Yan-Tao. Now go see to your chores outside while Elizabeth and I talk."

His small hand trembled in hers, telling her he knew exactly what they had to discuss. To his credit, he simply nodded and excused himself to go outside. As Mei Lien watched him go, she felt the words to call him back clamoring inside her throat, but she kept silent.

After he disappeared, she turned her attention to her tea, using all her strength to keep the cup from clattering against the saucer as she lifted it and brought it to her lips. Over the rim of her teacup, she saw Elizabeth watching her. In her eyes were the questions Mei Lien expected. It was time.

Shaking, she set the tea back down with only a small amount spilled over the rim. "Elizabeth, I asked you to come here not only to tell you about your brother, but to tell you that I am dying."

Elizabeth nodded as though she'd known that fact all along. That was when Mei Lien realized how awful her appearance must be. She brushed a wrinkle out of her skirt and got to the point. "As Yan-Tao's only living relation, I'd like you to take him with you when you leave here."

Elizabeth's cup clattered into the saucer as she set it down on the side table. "You what?"

"I need you to take Yan-Tao, give him a home until he is grown."

"I can't do that!" Elizabeth jumped to her feet and paced to the window, which she slammed shut, then spun to face Mei Lien, her hands wringing at her waist. "I'm sorry, May, but you know my husband would never allow him in our home."

"He is your brother's child, Elizabeth," she reminded her, trying very hard but not succeeding in keeping anger out of her voice.

"No, this is not the solution." Elizabeth went on as though Mei Lien had not spoken. She paced the room, her head down. "There has to be another way."

"Yan-Tao is a hard worker. He'll be a big help with chores or at your husband's shipyard. He'll earn his keep. Plus, I have a purse I'll give you for his care."

At this Elizabeth's head shot up. "How large a purse?"

"Five hundred dollars," she answered, subtracting the cost of the telegram and few groceries they'd purchased in town, along with the amount she planned to put directly into Yan-Tao's pocket. "I sold the farm to the neighbor."

Mei Lien could not stop the way her body tensed up at the thought of Campbell and the way he'd knocked on her door precisely five days after their agreement. Without a word, and with his typical arrogance, he'd handed her the cash and a roll of papers. One glance at the papers had confirmed what she'd feared—he wanted her to sign her name transferring ownership to him. She'd allowed him to see her illness that day and managed to get him to leave without signing anything. She didn't know if it would work, but she hoped not signing any documents would make the sale legally questionable should Yan-Tao wish to return someday and reclaim the property. Her tactic was underhanded, she knew, but she didn't care. She was doing what little she could to secure a future for her son.

"I admit the money would help," Elizabeth said as she dropped back into her chair, her gloved hands still wringing. "But I don't think Kenneth would be happy with us. He's…he's not like us."

Anger welled inside of Mei Lien so hot she had to throw off the blanket.

*No*, she told herself, catching her temper just in time. *I cannot spoil this. This is Yan-Tao's only chance.*

Pain stabbed through her belly so intensely she curled into a ball on the sofa. Ignoring the horrified expression on Elizabeth's face, Mei Lien continued her argument with a level voice for her son's sake. "All I ask is that you keep him safe, fed, and clothed until he comes of age. Please, Elizabeth. For Joseph."

At her brother's name and the reminder of his death, Elizabeth wilted into her chair. Gone was the starched back, thrown back shoulders, raised nose. For the first time, Mei Lien saw a side of Elizabeth that proved she was more than an uptight, judgmental bigot. She was a sister who'd lost her brother and she was hurting.

"I want you to go through Joseph's things," she told her as Elizabeth dabbed at her eyes with a handkerchief she pulled from her skirt pocket. "Take anything you want."

"Thank you." Elizabeth sniffed as she got to her feet with her face still hidden behind her handkerchief. "I'd like to be alone. Where am I to sleep?"

"In my and Joseph's room. I can't manage the stairs any longer."

Elizabeth nodded and started to turn away. Mei Lien spoke quickly before she could go. "What about Yan-Tao? Will you take him?"

Elizabeth dropped her hand from her reddened face and Mei Lien saw there were new lines of grief etched around her mouth. "Oh, May..." She sighed loudly and wouldn't meet her gaze. "Let me think about it."

Mei Lien watched her disappear into the kitchen and listened as she trudged up the stairs, all the while clasping her trembling hands to keep them from throwing something at the wall. Elizabeth sounded like she was going to refuse and, in doing so, she would be ensuring Yan-Tao's death. Once Mei Lien was gone, he'd have no one. He'd have no home.

She knew what Campbell would do if he found Yan-Tao living here past their agreed upon date.

Suddenly, she felt like her skin was being peeled from her body. She grabbed a pillow and held it to her chest, curling her body around it. The pain wouldn't ease.

Very much aware that Elizabeth was right overhead, Mei Lien buried her face in the pillow and moaned.

Joseph's sister had been her only plan for Yan-Tao. She had nowhere else to send him, no one to watch over him.

The tea curdled in her stomach and shot upward. Throwing off the pillow, she fell to her knees on the floor beside the couch, her head hanging over the ever-present bucket, and threw up until there was nothing left.

Too exhausted to care what Elizabeth would think when she came downstairs, Mei Lien curled up on the floor.

She fell asleep searching her mind for a way to save Yan-Tao's future, his very life.

"May, drink this. It will help."

She felt a cup at her mouth and liquid dribble down her chin. The voice kept talking to her, pulling her out of the dream she was having of riding with Joseph in his rowboat. He was telling her something important, but that irritating voice kept distracting her.

"May, you need to wake up. Wake up!"

She moaned in protest, but the owner of the voice slapped her cheeks, causing a spurt of tears to fill her eyes. She blinked them open.

Elizabeth was propping her up with one arm around her shoulders. She was lying on the sofa again, her blanket tucked around her. Black filled the window above the sofa, telling her it was nighttime now. She'd slept the day away. She'd wasted time better spent working on the embroidery, or holding Yan-Tao's little body before she could hold him no more.

"Yan-Tao?" She struggled to sit up all the way.

"He's asleep. It's the middle of the night." Elizabeth reached for something on the table and returned with a cup of water. "Here, drink this. You were coughing in your sleep. You need water."

Mei Lien sipped as the cup touched her lips. When the water hit her sensitive stomach, she choked and turned her head away. "No more."

Elizabeth set the cup down then settled Mei Lien back onto her pillow. "You are quite ill, aren't you?"

"Just as I told you."

Elizabeth's lips pursed in displeasure, but Mei Lien did not regret the censure in her voice. Her sister-in-law had already refused to keep her son safe. There was no need to remain civil any longer.

"Go to bed. I don't need you as nursemaid."

Elizabeth pulled her shoulders back then marched into the kitchen. Mei Lien heard her in there clattering dishes and pots but she ignored her. She had a more important matter to attend to.

Moving slowly because quick motions drained her, Mei Lien shifted to sit at the end of the sofa where her embroidery frame waited with the robe draped over it. Carefully she eased the protective cloth back to reveal the silk and the patterns she'd carefully sewn onto it these last seven years.

She grasped her needle between her thumb and finger and was about to pierce the fabric and continue with her pattern when another section caught her attention. Gently, she set the needle down and shifted the robe for a better look. On the body of the robe, just inches from the sleeve where she currently worked, was the section where she'd embroidered her life with Joseph.

For the first time she looked at the piece as if looking at the work of another woman. The background was the blue of the silk she worked on, but embroidered onto it were so many colors and patterns the blue was not visible across much of the cloth.

Grandmother would never recognize the hand that had created this. When they'd last worked together, Mei Lien was making perfect small, even stitches as she'd been taught. But, at some point over the years, she had strayed from her training and stitched without discipline. Here, where she'd depicted the house, the stitches were small, tight and even as they should be, which helped her see the grain of the wood on the porch post. But over here, where the forest behind the house grew, her stitches had abandoned convention. Next to a small, straight stitch, was a longer one double its length and shooting off at an angle. The stitches looked loose, jumbled, out of control. Disrespectful.

Mei Lien closed her eyes to block out the images. She didn't have time to redo this work. She didn't have time to fix her mistakes and still finish the whole story before her strength failed her.

Not finishing was not an option. She'd wanted to be finished by now so Yan-Tao could take the robe with him, but she hadn't been able. That was fine, because she'd figured out that part of the plan too.

Her plan was precise. It left no room for error, and so far she'd discovered two errors: Elizabeth's refusal and her shameful work.

She should give up. Right now. She should wrap up the embroidery and sink it to the bottom of the sound for it was not fit for human eyes. Any eyes, but most certainly not her son's eyes. This was to have been a gift for him, his one link to his ancestral past and to the story of how he'd come to be. This embroidery, which she'd planned for her son to wear at his wedding, was his road map to his origins and the answers to questions he might someday have.

But she'd failed.

"Oh, isn't that nice?"

Mei Lien jerked her head up and her eyes flew open. Elizabeth stood over her wiping her hands on a dish towel as her eyes raked over the evidence of Mei Lien's shame.

Immediately, Mei Lien reached for the covering cloth to hide it from sight.

"No, wait. What's this here? Is that Joseph?"

Even as she let the cloth fall back again, Mei Lien hated the way she'd always felt like a servant to her sister-in-law. She hated that, even now, she obeyed Elizabeth. "Yes, that's him, holding Yan-Tao as an infant. I found them standing in the field like that one day the summer after Yan-Tao was born. It looked to me like Joseph was showing his son around the farm so that Yan-Tao knew where his soul had landed."

"Joseph looks happy."

Mei Lien tried again to cover it up. "How can you know? It's just an embroidery."

Elizabeth grabbed the covering cloth and prevented Mei Lien from pulling it over the fabric and hiding it away. "You don't see it, do you?"

She dropped her hands to her lap in defeat. "See what?"

Instead of answering, Elizabeth lifted the robe from the frame, ignoring Mei Lien's protests, and carried it across the room where she held it up. "Look now," she commanded. "Do you see it?"

Instead of looking at the embarrassing embroidery, Mei Lien stared at her sister-in-law. "Be careful with that."

Elizabeth lifted the robe higher. "May, look at Joseph. This could be a photograph, but in color. I had no idea you could do this."

Mei Lien did look, and felt her heart catch. Seen from this distance, Joseph appeared alive as he smiled at her. Joy and pride radiated from him as he held his newborn son. Tears blocked her vision and Mei Lien had to close her eyes to shut out her husband's image.

The water shouldn't have taken him. He should be here with their son, helping Mei Lien fight whatever was killing her. He should be here holding them together.

But he was gone and soon she would be too.

"Please, Elizabeth," she begged, still with her eyes closed. "Please take Yan-Tao with you when you leave. I don't have the strength to find anyone else. Do it because your brother loved his son so much. Please."

Silence. The silence stretched for so long Mei Lien was sure Elizabeth had left the room. When she opened her eyes to make sure, she found her standing next to the embroidery frame, her eyes on her brother's face on the cloth.

"I'll take him," she whispered. Then, before Mei Lien could react, she pivoted to face her. "I'll take him," she said again, louder now. "But I won't let people know he is kin. You don't know what my husband would do if..." She left the sentence unfinished.

"Thank you, Elizabeth." Tears boiled behind her eyes again. "I'll make sure he's ready to go whenever you like."

Elizabeth showed no emotion. She simply nodded, then hurried from the room. "We leave in the morning," she said over her shoulder before disappearing into the kitchen.

Mei Lien felt a hole open up in the ground beneath her. This was her last night with her son in the house. Tomorrow would be her last morning to lay her eyes on his sweet, gentle face, kiss his soft cheeks, hold his lanky body.

"Elizabeth," she called as she pushed to her feet.

"What?" came the irritated reply from the kitchen doorway.

"Help me up the stairs. I need to sleep with my son tonight."

The grooves around Elizabeth's mouth deepened, but she didn't say anything as she helped Mei Lien up the stairs in the dark.

Exhausted and shaking from the effort, Mei Lien lay down on Yan-Tao's bed and curled her body around his smaller one as he slept. Determinedly, she focused on imprinting him into every cell of her body. His every breath she breathed into her own lungs. His sweaty boy smell she took in so that it filled the darkest reaches of her soul.

No mother should ever have to say good-bye to her baby.

Morning came too fast and with it the hurried packing to get Elizabeth and Yan-Tao to the steamer dock in time for the single passenger and cargo pickup of the day. For Mei Lien, every moment leading up to her son's departure was more painful than the last. Her bottom lip stung and she could taste blood from where she'd been biting it so hard.

There was too much left to tell him, too much yet to do.

Not enough time.

She lay on his bed, directing him in packing his belongings into the trunk Joseph had made her for her own clothing when they were newlyweds. *Joseph, you should be here*, she thought, not for the first time this morning.

"Mama, can Mutt come too?" he asked, referring to the dog trailing his every move.

"That's not up to me. You'll have to ask Elizabeth."

Yan-Tao carefully placed the toy boat Joseph had carved for him into the trunk then closed the lid with a huge sigh. "Are you certain I must leave with her today? Who's going to care for you?"

Knowing there would be enough time later to rest, Mei Lien forced herself to her feet so she could go to him. "My son," she began, with her hands on his shoulders. "I'll get by. When you leave here, I want you to remember me with life, not this wasting away shell that I've become."

The flood of pain caused not by her body, but by her heart, made her knees shake, forcing her to sit on the edge of the bed. She gathered her son into her arms, bringing him to sit on her lap like he used to do as a small child. "Son, live happy and love deep."

Her voice caught on the words as she heard the echo of her father's voice saying them to her not so many years before. She squeezed her son against her. "Promise me, Yan-Tao. Promise to be strong and honorable. Work hard like your father and look for signs of us in the world around you. When my time comes, I'll find a way to be near you."

His body trembled and he sniffed. Mei Lien felt her own tears well up in response, but she pushed through the emotion. Now wasn't the time. "Look for me in the leaves, the clouds, the birds. I don't know how I'll come to you, but I'll be there. You will never be alone, Yan-Tao. Ever."

Sobs burst out of him as he twisted around and flung his arms around her. His tears soaked her neck and she closed her eyes to better remember how they felt. Her hands rubbed up and down his back, feeling his bony ribs that would one day be covered in muscle. Agony rolled through her.

No. She opened her eyes. No, she must not give in yet. She must be brave for her son.

A noise in the doorway caught her attention and she turned to find Elizabeth standing there with a gloved hand over her mouth, her eyes surprisingly damp. But then she noticed Mei Lien watching her and she quickly dropped her hand and lifted her chin. "It is time," she said with a catch in her voice. Her gaze shifted away and she busied herself with her hat.

Mei Lien squeezed her son against her one last time. "Don't forget all that I've taught you. Don't ever forget. Promise?"

He nodded as she set him away from her, his tear-streaked face twisted in anguish. "I p...promise." His breath spasmed, nearly dragging him into another fit of crying, but he pulled himself together.

"Kenneth, can you carry the chest?"

Yan-Tao looked over his shoulder at his aunt then back to Mei Lien and she knew he was thinking of the name his aunt called him. Starting today, he would never again be Yan-Tao.

Mei Lien felt her own lungs spasm, but she swallowed hard and kept the sob from escaping.

"Yes," he said bravely.

"Yes, what?" Elizabeth asked, eyebrows lifted.

His head bobbed. "Yes, ma'am. I can carry the chest."

*And so it begins*, Mei Lien thought, wishing there was another way.

As Yan-Tao struggled with the chest, dragging it down the stairs so that it bumped against each step, leaving dents and deep scratches, Mei Lien followed behind, leaning heavily on Elizabeth's arm. The dog ran in circles in the kitchen, excited by all the commotion.

Outside, Mei Lien saw Elizabeth had already loaded Joseph's wagon with boxes of his clothing, the mirror he used to shave by, the rocking chair he'd made when Mei Lien was with child. Mei Lien looked at each item, jumbled there in the wagon, feeling each one in her memory like she was touching them now.

But it was just as well that Elizabeth was taking them. Better her than Campbell.

A flame of anger shot through her and she clung to it, knowing it would fuel her through the coming moments. Better to be burning with rage than melting with sorrow.

"Wait!" she said as she remembered. "Don't go. There's one more thing."

As quickly as her weakened body allowed, Mei Lien made it to the sitting room and her embroidery frame, where the silk robe lay where Elizabeth had left it the night before.

Without stopping to consider her decision, she snatched up her shears and severed the unfinished sleeve, which she left hanging on the frame, tattered edges drooping toward the floor.

Carefully, she folded the rest of the embroidered robe into a small bundle, then wrapped it tightly in the protective covering cloth and tied all of it with a skein of embroidery floss. When she turned around, Elizabeth and Yan-Tao stood shoulder-to-shoulder in the kitchen doorway.

"Yan-Tao, this is for you. This is our shared legacy and the most important thing I have ever given to you. Keep it safe." She looked at Elizabeth. "You will help him protect this?"

Elizabeth nodded, silent.

Satisfied, Mei Lien placed the bundle in her son's hands. "I wanted to present you with a finished robe, but there wasn't time. The story told there is not finished. I will finish the sleeve and I will leave it for you in your secret hiding hole where the *Bok Guey* cannot find it. You will come back and get it when you are grown, yes?"

He nodded, his red-rimmed eyes staring up at her. "You know about the hole?"

She smiled. "Of course. I am your mother." She had to stop now and take a slow, deep breath before she could continue. "Go now. You don't want to miss your boat."

Yan-Tao put his head down and dove toward her, bouncing against her chest so hard she fell back a step but was able to stop them both from falling.

One last time she allowed herself the pleasure of holding her child. "I love you, Yan-Tao. If you remember only one thing, remember that."

"I love you, Mama." He hiccuped, crying again.

"We must go now," Elizabeth grumbled. "The schedule says departure is at ten o'clock. We're going to be late."

"Good-bye, Yan-Tao." Mei Lien set her son away from her and forced herself to drop her hands away.

He shook his head through his tears. "No, I can't go. I'm not leaving you."

"You must go. You cannot stay."

His face crumpled. "But, Mama, I can help you. I can make you better. You'll see!"

Mei Lien felt her insides twist painfully and the familiar nausea well up. She put her hand on her stomach and hunched her shoulders to relieve the pull. "The only way you can help me is to leave and give me the joy of knowing you have a future to live. Now go."

"No, Mama!" He threw himself against her again but she didn't relent. She caught him by the shoulders and stopped his headlong rush.

"No, Yan-Tao. You can't stay. Go." Gently she turned him so that he faced away from her and gave him a nudge in the back. "Go."

Elizabeth pivoted to lead the way out the back door to the waiting horse and wagon. Yan-Tao followed more slowly, his head turned to keep his mother in his sight.

"*Zài jiàn,* Yan-Tao."

"*Zài jiàn,* Mama." With his head hanging so low his black hair hung into his eyes, Yan-Tao dragged his feet into the yard and climbed into the wagon next to Elizabeth. His dog jumped up beside him. Elizabeth let him stay there.

Mei Lien leaned against the kitchen doorjamb feeling like her heart had been ripped from her body and tossed into the wagon with the rest of her life. She watched her son hug the embroidered silk to his chest as he swayed to the movements of the wagon and wished with every hair on her body that she could call him back.

But he needed to go. This was his only chance for a future.

As the wagon headed out of the yard, Yan-Tao twisted to look back at her, his little hand lifted bravely to say good-bye. Mei Lien lifted her own hand and then, because they were torturing each other, she turned and shut the door, blocking him from her gaze and her from his.

As she leaned against the door, she closed her eyes. Suddenly she wasn't standing in her own house, but on the deck of a steamship in the dark of night. She saw herself, perched on the railing, ready to jump into the cold waters below. Standing behind her was her father, his face bruised and bloody, but twisted in pain, not from his injuries but from the good-bye he was saying to her. As Mei Lien watched, her younger self reached a hand up to her father, begging him to let her stay but he shook his head, schooling his features to hide his sorrow.

And then, he lifted his hands and shoved her off the railing into the swirling ocean below.

Watching from this vantage point, Mei Lien now saw the way his whole body seemed to collapse into itself. The railing was the only thing keeping him upright as his eyes searched the water for his daughter.

"*Zài jiàn*, Mei Lien," he whispered into the cold night.

Now back in her kitchen, Mei Lien felt the familiar dark void pulling her down. Unable to fight it, she slid to the dirty wood floor and whispered, "Good-bye, Father. Good-bye, my son."

# Chapter Twenty-Six

*Saturday, August 18—present day*
*Rothesay Estate, Orcas Island*

A nd here we thought all these years he didn't talk about his past because he was a paper son." Margaret scooted forward to take a scone from the plate Inara placed on the coffee table.

"What's a paper son?" Inara too took a scone still warm from the oven and bit into it as she sat down next to Daniel. Despite pushing him away the last few days, she was happy he was here now.

It was Vera who answered. "During the time of the Exclusion Act, only a limited number of Chinese citizens, such as merchants or diplomats, were allowed into the U.S. One way many Chinese got around the law was to purchase papers that identified them as the son of an American citizen."

Margaret jumped in. "Let's say there was a Chinese merchant with U.S. citizenship status. He would travel to China for a few years, and when he returned, he would claim to officials that he had gotten married and had several children in the time he was away. In reality, all he did was sell identity papers, which, years later, upon reaching America, the purchasers produced, identifying them as sons of the merchant. They were sons on paper only, but it worked."

Inara nodded as she let the explanation sink in. Too many people had worked hard to get to this country only to be treated cruelly once they arrived. It was heartbreaking.

She listened as Daniel continued to bring his family up-to-date on his team's Yan-Tao/Ken research. She was nearly as behind as everyone else since they hadn't spoken in days. It had been easier that way.

She planned to tell Daniel that night about losing her father's loan. She shouldn't have avoided him like she did the past few days, but she'd needed the time to process the fact that she'd failed at the one thing in life she'd ever really wanted.

Just thinking about it again sent gnawing shame burning through her. Her own father thought her incapable of building and running a hotel. To him she was only good for going to work for an established company where she'd be led by the hand if necessary. Obviously, he thought it necessary.

If only she hadn't spent so many years doing what he expected of her, she might have discovered sooner this passion for the islands and the hotel business. If only she'd worked while going to grad school and paid down her student loans, maybe she'd qualify for a loan of her own. If only... if only.

Now that Daniel was here, she yearned to talk to him about it all, get his perspective, feel his support. She needed to know she wasn't alone.

But later. Without his family around.

She leaned into his side as they sat together on the couch under the window in her living room—no, Dahlia's living room, she corrected herself. It wasn't hers anymore.

She slid her hand into Daniel's, needing an anchor for her mixed up emotions. He looked at her and his face softened into a smile. Then he squeezed her hand and resumed talking to his family, who had gathered here after settling their belongings in the guest rooms upstairs.

"Because I believed Ken Chin was a paper son and Yan-Tao a natural-born citizen," Daniel told them, "I never thought to check immigration records for either name. So this week, just to be sure, I sent my assistant to NARA, the National Archives and Records Administration facility on Sand Point Way. As I expected, she found nothing."

"What about his birth certificate?" Cassie sat in the armchair next to the fireplace Duncan had added to the house. Her long hair was pulled into a carefree bun and she had her designer-jeans-encased legs tucked under her. She seemed completely at home here and Inara wondered, if she squinted her eyes, would Cassie look like Mei Lien sitting in this house?

Daniel nodded in response to his sister's question. "It's in state records under the name Yan-Tao Kenneth McElroy. We still don't know where the name Chin came from, other than the hypothesis that he chose to change it when he ran away from the orphanage to keep anyone from finding him."

"It is a common family name," Vera told them from her perch on the opposite couch from Inara. She sipped at the oolong tea she'd brought as a gift, which Inara had promptly steeped to serve with the store-bought scones.

"You know," Inara said now as she looked at the scones. "I hadn't consciously thought of this when I decided to serve you scones, but we're enjoying refreshments from both sides of your ancestry. McElroy was Scottish, right?"

Apparently none of the Chins had thought about their Scottish ancestry because they all looked at her with various expressions of stunned surprise.

"Mei Lien should've embroidered a kilt," Cassie quipped.

Margaret turned to her mother-in-law. "Why did we believe the family stories going back to ancient China? Who came up with them?"

Vera's lips pressed together and her gaze darted out the window. "Perhaps the stories from Ken's wife's family got mixed up with his. She was the daughter of one of the wealthiest and most influential Chinese families in Seattle at the turn of the century, you know."

They all nodded as though her explanation made sense, but Inara saw the way Vera avoided looking directly at any of them. Perhaps it had been Vera herself who'd made up the stories.

"Vera," she ventured hesitantly, because the woman still hadn't warmed up to her. "Can you tell us more about Ken, your father-in-law? What was he like?"

Vera's scrunched-up eyes were locked on the windows and the driveway outside but Inara knew she was looking back in time. "He was a man who carried the weight of a heavy past everywhere he went." Her arthritic fingers absently rubbed together on her lap. "I once asked him about his parents, hoping he'd slip and admit to being a paper son or, at best, tell me about his childhood in China. He did neither. He turned away from me without saying a word but not before I saw sadness come over him. It was as if the thought of his parents caused him physical pain. My husband told me never to ask such questions again. I didn't."

"But some things I did know," she went on, looking directly at Inara. "He was fascinated by water but was deathly afraid of it. He loved fountains, going for walks along the sound or lake-front, even loved washing his hands in the faucet, but he flatly refused to go swimming. No one ever knew why."

"Because the water took his father away," Inara breathed, caught up in Vera's description. For several long moments no one spoke.

Finally, Margaret shook her head and whispered, "That poor boy."

Now it was Inara's turn to look out the windows, her mind roaming the property, wondering if Mei Lien was buried out there somewhere. Had her son watched her die by Duncan Campbell's hand? Would they ever know for sure what had happened?

"His time spent in this house must have been happy, I think," Daniel said, breaking the heavy stillness. "For seven years he had both his father and mother and all this land to play on."

Inara turned away from the windows to see Vera nodding matter-of-factly as though she'd made up her mind that Daniel spoke the truth.

She cleared her throat of the lump still there and forced lightness in her voice when she said, "How about a tour of the estate?"

The Chin women jumped to their feet as if they'd been waiting for her to ask.

She started with Dahlia's house, showing them where she'd found the sleeve under the stairs. Everyone took a turn peering into the hole with a flashlight. Cassie asked about the scratch marks and dents on every stair tread, imperfections that Inara had only recently discovered after Tom ripped out the carpet runner. "Maybe the marks were from Mei Lien's time in the house," she mused. "It's possible."

Then she showed them the upstairs and explained how later generations had added the wing to the main house, which changed the configuration of the tiny bedrooms and added a sitting room for the servants who lived there.

She then showed them the kitchen garden since she was confident Mei Lien and Yan-Tao had worked here, judging by the picture on the robe. Margaret spent several minutes poking through the herbs and vegetables Dahlia had planted and Inara had resurrected. She was so enthralled with them that Inara promised her a bag of whatever she wanted to take home with her.

She was just about to lead the group into the main house through the kitchen door when she changed her mind and instead led them around the back and into the forest. When they reached the crumbling cabin she stopped. "This is where I believe Joseph and Mei Lien first lived together before he built the house."

"Was Ken born here?" Margaret, in her cream-colored slacks and gold blouse, looked out of place standing in dappled sunlight on a carpet of fir and cedar needles.

Inara shook her head. "The property records I've been able to find say the house was built in 1886. He was born the following summer, so it's safe to say he was born in the new house."

Vera stood with her hands on her narrow hips, her eyes taking in everything that surrounded them. "How did they make a living here? It's nothing but forest."

"Joseph was a farmer," Inara explained. "Where the main house and garage stand now is where I believe the McElroy's had a barn and animal pens. The garden was probably bigger than it is today too."

She pointed to the east. "The tract of land across the road where my builder Tom lives now used to be the McElroy family's orchards. Maybe he'll let us walk over there later, if you're interested."

Vera nodded. "I am."

"Want to see the beach?" Inara asked, suddenly feeling uncomfortable. Here she was showing this family around property that had been in her family for over a century, yet she felt it belonged more to them than her. This was Mei Lien's land, not Campbell/Erickson land.

And soon it could be someone else's land.

But she couldn't think about that now. Today was about the Chin family. She turned toward the path leading to the beach. "Come see the bay. It's my favorite place on the whole estate."

They fell into single file behind her as she led them through the forest to the crescent-shaped beach where she'd spent much of the past two days thinking.

The instant she stepped down the slight embankment onto the rocks, she felt a sense of peace come over her.

This beach was special. She was going to miss it the most.

Blinking to clear her mind, Inara turned and found that Margaret and Vera had spotted the eagle nest high above the beach and were looking up and pointing to it. Cassie had wandered along the shoreline and was throwing rocks into the water. Daniel smiled at Inara, his eyes full of gratitude, and squeezed her hand.

She smiled back and leaned into his side. This was the family who should own this property, she thought. Daniel and Cassie carried Mei Lien's blood in their veins. They were the ones who should move in and make this place something meaningful again. They should carry on where Mei Lien left off as though the Campbell/Ericksons never existed.

But could they afford it? Sure, Margaret owned two successful restaurants but Inara had seen her house. The woman wasn't wealthy and the person to invest in Rothesay needed deep pockets to keep it afloat until the hotel hit black.

And yet… Inara swallowed as a new thought struck her. Maybe she'd been going about this all wrong. Maybe it wasn't a hotel investor she needed, but a restaurant investor. Someone looking to open a fabulous new location on Orcas Island that also happened to have a boutique hotel attached to it. Even if they didn't provide enough capital for the entire hotel project, it would be a start.

And maybe they could focus on opening the restaurant this fall while construction continued on the hotel. If she planned carefully, and maybe found a roommate to share living expenses, income from the restaurant could help them qualify for a business loan for the rest.

But what about her student loans, the first payment due next month?

A deferment. Why hadn't she thought of that sooner? She'd apply for a deferment of her payment due to financial hardship to put off having to pay for a few more months. Hopefully, until the hotel was making money.

And she wouldn't have to sell right away, after all.

Hope, however tiny it might be, sprang back to life in her heart and she welcomed it. She turned to tell Daniel but saw Vera making her way to them, so she kept silent.

"Thank you for bringing us here," Vera said, her sad expression reminding Inara of all this family was going through as they learned of their history. She watched as Vera turned back to face the water, her eyes searching the glossy surface.

Was the old woman searching for her lost great-grandmother?

As Inara let herself and Margaret into the main house's kitchen, tendrils of fog curled through the trees, playing hide-and-seek with the morning sun that would soon burn it away. They were there to give Margaret another chance to see the restaurant space since fading light and a quickly approaching dinner hour had cut their time short the night before.

Inara flipped on the panel of light switches and watched with satisfaction as Margaret's face lit up. Except for the finish work, the kitchen and restaurant space that now took up the back half of the first floor was complete.

Margaret clearly delighted in everything she saw as she moved purposely through the space, touching vent hoods, prep stations, bakers racks. "You have a Vulcan Hart range! It's what I use in my own restaurants. Are you working with a professional chef?" Margaret ran her fingers along the cold steel edge of the stove.

Inara wrapped her own freezing hands around the mug of tea she'd carried over with her. "No. I researched what was the best on the market right now."

Margaret nodded and moved to the walk-in cold storage and then the dry pantry, peppering her with questions as she went. Inara answered every one, growing more and more certain of her next steps.

She'd had three days to get used to the idea of losing the hotel and she was far from accepting it. She didn't want to leave for many reasons but the biggest was that she had unfinished business here. She owed it to Mei Lien to keep discovering her story. She owed it to Dahlia to see her dream come to life. She owed it to her mom to fill Rothesay with happy voices and life.

And she owed it to herself to fight for her own happiness. She was happy here. She wasn't ready to give up, and maybe her idea meant she didn't have to.

"What is this space for?" Margaret called to her, bringing her attention back into the kitchen. Margaret stood back in the shadows near storage rooms where walls had recently been torn down and ceilings opened up three floors to the attic.

Inara wandered over. "It's where we're going to install elevators both for ADA compliance and to make it easier for guests and staff to get around. Expensive as hell."

They returned to the kitchen where Margaret stopped at the picture windows to look out on the patio and back lawn where sun rays speared across the dew-covered grass. "Wow, imagine working with that view every day."

"Why don't you?" Inara smiled at Margaret's confusion. "Any chance you'd be interested in running a restaurant here and, maybe, having a stake in the hotel?"

Margaret's brows creased. "What do you mean?"

Suddenly nervous, Inara rubbed at an imaginary spot on the counter. "I don't have the money to keep going. I sent my crews home two days ago. Without a partner I have to sell everything. You have experience, contacts—"

"Are you asking me to be your partner?"

She nodded then forced herself to meet Margaret's gaze. "If you have the funding, or at least the credit for the loans we'd need." She realized she was getting ahead of herself. "There are a lot of details to work out but if you're interested, I'd love the opportunity to sit down and discuss it with you. I already know I love your food, and even though I've only known you a week,

I have a good feeling about a partnership between us. That is, if you're interested in working with me."

This was stupid. Why would Margaret want to go into business with her any more than the other investors who'd turned her down or her own father? "Look," she said before Margaret could say anything. "Forget it. I'm making you uncomfortable. Let's just go back to the house and get some breakfast."

Margaret didn't move and she didn't say anything as she tilted her head to the side and looked around the kitchen as if considering. When she finally spoke, it wasn't what Inara was expecting. "I'm thinking a fusion of Asian and Pacific Northwest. Farm to table, seasonal, locally sourced as much as possible."

Inara froze. "Are you saying what I think you're saying?"

Margaret smiled wide. "I'm saying I'm intrigued by the idea and am definitely interested in learning more about it. I'll have to talk with my financial people first, of course."

Inara could kiss the woman, but she settled for a hug. She threw her arms around Margaret, overcome with gratitude. "Oh, thank you! We have so much to talk ab—"

"What's going on in here?"

Inara turned to find Daniel standing just inside the door, wearing baggy gray sweatpants and a purple UW T-shirt that stretched across his chest.

She beamed at him. "Your mother and I might become business partners."

He came to her and slid his arm around her shoulders. "What about your dad?"

She shrugged as if it was no big deal. "He called in the loan."

Daniel's eyes darkened, and she knew he wasn't fooled by her act that she wasn't hurt. "I'm sorry. Why didn't you tell me?"

She'd wanted to last night, but they'd stayed up late with his family and she never got the chance. She stepped back and crossed her arms. "I don't know. Embarrassed, I guess."

"Well, regardless," Margaret said, joining them by the door.

"We have a lot to discuss, but I'm first going to call my accountant and my lawyer, if I can get either of them on a Sunday morning." She started for the door but paused to face Inara again. "I'm excited about this."

She smiled back. "Me too."

Just then Inara remembered Mei Lien and the part of the story she'd been keeping from Daniel and his family. She had to tell them everything and she had to do it now. She'd waited too long as it was. She'd deal with her dad later. The Chins had the right to know. "Wait, Margaret, don't go yet. There's something I need to tell you both."

Feeling like she was standing on the edge of a cliff that dropped into the bottomless black water of the Salish Sea, Inara turned away to look out the window as she gathered her thoughts. "You know the scene on the sleeve where all those people are in the water surrounding the steamship?"

"Of course," Daniel answered with a note of bewilderment.

Before she could lose her courage, she blurted it all out. "My great-great-great-grandfather, Duncan Campbell, murdered every Chinese person on board. He had them thrown into the water. As far as I can tell, Mei Lien was the only survivor."

She looked down at her fingers, which she was twisting together, and wished she was anywhere but here. "My father told me Duncan was a racist who thought the Chinese were too dirty to be on his boat. He was more interested in making money off of white passengers and profitable freight than he cared about the lives of innocent Chinese. Your ancestors."

Margaret gasped. Her hand flew up to cover her mouth and she stared at Inara in horror.

She had to make sure she said everything before more time passed. "That's the kind of man who built this manor and, I'm ashamed to say, the kind of person I'm descended from. My father wants to keep the truth hidden, but I had to tell you. If this changes your mind about the restaurant, I understand."

Daniel didn't move, but as he stared back at her, she saw anger growing inside of him, hardening his features, cutting her out of his heart. "You didn't think that was something you should have mentioned to me earlier?"

"I wanted to, but I was scared of what you'd think, or do. The information would ruin my family. It would ruin PMG and put a lot of people's jobs in jeopardy. Please understand. I couldn't tell you."

Daniel closed his eyes as if to block her out of his vision. His arms crossed over his chest and he seemed to be vibrating with anger, even though he made no further movement. "How do you know he murdered them?"

Inara explained about the records she'd found in the PMG company archives and her conversation with her father, leaving nothing out.

Margaret's lips pressed into a tight line, but she said nothing, just cast worried glances at her son. Daniel shifted his weight then shook his head at her. "I can't fathom how anyone could be capable of something like that, particularly a relative of the woman I love. And I really can't understand how your family, how you, could keep it a secret." His words trailed away as he continued to shake his head as if at a loss.

The woman he loves? He loved her? "I...I should have told you." She started to reach for him, but when he visibly stiffened, she crossed her arms over her chest. "I'm so sorry."

When Daniel continued to stare at her with an expression void of emotion, she turned to Margaret. "Do you understand?" God, she sounded like she was begging. She was, she realized. Her future hung on this moment.

Margaret studied her son before turning back to face Inara with a sigh. "My family and I have much to discuss, but I have to tell you that I'm very disappointed. I think I'll leave the two of you alone." With a gentle squeeze on Daniel's arm, she slipped quietly out the door.

When he didn't say anything for a long time, she begged, "Please, Daniel."

"I really thought you and I had a chance," he finally said, his voice hoarse. "I really did. But I can't be in a relationship with someone who isn't honest with me."

His meaning stabbed into her. It was exactly what she'd feared. "But—"

"We're through." His expressionless eyes bore into hers. "You should have told me, Inara. But you didn't. And now I need to consider what is best for my family, which means I will be researching further into what actually happened that night. With or without your help."

"What else could I have done?" She realized she was yelling but she didn't care. "This has been burning inside of me and I wish I could find a way to undo what happened, but I can't. There's no way to fix it."

He shook his head in disgust. "You and your family could own up to it. Say you're sorry to the families of the victims."

With that he pivoted on his heel and made it to the kitchen door before he turned back. "Oh, and you can forget about working with my mother." He slammed the door behind him.

Inara felt frozen in place, afraid to move lest she shatter into a million pieces.

At that moment, like no other moment before in her life, she wished her mother was there to comfort her and tell her what she should do. Her whole life she'd been like a person walking around with a gaping wound, pretending to be normal, and wondering why no one could see how much she bled. She'd lacked the northern star that was a mother's guidance, and she felt that lack right down to her smallest cell. She'd messed up. When she'd finally decided to live life on her own terms rather than her father's terms, she hadn't been good enough.

She wasn't good enough to succeed with the hotel, wasn't good enough to keep Daniel's love, wasn't good enough for her father to believe in her. She wasn't good enough to make right a wrong done generations ago.

All hope was gone now. She'd gambled and lost everything.

# Chapter Twenty-Seven

*Thursday, August 23—present day*
*Rothesay Estate, Orcas Island*

I nara kicked at a lone pinecone on the lawn and watched it bounce into the tangle of blackberry vines along the side. She walked farther, right up to the edge of the lawn where it turned into dirt before the sharp rocks took over and kept the tides at bay. The tide was in, the hungry water lapping a dozen feet below her tennis shoes.

She wanted to get closer.

Pivoting on her heels she headed for the path that led to the beach. As she emerged from the forest, she startled a blue heron that had been standing in the shallows looking for a meal. It rose out of the water with a honking sound and took flight over the trees. A shiver took hold of Inara and reminded her to grab a sweatshirt when she came back to the beach tomorrow.

On the day Daniel drove away with his family, she'd realized her last chance at keeping the estate had also deserted her. She'd called Luxe Realty the next morning to list the property and then she'd done almost nothing else since but go to the beach every day. Sometimes she sat in silence, thinking. Occasionally she threw rocks into the black depths, seeing if she could throw farther than the most distant rock that stuck out of the water at low tide. Twice she'd dragged an old kayak down here and took it out on the sound, paddling until her arms ached. Sometimes she cried. Sometimes she napped. But she never left the beach until darkness fell.

She thought of careers she could take up, books she could write, distant lands she could visit. She pulled up childhood memories, trying to dissect them for clues to explain her father's need for control, her mother's deep strength that allowed her to do what Inara couldn't—keep the family secret and help so many people because of it.

But mostly, she thought about Mei Lien and the embroidered sleeve that still haunted her thoughts and her dreams. She knew she would probably never see the sleeve again since Daniel had it and she hadn't heard from him. And that was okay. He should keep it.

The For Sale sign had gone up on Wednesday, and that night, when she'd gotten back from the beach, she'd found agents' business cards on her kitchen counter—evidence potential buyers had tromped through Rothesay.

Even though she expected them, needed them for their money, she felt violated by their presence, as though they were thieves sneaking into her sacred space when she was most vulnerable.

So she stayed on the beach, alone, and waited for the phone call that would tell her there was a buyer. The phone call that would be the end.

To make her feel even worse, this morning she'd received a check in the mail from the University of Washington that was the stipend Daniel had promised for the loan of the sleeve, which she'd completely forgotten about. The fifty-dollar check was now shredded and stuffed in her garbage can under a banana peel.

A light breeze ruffled the top of the water and carried the smell of wood smoke to her nose. Someone on the other side of the sound had a campfire going. She should make one, Inara decided. Just like her mom used to do here on the beach.

Her cell phone started ringing from where she'd left it in her bag on the rocks. The sound set off a cramp in her stomach. Turning her back to the water, she dug the phone out. "Hello?"

"Inara, it's Nathan."

She forced herself to sound happy. "Hey, big brother. Tell the kids I have the kayaks ready for next weekend!" She'd invited them to come Labor Day weekend so they could enjoy the estate one last time before it sold. Olivia was planning to bring her family too.

"Listen to me. It's Dad."

She felt her smile fall. "What?"

"Dad's in the hospital. It's bad."

Suddenly she was no longer a twenty-four-year-old woman, but a girl of fifteen being told her mother had died.

"What happened?" she whispered, unable to manage more.

"He had a heart attack this morning at work. They've got him hooked up to machines that are keeping him alive, but it's touch and go. He might not make it through the night. You should come."

"Of course. I'll catch the first flight off the island." She hung up and dropped her hands to her sides, her eyes closed. This wasn't happening. Her dad couldn't die. She'd been so mad at him this week she'd been ignoring his phone calls. When had she last told him she loved him?

She stared at the water as she fought to gain control of the panic coursing through her and threatening to explode. *Dad! Dad needs me.* She turned and ran.

When she got to the asphalt driveway and saw the full-force view of the estate, she jerked to a stop as the truth slammed into her.

It hadn't only been a hotel she'd wanted. She'd also wanted to give her family a place to be together again where they could recapture that closeness they'd had when her mom was alive. She'd wanted her dad to come here, see how she'd put love into the old building, and decide he wanted to be a part of it all. Nate and Olivia too. One big happy family.

That might never happen now.

# Chapter Twenty-Eight

*Thursday, August 23—present day*
*Harborview Medical Center, Seattle*

The blinds were drawn against the setting sun, making the single light burning over the hospital bed shine like a spotlight on the fragile form covered by a white sheet. Sobs tore from Inara's throat as she saw from the doorway how small and weak her dad looked with tubes going up his nose and into his arm. The machine next to the bed beeped softly with each timid heartbeat. She crossed to his bedside. "Dad?"

"He's sleeping." She turned and found her brother coming toward her from the shadows in the corner, looking like he'd aged twenty years since she'd last seen him. His suit jacket and tie were missing and his dress shirt was rumpled. His hair stuck out and a gray pallor dragged his face down, causing dark pockets under his eyes. "Glad you made it."

She leaned into his hug without taking her eyes off her dad. "How is he?"

Nate's chest rose and fell in a sigh. "Not good. Too much damage. It's just a matter of time."

She pulled away in anger. "Why aren't you finding someone

who can help him? What do you mean it's a matter of time? I'll find someone." She reached into her purse for her cell phone so she could locate the country's leading cardiac surgeon.

Nate put his hand on hers, stopping her movements. "There's nothing anyone can do, Nara. His heart is too weak for surgery."

Everything inside of her froze and a silent scream filled her ears. "He's dying?"

Nate's Adam's apple bobbed. "At least we get to say good-bye this time."

The reminder of their mother nearly made her legs give out, but it accomplished what Nate intended. Feeling raw, she reached for her father's hand and lifted it to hold between both of hers. "Hey, Dad. It's Inara." His skin felt warm, but it didn't feel like her father's hand. His was stronger. His would squeeze back.

"They don't expect him to last through the night." Nate went to the other side of the bed and laid his hand on their father's head like he was the parent. "Olivia and Jen went to get the kids and Adam's in surgery. He still doesn't know."

"They're bringing the kids here? Are you sure that's a good idea?"

Nate didn't take his gaze from their father as he shook his head. "I don't know, but I think they need to say good-bye to Grandpa, even though they won't really understand what's going on."

A fresh wave of pain made tears overflow and roll down her cheeks. Grandpa. Her dad was a wonderful grandfather who loved those kids so much. They were so small they probably wouldn't remember him in a couple years. Maybe Will, Olivia's oldest, would, but he was only nine. Even he wouldn't remember all the times Grandpa played cards with him or taught him how to hit a golf ball or played hide-and-seek, hiding in plain sight so the younger kids wouldn't get scared.

If she had kids of her own someday, they wouldn't know him at all.

"Hey, what's that all about?" Her dad sounded out of breath, but his voice was surprisingly loud in the quiet room. "No crying allowed."

"Dad!" Careful of his tubes, she leaned down and hugged him, grateful he was still here. "How do you feel?"

His hands weakly patted her back and she knew it was all he could manage. She stood back up, but grabbed a hold of his hand again. "Nate says the kids will be here soon."

"Good, good." He coughed then scrunched up his face in pain. "Water."

She helped him sip from the tiny white cup and straw sitting on the table next to the bed. When he was finished, he laid his head back and closed his eyes. Pain etched a white line around his mouth. She'd never felt so impotent in her life. "Go back to sleep, Dad. Rest."

He shook his head. "Need to talk to you, Nara."

She looked at Nate in question but he just shrugged. "What about?"

His gray-blue eyes pierced into her. "Starbucks."

*Oh, please, no.* Before he could say more, she had to tell him. "Dad, I never wanted to be in international business. I only did it because it's what I thought you—"

"I know," he interrupted her. "I knew all along and I let you do it anyway. But now you need to do what will make you happy. Are you sure about the hotel?"

Surprised, a laugh escaped her before she could stop it. "Yes. Are you serious?"

Her dad squeezed her hand, sending a fresh spurt of tears to her eyes. "Then that's what you should do." He coughed again. "When I'm...gone, you'll have everything you need, as will Nate and Olivia. I saw to that. If the hotel is what you want, then do that. I support you."

Inara's mind raced as her dad fell silent. She could keep the hotel. It's what she wanted, but she never wanted it to happen like this.

"Sorry I meddled." Her father's voice sounded weaker and she knew he was using what little strength he had to talk to her.

"Shh, Dad. It's okay. You don't need to talk."

He shook his head and pulled at her hand until she leaned closer. "After you found that sleeve, I was so afraid," he whispered. His watery eyes pleaded with her to understand. "I saw what the truth did to your mom. It changed her, dimmed her. Didn't want that for you. Thought if I got you off the island, the whole thing would go away."

"This was about the sleeve? Even calling in my loan early?" Bewildered, she shook her head and was about to say more, then remembered that Nate was here and he didn't know anything about the family secret. Careful of her words, she asked, "It was all because of the...because of Duncan?"

Her father's tired eyes went to Nate then back to her. His lips pressed together and then he said, "Tell him. Olivia too. They need to know, but later." He struggled to bring his other hand across his body so he could hold her with both hands. "You remind me so much of your mother, do you know that? So much like her. I'm so damn proud of you." His bottom lip quivered.

She was crying now and could only nod in response.

He let go of her hand and wiped at his eyes. "I wish I could have seen your hotel."

"You can see it, Dad," she insisted. "Just hold on longer."

He gave her a sad smile and closed his eyes again. "Can't, Nara-girl. Too tired."

Inara couldn't hold back the sobs. Nate reached across Dad to rub her shoulder in comfort but it did little to ease her pain.

When she finally got herself back under control, she saw that her father's eyes were still closed so she turned to find a chair to sit in. His voice stopped her. "Nara. Book...on my nightstand."

Confused, Inara looked at the bedside table and found only a tissue box and her father's water cup. "What book, Dad?"

"At home. You'll know."

And then Olivia arrived with her two kids and Jennifer was soon after with hers. The family crowded in the tiny room to wait, going in shifts to take the kids for walks down to the cafeteria or outside. Dad drifted in and out of consciousness and by ten o'clock the doctor told them he was in a coma and would not likely waken again.

By eleven, he was gone.

Inara pushed open the double doors that led into her father's bedroom. The last two days had been busy with phone calls to friends and family, meetings with the funeral director and her father's attorneys and financial adviser. Flower arrangements and cards seemed to arrive nonstop, as did phone calls she let go to voice mail. The local news station interviewed Nate for their story on Dad, but thankfully, Inara didn't have to be part of that. With arrangements finalized for the next day's service, she realized there was nothing left to keep her busy.

And then she remembered the book.

When she opened her father's bedroom door, the spicy, sweet scent of his cologne filled her head and made her eyes sting with tears she didn't know she had left. Maybe it was a bad idea.

She was a mess. If it wasn't something about her dad that set off her tears, memories of her mom, and even Daniel, did it to her. Losing her dad brought the pain of her mother's death into sharp focus, and then, to make it worse, she found herself reaching for her phone time and time again to call Daniel for comfort, only to remember they'd broken up. She was alone in her grief and barely hanging on.

She closed her eyes and breathed deeply, letting the feel of her father's presence wrap around her. For a moment she let herself pretend he was here with her, propped in the bed reading the newspaper. As a little girl she'd come in on weekend mornings to find both her parents lingering under the covers with the paper. She'd launch herself in between them and snuggle into their warmth, feeling safe and content, surrounded by the scent of her father's cologne and her mother's lavender hand cream.

Her mother's scent had disappeared years ago—God, she missed that smell—but her father's was still strong, as if he'd just splashed it on before heading out for the day.

Sighing, she opened her eyes and crossed the plush carpet to the bed. There, again, emotion snuck up on her. His reading glasses lay on the polished wood surface of his nightstand. The red light on his digital clock indicated the alarm was still set for five a.m. A single pill sat beside an empty water glass as if her dad had forgotten to take it that morning. And next to the lamp lay an old book that didn't look like her father's usual reading material, since it wasn't covered in a glossy book jacket graced with the smiling face of a well-known business executive.

It must be the book he wanted her to have.

She picked it up and turned it over in her hands as she eased down on the edge of the bed. It was made of scarred brown leather and had a leather thong wrapped several times around the middle. A journal? Had her dad kept a journal?

From between the frayed pages, a yellow sticky note poked up, showing the letters *ARA* in her father's handwriting.

*ARA*. Ara. Inara?

Taking a deep breath, she undid the leather thong and opened the fragile pages to the one marked with the sticky note. There she found the words *Give to Nara*.

*Okay, Dad. What did you want me to see?*

She pulled the note off and looked closely at the page, feeling her breath catch at the date written in a female hand at the top. *February 3, 1895.*

Whose diary was this? She flipped to the front page and, in awe, read the name *Gretna MacTavish Campbell, Orcas Island, Washington State.*

Gretna Campbell had been Duncan Campbell's wife and Dahlia's grandmother. She was the one who'd had the nervous condition that kept her on the island full-time while her husband traveled back and forth to Seattle for business. She would have been Mei Lien's neighbor and the first woman to live in Dahlia's house after Mei Lien left.

Her dad had told her there were no records like this, or if there had been, he'd told Dahlia to get rid of it all. He'd lied to her.

Feeling a sense of urgency, she clicked on the lamp and then held the book under the light to better see the faded handwriting...

> The new house, while bigger than our last, is not enough for my husband. He talks of adding on so that our home is fit for entertaining guests, as he puts it. I must admit, I much prefer the quiet that we have now and do not look with eagerness upon the time when our home is overrun with strangers.

Inara paused. She was sure Gretna was talking about Mei Lien's house here. Apparently Duncan had planned to build Rothesay right from the start. She kept reading...

> The new house is wonderful. Even though that Chinese woman lived here before us, a fact that irks Duncan to no end and was the reason he insisted the servants scrub every inch of it before we moved in last month, I very much like the amount of space we now have. The kitchen opens onto the garden, which is itself quite large compared to the plot I had on our old property. The kids love all the land outside to run and play after chores are done.
>
> Speaking of the Chinese woman, I really mustn't laugh, but it amuses me greatly to watch Duncan jump at shadows. It seems the woman disappeared without word to

anyone. Duncan told me the last time he saw her was when he delivered payment for the property to her. He didn't notice anything amiss and he did not linger. No one saw her again after that day, and he knows because he asked around, so driven was he to find her and ensure she had indeed vacated the premises. She simply disappeared. I have to believe he thinks she fell victim to misfortune and is now haunting our new home by the way he flinches at every noise and shrinks from shadows.

I'm sure this will encourage him to build his grand estate that much faster so he doesn't have to live within these walls. As for me, I'm quite content.

Inara let the book drop to her lap as the realization hit her. Duncan hadn't known Mei Lien's fate. Which meant he hadn't killed her.

Duncan hadn't killed Mei Lien!

She still didn't know for sure what had happened to Mei Lien, but she did know that her great-great-great-grandfather had not murdered her. Sure, he was still guilty of killing hundreds of other people, but not this one woman whom Inara had grown to know and care about. Crazy as it was, that fact meant a lot.

"Inara? You okay?"

She looked up to find Nate filling the doorway. Only then did she notice her face was wet with tears. She wiped them away with her fingers and laughed. "He didn't kill her, Nate."

As shock registered on his features, she realized her brother had no idea what she was talking about. She patted the bed beside her, and when Nate joined her, she told him her secret fears that their ancestor had murdered Mei Lien for her land. "But Dad had this diary that says Duncan didn't know Mei Lien's fate, so that means he didn't kill her. Isn't that wonderful?"

Nate lifted his eyebrows and gave her a look that said he

doubted her sanity. "Why in the world would you think Duncan murdered her in the first place? He had enough money to buy any property he wanted."

"You two having a cry fest without me?" Olivia asked as she swept into the room dressed in pressed slacks and a starched blouse. She bounded onto the bed with them. "I want in."

Inara laughed as she scooted up to lean against the headboard next to her sister. "What are you two doing here anyway?"

Her siblings looked at each other before Nate carefully said, "I tried calling you but you didn't answer. I thought we should meet here and start making decisions on what we're going to do with all of Dad's stuff, and the house too."

"Did he leave it to the three of us?"

Nate nodded.

Inara wasn't ready to think about any of that yet so she was relieved when Olivia changed the subject. "Did I hear you two saying someone murdered someone?"

Reminded, Nate scowled at Inara. "She thought Duncan Campbell killed the Chinese woman who made the sleeve she found. Why would you think that?"

Inara hugged her knees. "In researching the sleeve, I learned something that Dad wanted me to keep secret, something Duncan did. Mom had even known about it and didn't tell anyone. Before he died Dad told me to tell you. I think he realized the truth needs to be told."

When her siblings exchanged confused glances, she launched into the story, telling them everything she knew about the night Duncan ordered three hundred fifty people thrown overboard to their deaths. As she spoke, Olivia covered her mouth with her hands in horror. Nate shook his head in disbelief.

"I think we need to tell the truth, even after all this time," she told them now. "Think about all those families who never knew what happened to their loved ones. And even though it might change how people remember Mom and Dad and all the

Campbells before them, I still think it's important that the world knows the truth of what happened."

Thinking of Daniel she added, "We need to apologize."

"I agree," Nate said. Olivia nodded.

Inara caressed the journal cover. "I think the truth ate at Dad like it's eaten at me. I think that's why he wanted to give this to me. To say that he changed his mind about the secret."

"I think you're right," Olivia said, reaching for her hand.

With a grateful smile for her sister, Inara squeezed her hand. "Believe it or not, there's more to tell you." She swallowed. "We found out that Mei Lien's son was Daniel's great-grandfather and I had to tell him the truth of what happened. Because I'd lied, we broke up. I'm not sure how his family feels about everything, but I'd like one of you to reach out to them and see if they'd help us tell the true story."

"Of course," Nate agreed. "That's an excellent idea."

Olivia had a strange look on her face as she looked at Inara.

"What?" Inara asked, feeling defensive all of a sudden.

Olivia shook her head as a smile spread her pink-glossed lips. "I'm so proud of you. I don't know if I've ever told you that before now, but I am."

The unexpected compliment started off another spurt of tears but Inara smiled through them and hugged her sister. "Thanks, Liv. Does this mean you'll help me?"

"Absolutely. And I think you're right. Dad probably realized the truth had to be told." She patted the diary on Inara's lap as evidence. "But can we figure it out after the funeral?"

"Good idea." Inara picked up the diary and hugged it to her chest to soothe the ache that started up there again at the mention of her father's funeral. "Nate, are you okay with this? You'll take the brunt of it all, being the new CEO of PMG and all."

He ruffled her hair like he'd done when she was a kid. "I'll manage."

"Thanks, Nate." She squeezed his hand then reached for

Olivia's. "You too, Liv." Holding them, she breathed in her father's scent again and wished he was here with them.

"I don't know about you two, but I'm not feeling like making any decisions today after all." Nate got to his feet. "I vote for dinner and a movie at my house. You in?"

"Excellent idea." Inara headed for the door with her siblings.

Nate paused at the threshold and turned back to look at the bedroom. "Feels like he just stepped out, doesn't it?"

In answer, Inara slid her hand into his and wordlessly switched off the light.

# Chapter Twenty-Nine

*Wednesday, December 26, 1894*
*McElroy Farm, Orcas Island*

With shaking hands, Mei Lien snipped the thread and fell weakly back against the sofa.

Finished.

Finally.

For forty-six days, since the morning Yan-Tao left, she'd done nothing but embroider. When she was hungry, she reached for the bowl of cold rice she kept next to the embroidery frame. When she was sick, she threw up in the bucket on the floor, not bothering to empty it for days at a time. When she was tired, she slept for as little as she could for there was more work to finish. When she was in pain, she worked through the pain.

She'd had to take to wearing gloves while she worked because her fingers had developed blisters from the constant rubbing of the needle and embroidery floss. Eventually the blisters had popped and bled and she hadn't wanted to drip blood on the silk. She'd never had any other use for the white woman's gloves Joseph had bought for her.

Her entire body ached. Her eyes burned. Her skull pounded.

Nothing mattered but finishing the embroidery before it was too late.

And now she was finished. The scene lay before her with every last detail in place. It was the scene she'd started seven years before but had never felt was truly finished. Now, it was. The entire story was told, including the story of her death, which she could clearly see.

She sat still, moving only her eyes as she took in the embroidered scene. It was of the night that changed everything. The ship. Campbell. Father. Grandmother. Water—swirling, pulling, taunting. Beneath the waves was Mei Lien herself, floating on the current with arms and legs splayed, smiling.

The smile hadn't been planned. She'd meant for the scene to portray all the horror and agony the night had inflicted upon her. She'd planned to embroider no facial features at all to show the loss of herself. But right at the end, just a few minutes ago, she'd added that smile and only now, after, did she know exactly why.

That night and all of its horror had given her Joseph and eventually Yan-Tao, which meant the story ended in happiness. But that was only half of it.

The other half was yet to come. She'd felt the call of the water all these years. She'd heard her ancestors calling for her in the waves and reaching for her in the currents. Finally, tonight, the water would get what it was cheated out of eight years ago. Tonight, it would get Mei Lien.

She smiled about that because the water was her destiny and there was no denying destiny. The water held Father, Grandmother, and Joseph, and in the water she would be with them again.

Carefully she cut the ties holding the silk to the frame and folded the finished sleeve into a tiny square. If only she could give this to Yan-Tao to go with the rest of his robe, but at least he had most of the story in his possession, and he would return one day for the rest.

Then, as gently as though she were swaddling a child, she wrapped the sleeve inside the shirt of Joseph's that she'd kept aside for just this reason. There was nothing special about the shirt other than the fact that Joseph had worn it his last day on the farm. It's what Mei Lien pictured him wearing when she thought of their last day together. She hoped Yan-Tao would remember it too when he came back to find the embroidery.

Finally, she got to her feet and limped into the kitchen where she found a piece of oilcloth to wrap around the bundle and kitchen twine to tie it all closed.

Before her strength failed, she made her way to the stairs that led up to the bedrooms and mostly fell onto the bottom step, so weak were her legs. Before her was the second step, its wood scuffed from years of use. A new scratch from Yan-Tao's travel trunk scarred the middle. The nails holding the step to the supports below had loosened, or been pried loose, she wasn't sure, and now sat at angles in their holes. She ran her hand over the nails but couldn't bring herself to pull the board up.

She'd never opened this secret compartment. It belonged to Yan-Tao and held whatever a young boy considered his treasures. She had no idea if he'd taken anything from here before he left, or if she'd find everything he'd stashed away along with dreams and young-boy secrets. She didn't know if she wanted to find treasures or emptiness; both would hurt.

She shook her head at herself. She didn't have time to be sentimental.

With a hard yank she pulled the tread up, jiggling it until the nails pulled free and the entire board came loose in her hands. She set it on the step above and peered inside.

Dark, but not empty.

Placed carefully in the hole created by the first and second steps were pinecones, rocks, and twigs that must have held special importance to her son. On the floor, wedged under the first step was a faded green blanket he'd carried around as a toddler.

Dirt and holes made it nearly unrecognizable, but she knew immediately what it was.

In the dancing light of the lantern flame, she spotted something hanging from a nail tacked into the side of the compartment. With her aching body protesting, she balanced her weight on one arm and leaned with the other into the hole to reach the thin rope and pull it free. Fresh tears stung her eyes as she saw what Yan-Tao had hung there.

Her father's embroidered coin purse. The one he'd thrust into her hands on the steamship and told her to hide in her chest bindings. She'd forgotten all about it.

The lump growing in her throat burst free and she found herself sobbing. Yan-Tao should be here. Her young son should never have been forced to leave his mother so soon after losing his father. He should still be here, storing treasures in his secret compartment.

It wasn't fair. Her whole adult life had been one cruelty after another and now that cruelty had scarred her innocent child.

She plunged her arm into the hole again, grabbing his forgotten blanket and balling it in her hands. Bringing it to her face, she sobbed into the soft cotton, her heart shattering at the pure torture of feeling near him one last time but it not being enough. A hint of his little boy scent lingered. She clung to the blanket, needing it more than life, and wept.

When nothing was left inside of her but a great emptiness, she wiped her tears with her skirt and remembered why she was here. To leave her son's legacy where he could find it.

She picked up the bundle containing the embroidered sleeve, leaving Yan-Tao's blanket in its place on her lap, and carefully wedged the bundle under the front step where the blanket had been. Then, bringing two trembling fingers to her lips, she kissed them and pressed them to the bundle, hoping Yan-Tao would feel her love the day he returned to find the package.

She moved to place Yan-Tao's blanket next to the bundle,

but hesitated. She couldn't give it up. She'd given up so much already, surely this one token she could keep with her. Surely Yan-Tao would understand and forgive her.

Her mind made up, she stuffed the blanket into the bodice of her gown to keep it close to her heart. The blanket slipped down to her waist. Only now did she realize how her dress gaped from her body, how thin she'd become. Her ribs poked out like a street dog's, her wrists looked thin as twigs and just as fragile. She knew if she looked in a mirror—which she would not do—she'd see a woman she didn't recognize.

She was surprised to realize she wasn't bothered by her wasting body. She would soon have no more need of it and the spirits who loved her and were waiting for her would recognize her soul without the trappings of skin, hair, and bones.

Reaching into her bodice, she pulled the blanket up and tied it around her neck. There, that was better anyway. It kept Yan-Tao even closer to her, where she could smell him. On top of this she hung Father's coin purse around her neck. It too should return to the water where it belonged.

She lifted the stair tread back into place and carefully fitted the loose nails into their holes. Now she needed to secure it to keep it hidden and safe from Campbell and anyone else. She'd thought very carefully about this part of her plan for if Campbell found the compartment, he would destroy everything inside.

One more task. *You can do it*, she told herself. She had to.

She found Joseph's crate of tools right where she'd left it tucked next to her canning supplies behind the stove. It felt much heavier than she remembered from two months ago when she'd left it there, but she managed to push and pull it across the floor to the stairs. Sweat dripped off her but she refused to stop.

With strength she didn't think she had, she hammered nails into the step, securing it tightly to the supports underneath while being careful not to make it appear different from the other steps. Then, for good measure, she added more nails to the bottom step too.

It was all she could do. It would have to be good enough.

"You've done good, May."

Though it should have startled her, the sound of a voice in the room didn't surprise her at all. It was like she'd been expecting him all along.

She turned, the hammer still in her hand, and found Joseph standing behind her. He smiled down at her with a look of such love she could not help but smile back through her tears. "I knew you'd come back for me."

He reached his hand toward her. "I never left you."

She reached up to grasp him. Just when she should have felt his touch, her hand went through his and she was reminded that Joseph was a spirit now.

Still smiling, she packed the tools back into the crate and tugged it back to its place behind the stove. "I'm almost ready, Joseph," she told her husband's spirit as she gave the crate one last push.

"Your mother is eager to see you," came her father's voice in reply.

Mei Lien jerked around and found Joseph's spirit had gone and in his place stood her father, looking strong and healthy as she remembered him when they'd lived in Seattle. "Father! I missed you." She limped toward him but stopped halfway, knowing she wouldn't be able to hug him as she so badly wanted. "Are you well?"

His smile faded. "I wish things could have turned out better for you, my daughter."

Mei Lien shook her head. "No, Father. It is as it should be." She looked around the kitchen and realized she had no reason to linger. Her duties here were done. "I am ready to go now."

When she looked back to where her father stood, he was gone again. "I'll see you in the water," she whispered to the empty room.

Carefully she went through the house, extinguishing the few

lanterns she'd been using. Then, to any spirits that might reside here, she said, "Please keep my embroidery safe for Yan-Tao."

In answer she felt a wave of peace wash over her and she knew her wish would be granted.

It was time. She slowly, painfully, made her way to the back door and outside to the dark yard. The moonless sky twinkled with thousands of stars but the forest around the house looked like a black void.

She didn't hesitate. She knew where she was going and she knew nothing hiding in the dark would harm her. She had a purpose for being here. Her family was waiting.

At the water's edge she stopped and listened. The waves lapped against the rocky beach. Something scurried about in the dried leaves of the forest behind her and an owl hooted from somewhere up the mountain. Otherwise there were no sounds. Not her father's voice, not Joseph's.

Still, she talked to them as she stepped fully clothed into the inky water. "I'm coming. I'm coming," she whispered over and over as the cold wrapped around her limbs and pulled her in deeper. She could see her breath on the frigid air. "I'm coming."

Her stomach revolted at the shocking cold, but she didn't stop. Her limbs were shaking now and her teeth chattered as she spoke, but she knew it was only temporary.

As the water reached her neck and Yan-Tao's blanket tied there, she finally saw them. Joseph. Father. Grandmother. Even her own mother. As though they'd always been there waiting for her, they surrounded her, filling her with warmth and light.

With one step more, the water closed over her head.

# Chapter Thirty

*Wednesday, August 29—present day*
*Lake Union, Seattle*

Early on the second morning after her father's funeral, Inara had Nate drop her off at the Kenmore Air seaplane terminal on his way to work, which meant she was an hour too early for her flight. Luckily, there was a Starbucks on the other side of the parking lot where she could kill time, so, after checking in with the reception desk, she headed there.

She ordered a tea latte and chose an outdoor table to watch the morning take shape over Lake Union. From her vantage point, she could see the southern shore of the lake where the Museum of History and Industry would later be drawing tourists but for now sat empty. Maybe someday, after she and her siblings revealed what they knew, the real history of Seattle's Chinese would be displayed in that building. Maybe she'd contact the museum and suggest it.

Shifting her gaze, she saw the sun had crested the top of Capitol Hill to the east and would soon bring heat to the air that still held the cool freshness of night. A ribbon of traffic wove around the base of the hill, heading to another workday in the city.

As beautiful as Seattle was, she ached to be on her beach away from the people, noise, and congestion. She wanted to hear the breeze blowing through the forest, not the hum of traffic or the cry of seagulls rooting in garbage cans. She wanted to watch the sun rise over Mount Constitution, not the steel and concrete that made up her eastern horizon now.

She needed to be alone to process everything that had changed in her life in the last few days. She missed her father. Was still working through the fact that he was gone.

And she missed Daniel. Missed his one-dimpled grin and that lock of hair that always fell over his eye. Missed hearing his voice at the end of every day.

She sipped her latte and watched the sky lighten to the robin's-egg blue of summer. It was probably for the best that Daniel broke up with her. She needed time to be alone to mourn her father, to rework her hotel plan to fit the budget she now had with her unexpected inheritance.

The dichotomy of joy and pain she felt was tearing her apart. On one hand she couldn't be happier that she got to keep the hotel. She would see her dream come true! But on the other hand, it had taken losing her father to get it.

She'd rather lose Rothesay a hundred times over.

She checked the clock on her phone. Forty-five minutes until her flight. She groaned under her breath and consoled herself with the reminder that by lunchtime she'd be home. In fact, she should call Tom and have him meet her at the house so they could get to work right away. She dialed his number.

He was surprised to hear from her but, thankfully, was available that afternoon. She hung up and slipped her phone back into her pocket, glad he hadn't offered condolences. She was nearing her breaking point on condolences.

"Inara!"

She turned at the sound but didn't see anyone. Then the call came again: "Inara, over here."

She looked in that direction and was shocked to find Margaret Chin, of all people, heading toward her from the air terminal. She waved to Inara with one hand as the other clutched a gold purse to the waist of her tailored burgundy skirt and jacket.

Inara got up and went to meet her, wondering all the while why Margaret Chin was at Lake Union at this time of day dressed like she was heading to a business meeting. "Margaret, good morning," Inara said in way of greeting as she hugged the woman who had been nothing but kind to her in spite of the hurt Inara had inflicted on her son. On their whole family.

"You're a hard woman to get ahold of," Margaret told her as she hugged her back. "Don't you ever answer your phone?"

Inara flinched. "It's been a difficult week."

A look of sorrow came into the older woman's eyes. "Yes. I'm so sorry about your father. I heard the service was beautiful."

Inara nodded her thanks but said nothing.

"Your brother told me I'd find you here." She motioned toward the table Inara had just vacated. "Can we sit?"

A tremor went through her as she returned to her seat. "Is Daniel okay?"

Margaret patted her hand. "Daniel's fine. This is about you and me."

"What do you mean?"

Margaret crossed her toned legs and regarded Inara with a small smile. "Did you mean what you said that morning about us working together on your hotel and me running the restaurant?"

Inara let the question sink into her brain. Was she hearing Margaret correctly? "I...I meant it, but I have to admit, my financial circumstances have changed now."

Margaret pressed her lips together and seemed to be considering something. Then she opened the bag on her lap and pulled out a one-inch binder, which she opened and set in front of Inara. "This is a report I've put together showing you some sample menus, staffing needs, ideas for decor, and, most importantly, financial projections for the restaurant. The way I figure it, your hotel still needs a restaurant, and I'm the best you'll find. Plus, I'm dying to relocate to Orcas part-time and work with you, if you'll have me."

A bit overwhelmed, Inara flipped through the pages in the binder, growing increasingly intrigued by everything she saw. "I'm not promising anything, but if we were to do this, I suppose we could renovate a space on the third floor for you to live in."

Margaret waved her hand in the air. "No, no. I already have my agent looking for condos in Eastsound."

"What about your restaurants here? Your family?"

"I'll commute back and forth but can commit most of my time to being on Orcas for the next few years until I find a chef I can trust with the menu and whom you and I both like."

Margaret had yet to mention the biggest obstacle Inara could see. She looked down at her lap. "What about Daniel? Does he know you want to work with me?"

"He told me I'd be stupid not to pursue this. In fact, he wants to talk to you himself. He drove me here."

Inara jerked her chin up and followed Margaret's gaze toward the parking lot. Daniel leaned against the metal railing, watching them with his hands tucked into his pockets. A lock of black hair hung in his eyes, just the way she loved. Her fingers itched to brush it aside.

Somehow she got to her feet despite the nervous shaking that had overtaken her body. She didn't remember moving, but she was suddenly in front of him, her body straining to touch him and barely holding back. "Daniel. It's good to see you."

Those smooth lips she loved so much spread into a smile that could have broken her heart had it not been broken already. He didn't move to touch her, but his eyes were warm as he said, "You too. I missed you."

His words shot straight to her heart, her eyes stung with tears. She took a step forward, reaching for him, but stopped. Too soon.

She stepped back and looked down at the pavement, noticing that someone had dropped a nickel. "Daniel, I'm so sorry I didn't tell you about—"

"Look, I need to apologize," he interrupted her. "I handled things between us horribly, and for that I'm sorry. Inara, look at me."

What if he was just playing nice for his mother's sake? *Don't get your hopes up, Inara.* Still, her chin lifted; her eyes met his. His face softened into a smile filled with all the memories of their days working together, their nights in each other's arms.

With the sound of commuter traffic and piercing seagull cries surrounding them, Inara allowed herself to admit the truth—she still wanted to be with him, despite all that had gone wrong between them.

"Your brother called me last night. He told me you're planning on revealing what Duncan Campbell did." He shifted his weight to the other foot and kicked at a tuft of grass growing in a crack in the pavement. "Don't tell the story on my account, please. I don't want you or your family hurt."

*He still cared!* "Thank you, but Nate and Olivia and I have talked, and we think it's time. We're going to make the announcement next month." She crossed her arms to hide her awkwardness. "It would mean a lot to me if you were there."

His eyes gleamed. "I'll be there. My whole family will be there." His hand came up, his warm palm cupping her cheek. "I missed you so much."

She leaned in to his touch and closed her eyes. Suddenly his lips were on hers, and she forgot all else except how right it felt to be in his arms again. She melted into his kiss and let her body fit perfectly against his.

It was only the loud clearing of a throat that brought them back to the present. They looked at each other and laughed before turning toward Margaret, who had remained at the table. She was smiling, and Inara would have sworn her eyes were damp.

"Before you two get carried away, let me remind you that Inara has a flight to catch and I still need an answer from her."

The restaurant. She'd forgotten all about it when she'd seen Daniel.

With Daniel's arm around her, and Margaret and her binder of ideas, Inara felt the rightness of it all. She'd wanted her hotel to be a place where her family could come together again. With her father gone, her vision would never come to fruition, but that didn't mean her definition of family couldn't evolve.

The Rothesay Hotel would be a place for family—hers and the Chins, and all the families who would come to stay over the years.

"Inara? Your flight?" Margaret reminded her.

*Her flight!* Panic chased away the warm fuzzies. She pulled out her cell phone and saw it was time to head to the floatplane dock or she'd risk missing her flight. "I have to go," she told them, for the first time wishing Tom wasn't waiting for her. "But my answer is absolutely yes. I want nothing more than for you to run the restaurant. How soon can you be there?"

Margaret jumped to her feet and grabbed Inara for a hug. "Thank you! This is going to be wonderful!"

Inara squeezed her in return. "Thank you, Margaret. For everything."

Margaret drew back and smiled in a way that showed she understood. "You're welcome. Now go, catch your flight. I'll call you tonight."

Torn, Inara looked toward the dock and back at Daniel. Seeing her struggle, he gave her a nudge. "I'll come up to see you this weekend. We have some time to make up for."

At that she stood on her tiptoes and gave Daniel a kiss that would have to keep both of them satisfied for the next two days. She grabbed her bag and ran for the floatplane that would take her home.

# Chapter Thirty-One

*Saturday, October 6—present day*
*Waterfront Park, Seattle*

Inara listened as Nate addressed the crowd assembled for the dedication of the new waterfront park. The press releases they'd sent out had promised an unexpected announcement at the dedication ceremony but she could tell by the shock on most faces that none of them had expected anything like what they'd just learned.

With Elliott Bay sparkling in the autumn sun behind her and Mount Rainer hovering in the southern distance, Inara had revealed Mei Lien's tragic story and her great-great-great-grandfather's role in the murders of hundreds. She'd left nothing out as the news cameras recorded everything, and she knew—they all knew—that the news would spread around the world, sending shock and outrage back to her family and PMG. They hoped the statement Nate was reading would help people understand their own family's sorrow and how deeply sorry they all were for their ancestor's actions.

"This park is not being dedicated to the memory of Duncan Campbell as originally planned," Nate was saying and Inara held her breath for the rest. "This park is dedicated in memory of all who lost their lives that tragic day and is being named in honor of the woman who made sure the truth would not be forgotten. Ladies and Gentlemen, I give to you the Mei Lien McElroy Memorial Park."

With that the cloth was pulled from the statue at the center of the park to reveal a bronze Chinese woman staring out to sea, a sad look in her eyes and a bolt of cloth in her hands. Inara heard Margaret gasp beside her and knew she'd caught sight of the face. She'd given the artist a picture of Cassie to use as a model for Mei Lien. He'd only had a month to create this new sculpture and it had cost an exorbitant fee, but it was worth it for this single moment of awe.

"Oh, Inara, it's beautiful!" Margaret pulled Inara against her for a hug but her eyes never left the statue.

"I'm happy you like it."

"Why'd you make her look like Cassie?" Daniel asked from her other side as they watched Cassie pose for a picture next to the statue while news cameras rolled and reporters fired off questions to her about her newly discovered ancestor.

Inara laughed. "Do you think she minds?"

"Not at all." Something in Daniel's voice made her glance at him and she found him looking down at her with a tender expression. "Thank you for this. All of this."

She knew he understood how difficult the next few days and weeks would be for her family. She also knew he'd be right there beside her during the worst of it. She stepped to him for a kiss. "Thank you."

With his forehead to hers, he murmured, "I have a surprise of my own waiting for you back at Rothesay."

She pulled back. "I hope to be back next week, but I have to stay to help Nate and Olivia deal with the fallout for however long it takes—"

"Don't worry," he interrupted. "It'll be there whenever you

go back, and when you do, I'm going with you. No hurry. For now, though, I think you're needed." He nodded toward Nate who was surrounded by a knot of people flinging questions and accusations at him as though he, not Duncan, was the guilty party.

"I'd better go help him. I'll see you later at Toisan, right?"

"Mom promised to hold dinner until you all get there. Take the time you need to deal with this." With one last kiss, he nudged her toward the waiting crowd.

Gathering her strength, she stepped beside Nate with a hand on his back so he knew she was there and then she pasted on a smile for the crowd. Olivia stepped to his other side. Together they'd face what came and they'd do whatever it took to bring peace to those shattered by their news.

"I'm exhausted, but so happy to be back," Inara told Daniel as she climbed out of his car in front of Rothesay a week later. After all that had happened, she finally felt confident in thinking of the house as hers. She was home. "Thanks for driving."

"No problem. Hey, my mom must still be here." He nodded toward the car parked in front of the main porch and the lights shining through the front windows. "Let's go say hi."

She left her bags in the car and came around to slip her hand into his and walk through the cool blue evening to the hotel. She couldn't wait to see what Tom's crews had accomplished during the three weeks she'd spent in Seattle. She would have stayed longer, but Nate had practically packed her bags for her and pushed her out the door.

"We've got it under control," he'd said in reference to the public relations fiasco their announcement had caused PMG. "I've hired Daniel's research team to start identifying the victims and tracking down any living family. We're over the worst of it. Go. Be a hotelier."

She'd laughed at the title as she'd hugged him good-bye. Hotelier. Yes, that was what she was. It fit, she decided.

"Mom, you here?" Daniel called as they entered through the front entry.

"She's probably back in the kitchen and can't hear you…" Her words dwindled away as she caught sight of Margaret standing in the newly tiled lobby between the reception desk and a large glass case Inara had never seen before. Margaret's gleeful grin made Inara take a second look at the case and what was inside. Her breath stuck in her throat. "Is that…"

"Yes, your surprise," Daniel answered without hearing the full question. "We had the robe cleaned and hung on a floating form with your sleeve. It's a temperature- and humidity-controlled case so it should keep well here in the hotel, if you like it."

Somehow she made it down the steps and across the lobby to the case where the full impact of the robe and sleeve hit her. They were together, here on the property where Mei Lien had poured her heart and soul into them.

Even though the robe had been cleaned, it was still yellowed with age and bare in places. The contrast between it and the sleeve was remarkable and showed how intensely the robe had been loved. Worn on his body or not, Yan-Tao had clearly treasured the robe, probably because his mother had made it for him. The hem was even frayed, like it had been dragged on the ground.

She still couldn't figure out why Mei Lien or Yan-Tao had cut off the sleeve and hidden it. *But, really, does it matter?* She was glad they did it because she, and now anyone visiting the hotel, could see how breathtaking the colors had once been. The sleeve practically glowed under the lighting Daniel had set up in the display, the vibrant colors telling their story in a way that was almost three-dimensional.

The robe itself had many stories to tell too. More than she realized, she thought now as she circled the display and got the full view of all sides. She'd have to spend some time studying it over the next few days, she decided. Was that a rabbit? *Later.* She'd study it later.

She turned to find Daniel and Margaret watching her. "Are you sure you want to give them to me? Doesn't Vera want them? Or the museum?"

Margaret squeezed her shoulder. "We think you should have it. It's our way of saying thank you for connecting us with our family history."

"It's perfect." She pulled Margaret to her for a hug. Over Margaret's shoulder she smiled at Daniel. "Thank you so much," she said again.

Later, she and Daniel made their way to the beach through the dark forest. After the emotional and hectic last few weeks, Inara needed to reconnect with the peace the beach always brought her.

"I'm so glad we revealed the truth. It just feels right, you know?" she said to Daniel as they came out of the trees onto the beach, her breath showing in the cold night air. She switched off her flashlight since the moon lit the night nearly as bright as day.

They walked in silence to the edge of the low tide where they stood in a path of moonlight stretching across the water. "You know," she said in a muted voice since the night seemed to call for quiet. "It's strange that of all the people I might have gone to for help identifying the sleeve, I found you and you ended up being connected to it."

"I was thinking about that too," he admitted, holding her close to his side for warmth. "I think Mei Lien and Yan-Tao had something to do with that, if you can believe in such things."

Just like how Dahlia brought her back to the place where she belonged so she could find the sense of self she'd lost along with her mother. "Yes," she told Daniel. "I think I can believe such things."

She looked up at the bright moon and wondered aloud, "What do you think happened to her, really? We know Duncan didn't kill her."

She felt Daniel shrug, though she didn't take her eyes off the moon. "We may never know for sure," he answered softly.

A sudden thought occurred to Inara and she turned to look at him. "What do you think Mei Lien would think about us being together? Do you think she'd hate for you to be in a relationship with a Campbell relative?"

Daniel seemed to mull it over as he stared at the water, his features highlighted by moonlight. Then his face softened. "You know, I think she approves. I think she's forgiven your family."

Inara laughed. "You talk like she's still here."

Daniel didn't laugh with her. Instead he turned his face to her and she saw he had a thoughtful expression there. "I think she is," he told her. "Don't you feel it?"

Inara's laughter faded. "There's something about this beach, isn't there? I didn't know anyone else felt it."

Now Daniel did smile, but it was one directed back across the years to the woman who'd left them her story on an embroidered sleeve. "I feel it."

He pulled her into his arms and tilted her face up to his. "You found her story and you brought her family back here to her home. You've also made her great-great-grandson a very happy man."

His lips came over hers, warm and demanding. Inara sank into his embrace, responding to his hunger with her own.

From somewhere out in the water, the sound of a splash echoed to where they stood wrapped together on the beach and she knew Daniel was right.

Mei Lien approved.

# Author's Note

The inspiration for this novel sparked as I was researching the history of the San Juan Islands and came across a story in an old settler's diary telling of nineteenth-century smugglers in the islands. One smuggler, it was rumored, had caught sight of a revenue cutter chasing him. Not wanting to be caught with illegal Chinese immigrants on board, he bashed their heads with a club and dumped their bodies overboard.

The story stuck with me for years, along with many questions. Why were they smuggling Chinese people? Why murder them? What was the story behind all of this?

And then I learned of the Chinese Exclusion Act of 1882, which was an immigration law excluding people from the United States based on their Chinese race, although still allowing entry to some merchants. This was followed by the Geary Act of 1892, which discriminated equally against all Chinese immigrants. These acts were not repealed until 1943 with Public Law 199, which allowed Chinese to enter the United States under a rigid quota system. With anti-Chinese sentiment high in the latter half of the nineteenth century, white citizens in towns from Southern California to British Columbia and east to Wyoming and Colorado forcibly, and often violently, drove all Chinese out. Lynchings, shootings, and homicidal beatings were common.

The more I learned, the more I became horrified at the ethnic cleansing that had occurred and that was left unmentioned in all of my history books in school.

Although this story is a work of fiction, it draws from factual events. The Chinese residents of Seattle, more than three hundred fifty of them and many legal U.S. citizens, really were driven out of town on February 7, 1886. Fearful for their lives, they bought passage on the steamer *Queen of the Pacific*, which was bound for San Francisco. However, before the steamer could leave dock, Territorial Governor Watson C. Squire intervened, ordering the anti-Chinese mob to desist the violence and declaring martial law. Judge Roger S. Greene interviewed every Chinese person, including those who had paid for passage on the steamer, and informed them of their right to leave or stay in Seattle. If they chose to stay, they would be protected.

The Chinese people who chose to stay were escorted back to their homes by the Home Guards, the Seattle Rifles, and the University Cadets, all there to protect the Chinese from the angry mob still rioting in favor of driving them from the city. After several months of unrest, peace was restored. Only one death occurred during the riots, that of a white rioter. Those who chose to leave reached San Francisco safely.

Since Seattle was an exception, I chose in this story to represent and honor all those whose lives were taken in other cities and towns by giving my Seattle Chinese a similar fate.

# Reading Group Guide

1. Discuss the role of race in this novel. What are some examples of racial discrimination you have experienced in your own life? Do you feel race relations have improved in the more than a century that has passed since Mei Lien's time? Why or why not?

2. Discuss Mei Lien's decision to hide herself and her son away on the farm to avoid contact with other people. In her shoes, would you have done the same thing or something different? Why?

3. Before reading this novel, had you already been aware of the "driving out" of Chinese people from American and Canadian towns? Share what you know. If you weren't previously aware of these events, what was your reaction to learning of these racial purges?

4. Family relationships are a key theme in *The Girl Who Wrote in Silk*. In what ways do you think Mei Lien and Inara have similar familial experiences? In what ways are their experiences different?

5. Both Mei Lien and Inara struggle with the death of loved

ones. Discuss how their methods of mourning and honoring their lost loved ones differ or are similar. Is there anything they do or do not do that surprises you?

6. The island setting is an important one in both time periods. Do you think that Mei Lien and Inara experience Orcas Island in the same way or differently? What causes these similarities or differences?

7. Compare and contrast the father-daughter relationships in the story. How do you think they might have been different if the women's mothers had lived?

8. After finding her grandmother's body on the beach and realizing that her family had indeed been killed, Mei Lien feels that a part of her heart has died, a part that will forever keep her from loving Joseph fully. Do you think this comes to be true for her? Have you lost a loved one and felt that a part of you is now lost forever?

9. Inara struggles with accepting the fact that her ancestor committed a heinous crime. Do you think she is able to absolve her family of this shameful act? What would you do if you discovered an honored ancestor of yours had done something shameful?

10. The "driving out" of Chinese occurred loosely about the same time in U.S. history as when Native Americans were forced onto reservations. If you had been alive at the time, how do you think you would have felt about these events? Can you think of similar ethnic cleansings occurring in today's time, in the United States or in other countries?

11. Inara turns down the Starbucks job to renovate and eventually manage the boutique hotel on Orcas Island. What motivates her to make this decision? What decision would you make in a similar circumstance? Keep in mind issues such as security, family obligations, location, social obligations, and financial peace of mind.

12. Which character, Mei Lien or Inara, did you feel more connected to? Why? Is one more or less authentic than the other?

13. If you inherited a large family estate, what would you do with the property?

14. Inara thinks of Aunt Dahlia, Gretna Campbell, and herself as the family "oddballs" because of their unique ways of relating to the world around them. Have you ever felt like an oddball? Were you able to embrace it as Inara does? Explain.

15. Mei Lien sees her loved ones in the animals around her. In the final scene of the book, Daniel and Inara hear a seal splash in the water and feel it is Mei Lien giving her approval for their relationship. Do you think loved ones could return as animals that can interact with us? If you could come back as an animal, what would you be and why?

16. What do you imagine happens next after the novel ends? Will Inara and Daniel stay together? Will the hotel and restaurant be successful? What effect, if any, will what Duncan Campbell did have on the characters' lives?

17. Finding the embroidered sleeve changes the course of Inara's life because the intricate beauty and mystery won't let her go. Have you ever come across, or do you own, an object that had a similar effect on you?

18. Another theme of this novel is belonging and acceptance. Mei Lien is ostracized because of her race. Aunt Dahlia was sent to live on the island because of her sexual orientation. Inara chose a field of study to please her father and live up to the professional success of her siblings. In what ways have you struggled in your life for acceptance?

19. Inara agonizes over whether to honor her father's wishes and keep the truth a secret, or tell the truth and know it will hurt people she cares for. If you were in a similar situation, what would you do?

20. If Mei Lien had lived, what do you think she might have done to support herself and her son? Where would their story have taken them, and what would have been different for Yan-Tao?

21. Mei Lien dresses as a boy to move freely and safely around Seattle. After she marries Joseph and starts dressing as a woman, she never really feels comfortable. Do you think her preference in clothing represents a deeper gender issue? What else might it represent for her?

22. We get hints at what Yan-Tao/Ken's life was like in the orphanage based on the curriculum taught there and about his life in Seattle based on what Vera tells her family. Do you think he found happiness? Given what you know from the story and world events of the twentieth century, what do you think his life was like?

23.  Inara suspects that Vera Chin made up the Chin family's false background that Ken grew up in China and then immigrated to Seattle in the early 1900s. Vera claims it must have been a mix-up, but Inara wonders if Vera's sense of pride motivated the stories. Think of your own family history and the members of your family who are the keepers of stories. Is the validity of any of your family stories suspect? Are there any that are outrageous, but you know them to be true?

24.  Do you think Yan-Tao/Ken ever went back to the island to attempt to retrieve the sleeve his mother left for him in his secret hiding hole? Why or why not? If he did go back, why might he not have been successful?

# A Conversation with the Author

**What was your inspiration for writing *The Girl Who Wrote in Silk*?**

In 2002, I was researching the history of the San Juan Islands for a historical romance I was writing when I read of a smuggler who, rather than face getting caught with his illegal cargo of Chinese people, chose to bash them on their heads with a club and throw their bodies overboard. Over the years, the horror of that story stuck with me. Once I learned of the attempted purge of all Chinese from Seattle, pieces started falling into place, and soon I had Mei Lien's story.

I've always been fascinated by stories that recount history and its effects on contemporary characters, so I knew I wanted this story told in both time periods. Inara's story grew out of the connection to Mei Lien through the house and the sleeve she finds there (more on that below), as well as the personal family connection she discovers while researching the sleeve. I chose to have Inara create a boutique hotel because I've always loved travel and tourism and think it would be fun to run a small hotel, so I had Inara do it for me.

**Why did you have Mei Lien use embroidery to tell her story?**

I was really stumped at first on what that "thing" would be that connected my historical and contemporary story lines (other than the house), so I took the issue to my plotting group.

One of my plot helpers, Carol, told me of a framed, embroidered Chinese sleeve that she owned. Upon further research, I learned that wide, embroidered Chinese sleeve bands are often sold in China as souvenirs. These sleeves, however, are much different from the one Mei Lien creates. I had her pattern her entire robe, including the narrow sleeve with a horse-hoof cuff, after the court dragon robes worn by ranking officers in dynastic times because I liked the idea of Mei Lien's grandmother telling her stories of life in China and Mei Lien choosing to honor that heritage in the garment for her son. The idea of a solitary sleeve stuck, however, and is why that was all Inara found under her stairs.

**This story is told in both historical scenes and contemporary. Did you find one or the other more difficult to write?**

I found Inara's scenes, the contemporary ones, the most difficult. When writing in Mei Lien's point of view, I could completely immerse myself, mentally, in that time period and its unique challenges, speech patterns, dress, etc. I loved researching what people ate in the 1880s and '90s, what they wore, how they traveled, etc. I also found myself fascinated by the cultural differences of the time. And, though it was true to the period, I cringed every time I typed a racial slur, which made me so thankful I live in a time when Americans are more accepting of all races, genders, religions, sexual orientations, and ethnicities. Or, at least, making progress toward acceptance.

I think the challenge in writing the contemporary scenes came more from making those as compelling as the historical because there was so much I found interesting and challenging about the historical story line. To make it easier, I completely wrote all of the historical chapters first and then wrote the contemporary chapters as though they were a separate book. Then I went back and wove them all together, even rearranging the chapters a few times until the flow made sense.

**Why did you choose to set Mei Lien's story on Orcas Island?**

I knew I'd have her end up on one of the San Juan Islands because of the smuggling of Chinese immigrants through the islands and also simply because I adore that area and love spending time there, even if only in my head. I chose Orcas Island specifically after reading a fascinating settler's diary that put me right on the island during that time period. If you're interested, the book is *The James Francis Tulloch Diary 1875–1910*, compiled and edited by Gordon Keith. For those of you with sharp memories, yes, this is the same James Tulloch I have take over the mail carrier position when the islanders take it away from Joseph.

**Did any characters in the book really exist, or did you base any characters on real people?**

Yes, and I found it quite fun to slip real people into my story. Besides James Tulloch mentioned above, there was also:

- Captain Herbert Beecher, who took Joseph and Mei Lien to Port Townsend. In real life, he was a steamer captain in the islands and the son of the famous protestant preacher and abolitionist Henry Ward Beecher and nephew to Harriet Beecher Stowe, author of *Uncle Tom's Cabin*. I got a kick out of having Herbert help Mei Lien since he came from a family known for helping victims of racism.
- The Baron, the store owner in Port Townsend who helped with the arrangements for Joseph and Mei Lien's wedding, had the principal ship chandlery in Port Townsend and was one of the chief supply houses for the extensive lumber and logging interests in Puget Sound. Many loggers made his firm their bankers, as well. His real name was D. C. H. Rothschild and, as of this writing, his home is still open to the public as a museum.
- Preacher Gray, whom I have Joseph mention in passing,

really did go door-to-door on Orcas Island, asking residents for money to build a new Episcopal church in Eastsound. That church still stands today.

**What research did you do to write this book?**

I read everything I could find on Chinese embroidery, Chinese clothing and customs, the history of the San Juan Islands, the history of Seattle, how we ate in the late 1800s, construction methods of the 1880s and '90s, Chinese food, steamships, the purges of Chinese from U.S. towns, and on and on. I visited the Wing Luke Museum of the Asian Pacific American Experience in Seattle to read the information they had on the anti-Chinese riots, as well as the transcripts from oral histories of people who witnessed the event. While at the museum, I also toured their archive room to learn how textiles are safely stored and handled. I visited the history museums of both San Juan Island and Orcas Island and came away with tons of notes and pictures. I read stacks of books on historical homes to find just the right one to represent Rothesay and then decided to loosely base it on the house used in the movie *The Sound of Music.* I read countless novels with a Chinese protagonist and nonfiction about Chinese settlers in the Pacific Northwest or Chinese women anywhere in the United States to better understand their experiences. Through all of this research, I came to embrace the belief that the more you know about a topic in which you previously had little interest, the more you grow to love it.

**What was the most interesting experience you had while researching this book?**

In a moment of serendipity, just as I was researching the Chinese experience in America, I learned of a special dinner the Wing Luke Museum was hosting, and I quickly signed up. On a warm July evening in 2010, I attended this dinner, called "Pigs' Feet, Olives, Watermelon Seed: Chinese American Food of the 1880s," featuring Seattle food anthropologist and cultural specialist Maxine Chan, who guided us through each course with stories and explanations of the foods before us. Some of the dishes I ate were preserved pomelo peel with pork, steamed egg, pigs' feet, and much more. You'll find more information and pictures from the dinner on my website at www.kelliestes.com.

**Which character do you feel most closely connected to?**

One might think my answer to this would be Inara since we are both Caucasian and living in the twenty-first century, but actually, I felt closest to Mei Lien. From the very first word I wrote in her point of view, I cared for her deeply and hated all the horrible things I was making her face. She and I are both mothers, and when I wrote the scene of her saying good-bye to Yan-Tao, I imagined having to do that to one of my own boys, and I felt her pain deeply. In fact, as silly as it may sound for an author to have such a reaction to her own writing, I still get a lump in my throat when I read that scene. Mei Lien's struggles are not my own, yet I felt her pain as she lost her family, both times, and found the strength to do what was needed.

**This is your first published novel. What was your journey to becoming an author? Did you always want to be a writer?**

I always loved reading, voraciously, but never once considered that I could write the books I loved so much. To me, writers were people who lived a faraway magical life that had nothing to do with anything in mine. That changed when I met the woman who would later become my sister-in-law and she told me she was writing a romance novel. Here was a real live person who was writing a book? It could really be done? And so, I tried it and knew that, even though I had a huge learning curve ahead of me, it was exactly what I wanted to do with the rest of my life.

I graduated from Arizona State University with a degree in business management and went to work for an airplane manufacturer as a buyer and contract administrator. Though I enjoyed the work, I wasn't passionate about it, which is why I found it easy to walk away when my husband offered to support me as I became a writer and stay-at-home mom. This experience made it easy for me to relate to Inara when she realized working for Starbucks wasn't her passion. In the fourteen years between quitting that job and selling this novel, I wrote six manuscripts, attended countless writing workshops and conferences, and raised two boys who are now in school all day, which allows me to focus on writing. There's that serendipity again—giving me more time to write just as I launch my publishing career!

## What is the most challenging part of being a writer?

For me, the most challenging part of being a writer is finding balance between writing and everything else that needs to be accomplished in a day. It seems like just when I achieve that balance, something changes and I need to start all over again. While my kids are still living at home, they will always be my priority. If I'm not careful, I could easily fill a whole day with volunteering at the kids' schools, running errands, making dinner…and suddenly there's no time or energy left to write. I've learned to schedule writing time every day in my planner, the earlier in the day, the better (the same is true for exercise), and to set weekly goals and make it a rule that if those goals don't get accomplished, I don't get to relax on the weekend.

## Where do you get your story ideas?

Ideas come from everywhere, and I find it an adventure to pay attention to everything and everyone around me for nuggets of inspiration. From television shows and movies to overheard conversations at the grocery store to magazine articles and plaques on the side of a building…everything is a potential story.

I keep a file of articles and notes of things I find interesting—anything from job descriptions to pictures of jewelry to whole plot ideas. When I'm ready to start working on a new book idea, I'll open this file and see what ignites the flame. Usually I'll pull together several ideas that I'd previously thought were each a book themselves but really are just one aspect or one plotline of a much more complicated story. I also like to make a list of things I'm passionate about at the time and work those into my story to keep it fun. For this book, things from that list were San Juan Islands history, driving out of Seattle Chinese, Seattle history, boutique hotels, summer, water, and forest. My next book will likely include exercise, vegan food, and female friendships.

**Do you know how to create embroideries?**

No, I don't have that talent. Embroidery wasn't something I was ever interested in until after I started researching it for this book. Like all things we think we don't like in life, I found that learning more about it made my fondness grow. I now own clothing with embroidery and recently received an antique embroidered Chinese sleeve as a gift from the same sister-in-law who inspired me to start writing. As for creating something embroidered myself... Who knows? Maybe someday I'll learn how.

**What advice do you have for aspiring authors?**

Begin by writing as often as possible and learning as much as possible by attending workshops, conferences, and critique groups. Be open to feedback. Read books on craft. Read your favorite authors and pay attention to structure, word choice, plot, conflict, character development, etc. Write more. And then, once you have a good understanding of all the writing "rules," give yourself permission to ignore it all and be true to your own voice and your own story. I wrote four romances and one women's fiction before this book, paying close attention every time to the rules, and when I started writing this one, I let all that go and had no idea where it would even be shelved in a bookstore. During the revision process, it started to come together. Trust yourself, trust your voice, trust the story that comes to you, and you'll find success. Also, don't rush. It will take longer than you think to have a finished book, and that's okay.

# *Acknowledgments*

There are many people who helped inspire, shape, and encourage this story and I am so thankful to each of them.

My deepest thanks to my husband, Chad, and our two boys, who believed all along that I would become a published author. They celebrated every milestone of every unpublished book I ever wrote, and they especially celebrated this one with me, from finished first draft to contract signing to final manuscript submission. Thank you for loving me and for giving me the time and space to write. (On that note, thanks also go to Xbox and LEGO for keeping my kids happily occupied while I wrote!)

I cannot thank my agent, Beth Miller, enough for seeing the soul of this story early on and helping me whip it into shape. Thank you for believing in me.

I also am so grateful for my editors, Shana Drehs and Anna Michels, for loving my story and for making it shine. I am thrilled to be working with you! The whole team at Sourcebooks are superheroes, in my opinion, and my thanks go to everyone who had a hand in bringing this book to life.

Huge thanks go to my writer friends, who've helped me brainstorm plot or work out problems with the manuscript. Thank you: Cherry Adair, Christina Arbini, Kira Brady,

Kristine Cayne, Rebecca Clark, Carol Costantino, Lesa Dragon, Carolynn Estes, Heather Higgins, Julia Hunter, Emma Locke, Laurie London, Dona Sarkar, and Shelli Stevens. Your friendship, plotting sessions, and support mean so much to me. Carol, thank you for introducing me to embroidered Chinese sleeve bands, which inspired the embroidery in this story. Thank you!

Any inaccuracies or oversights in research are mine alone. Thank you to the following experts for your help: medical examiner William Barbour for information on dead bodies and decomposition, Eirena from the Orcas Museum, Bob Fisher from the Wing Luke Museum, and the authors of the settlers' diaries that brought the San Juan Islands of the late 1800s to life.

Some very dear friends read early versions of this manuscript and gave me detailed critiques that helped me find focus and direction for the story. Ladies, I hope you know how much I treasure your honesty and thoughtful feedback. Thank you, Rebecca Clark, Melynie Elvidge, Laurie London, and Dona Sarkar.

Dona, you were the first person to make me believe I was a "real" writer, and you never once let me think otherwise in all the years since. I hope you know how huge that is.

And last, thank you to the Romance Writers of America and the Pacific Northwest Writers Association. Both organizations taught me so much about the craft and business of writing.

# About the Author

Photo by Chad Estes

Kelli Estes grew up in the apple country of eastern Washington before going to college at Arizona State University, where she learned she needs to live near water and where all four seasons can be experienced, so she moved to Seattle after graduation. There, she bought airplane parts for four years before finally getting the courage to try her hand at writing. Six manuscripts, two babies, and fourteen years later, her dream of a writing career came true with the publication of *The Girl Who Wrote in Silk*.

Kelli now lives thirty minutes from Seattle with her husband and two sons. When not writing, she loves volunteering at her kids' schools, reading, traveling, going out to eat, exercising (because of all the eating), and learning about health and nutrition. Connect with Kelli at www.kelliestes.com.